STEALING
HEAVEN

The Love Story of
Heloise and Abelard

BOOKS BY MARION MEADE

Stealing Heaven

Eleanor of Aquitaine

*Free Woman: The Life and
Times of Victoria Woodhull*

STEALING

HEAVEN

*The Love Story of
Heloise and Abelard
by MARION MEADE*

William Morrow and Company, Inc.
New York

For Alison

May 16, 1163 ❦

"Open the shutters, will you?"

The bowed head next to her bed snapped erect and she heard the sound of rosary beads clattering to the floor. "My lady—?"

"The shutters. Open them, please." Through the small, high window, she could see a sliver of moon glinting hard and clear; the sky was drenched silver with stars. Staring, she felt the crystalline drops draw close enough to touch, their phosphorescence blinding her. She blinked feebly, and when she looked again they had retreated, playful and aloof, beyond her grasp once more.

How long had she lain there? Weeks? Perhaps only days. She did not know, nor did she care enough to ask. Earlier this evening, after vespers, the nun who sat by her bed had suddenly gasped and run to fetch the board and stick. She had heard her race into the cloister, furiously beating the death board, and soon the infirmary had begun to fill with women, ready to start the litany. But Sister Claude had come and bustled them away, briskly sending them back to their suppers and muttering in gentle reproof to the precipitate sister still clutching the splintered board. Heloise had laughed to herself. She was not ready; she would not be hurried. For so long she had hungered to embrace this moment, prayed for it, ached with anticipation, and now that the time had arrived, she felt, perversely, no need to hurry. Only our beginnings and endings are truly worthy of the name mystery; one cannot be conscious of birth, but death, if one desires, may be lived. She wished to savor her end, or at least experience it. She would not permit them to hurry her into darkness.

A balmy night breeze from the river streamed through the window and eddied along the plain stone walls. In the corner, a blue flame trembled convulsively beneath a crucifix. Eyes half closed, she listened to the rustling murmur of the water nearby, its sonorous ripples racing in time with her breathing. A choir of frogs chanted ecstatic plainsong from among the tangled reeds.

"My lady abbess," a voice murmured, "a sip of gruel." Arms lifted her head. Obedient, she strained to open her mouth, but the greasy liquid flowed down her chin, and finally they rested her head against the pillow again.

Her body felt strangely weightless, as insubstantial as the configuration of smoke; she could feel neither her legs nor the stabbing pain in her belly that had tormented her these many months. I shall not be unhappy to abandon this body, she thought; it has mocked and destroyed me.

She sighed and closed her eyes. Behind her lids immediately danced a ghostly face: a pair of great, lustrous eyes the color of heliotrope framed in a cloud of pale hair, roseate mouth sensually crooning, "Bunny, sweet bunny." It was that elusive, unknown face she had sought so determinedly for sixty years, always rearranging the features into different patterns, always uncertain that she had fitted them together correctly. Ah, she thought, so that is what you looked like; I remember now. The woman faded, and in her place marched a slow procession of familiar figures, long dead, each moving into the center of her vision for a few moments, then sweeping aside to make way for the next. A lean woman in black, in her hand a switch raised menacingly. A grimy child, merry-eyed and hilarious, holding aloft a half-eaten honey bun in sticky fingers. A marble-faced man, thin lips drawn tautly together, who embraced her fiercely and then thrust her away in disgust. A sleeping newborn infant, fretted blue veins etched on the vellum lids, his smile trailing clouds from other realms. And lastly a prancing skull-faced man, his lipless mouth stretching into a terrible grin, feet executing an obscene dance on skeleton toes. In his outstretched hands he held a knife dripping red streamers and a wrinkled mound of bloody flesh. First gracious, then insistent, he pressed on her his monstrous gifts. A scream ripped through her throat. "Aristotle!"

"My lady—"

Weak, she opened her eyes. In the milky light, cowled shadows bent over her, comforting, stroking, pressing a cool towel against her forehead. Their voices tumbled softly above her. "She speaks of Aristotle now!" "Shhh." "Jesu, mercy—Jesu, have mercy on her soul—"

"Where is Aristotle? Call the naughty girl. Ceci, look under the bed."

The nuns exchanged glances. They were silent a moment, and then one of them said, "Sister Cecilia is not here, lady."

Shutting out the hum of the voices, she moved her eyes to the flame and then slowly upward to the crucifix with the man's slack body glued to the cross. The flame stirred and heaved, its glow throwing up arms of vivid citron and azure and amber around the crucifix. The stone walls were bathed in mute lilac shadows. She looked away from the corner and saw clearly the walls of the room, stark, gray, ugly, and listened to the distant rustle of the nuns' skirts. The earliest things she could remember were stony walls and black-robed women murmuring in whispers. The peace of the sepulcher, she mused. For only a few short years had she been reprieved, thrust innocent and naked out of that immuring grayness into the blazing white light of the world.

Once she had tasted freedom, or the illusion of it, but then his invisible hand had reached out and pulled the fugitive back. *Oh God! thou who made this world and all that is in it, why did thou condemn me to gray walls and an existence I always loathed? What lessons did thou mean to teach me and why did I, who greedily absorbed all human wisdom, learn so late to discern thine?*

Somehow she had lived through sixty-three summers, playing her tedious roles, forever smiling and dissembling, never allowing the world to glimpse the real woman. Quickly, she corrected herself. To him she had revealed her true self. Sometimes. But even he could not accept her. The letters, those shameless shreds dredged from the bottom of her soul, those offerings of truth delivered up to his aghast silence; her hands clutched the coverlet in stinging memory. Ah, my very sweet friend, she thought, you didn't understand my love. In the end, you learned to love God, even, in your own way, to love me. But it had taken so long.

The years rolled back, and she could hear the melodious ring of that voice that had hypnotized so many adoring thousands. And she could hear her own voice, high-spirited and reckless, the diamond-sharp voice of a young girl who gloried in rebellion and who did not care if the world ended tomorrow as long as she had her lover. They were lying in a grassy meadow on the road to Saint-Victor. It was an afternoon in midsummer, and they had crossed the Petit Pont and followed the vineyard-bordered Rue de Garlande, carrying with them a skin of good red claret and a basket of flaky pasties filled with soft cheese and eel. Along the road, they had picked wild raspberries and gathered poppies and yellow buttercups. In the rippling grass, she had strewn the blossoms into the shape of a gold and scarlet bed, and then they had pulled off their clothes and thrown themselves, flushed and naked, atop the flowers. Afterward, they had fed each other berries, laughing softly at their carmine-stained mouths and listening to the sawing of the grass-hoppers in the green-latticed sunlight.

You will never reach paradise, he had teased. And she, wanting no more of paradise than she possessed that afternoon, had answered, amused and defiant, that heaven did not mean a peppercorn to her. She had declared, I don't care to go there unless I have you, my dearest friend whom I love so much. Do you know who goes to paradise? I'll tell you, my honey sweet. There go priests and old cripples and the maimed and ugly who are shriveled in body and soul, those who crouch day and night before altars and ancient crypts, who are naked and shoeless and covered with hideous running sores, who die of hunger and wretch-edness. These people go to heaven, but I want nothing to do with them. I'm willing to go to hell, because to hell go the famous scholars—yes, it's true—and the courteous knights who die in tourneys and glori-ous crusades. With them I'll gladly go. And there go the fair ladies who have lovers besides their lords. And do you know who else goes there? The harpers and jongleurs and lute players and the great kings and queens of Christendom. With all these will I go, if only I have for com-pany my own love with the black curls, my Abelard. And when she had finished, he clasped her in his arms and pressed his greedy mouth to her eyes and her mouth and her forehead and throat.

Faintly, she could hear the rising and flickering sound of someone praying.

"Lady, you have a visitor. Father William is here and he—lady?"

When Heloise did not open her eyes, the sister broke off and backed away from the bed. She heard a man speaking, and then the prayers re-sumed, this time with the heavier counterpoint of the priest's droning voice. Curdled with irritation, she bit down on her urge to scream at them. She refused to allow these sisters and brothers of death to escort her to the edge. No, she would go skipping and dancing to the melody of a lute with a summer breeze floating her hair behind her like an an-gel's wings.

She swallowed and opened her mouth to speak. She said, Leave me alone. But the words whistled vainly through her teeth, and she did not try again. Once more the jeweled visions tumbled and somersaulted through her mind, and she hurried to chase after them before they es-caped. If only she might catch them, she would be young again. Her hair would be the color of wild wheat and she would wear a blue gown girdled with a rope of damascene gold. She would not fear Death's

5

crushing claw; she would not even acknowledge its existence, because between her and Death swirled a thousand rainbows, ten thousand pink-tinted dawns heralding days of sunlight and music. She was more than a child but not yet a woman, and life beckoned.

1 ⚘

SHAPELESS BLACK SHADOWS stretched out on all sides; the hammering sound of rain laid a mantle of fog over the cot. In the heavy, deep darkness, a chorus of snores whistled softly before dying away, the stirring and breathing of sixty women and uncounted animals, uneven and flute-shrill against the monotonous rasping of water dripping on the roof overhead. For thirteen years, she had been awaiting this dawn, but she had not imagined the rain.

"Heloise?"

"Yes."

"Are you awake, sweeting?"

"Yes."

She drew a deep breath and rolled to the edge of the cot. Next to her, she felt the blanket lift for a moment and then Ceci's cool, naked body slipped in beside her. She curled her legs around the girl's and moved her hand caressingly over the supple waist. "It was raining the first day I came here."

"Nonsense," Ceci said placidly. Her voice was husky and nasal, as if she had a cold. Or had been weeping. "You were only a babe. You can't remember."

Heloise dragged the coverlet around their ears and hid her face in Ceci's thick black plaits. Her throat tensed. She thought, How can a person live in a place almost her whole life and yet never think of it as home? She had been well treated; there was no cause for complaint. "I don't want to argue with you," she said, her mouth next to Ceci's ear. "It was cold and wet the day Uncle brought me. My hair was soaked, and Lady Alais sat me by the fire in her parlor and fed me hot licorice wine."

Ceci sniffed. "I thought you said Agnes brought you here."

"Whoever." Each January, before Epiphany, Agnes would make her annual visit to Argenteuil. Her uncle's housekeeper was round and enormous, her face as bloated as an unbaked loaf of bread with two sunken raisins for eyes, her voice as deep as a man's. From under her voluminous cloak, she'd bring out the eagerly awaited bundles—oatcakes and gingerbread, currants and candied oranges, a small bag of deniers for Heloise's tuition, and always a new bliaut. Unfortunately, she never failed to deliver the same lecture: how lucky Heloise was to be a pupil at wealthy and fashionable Sainte-Marie of Argenteuil, where Charlemagne's daughter had once been prioress. Master said that its reputation for learning compared to the famous German convents of Gandersheim and Landesberg. Count your blessings, lamb, she'd pant in a stentorian tone.

And so forth. Heloise had heard the admonitions so often that she no longer bothered to listen. She would hold her breath until Agnes had raced off to the abbey church to gawk at *la sainte tunique,* the tunic woven for Christ by the Blessed Virgin. She hated relics. Disgusting old bones and ridiculous splinters of wood that the ignorant slobbered over. The tunic was somewhat better—at least it might possibly be authentic. Except that she doubted it.

The darkness had begun to scatter. Through a high window, far away, she could see a leaden square of sky. The rain had subsided to a thin hiss that she could barely hear. She was tired. Numb, too, although this she did not wish to admit. Last week, when Lady Alais had summoned her and announced that Uncle had sent word she should come to Paris, she had sprinted into the cloister and rolled on the grass. She had sobbed hysterically, as much from relief as happiness. Now, for the first time, she felt uneasy about leaving Argenteuil. Something occurred to her. She knew nothing of life in Paris. For that matter, what did she know of life anywhere, except behind these walls?

Abruptly, she jerked her arm from Ceci's waist and rolled to the far edge of the cot. She burrowed deeply into the safe blanket.

Ceci said, "Don't go today."

"I must. Lady Alais has arranged for me to ride pillion with a butcher who's traveling into town."

"Go tomorrow instead. One day won't matter."

"It will."

"Why?"

Heloise thought of the ride and of Paris. Beyond the crenellated walls of the convent squatted the village. And beyond the village was—what? Plowed fields, vineyards, more villages. She shrugged irritably. "You would keep me here forever if I let you. You know I must leave today. Uncle will be expecting me."

Neither of them spoke. After a long while, Ceci said quietly, "I want to go home."

Heloise glanced at the pale face next to hers. "You will. Soon your father will send for you. Then you can go back to Angers and marry your Rannulf or Geoffrey or whatever his name is."

"Girard. I don't know, maybe he's married someone else by now. I've had no letter from Father since Michaelmas." She sighed noisily. "Girard won't have me without a dower, and with four older sisters I—"

"Well, marriage isn't so important." Hearing Ceci's sharp gasp of indignation, she grinned. "God's toenails, how boring to be a woman!"

"You're in a pretty mood. What would you be then? A man?" Her voice was thick with sarcasm.

Heloise hoisted herself on one elbow. She turned to the girl and tugged at one of her plaits. "Listen to me, Ceci—"

"I'm listening."

"Do you ever think about the future?" She paused, searching for words that Ceci would understand. "I mean, do you ever wonder what your life will be like twenty years from now?"

"You sound like an astrologer."

"Do you?"

The subject made Ceci uncomfortable. She bit her lip and turned unsmiling eyes on Heloise. "What's there to think about? When I go home, I'll marry Girard. Or someone. We'll sleep together and I'll have a son. The next year—"

Heloise closed her eyes and stirred impatiently.

"—the next year, I'll have another son and then maybe a daughter." Her voice rose to a triumphant bleat. "And in twenty years, I'll have a lot of grandchildren."

It was a bad subject to have brought up this morning. In a few hours, she would be gone. She would miss Ceci. She thought, I should tell her that and make her happy. Musing, she felt her eyes grow heavy, and she started to doze; in her sleep, she heard someone playing the lute, badly. A moment later, Sister Adela's greyhound jumped on the bed and began climbing over her chest, his wet tongue lashing her neck. Absentmindedly, she pushed him to the floor. Sister Adela's hound had a habit of making water on people's beds.

Ceci pushed down the bedclothes and sat up. She regarded Heloise with teasing black-rimmed eyes. "And where do you see yourself in twenty years, madame?"

"You wouldn't understand." The girl, two years younger than she, was still a child—Heloise was fourteen.

"Yes, I would. You can tell me."

Heloise glanced around the dormitory in the wavery light. Even though the bell for prime had not yet rung, the mounds under the blankets were beginning to stir. There was a low torrent of coughs and catarrh, and she saw Sister Judith waddle toward the privy, her rump swinging loosely behind her. Solemn, expectant, Ceci leaned toward her. With her compact body and eyes as dark as berries, she sometimes reminded Heloise of a gypsy. She wondered how Ceci would manage at Argentcuil without her; for eight years she had followed Heloise like a worshipful puppy, imitating her and hanging on every word with little-sisterish adoration. "I won't be a bride. Neither of man nor of Christ."

The girl began to giggle. "You don't want to marry."

"That's right." Heloise smiled.

Ceci looked bewildered. "Then you must return here and take your vows. There is nothing else."

Heloise saw the subsacristan appear at the far end of the dormitory; bleary-eyed, she began to wag the little bell for prime. She crept down the aisle between the cots, keeping to the center lest someone trip her. No one looked at her. Ceci rolled out of bed and stared down at Heloise before leaving. A few minutes later, she returned carrying her clothing and shoes. Heloise had not moved. She stared up at the ceiling with expressionless eyes.

"Aren't you getting up?" Ceci asked nervously.

"No." All in a burst, the sun had risen and she could hear someone gurgling about the fine day. Suddenly, the room was full of women hurriedly pulling on black robes, unplaiting hair, arguing hoarsely. Always wrangling, forever wrangling. Ceci sat down on the edge of the bed and began tugging at her shoes. "Your uncle won't keep you at home forever," she said breathlessly.

"He might." No, he would not. Not for nothing had she listened to Agnes's doleful plaints the last dozen years. Fulbert was a money-hungry, pinchpenny miser. Which was why he was rich and owned farms and vineyards near Melun. But Heloise's mother had left her some money, how much she did not know exactly. She did know that the fees Fulbert paid Lady Alais for her education came out of her own money. She thought, Those few sous each year couldn't have exhausted my inheritance. There must be a great deal left. I must speak to Uncle about it. "I won't marry. I'll read Greek and become a great philosopher. Like Plato."

Ceci stopped combing her hair and gave a gleeful little cackle. "Oh. Well, yes. Prioress says you have a mind like a man." She shook her head violently. "But you're not a man, sweeting. So you must be a woman and marry a man."

"I'm not interested in men," Heloise said heavily. All Ceci thought of was men, she thought, suddenly angry for no good reason. But she was no different from any of the others at Argenteuil. Their chief topic of conversation, after their pets, was men. Bishop this—brother that. She put her hands to her face, rubbing her eyes and trying to shut out the lemon sunlight.

"You've never known any men," Ceci said loudly and pointedly. "Wait. Paris is full of them. Thousands of students from all over. They say there are more students than people in Paris. Mark me, you'll change your mind."

Heloise made a noncommittal grunt in her throat. She didn't dislike men, so that was not why she had no desire to marry. She didn't want to talk about it to Ceci. When she looked up, she met the eyes of Sister Judith standing over the cot.

"Why aren't you dressed?"

"What?"

"Clean out your ears. The bell for prime rang fifteen minutes ago. Didn't you hear?"

Heloise made a face and pulled the blanket over her chin. "I'm not coming."

"Are you mad? Lady Abbess will be furious."

"Let her."

The dormitory had emptied, save for a handful of nuns who had stayed up late after matins drinking and gossiping and who, naturally, could not manage to rouse themselves. Heloise crawled out of the cot and pretended they weren't there. She hurried to the lavatory to wash, and when she came back, she pulled a wooden clothes chest from under the bed. Inside, hidden among her tunics, was a white linen shift and a pale-blue bliaut, neatly folded, and a coiled embroidered belt. This treasure, concealed for the past year, she had garnered from the maid of a rich lady who had stopped the night at Argenteuil. The maid had seemed surprised when Heloise begged for shabby clothing fit only for the fire. It was true: the shift had been badly ripped and the faded bliaut stained with grease spots and mud. But Heloise had mended and stitched, and she had scrubbed the stains with verjuice until the dress looked presentable. It had remained hidden in her coffer against the day when she might have occasion to wear such frivolous apparel.

She pulled the shift over her head and wriggled her arms into the long, tight sleeves of the dress, pulling it down sleekly over her breasts and hips. The belt she passed twice around her waist and knotted low on her hips. There was something wrong; she wished that she could see herself. The dress felt considerably more snug than when she had first acquired it. When she looked down, she saw that it barely covered her ankles. Last year it had fitted, but now she realized that she must have grown.

"God's death, why am I so tall?" she swore aloud. Already she towered by half a head over the tallest nun at Argenteuil. It was bad enough to be an orphan, but to be a tall orphan seemed a cruel and gratuitous insult on the part of fortune.

There was nothing she could do about the bliaut now. Quickly she unplaited her hair and let it stream down her back. From the chest she pulled her cloak and spread it flat on the cot. She began emptying the chest. In no time, everything she owned had been placed in a mound, and she tied the cloak into a bundle. Kneeling, she reached into a hole in the mattress and drew out a grimy silk purse. The contents she dumped on the bed, and began to sort the motley collection of bits and pieces into two piles. On one she threw a handful of shiny pebbles she had collected along the Seine, a cheap brooch, a length of yellowing lace, and a fistful of almonds. These she stuffed back into the purse and went over to slide it under Ceci's pillow. Into her bundle went the remaining items—an ivory comb missing several teeth, an orange and black butterfly mounted on a scrap of parchment, two needles and a thimble, and a vial of rose water she had concocted herself last summer. And, most precious of all, her writing implements: knife for scraping parchment, quill pen, biting pumice, and ruler.

She left the parcel on her cot and headed toward the night stairs leading to the south transept of the church. A voice from one of the cots behind her shouted, "Wait till Lady Alais gets a look at you in that thing!"

Heloise did not turn around.

"Slut!" The voice rose to an angry wheeze.

The stairwell was dank and chilly. Under the fitted sleeves of the gown, she felt gooseflesh rise on her arms. Suddenly her stomach wrenched violently and she felt like vomiting. Halfway down, she stopped and leaned against the damp stone wall. How many hundreds of nights had she crept, dazed and soft with sleep, down these dark steps to say matins and lauds, how many hundreds of dawns for prime? As a young child, she had not been required, or even permitted, to get up for the night office at two A.M. But of course the forbidden always lures, and she had begged the nuns to take her along as a treat. By now it must have been eight or nine years since she had slept the night through, and she could hardly imagine a night of unbroken rest.

She went on down the steps. In the cool, dark shadows near the choir, she pressed against a pillar and watched the nuns gabble their way through a psalm. This morning they were skipping sentences to get the service over quickly. One side of the choir had omitted a pause between verses and were already mumbling their way into the next verse before the other side had finished the first.

Still, they were behaving better than last year at Pentecost, when they had giggled and joked during services and dropped hot candle wax from the upper stalls on the heads of those below. After that, the bishop had severely chastised Lady Alais for negligence and commanded that she restore discipline among her women. Heloise wrapped her arms around her chest and shivered. She thought of taking her place in the choir one last time but decided not to. She could think of nothing but Paris. Besides, there was the matter of her dress. She edged her way along the wall to a side door and opened it carefully. As she turned to close the door behind her, she caught a glimpse of a bilious-looking Sister Judith, eyes closed, mouth hanging open in a silent snore. Heloise choked off a laugh. She thought, Most of these women wouldn't be here if the choice had been theirs. Obviously.

The cloister was deserted. Along the east walk she broke into a run, passing the bakehouse and kitchens, and let herself out through the postern door which led to the vegetable gardens. The brightness of the air made her blink; she didn't remember May to be this hot. Before her swept the farm and pastureland belonging to Argenteuil. Robin, the oxherd, was veering his bulls toward the west pasture; over by the pens, the dairymaid screamed at her heifers and calves. The air smelled faintly of rosemary, rankly of manure.

Argenteuil lay on the north bank of the Seine, and the path down the hill to the river took her by the convent's fishponds and then through tall, lush grass and a grove of willow trees. Under the arching branches, the noises of the farmyard faded; the air was colder and the grass wet and glistening from last night's rain. With a rush of joy, she ran along the muddy path, hair blowing behind her.

In the woods grew banks of violets and gillyflowers, and between the moss-footed tree trunks she caught flashes of the river, steel-gray, and then in a burst of sunlight, brilliant cerulean blue. As a child, her greatest delight had been to steal away from Sister Madelaine and run to the riverbank to dream her secret dreams. At the water's edge, she scrambled up on a shelf of searing-hot rock and threw herself face down. Squinting, she watched a barge skimming downriver toward Paris, raising clouds of spray in the bobbing water.

In the distance, across a loop in the river, she could see the red-tiled roofs of the abbey of Saint-Denis, the monastery favored by the royal house of Capet. Sister Judith had told her that King Louis had studied there as a boy and it was very famous. Heloise didn't care about that; she was only interested in the annual fair held in the little town that had grown up outside Saint-Denis's walls. For two weeks every June, the lay workers at Argenteuil talked about nothing but the Lendit. Colorful tents were laid out in streets, and if you had sous in your pocket, you could roam around and buy plenty of pasties and fruit and fish and cakes. There were jugglers and trained bears and storytellers who recited every single verse of the *Chanson de Roland* and made everyone weep. Minstrels brought their viols and strolled about the tent streets playing lays to maidens who painted their cheeks. It was all madly exciting. Or so she had been told; she had never been there.

Thirteen years here. How little I have seen, she thought. Nothing but women and yellowing parchment manuscripts. Surely there is more poetry to life than is contained in the verses of Virgil and Seneca, as intoxicating as they may be. I'm old already and I know nothing, she told herself. She thrust the thought away with a sudden surge of resentment. Let Sister Madelaine get herself another prize pupil. Let all of them go to the devil. Even Ceci.

Her back and scalp were beginning to prickle from the stinging fire of the sun. She closed her eyes and lay very still for a few minutes before leaping to her feet and starting back up the slope to the convent.

Prime had ended and the cloister rumbled with the hum of women's voices, gossiping and laughing. Heloise brushed past unseeing and ducked into the library, which also served as scriptorium and schoolroom. There was no one there. In this room, when hardly more than an infant, she had held a wax-coated tablet on her knees and carefully traced the alphabet with an ivory stylus. And here, too, she had labored over her Latin, Greek, and Hebrew. She slid into a carrel next to the window and stroked the grain on the slanted wooden desk with a thumb.

During Sister Madelaine's thirty years as prioress, she had assembled an excellent library of nearly a hundred volumes, few of which the nuns of Argenteuil ever bothered to open. Not only did she have Aristotle's *De interpretatione* and Boethius's *De musica,* but in her locked cupboard could be found all the ten books of Livy, Plutarch's *Lives,* and Caesar's *Commentaries,* as well as a wide variety of the heathen poets: Terence, Virgil, Seneca, Lucan, Plautus. Even Ovid's *Art of Love,* which, by rights, no nunnery should even know about.

Sister Madelaine came into the room quietly. "You've come to say goodbye," she said in a raspy voice. The thin lips, outlined by a faint down, bore a smile, but there was no warmth in it today.

"Did you imagine I wouldn't?" She could not endure this farewell, but she could not endure not coming either. Everything that she knew she had first learned from Madelaine, until finally the day had arrived, several years back, when the prioress had had no more to teach her.

"Now you will go to Paris, where your uncle will find a rich lord who needs a decoration for his household." She pulled over a stool and slammed it down next to Heloise. "And soon you will spawn a castleful of brats and forget all about philosophy." She sank down heavily, frowning at the floor in accusation.

"No," Heloise whispered, bruised inside. "Is that all you know of me?" Madelaine would not spare her; she had known it.

The prioress laughed, lightly. "Ah, it's not that I lack understanding. I know that your pretty head is befuddled with dreams. Don't toss your hair at me, missy. If I fear for you, it's because I love you."

Heloise turned to the window and watched Sister Adela's hound doing its business on the velvety grass under the abbess's favorite lemon tree. There would be trouble about that later. "Thank you," she said over her shoulder. "You can always pray for me." And then, because the words had come out edged with sarcasm, she added gently, "You needn't worry that I'll marry. I have other plans."

"Such as?" The prioress glanced up suspiciously.

"Oh. You know."

"Be specific."

"You wouldn't understand." She swiveled around and waved her hand in dismissal. But Madelaine sat there, stony and unyielding, her brittle little face twisted into a silent command. "I'll continue my studies of course. At the cloister school if Uncle permits, or else I shall study at home." She stopped and breathed deeply for a long moment. "And then I'll take students of my own."

Madelaine bristled. "Excellent," she said angrily. "That's exactly what I meant when I spoke of your foolish daydreams. For all your learning, you have the sense of a flea when it comes to practical matters."

"I told you that you wouldn't understand." Most people wouldn't understand. But she had thought that Madelaine might. She stood up and went to a cupboard where Madelaine kept the least precious of the convent's manuscripts. She took out Bede's *De arte metrica*, the old textbook she had used in learning to write Latin prose and verse. "I'm not so stupid as you imagine. Madelaine, listen, I could teach girls."

"Faugh!" Madelaine grunted. "What kind of twattle is that? What need have girls of Latin and—" She stopped and closed her mouth with an audible click.

Furious, Heloise slammed down the book. "I don't believe it!" she shouted at the nun. "You wouldn't have wasted your time on me for nothing."

Madelaine laughed cautiously. "Perchance I'm as big a fool as you. But a pupil like you comes along once in a teacher's lifetime. If she's lucky. How could I leave such an extraordinary field to lie fallow?" Impatient, she waved her arm. "But I never promised that your knowledge could be put to use. Or that it would make you happy." She took a jar of ink from a table and began to make her way along the carrels, filling the inkhorns. "I'm sorry if I misled you."

Heloise shrugged. "Never mind. Books are my life. Think you that I'll be stirring pots of soup and suckling babes?" She realized that she was clenching Bede's manuscript; she made herself take it back to the cupboard and replace it carefully. "Somehow I'll manage, I'm sure."

The prioress set down the ink jar and regarded Heloise quietly. "God forgive me for saying so, but he should have made you a man. Then everything would be simple." She came over to the girl and grabbed her by the shoulders. "Listen to me, child."

Heloise's head flew up.

"The only place for a man with a brilliant mind is in the Church and—" When Heloise tried to wrench away, she held her tightly. "No, mark me. And the only place for a gifted woman is also in the Church. For God's love, stay here!"

"No!"

"One day you could become an abbess. If not at Argenteuil, then at an even greater convent."

"No. No. No." Heloise's voice cracked with hot rage. "You— Why are you saying these things? It's cruel. You know that I have no calling for religion. Don't you know that I hate this place? I want to live." She gestured wildly. "This isn't life."

"Heloise," Madelaine said softly, "you're a special child. But even geniuses can't remake the world to suit themselves. You believe the outside world to be such a fine place. Well, you will see for yourself and God's will shall be done." She sighed heavily. "As always."

She straightened and went over to her locked cupboard. Taking a key from her belt, she unlatched the door and lifted out a leather-bound manuscript. "I've been saving this for you—St. Athanasius."

"Oh, Sister Madelaine, you mustn't." Heloise looked quickly around. "It belongs to Argenteuil. What if Lady Alais—"

"Now, how would Lady Alais ever miss it?" said Madelaine. "In thirty years you've been the first one to learn Greek. The first and no doubt the last. Take it."

Uncertainly, Heloise reached for the book. She had never heard of a girl having a book of her own; at any moment Lady Alais might sweep in and beat her for red-handed thievery. As she stroked the leather cover, her eyes kept flicking nervously toward the cloister. "I don't think—"

"Don't stand there mewing," Madelaine told her. "Run along and hide it among your parcels." When Heloise did not move, she came over and stood before her. She kissed her hair before giving her a push toward the door. "Go, or I'll take my switch to you!"

Heloise caught a deep breath in her chest and plunged through the refectory door. The long oak tables were almost filled, and she maneuvered her way into an empty space on a bench next to Ceci. When Ceci turned and saw her, she gave an involuntary gasp. "Mother of God, where did you get that?"

"What?"

Ceci twisted around and stared, as if her eyes were ready to fly off her face. "Oh, Heloise," she whooped, "it's a real dress! You're so beautiful!"

She knew that she looked terrible, so she shrugged the compliment aside. "It's just a dress." She was thirsty; a pitcher of ale was sitting on the table, but fast could not be broken until Lady Alais arrived for the benediction. The nuns across the table were watching her; their eyes were critical.

"Well, what are you staring at?" she demanded sharply.

One of them laughed. "You can ask that when you've gotten yourself up like a knight's doxy."

"What did you expect? A black veil?" She had not intended to be nasty but it had slipped out. This morning nothing had gone right. Everyone was being spiteful and vicious. They couldn't stand the thought that one of them had been reprieved.

"I'm a bride of Christ," bellowed the woman, eyes hard as agates, "I like the nun's habit."

Heloise mumbled softly between her teeth. "Shit."

"What did you say?" said the nun, surprised.

"I said you're jealous." A kitchen scullion was trotting around, dropping round loaves of bread on the tables—the hot yeasty aroma made her stomach feel queasy. She bowed her head, hoping to discourage the woman, who clearly wanted to start an argument. Who, in fact, had already begun one. Quarreling was a favorite recreation at Argenteuil. She thought, We can't help but get on each other's nerves.

"Excuse me. Jealous of somebody who looks like the very devil? You should see yourself. That dress is so wanton that everybody can see the outline of your breasts." She paused to take a breath. "Disgusting. You look like a strumpet, a harlot from the back alleys of Sodom, a—"

Heloise grinned. "Oh, shut up." She felt her good humor returning.

"—a whore who throws up her skirts for any—"

"I get the idea," Heloise said, laughing.

Winging down the table came Sister Judith's warning voice. "Leave her alone. She's taken no vows and she's leaving today. She can do as she wishes."

Heloise leaned against Ceci's side and relaxed her weight. Strict silence was supposed to be observed in the refectory. If a nun wished to communicate at table, she was to do so by means of signs. When Heloise had first come to Argenteuil and watched the women wagging their hands like fishtails and rubbing their thumbs against their noses, their dumb show had made her snicker. There were over a hundred signs, all of which she knew by now, but the rule of silence was never observed until Lady Alais made her appearance at the head table.

"Don't quarrel today," she said to the nun sitting opposite. "I want to leave with pleasant memories. Don't spoil it. Please."

The woman jerked her head. "As you wish." She fixed Heloise with a sour smile. "What is Paris like?"

"I don't know."

"But you came from there."

"Yes," Heloise said pleasantly. "Yes. But I was a babe when I left."

"Your uncle has never brought you home for a visit?"

Heloise kept her gaze steady. "No."

"Why not?"

Under the table she felt her hands begin to tremble. "I don't know," she said evenly.

Happy, the nun began to dig like a dog hot on the scent of a buried bone. "That's exceedingly strange, isn't it? Your own kin—"

"I expect he had more pressing matters to attend to." From the corner of her eye, she saw Ceci watching her uneasily. "He's a canon at Notre Dame, you know."

Ceci said, defensively, "Her uncle sent her here to be educated like a great lady. Now that she's grown, he's going to present her at court and betroth her to a rich baron with three castles."

Heloise shook her head, blushing. "No, Ceci. That isn't true."

The girl reached out and touched her arm. "Well, you don't know. It might be true. Mightn't it?"

"No. I'd like to study in Paris."

"What for?" called someone from the other end of the table. "Don't you know everything already?" The whole table broke into a good-natured roar.

At a loud hiss, everybody stopped talking. Lady Alais was coming in the door and taking her place. Methodically, she swept her eyes up and down the tables, checking for absentees. When she reached Heloise, she stopped and her eyes widened; then she moved on. At last she slouched her neck and gibbered a perfunctory blessing, not a bit like the sort she said when guests were present. After the abbess had finished, water bowls were passed and each nun washed her hands. By the time the bowl reached Heloise's end of the table, the water was gray and oily. Then the only sounds to be heard were teeth crunching bread and the clattering of the ale pitchers.

Heloise poured the pale, weak ale into her cup and took a long drink. The bread was black and burned on the bottom crust, but inside it was warm and moist. She ate around the scorched part, trying to think about what sort of food Uncle might serve at his table. White bread, no doubt. Perhaps soused herrings and roast mutton with mint and tansy sauce.

Certainly frumenty and baked figs in syrup of honey, because Agnes often told her that Uncle loved sweets. She still couldn't believe that by tonight she would be in Paris finally, that she would never eat another silent meal in this hall. She thought, I must ask Uncle to buy me proper clothing, the styles they are wearing in Paris. Under the table, Ceci was tugging insistently at her skirt.

"Heloise," she whispered.

"What?"

"Take me with you."

"Don't be stupid," she said mildly.

When the meal was over, she rose quickly, but a scullion stood in her way. "Cook wants you, mistress."

Heloise went down the passageway and pushed open the door to the kitchen. A wave of heat slammed her in the face. The huge fireplace was blazing; blackened caldrons bubbled on tripods above the open flames, but the spit was empty. On a table in the center of the room were heaped mounds of minced cabbage, and also lentils, millet, onions, and garlic. The cook was standing in the doorway to the storeroom swearing at someone inside. "Of course it's there. Are you blind? Look again." When a small, dirty boy emerged with a cheese, she gave him a stinging cuff across the ear. "Turd-head."

As she turned and noticed Heloise, her broad face widened into a grin. "By St. Denis, so you'll be leaving this hellhole of cunnics today."

Heloise threw her head back and burst out laughing. "If Lady Abbess could hear the way you talk back here, you'd be looking for a new job."

Cook attacked the cheese with a meat cleaver. "Piss on her ladyship," she said cheerfully. "She'd be doing me a favor. There are plenty of castles needing cooks—and willing to part with a few more deniers than this miserable place."

She hacked off a good-sized chunk of goat cheese and wrapped it up with a loaf of bread; from a bucket in the corner, she filled a wine-skin. "You'll be needing something to eat on your journey," she said. Heloise slid her arms around the cook's sweaty neck. The woman patted her back kindly. "Now, now, little damsel. Don't go pulling a long face. Our Blessed Lady in heaven has answered your prayers and reached down to pluck you straight out of here. 'Tis a happy day."

"Yes," said Heloise. Outside in the passageway, she began to smile.

*   *   *

After breakfast, they all gathered in the great courtyard near the portress's lodge to hear the abbess deliver her farewell blessing for Heloise. Near the gatehouse clustered the guests who had spent the night at Argenteuil—a few poor pilgrims, a group of merchants and men-at-arms, contentious and bragging, a noble dame with her maids. Across the yard milled a clump of beggars squirming impatiently for the almoner to distribute bread. This morning they babbled in excitement, because not every day did they have a chance to gape at Lady Alais herself. Soon she entered the yard on narrow, dainty feet, trailed by a small girl of seven or eight carrying a parrot. She was an aristocratic woman, this abbess, a lady born and bred, and one had to look closely to make certain that she was not a duchess or a countess. For that matter, she might easily have been one if her father had not had three daughters to marry and a son who spent money on tournaments and fashionable cloaks.

Heloise, flanked by her bundles, stood in the front row of nuns and studied Lady Alais's appearance. Everything that she knew about fashion she had learned from observing the abbess. She marked the low neck and long train on the dress, the gold pins holding her silken veil, the silver belt.

"Oh sweet Jesu," the abbess gravely intoned. Her straight nose, gray eyes, and little red mouth puckered into an expression of determined blankness. "The Son of God, the endless sweetness of heaven and earth and of all the world—" Heloise yawned with pain. A cramp was edging its way across her left ankle and up her calf. She dared not shift her weight to her right leg because she was in the front and everyone would notice if she fidgeted. Instead, she concentrated on Lady Alais's rings; her fingers glittered with garnets and rubies, and suspended from a necklace of snowy lace was a gold ring with one diamond. "—be in this child's heart, in her mind, in her will, now and forevermore."

Nonsense. God had had thirteen years to enter her heart at Argenteuil and he had not troubled to concern himself with her existence. If he could not find her here, she doubted if he would come searching for her in Paris. Trying to ease the cramp, she carefully flexed her toes inside her slipper. The cramp left but the sun was burning her shoulders. Already the dress was clinging, sodden, to her back. She wished that Lady Alais could have thought of a more inspirational message. But then the abbess was not known for her originality. She was given to laziness.

"Keep faith with God, my child. Even though you are one of the naturally weaker sex, formed from a rib of man, trust in the Father, and his holy grace will protect you from evil. Use your great knowledge of letters, the talents which he has entrusted to you, to glorify his name. Do not make the mistake of casting pearls before swine."

Heloise fought the impulse to laugh aloud. The abbess had never been enthusiastic about her studies. Once, after drinking many cups of raisin wine and becoming very slightly drunk, she had prophesied that Heloise's brilliance would lead to her damnation—how could it be otherwise when a woman's body contained a man's mind?—and she had fervently wished for Heloise an elderly and understanding husband. As Lady Alais ground on, the huge red sun stared down implacably on the courtyard. Crickets chattered in a clump of nettles near the gatehouse. The abbess's parrot began to squawk fussily.

"Jesu, as thou art full of mercy, Jesu have mercy on this child and on all mankind redeemed with thy precious blood."

Heloise thought, If I had to remain here the rest of my life I would go mad. I hope Uncle won't insist that I attend mass every day. God's death, if Lady Alais says one more word, I'll spit, right here on the ground—I'll spit and I don't care a damn what they think. From the corner of her eye, she suddenly caught a glimpse of Ceci. She was cleaning her fingernails.

"Jesu, amen."

They crossed themselves and everyone said amen. Heloise boomed a relieved amen in an extra-loud voice. Behind her someone said, "Oh God, I'm sweating to death and it's only nine o'clock."

At last it was over. Some of the nuns charged toward the inside gate to find coolness in the cloister before chapter meeting began. The others streamed up to Heloise to say goodbye. She greeted them awkwardly, uncertain whether to smile or look sad. Finally she pasted a smile on her face and held it there with effort. Lady Alais pushed her way through the crowd and tried to enfold Heloise in her arms, but since the girl stood a head taller, this was impossible. Instead, she rested her head against Heloise's shoulder and the soft red mouth crumpled into a grimace. "It seems like only yesterday that you came to us," she said, weeping. "All those golden baby curls and the thumb always stuck in your mouth." Her voice quivered prettily. "And now you've grown up. Now who will read all those dusty manuscripts in the library, tell me that, child."

Heloise said lightly, "There will be others, lady." Embarrassment flushed her cheeks, and she longed to make her escape before she began bawling. She moved back a step and swept her gaze around the yard. She could not see Ceci. Or any man who appeared to be a butcher.

"Ah yes, but there is only one Heloise." The parrot let loose with a hoarse, mocking shriek. "Oh dear. Baby wants his breakfast." Nervously, she twisted the diamond on its lace chain. "Remember me to your uncle, child."

"I will, lady."

The abbess smiled and a dimple appeared at the corner of her red mouth. "God be with you until next we meet."

Heloise gently corrected her. "Lady, I won't be back. It's not likely that we will meet again in this world."

"Oh." She appeared confused for a moment, and then she shrugged. "Just so." She turned and headed for the cloister gate, like a galley under full sail, the child in charge of Baby limping dutifully in her wake.

Heloise stared at their backs, especially at the child's. She was lame. One leg was several inches shorter than the other. She remembered the day that the little girl had been left here, the father lying broadly, solemnly assuring Lady Alais that his daughter had already had a calling from God, and so forth. Heloise remembered looking at the child's pinched, frightened face and then down at her withered leg, and a cruel rhyme had run through her head: "I was not good enough for man/ And so am given to God." Something about the disfigured girl had filled her with distaste, and she rarely spoke to her unless it could not be avoided.

She picked up her bundles and walked toward the portress's lodge, all the while looking for Ceci. At the doorway, the portress called out, "The butcher was here just a minute ago. Now, where did that scurvy knave get to?" She darted into a crowd of men saddling their horses. Through the doorway, Heloise could see Ceci huddled inside on a stool, her eyes rimmed with tears. As she came slowly toward the door, she blotted her face with the back of her hand. "I have to work on my embroidery now," she said vehemently. "Sister Judith said so."

Heloise stepped one foot inside and caught her by the shoulder. "Little fool. I'm leaving now. Kiss me goodbye."

"Goodbye."

"I'll miss you."

Ceci nodded wanly. "Heloise."

"What?" she asked.

"I'll always love you. And no matter what you say, I shall pray every day for your return."

"Crazy little fool." Heloise kissed her roughly and stumbled out into the glaring yard. The portress brought up a brawny man leading a packhorse. Without speaking, the butcher lashed her bundles to the saddle and boosted Heloise up onto a cushion. He mounted, and they started to ride out through the gate. Heloise turned and looked back. Ceci was still standing in the doorway of the lodge, her face dazed, and when Heloise waved, she lifted her hand in a weary farewell. After a while, Heloise twisted forward on the cushion and riveted her eyes on the butcher's back and, over his shoulder, at a strip of field being weeded by men with sunbrowned faces. The fragrance of herbs and moist earth and sweat fogged the hot blue air. When next she looked around, Argenteuil had vanished behind a hill.

2 🌿

FULBERT'S HOUSE STOOD on the far edge of the cloister at Notre Dame, where the Rue des Chantres meets the river. The ground pitched away steeply, sweeping down to the Port Saint-Landry; Heloise could see a cluster of boats tied up to the quay. Two fishermen were arguing as they hung their nets. Confused, she stared at the house, at the fishermen, and then back at the house again. It was not what she expected. Taller perhaps. Grander. When she looked closely, she realized that it was not one building but three, stuck together as if by a playful mason. Reluctantly, she slid to the ground and waited, wobbly-legged, while the butcher pounded on the closed door.

Immediately the door jerked open and a woman, her face flushed, impaled him with a baleful glare. "God's toenails! Took your good sweet time, didn't you! Did you come by way of Avignon?"

The butcher looked properly cowed. He began to mumble about traffic, but his words were drowned in a torrent of abuse. "The canon expected her before dinner," she shouted. "Here it's nearly nones." She called him villein, dog, and son of a whore before extracting a denier from her girdle and waving him away.

The butcher snorted at the coin. "May your tongue rot," he said mildly. He strode back to the horse and mounted.

Heloise lowered her eyes. When she raised them, she saw the woman lumbering toward her, arms outstretched, a tearful smile grooving jagged lines about her mouth. "Lady, lady, lady. Oh, my sweet little one, my lamb . . ."

Not until the calloused hands had begun stroking her hair did Heloise recognize Agnes. She could have sworn that her uncle's housekeeper had been fat. This woman was big-boned and muscular but far from obese. Over Agnes's shoulder, she saw, crouched in the doorway, a girl with white-blond hair squinting at her suspiciously. When Heloise caught her eye, she looked away, scowling.

Heloise wanted to tell Agnes that she was happy to be here, but the words demanded by custom and courtesy stuck in her throat. She was beginning to feel the queasiness in her stomach that she had experienced earlier in the day, and for a queer instant she could barely recall what Argenteuil looked like. "Agnes—"

Agnes smothered her neck with kisses. She did not seem to notice Heloise's silence. "God be praised!" she said, beaming. "What a joyous day for the master. And look at you . . . What a great bean pole you've become."

Heloise smiled stiffly.

"Come inside before you catch sunstroke. Master went to the cathedral after dinner, but I've saved you some quail." She led her by the hand toward the house. "I'm afraid the sauce has gone bad. In this heat you can't keep anything. Isn't that right, Petronilla?" The pouting girl clung to the doorway, apparently immobilized. Agnes raised a clenched fist. "Take the lady's bundle up to her room, and mind you don't touch anything or I'll box your ears. And see to a bath for your mistress. Hurry up!"

Her mouth dry with thirst, Heloise followed Agnes. Inside, the house was as cool and dark as a cave. Blinded, she hesitated and locked her hand under Agnes's arm to keep from stumbling. The vaulted passageway smelled of lavender and incense. And of a fermented silence. She wondered why, considering Agnes's propensity for gabbling like a magpie. The passageway ran alongside a solar, and, through an arch, Heloise caught a glimpse of an arras-covered wall. They skirted the kitchen and came out at the rear of the house into a garden strewn with fine white pebbles. A pear tree shaded half of the courtyard from the midafternoon sun. Through the foliage, hazy shafts of light struck the pebbles and burst into golden motes. At the base of a wall at the back of the garden, dragonflies swooned in beds of mint, basil, horehound, and sweet william.

Heloise sank on a bench under the pear tree. She felt very tired. All she wanted was a cool drink and a bed. Suddenly, boisterous shouts of laughter erupted on the other side of the wall. There were sounds of yelling and thrashing about; somebody cursed loudly. She looked quizzically at Agnes.

"Students in the close." Agnes's voice was almost bored. "You'll get used to them."

"Do they always make so much racket?" asked Heloise.

"Usually. Noisy whelps." She grimaced. "And it's been unbearable since Master Peter has come back." According to Agnes, this Master Peter was responsible for half the riffraff in western Europe settling in the Ile-de-France, with a goodly share of the rabble congregated directly behind the canon's garden wall. Paris, she panted bitterly, was no longer fit for decent folk. Still disparaging the students, she began moving toward the house. Heloise called her back.

"I'm not hungry, Agnes," she said. "Just a drink, please." Eyes half closed, she slouched against the tree trunk. It was hard to stay awake.

"As you wish, lady." Agnes brought a bowl of water from the well. "Slowly, now," she warned. "Best way to take fever is to drink icy water on a hot day."

Heloise held the bowl greedily, forcing herself to empty it in small gulps. She leaned back and stirred her toes in the pebbles while she considered asking why Fulbert had sent for her. Agnes would be sure to say that she knew nothing about it; no doubt she knew everything about it.

After a while, Agnes took her upstairs to a turret room on the third floor and left her with Petronilla. At first, all she could see was fat pillows on a great feather bed, and after a dozen years on a prickly straw mattress at Argenteuil, she couldn't help gaping. She had never seen such a bed; even Lady Alais's could not compare. Her uncle, she thought, must be rich as a king.

She ran to the window and peered down at the Seine, its massive surface rippling like gold in the sun. Upstream, she could see an island, a flat saucer on which herds of cows were grazing. Petronilla circled behind her and began to peel off Heloise's sweaty gown and shift. A tub sat in the middle of the floor, and when she stepped into it, water sloshed over the sides.

She soaped herself in silence. The girl was busy with Heloise's bundle, lifting out the crumpled gowns, inspecting them with undisguised disdain, and hanging them on the wall pegs. She looked to be about Ceci's age but, with the exception of the fair hair that flowed down her back, she was more ugly than not. Her nose was too long, her chin slightly receding, her mouth sulky. "How long will you stay?" she blurted out suddenly.

Heloise started at hearing a voice emerge from that sullen mouth. "I don't know."

"Did you like the convent?"

"No."

"Why not?"

Heloise bobbed her head under the water to wet her hair. The girl asked too many questions. "Boring."

Petronilla gave a knowing laugh. "Have you had a man?" she asked boldly.

"What?"

"I have. Five or six."

Heloise retreated into shocked silence. The girl must be lying; she was only a child. She forced her face into a blank expression for fear of eliciting further unwanted confidences. Surely the girl lied.

But Petronilla did not pursue the subject. She carelessly dumped the rest of Heloise's belongings into a chest that served as a window seat and slammed down the lid hard. Licking her lips, she said, "Everybody talks about you."

"Who?"

"Master. Agnes. Everybody."

Heloise stood up and motioned Petronilla to bring the towel. "What do you mean? What do they say?" She frowned a little, thinking nervously of the gossiping women at Argenteuil. No trivial incident, no personal idiosyncrasy, was too insignificant for them to chew to pieces. She knew no one in Paris; what could they possibly have to say about her? "What are you talking about?"

"You know." Petronilla yawned, her eyes never leaving Heloise's face. "That you can read and do sums."

She laughed out loud in relief. "Oh. Is that all?" She began untangling her wet hair with a comb. The girl squatted on the floor, arms folded over her knees, and slyly watched her every move. For lack of something better to say, Heloise asked if Agnes had been ill.

"No."

"You're sure?"

"Of course."

"But she's always been fat," Heloise insisted. "Now she's thin."

Bending double with laughter, Petronilla rolled on the floor. Heloise stared down with increasing annoyance at the childish horseplay and finally nudged her with a foot. Flat on her back, the girl gasped, "Can't you tell when a woman is breeding?"

In the haughty tone that the young take with a toothless grandam, Petronilla explained that Agnes was brought to bed nearly every year, but the brats invariably died before they were out of swaddling clothes. "Save myself, of course," she added, hauling herself to her feet.

"Holy Lady!" Heloise cried, forgetting her irritation. "Agnes is your mother!"

"Yes."

Her curiosity piqued, Heloise asked, "And who is your father?"

Petronilla did not answer.

"Come now, you must have a father. Don't you know?"

She raised her eyes and blasted a hard, mocking look straight into Heloise's face. "No, I don't know!" she shouted. "And I don't want to know, and if I did know I wouldn't tell you!" She burst into sobs, hiccuping and blubbering as runnels of tears coursed down the sides of her nose and into her mouth.

Startled, Heloise said nothing. The child was odd, anyone could see that. When she finally spoke, her voice was gentle. "Silly! Lots of people don't have fathers. Is it anything to cry about?"

Still sniveling, the girl refused to be consoled, and after a while Heloise turned away in disgust. She walked over to the bed and pulled down the coverlet. Between the cool white sheets Agnes had tucked bunches of lavender. Heloise clambered onto the bed. Before her head reached the pillows, she was asleep.

The voice of a man somewhere below in the house jerked her awake. The sun was flooding through the windows, rouging the room with a wash of crimson light. From the direction of the close skittered a confused murmur of voices, laughter, jangled snatches of a charivari. After Argenteuil, the rough male tones unsettled her. She was only beginning to realize the difference between the ordinary world and the convent, not that the nuns hadn't reminded her often enough. Her mind wandered to a day—she must have been four, five—when old Sister Marie had jabbed her and pointed to a goat. See that? she had cackled, lips stretched back over mirthless gums. There with the horns. Do you know what that thing is? That's a woman of the world!

Heloise had smiled dutifully, but she had not believed her, of course. She recognized an animal when she saw one. Still. What precisely had Sister Marie meant? For years afterward, whenever she saw a goat, she thought of the old nun's words and grew faintly uneasy.

When she came downstairs, Agnes motioned her into the solar and left without a word. Fulbert was standing by the window, and despite the warmth of the day, he was wearing a cloak of dark-red velvet. At the sight of him, Heloise felt a sharp, cold blade pass through her body, but in the instant it took him to turn from the window and walk slowly toward her, the sensation vanished. She was a little surprised to see a man of taller than average height—she could look into his eyes without lowering her head—with an extremely pale, clean-shaven face and silvery-blond hair. There was something striking in Fulbert's appearance; his handsome face had a hand-carved look, that angularity of cheekbones and chin that makes age indeterminable. She knew he must be close to forty, but he had the face of a much younger man.

"Agnes said you'd grown tall."

He came to her and kissed her on both cheeks. His eyes were a grayish blue, friendly but wistful, distracted even, and they made her feel self-conscious. She backed away from him and smiled vaguely.

He patted her shoulder and pulled up a stool for her. "Here, child. Sit down."

She sank down reluctantly and watched him as he looked her over. Suddenly she felt awkward and painfully aware of her shabby gown.

"Well, now," he said gently. "You've given me reason to feel proud of you. Lady Alais tells me that you're a genius."

Heloise colored deeply. Lady Alais only parroted what Madelaine told her. "I did what they asked of me." Then: "I love books."

Fulbert cleared his throat. "Heloise," he said, "is it your wish to take the veil?"

"No." Her voice was vehement.

Her uncle sighed. "So Lady Alais informed me. In her opinion, you have no vocation. Which is a pity. An immense pity because a learned woman is at a great advantage in the Church."

He went on at some length about Church politics and the opportunities for advancement when a girl could read Greek and Hebrew. He said that he knew of few grown men who had achieved what Heloise had already accomplished as a child. She lost track of what the rambling voice was saying. He could not force her to return to Argenteuil; if he tried she would run away. She folded her hands in her lap and listened to Agnes banging kettles in the kitchen and yelling at Petronilla to fetch eggs.

"Therefore, I suppose I must see about finding you a husband."

The statement nearly propelled her off the stool. "A husband!" she cried. "I don't want a husband!"

Fulbert didn't seem to have heard her. His face was as matter-of-fact as though he were selecting hymns for vespers. "You are fifteen—"

"Fourteen," she interrupted.

"—almost fifteen, and of an age when it's proper that a woman be married." He walked to the doorway and called for Agnes without raising his voice. "You come from good stock. Be assured that I'll give you to a man of sufficiently high rank"—he cleared his throat again—"that is, the highest possible rank for a girl with no dower to speak of."

Agnes appeared in the doorway, wiping her hands on her apron.

Fulbert spoke without looking at her. "Have Petronilla set up the trestle in the garden tonight. It's much too warm to dine indoors."

"Yes, my lord."

Heloise slumped on the stool, sluggish. Fulbert made everything sound so simple. Black and white, convent and marriage. She felt a torrent of involuntary fury surge over her, but it was directed entirely inward. In bed sometimes at night, after coming up from matins, she would make up lives for herself, and in her mind she often saw herself as the Margravine Ida who had ridden to the Holy Land at the head of her crusading army. Some said that the Austrian amazon had perished, killed at the same massacre in the hills of Asia Minor where Heloise's father had died; others swore that she had been captured and taken away to live in some emir's desert castle. But later, after Heloise had studied Greek, her dream-fantasies were all placed in Lesbos or Athens, where she pictured herself as the sweet-tongued lioness, Sappho, or as Aspasia, lovely and wise, strolling among the fluted columns of the Parthenon with her lover, Pericles. Yet these were the foolish mirages of a child, and for several years she had known it, even though she continued to dream, eddying on a phantasmal river that made life bearable. She thought sorrowfully, I'm too old for make-believe.

The moment of panic skittered away. All she felt was shame. She fully expected Fulbert to be furious with her, but he was still standing there, smiling amiably. Apparently he had already devoted some thought to this problem of a husband, for later, over supper, he spoke of little else. What he sought was a man of good family, a man somewhat learned himself who would appreciate the value of a young woman on whom he could get intelligent sons, someone to keep the household accounts in perfect order and read aloud in the evenings. Ideal would be an older man, preferably a widower seeking the exotic in a second or third wife.

Unfortunately, Fulbert confessed to her, he had been unable to think of anyone remotely approaching this description. Heloise, ravenous, ate and said nothing.

After the meal, on her way up to bed, she overheard him telling

Agnes that Heloise was too big for a woman, but, God be thanked, she was at least pretty. A girl both ugly and learned would be nigh impossible to dispose of, she would be eating his bread until the day he died.

"She carries herself like a duchess," Agnes replied.

"Too tall."

3 🌿

AT FIRST, Fulbert talked a great deal about Heloise's marriage, and so did Agnes and Petronilla. But on the second Sunday of June took place the Procession of the Relic, when Notre Dame displayed the piece of the True Cross that it had acquired a few years earlier. Since relics were Fulbert's chief passion, he was busy with arrangements for the feast day. On the Thursday after St. John's Day, he rode down to Melun to collect overdue rents from his tenant farms, and after he returned it rained steadily for a week. The coverlet on her bed began to smell of mildew, and the streets of the Ile turned into lakes of mud until horses floundered up to their fetlocks. On the main streets, planks had been thrown down at the crossings, but nobody went about much unless he had to. Heloise noticed that Fulbert no longer mentioned the betrothal. Probably he had forgotten, and she had no intention of reminding him.

During the first summer in Paris, life seemed to settle into a pattern, but unlike the oppressive rituals at Argenteuil, it was a routine that filled her with an immense peace. Fulbert owned a fine library; she would spend the mornings in his study or take the books to her turret chamber and read by the window, turning the parchment pages and memorizing whole passages from Seneca and St. Jerome. The more she read, the more she became aware of all she had not read, and she devoured books the way Petronilla bolted down Agnes's cardamom cakes.

Fulbert puzzled her. He was responsible for selecting the music at three of the seven daily services, but he hired others to do much of the work. Most of his time was spent dealing in relics, at which business he made considerable profit (with the exception of Christ's baby tooth, and in that case he claimed to have been cruelly swindled), and he was constantly adding to his property holdings near Melun. His canonical duties were performed as a sort of afterthought, or so it appeared to Heloise.

What gradually became clear to her was that Fulbert was growing fond of her. The moment he stepped foot in the house he would call for her, and they would sit under the pear tree while Agnes babied him insanely. She would seat him in a cushioned chair and slip a pillow under his feet; for that matter, she was on the run for him at all hours, massaging his feet with unguents, dosing him with broths of medicinal herbs, fetching his toothpick or a silver henap filled with Macon. Fulbert was a man who demanded, and received, good service from his women. The lesser sex might be gateways to the devil, but God had put women on earth for a purpose—to bear children and provide food, drink, and other sundries for men. As for his niece, he valued her for other reasons. Hearing her read aloud gave him pleasure, and after dark he ordered candles, instead of the rushlights they ordinarily burned, so that Heloise should not ruin her eyes.

According to Agnes, this in itself was remarkable, because Master was forever grumbling about the expense of candles, just as he grew anguished over any unnecessary expenditure. Petronilla said he was stingy, but Heloise believed it merely thrift. Certainly Fulbert esteemed money; he dressed in fine velvets and brocades and decked his fingers with rubies and emeralds so that he looked more lofty than a bishop.

This quirky passion of his for listening to her read embarrassed Heloise a little in the beginning, especially at his monthly "evenings," when he entertained his fellow canons and some of the local barons. These recitations being very nearly in the nature of public performances, Heloise started to balk, but then she thought better of it. It was clear that these fine gentlemen, despite their education, in no way approached her storehouse of knowledge, and if it gave them pleasure to learn, she did not begrudge them. Agnes said it was a blessing to have Heloise at these gatherings because, before her arrival at the Rue des Chantres, the men wound up arguing, and Canon Martin, Fulbert's closest friend, invariably stalked out in a fury.

After Lammas, Fulbert began taking her across the Petit Pont to a flat field near Saint-Germain-des-Prés, where he taught her to ride. He said it would be a disgrace for a noble girl to be anything less than a fine horsewoman. The sluggish brood mare he first brought for her was about as exciting as a half-dead mule; she lumbered along until Heloise feared each step would be her last. Heloise protested, and the next time they went out, Fulbert had selected a dun gelding, lively and high-stepping.

The meadow ran alongside the Left Bank of the Seine, across from the king's palace. There was a landing quay at the tip of the island, and Heloise could make out mossy green steps leading up to a gate and beyond that what appeared to be a luxuriant garden.

The early-morning mist was beginning to lift, breaking into frail patches and drifting up in the sunlight. Fulbert lengthened the dun's stirrups. Sighing, Heloise called to him, "I wish I were a lark. I'd fly across the river and sit on a branch of one of those lemon trees, and I could watch all the court ladies."

He straightened with a laugh. "That's not necessary. In summer, King Louis opens the garden to the masters and students from the schools. They hold classes there and anyone may enter." He hoisted her into the saddle and handed up the reins. "Frightened, poppet?"

"No." The dun took two steps forward and happily bucked her into the wet grass. She sat there in surprise a minute before pulling herself to her feet. The dun looked back, snorting disdainfully.

Fulbert held out his arms to lift her up again. "This time, don't slam down your behind so hard. You're too rough."

Heloise stroked the dun's withers, talking to him softly in Hebrew. "See. He's a Jew. He likes me now."

Her uncle grinned. "Mayhap."

At a slow jog, they began to move down the field. Heloise relaxed in the saddle and felt the breeze streaming over her bare ankles.

"Sit up straight!" shouted Fulbert. "Don't flap your elbows around like a hawk." He spurred his stallion into a canter, and the dun followed.

From the corner of her eye, Heloise kept swinging her gaze over to the blue roofs of the Cité Palace, foolishly hoping to catch a glimpse of the king or his new bride, Queen Adelaide. "Do you think I could go there?"

"Go where?"

"There." She pointed to the king's garden. "To hear the masters teach."

Fulbert wheeled the stallion and galloped around her in a circle. With the haughty curve of his back and his fair hair streaming out behind in the glare of the sun, his head appeared speckled with a kind of luminous crown. Heloise thought that he looked like St. Michael, or one of those knights the jongleurs always sang about; he would have been a knight if his father had not sent him into the Church. He rode up behind Heloise. "Whatever for? My fair niece, you know more than the masters."

She doubted that. "I? You tease me."

"Indeed." He was gazing at her affectionately. "Oh, well. I suppose there are a few of them who might teach you something. Peter Abelard perhaps."

Before she could answer, he was halfway down the field. "Come on!" he yelled.

She still wanted to go; he hadn't said no.

They were coming to Pré-aux-Clercs, a strip of land lying between Saint-Germain and the river, and constantly disputed between the monks and the students. This morning the chewed-up field looked to be in the hands of the young people; they were dancing and singing, and some had gathered around a wrestling match. Heloise and Fulbert dismounted at the edge of the field and let the horses graze.

"Are you happy?" Fulbert asked kindly.

"I'm happy."

"I mean, living with me." He rested his palms on her shoulders. She could feel the warmth of his fingers through her dress.

"I'm happy." She swallowed. "It's been—"

"Good."

She caught his hand. "You won't send me away? I hated Argenteuil." She wanted to say more, to ask him never to send her away, but pride prevented her from drawing attention to her shameless insecurities. In all the empty places she must walk, he would stand between her and evil.

His fingers tightened around hers. "Don't talk about it."

She said tautly, "All right." It was funny, now that she thought of it, how people always wanted you to keep quiet about the things that mattered.

"You're only a child yet."

They ran toward the horses; on the way back to the Rue des Chantres, they talked of the petition the burghers were planning to draw up, requesting Louis the Fat to cobble the streets of the Ile.

Summer ended. Small whooping boys stopped diving naked off the Petit Pont, and the chestnut leaves in the cloister turned burnished red. Each day more and more students swarmed into the city, something Heloise had not believed possible. Michaelmas came and went, and now the evenings were too crisp to sit in the garden. She and Fulbert moved inside to a fire in the canon's private apartments, and they would talk long after the watchman had drawn the chain across the Rue des Chantres. Rarely, if ever now, did she brood about the future; there seemed to be an unspoken agreement between her and Fulbert. He did not again refer to the morning at Pré-aux-Clercs, yet it was taken for granted that there would be no husband, not now at least, and that they would skim through time together, snugly wrapped in a cocoon of their own making. They never talked about it.

Nevertheless, she knew that what she felt for Fulbert fell into some ill-defined category of love. She loved God, of course, and Jesus and the Blessed Virgin, but it was hard to say whether she loved any living person, and being uncertain, she rather thought not. The people one ordinarily loved, mother and father, brothers and sisters, had never existed for her. Sister Madelaine she had admired, but not loved, and Ceci she had tolerated, as one forbears to shoo away a dog forever curled around one's ankles. There was only Fulbert, who filled her with a kind of tranquillity, Fulbert with his pale hair and his fingers lightly stroking her cheek.

On a hazed-over morning in October, Heloise sat in the kitchen, her face smeared with one of Agnes's concoctions of lemon juice and goose grease to make skin smooth and white. The precise reason for these beauty treatments escaped her—there was no man she wished to impress, except perhaps Fulbert—but Agnes insisted. She made it a point of honor to advise her mistress on everything a young lady of good blood should know.

Agnes was rolling out pastry dough with floury arms and talking of how Queen Adelaide would have her lying-in at the Cité Palace instead of Compiègne, and how it was high time King Louis gave the Franks an heir, seeing as he had waited until the advanced age of thirty-five to marry.

Heloise yawned. "He must not like women."

"Oh, I imagine he likes them well enough," Agnes grunted. "He's sired at least one bastard." She began cutting the dough into circles. "True, it wouldn't surprise me if he did hate them, after Bertrada got done with him."

Agnes never ceased to astonish Heloise. She had a repertory of gossip, past and current, and given half a chance, she would chatter your ear off. "Bertrada?" asked Heloise. "Who's that?"

At the spit, Petronilla was turning, halfheartedly, a pair of fowls. She threw Heloise a jeering look. "Lady. You are dumb."

Heloise ignored her, but Agnes bounded across the kitchen and whacked the girl's face until she'd raised a liverish welt. "God's toenails, can't I trust you to do anything properly? Those hens are beginning to look like cinders." She went back to the circles of dough and started dropping spoonfuls of minced cheese on the moons. "Bertrada," she explained carefully, as if informing Heloise of some momentous battle, "Bertrada was Louis's stepmother, that is to say, the second wife of Old King Philip, God rest his soul. She tried to poison Louis so that her spindly brat could have the throne." Triumphant at the skill with which she had condensed years of complex history into a few sentences, she turned to Heloise with a smile and said, "You see? The point is, the old hag didn't succeed. Mind you, Louis was sickly for quite a time, but—" She shrugged, and immediately embarked on a dissertation about how to keep moths out of feather beds.

The aromatic warmth of the kitchen made Heloise drowsy; the greasy juice rolling down the sides of her cheeks made her skin itch. Propping her feet up on a wooden keg, she raised her face to the ceiling. Hanging from the beams were bunches of dried herbs—sage, mint, fennel, hyssop, all carefully extracted from the garden before the first frost. This room was Heloise's favorite part of the house. The fireplace stretching across one whole wall belched warmth; everything was permeated with delicious aromas. When she awoke in the mornings, even before she had opened her eyes, the smells were already drifting through the house —stews and soups, goose, frumenty, bacon and beans, minced beef and raisin pies. In the pantry were massed jars of wine that Agnes had made from cherries, currants, raspberries, and pears, and down in the cellar she kept the imported wines of Cyprus and Spain that Fulbert served to guests. Never had Heloise imagined such an abundance of food and drink. As though she had been starved all her life, she ate ravenously and sometimes stole to the kitchen between meals to beg Agnes for a taste of this or that. In only a few months, her cheeks and breasts had rounded and her hips were beginning to curve snugly inside her gowns.

From the hearth, Petronilla hissed belatedly, "I know why King Louis didn't die. He had a philtre from the Fairy Lady. And her magic was stronger than Bertrada's."

"So they say," Agnes answered. She looked hastily over at Heloise. "If you believe that mumbo jumbo."

Heloise sat up straight on the stool. "This Fairy Lady, does she make love philtres? Will she tell your fortune?"

Petronilla was prowling along the wall, hoping Agnes would not notice the untended spit. "She knows who a girl's true love is."

Heloise laughed uneasily. At Argenteuil, the nuns had gossiped incessantly about witches and fairies—after crossing themselves, of course. Madelaine had called it hocus-pocus, but Heloise always listened just the same. She believed all of it and none of it. How was it possible for a fortune-teller to scan the emptiness of time for that which is yet to be? It was not possible, she suddenly decided. Or if it was, then only God could manage such a feat. Wiping the grease from her face, she threw down the towel and turned her back on Petronilla and her Fairy Lady.

Later that morning, she walked over to Notre Dame. Coming back from mass she decided to walk past Saint-Christofle and return home through the cloister, a route she rarely took because of Agnes's warnings that it was dangerous for decent girls to go among the students. "Animals," Agnes called them, and it was true that their drinking and roistering created disturbances in the Ile and gave them a bad name with the burghers. But with so many of them crammed into one small island, it was to be expected that a few would misbehave. Heloise thought that probably most of the students were courteous young men.

A smell of burning leaves hung in the air. Trying to look inconspicuous, she pulled her cloak around her ears and tucked her chin into the collar. Everywhere there stood bands of gowned young men, but nobody paid attention to her; they were all too busy talking. She was marching briskly eastward when a boy disengaged himself from one of the gangs and began to skip alongside her. She threw him a stern glance and walked faster; with her long legs, she soon managed to outdistance him.

When she jerked around to look, she saw that he had stopped but was continuing to stare at her.

"*La très sage Héloïse,* greetings," he said. "Lady, forgive. I meant no harm." The boy was only half grown; he had apple cheeks and wisps of fuzz on his chin.

Curious, Heloise waited while he came slowly toward her. "How do you know my name?" she said.

"Everybody in Paris knows," he told her with a toothy grin. "The very wise Heloise they call you. You're Canon Fulbert's niece, and I've heard that you're the wisest girl in France. Mayhap in the whole world."

Heloise laughed. "And you're a very foolish boy. Do you believe everything you hear?"

"Lady, I've just begun studying with Master Abelard. I wish that I knew as much as you."

His look was so full of admiration that she stifled her smile. "Good," she said gravely. "Then go back to Master Abelard and listen well." She turned away, amused by the boy but anxious to go home.

He ran after her. "Lady, tell me something, please. Are you a Nominalist or a Realist?"

"My friend, all I can tell you is that I have no idea what you're talking about. Pray, what is a Nominalist?" She felt dumb for asking.

The boy spent ten minutes explaining that the Realists believed in the importance of universals—the Church, humanity, divinity—while the Nominalists thought particulars more significant—churchmen, individuals, persons of the Trinity. Apparently this was a fashionable intellectual controversy in the schools. No scholar could ignore it; one must, he informed her, take a side.

Heloise smiled at him. "I'm in debt for your information," she said lightly, "but does it really matter, after all, believing one thing or the other?"

"Oh, yes." He stood there, clumsily knotting and unknotting the girdle of his tunic. "Yes, it matters a lot."

"Ah, well—in that case." She moved off quickly. "Farewell."

Behind her, the boy was shouting, "God guard you, lady!"

The rest of the morning she spent in her room translating Lucan, a project that had occupied her for some weeks. But today she found her attention wandering, her mind trailing back to the boy she had met in the close. Not to the boy himself but to something he had said, his explanation of the Nominalists and the Realists. The controversy in itself she found of no great interest, yet she had to admit that the idea of debating such subjects intrigued her. She knew that she was weak in dialectic, and even though Madelaine had halfheartedly imparted the fine points of logical argument, thesis and antithesis, antecedent and consequent, she had had few opportunities to practice. Fulbert was heavily unenthusiastic, dismissing it as mere showing off.

The turret room was freezing. She padded down to the kitchen and asked Agnes to make her a cup of hot almond milk. Upstairs again, she crawled under the coverlet and sipped her milk thoughtfully. The idea that had been thrashing around at the back of her mind for hours suddenly forced its way into consciousness; she wanted to go to school. Immediately she began to sigh and berate herself for wishing the impossible. But was it?

She pulled the cover around her neck. Agnes once mentioned a niece of the Count of Montmorency who had attended classes at the abbey of Saint-Victor across the river; at the same time Heloise vividly remembered Agnes's scalding grimaces of disapproval and her mutterings about immodest hussies. Evidently, females rarely showed their faces in the all-male schools, and when they did, people talked about them. Knowing Fulbert, she knew he would not want that. Coughing, she got out of bed and checked to see if the shutters were securely fastened.

Something else occurred to her; that boy in the cloister knew all about her. How? Presumably through Fulbert's boasting and those of his friends who had met her. Uncle seemed to have no objection if the people of Paris admired his "wise" niece. Perhaps there was a way to get around him after all.

She heard the clump of the downstairs door and Fulbert's voice, then Agnes squawking waves of orders to Petronilla and the creak of running feet. Abruptly the hushed house sprang into motion. Before going down, Heloise brushed her hair down with her palms.

Already the trestle had been covered with a white cloth, and Petronilla was laying out the trenchers and goblets. The girl wore her usual surly expression. "Master was asking for you."

A few minutes later, Fulbert was blessing the table and reaching for the pitcher of Macon. "Come kiss me, child," he said.

Heloise trotted over and wound her arms around his neck. Unlike most men, who shaved only two or three times a week and had prickly cheeks, Fulbert had Agnes shave him every morning. His alabaster skin was always smooth as a woman's, and smelled of pine scent. She stroked a tiny wet peck on his cheek and ran to her chair.

Heloise poured a little of the Macon into her goblet and filled it to the top with water. While Agnes brought in the dishes, she studied Fulbert's face, searching for signs of his mood.

"What did you do this morning, sweet?" He doused a helping of roasted fowl with garlic sauce.

"Worked on my Lucan." She paused. "While I was out walking earlier, a young man came up to me. A lad really. He called me 'the very wise Heloise.'" She scratched her nose, keeping her voice bland. "He said that everyone in the Ile knew of me."

Fulbert shook his head at her. "An exaggeration, naturally. Still, I'm sure that a great many people know you by reputation."

"That doesn't bother you?"

"No." He took a generous portion of pease porridge, tasted it, and wiped his mouth on his napkin. "Why should it? Try a little of this porridge. It's superb."

She shrugged. Uneasily, she wondered if this might be the proper time to bring up the subject of school. Realizing that she had not yet touched her trencher, she hastily skewered a chunk of fowl on her knife and flicked it into her mouth. "I was wondering," she said quickly, chewing and talking at once, "what you would think of my attending one of the schools. I mean, becoming a pupil of some master. I—" She stopped to swallow.

"Yes? You what?"

She looked swiftly at Fulbert. "I'd like that."

He pushed aside the trencher and picked up his goblet. He held it for a little while before drinking, his eyes cloudy. She knew that look. It meant that he was searching for a tactful way to say something.

Smiling, he said, "This is a tender situation. A unique set of circumstances that we, uh, have to deal with."

Heloise crumbled a piece of bread into pellets and mounded them next to her trencher.

"I'm aware," he went on, "that a person of your intelligence should be attending classes. Now, if you were a young man, I would have signed you up with some master immediately." He threw up his hands with a loud sigh. "But what can I do? There's no place in the schools for women, and rightly so."

Avoiding his eyes, Heloise stared stiffly into her lap.

"Now, now, poppet, you're not going to cry, are you? Please don't cry. I know you're disappointed, but face facts. God didn't make women to be scholars. Now, you must admit that's so. It's not my fault, is it?" He rubbed his chin and smiled brightly, trying to jolly her into looking happy.

Her head snapped up. "I have heard that it's not totally unknown for a woman to attend classes." She strained to speak calmly. "There was a niece in the Montmorency family—"

"A strumpet. She didn't know A from B. Just interested in getting a master into her bed."

Heloise flushed dark red. Never before had she heard Fulbert refer to the sin of the flesh, and she was a trifle surprised. Nonetheless, she felt her advantage slipping and leaned forward to renew her attack with more force. "I'm a serious student, Uncle. If Saint-Victor could find room for a strumpet, surely they can tolerate my presence. Or—now, listen to this. With your influence at Notre Dame, you can find a way for me to attend the cathedral school. After all—"

Fulbert flung up his arms. "Listen to reason!"

"I won't!" Heloise cried hotly. She sat on the edge of her chair.

"By St. Denis, I see you have your grandmother's temper! There's no missing that."

Hearing the raised voices, Agnes hurried into the solar with apprehensive glances at both of them and deposited a flawn on the table. Heloise ate half the custard while haranguing Fulbert unmercifully. To his every groan of "Impossible, child," she had an answer, if not always a sensible one.

In the following weeks, she nagged him whenever she saw an opportunity, but he remained adamant, saying that she asked the unreasonable. Not until Advent had arrived and he'd begun talking about going to Saint-Gervais for the Christmas holidays did Heloise gradually subside in her demands. Excitement over the forthcoming journey soon driving all other concerns from her head, she pumped Agnes daily for information. How big was the castle? How many children did Uncle Thibaut have? And how did he get the nickname "the Lecher"? When had her grandmother, Mabile of Aspremont, died? Since Agnes had been born at Saint-Gervais and had come to Paris only when Fulbert received his canonry, she had plenty of stories to tell—in fact, several generations' worth. Nearly every day, Heloise trailed after her while Agnes aired feather beds and dusted, and she continued to plague her with questions.

It was during one of these interrogations that she discovered the reason for Fulbert's decision. Actually, it had not occurred to her that the excursion might be unusual; she assumed that Fulbert went back to Saint-Gervais every Christmas.

But Agnes said no. Ordinarily, he never left the Ile at this time of year because it was his busiest season, with many extra services at the cathedral. "It's for your sake, lady. Master says it's bad for you to stay cooped up with old people all the time. You need friends your own age. At home, there are lots of cousins." She scratched her head. "Let's see, Lady Marie's oldest girl must be about eighteen now. And there's Claude and Little Alis. I forget."

Heloise grinned at her. "You mean, Uncle wants me to meet normal girls who don't pester their elders about school."

"I didn't say that," Agnes answered lamely. "But you can't study all the time, sweet. It won't hurt to have fun once in a while."

Fulbert had Agnes make her two spectacular gowns, and he personally escorted Heloise to a furrier on the Rue de la Draperie, where he picked out a new cloak, raspberry velvet lined with marten. If there were ulterior motives behind this largess, for the cloak was extremely dear, his machinations met with overwhelming success. Obliging, for a time at least, Heloise dropped the subject of school. She had a curious feeling that something special, even important, lay in wait for her, and in this premonition she was right. At Saint-Gervais she met Jourdain for the first time.

The domain of Saint-Gervais lay on the fringe of the forest, an hour's ride west of Melun. The snow in the streets of the town had been whipped into beds of slush, but among the open hills, isolated and still, the woods were mantled with an unwrinkled layer of white powder. The sky hung heavy with snow falling steadily in a thin curtain, and crows flapped their wings above the frozen branches. Every few yards, Heloise flexed her mittened fingers, but the stiffness remained. When Fulbert offered her a handful of walnuts, she shook her head.

"How much farther?"

"Not much. Over the rise."

Twenty years earlier, when her grandfather, Rainard the Bald, had been castellan here, the place had glowed with an air of well-tended prosperity. But that had been before the great crusade, and now the accumulated wealth of generations lay strewn from the plains of Hungury to Jerusalem. It was not merely the horses, the fine leather saddles and costly armor that had rotted in the infidel soil, but the men of Saint-Gervais as well: old Rainard himself, who died of fever outside the walls of Antioch; his heir, Garnier the Young, and his wild-headed second son, William, both of whom had perished in the first assault on Jerusalem. True, those who had taken the cross were martyrs now and sat on God's left hand in paradise, but the living at the castle of Saint-Gervais were vouchsafed no such protection, and gradually most of the fief's southerly tracts had been mortgaged to the usurers of Melun. In the year of Our Lord 1115, the palisade had fallen into disrepair, and the keep could have used a coat of whitewash.

Over a creaky bridge spanning a snow-filled moat, they slowed to a walk and racketed into the ward. Everyone was waiting—the lord of Saint-Gervais, Lady Anne and Lady Marie, a half dozen cousins, knights and squires in service at the castle, varlets and servingwomen who had left their smithies and kitchens, all of them babbling at once. Heloise dismounted into a cluster of pages and grooms and barking dogs. The yard smelled powerfully of manure. A girl with flaxen braids made a dive for her hand. "Fair cousin . . ." Heloise heard her stutter, but the rest was lost in the thrum of voices.

Upstairs in the dark, smoky hall, formal introductions were made and acknowledged. Uncomfortable under the stares, Heloise glanced about uncertainly and tried to match faces with names, but they kept metamorphosing into smiling blobs. Everything about the castle confused her. After the peaceful house on the Rue des Chantres, where even the noise was noiseless, the castle presented a mosaic of barely controlled bedlam. Dozens of people milled around aimlessly; on the straw-covered floor, dogs and quarrelsome children yipped in shrieky voices, and in the flagstone fireplace whole sheep were roasting on the spit. Lady Anne, watery-eyed and looking constantly befuddled, gasped a torrent of orders to the squires.

Thibaut led Fulbert to a high-backed armchair near the hearth and seated him under the shield of Saint-Gervais. "Permit me to attend you, fair brother," he said. "You must be tired."

"Thank you, brother." Fulbert leaned back regally and stretched his legs.

This Thibaut, called the Lecher, was the fourth son of Rainard the Bald. He had inherited the fief quite accidentally after the deaths of his two eldest brothers in the Holy Land, while Fulbert, only ten months older, had been promised to the Church at birth. Heloise disliked Thibaut on sight. He was a largish man, bull-necked, with a faded yellow beard. There was something very nearly clownish about him, a slight slurring of his words, a fey expression around the eyes that did not match his protruding belly and massive thighs.

"Come over here, girl," he called to Heloise. "Let me look at you."

She drew nearer, smiling, trying to think of what Agnes had told her. Three wives, the first repudiated, the second dying under mysterious circumstances. Each wife had borne a son, and Thibaut had chauvinistically christened them after the kings of France—Philip, Hugh, Louis. Agnes had intimated that Thibaut was famous for treating his women badly, and judging from the remote look on Lady Anne's face, Heloise could imagine this might be true. "Sire," she said, bobbing a half curtsy.

Openly he studied her up and down, as if he were buying a brood mare. "So this is Hersinde's get," he rumbled to Fulbert. "Nothing of

our kin here. God's bones, brother, she must take after Guy-Geoffrey."
He went on talking about Heloise as if she were not there, addressing
his remarks to Fulbert, who nodded now and again and murmured
"Ummm."

Heloise said nothing. She admitted to no one, and sometimes not
even to herself, that she could not remember her mother. From small
things Agnes had told her, she had fashioned a portrait of a dainty
blond woman, all pink and white like some angel in a stained-glass window. Her father had died shortly after she was born. He meant nothing
to her; for him she had not even bothered to construct a face. Still, she
disliked the unpleasant inflection in Thibaut's voice when he mentioned
her father. Agnes had warned her not to expect them to have a good
word for Guy-Geoffrey of Rousillon, but when Heloise pressed for a
reason, Agnes had only shrugged. "He was from Poitou," she finally
said, as if that explained everything.

Thibaut was spraying spittle in all directions. "God, she's a tall one!"
he roared. "You'll have plenty of trouble finding a stallion for this
mare."

Fulbert smiled sourly. "I suppose."

A squire scudded up behind them balancing a tray of cups and a
pitcher of wine.

"A good breeder, surely," drawled Thibaut. "Strong."

Fulbert yawned. "Obviously." He rapped his fingers with ill-con-
cealed impatience on the arm of the chair.

Finally, a woman with a blight of pockmarks across her scraggy
cheeks came and hustled Heloise away. "My poor niece," Lady Marie
muttered. "Pay no attention. The old bastard's been drinking since
cockcrow." Heloise followed her aunt up a ladder to the solar; the
women's quarters, partitioned from the rest of the upper chamber by
hanging tapestries, was a congeries of pallets and feather beds. It was
hot and airless, and reeked of rose water and sickly-sweet lotions. On
the biggest of the beds flopped a half dozen chattering girls, giggling and
eyeing Heloise with undisguised curiosity. The girl with the flax-blond
hair who had greeted Heloise in the ward pushed one of them with a
volley of kicks. "Move, Claude, make room for our cousin Heloise.
Cousin, come sit here. There's plenty of room." Her face was flushed
with excitement.

Heloise sat down gingerly, careful not to disturb a young woman who
was giving the breast to a big boy of two or three.

"Mama," cried the blond girl, "can Heloise sleep with me? Please, Mama, say yes."

Lady Marie appeared not to have heard. "You favor your father," she said to Heloise. The fixed smile on her face was more of a grimace; she looked as though she had swallowed something bitter.

"That's what they say," Heloise replied, trying not to stare at her aunt's face. The craters made her cheeks look like a plowed field. Once she might have been pretty, like her daughter, but it was impossible to tell now.

After a moment, Lady Marie said mechanically, "Well then. Alis will look after you."

For all its seeming gaiety, its seeming country normality, there were things about Saint-Gervais that puzzled Heloise. That evening, which was Christmas Eve, everyone in the castle rode over the hill to the village of Saint-Gervais, where they heard mass in the church. Afterward, while they were braiding their hair for the night, Heloise noticed a girl huddled on a pallet in the corner. With her petaled black eyes and tousled hair, she looked remarkably like a doll that had been hugged shapeless. When Heloise smiled at her, she stared back, and then it became evident that the child had a humor: her face shone with a waxy pallor and smudgy violet shadows ringed her eyes.

"Greetings, friend," called Heloise, who was feeling merry from the wine and the mass. *"Joyeux Noël!"*

But there was no answer from the dark damsel, not even a glint of expression in the eyes.

Taken aback, Heloise nudged Alis. "What's wrong with her?" she whispered, motioning to the corner. "Is she deaf and dumb?"

Alis barely glanced around. "Oh. Don't bother with her. She doesn't speak the *langue d'oïl*." She was pulling off her shift. Her body glowed pink and soft-fleshed as a ripe peach. "She's from Castile."

"Really? What a long way from home."

Alis threw her a look of surprise. "Why, this is her home. She belongs to Thibaut. He bought her from a caravan of traders, a year ago Allhallows it must have been."

In silence, Heloise crawled under the coverlet while trying to digest and assess this news. She had never heard of a Christian buying another human being. Only the paynim kept slaves, and they lived on the other side of the world. Entranced, she propped herself against a pillow and stared at the girl. "I've not seen her downstairs," she said to Alis finally.

"Uncle forbids it. She's not to leave this chamber until you and Fulbert have returned to Paris." Alis crawled under the furs and huddled close to Heloise.

"Why?"

"She's breeding, didn't you notice? Six months or more." Alis laughed harshly. "Well, I guess she can't help it. She's only a whore."

Heloise shivered. The Spanish damsel appeared to be about ten years of age, although obviously her true age must be older. Still, she looked like a child. Heloise studied the girl's smoky eyes and the delicate curve of her heart-shaped face, and as she stared, she tried to understand what it all meant. Just as she was on the point of comprehension, the thought splintered and slithered aimlessly into a gaping void.

A servingwoman blew out the candle. In the darkness, Heloise twitched restlessly, her body bundled tightly between Alis and a second cousin. Their hospitality was all very fine, but she was accustomed to sleeping alone and felt miserably cramped. She wished that she were home again.

Alis stroked her hair. "Tell me something, cousin—how do you know when a man is in love with you? Oh, I wish somebody would fall in love with me, some handsome knight who plays the lute. But really I'll take anybody, so long as he's young. He wouldn't have to play anything." Breathing into Heloise's ear, her voice turned soft and tearful.

Heloise, uninterested, said placidly, "It should be perfectly easy for you to marry. You're very pretty."

"You don't know what you're saying!" wheezed Alis. "Thibaut—"

An exasperated voice interrupted. "Shut up, Alis. You'll keep us up all night."

"Shut up yourself." In ragged hisses, she whispered very fast into Heloise's ear. "If my sainted father hadn't been killed in the Holy Land, he would be lord of Saint-Gervais. And my lady mother would be mistress and we'd all have fine dowries."

"But surely Uncle owes you dowries—"

"Oh cousin, Thibaut is a pig. Didn't he marry Mabile to a man with one eye? And doesn't he keep threatening to send Claude to the convent of Sainte-Catherine?" She began to snuffle noisily. "I'm nearly eighteen, Heloise. Are you listening? Eighteen. God, I'm old! Nobody will ever take me without a dowry. I'll rot here, that's all!"

Heloise remembered seeing the one-eyed man in the hall. He had a gravy-stained tunic and caved-in cheeks and, when he laughed, his mouth showed practically toothless. She thought Mabile's husband repulsive. Shrouded in loneliness, she stared into the bubbling darkness a long time before she slept.

4 ❧

Two DAYS AFTER CHRISTMAS, Thibaut organized a hunt and took the men off to chase foxes in Saint-Gervais forest. Heloise was not sorry to see them go, especially Thibaut, who had pinched her bottom on the way to chapel the previous evening. Already she was counting the days until her departure; she suffered from constipation and dull pains in the head. By now, it seemed clear that she had nothing in common with her cousins. Thibaut's three boys, sly-looking youths with fleshy faces, had spoken no more than a few words to her. The eldest, Philip, wore a permanent sneer at the corners of his mouth. Mabile had troubles of her own with two infants and a third on the way, and her conversation was limited to complaints of sore breasts and pains in her lower back.

Alis and Claude and the rest of them gibbered constantly about clothes and boys. Heloise had been shocked to learn that Alis could write no more than her name and that she had never been taught to read. None of them at Saint-Gervais knew, and would not have cared had they known, about Heloise's studies. They only knew that Fulbert had brought her home from Argenteuil to be married, and nearly everything they said to Heloise centered on this one subject.

The morning, like all previous ones, dragged by sluggishly in a tiresome round of embroidery and gossip, most of which concerned persons that Heloise did not know. The laborious idleness, as well as the tattoo barking of the castle dogs, made her head throb, but she purposely said nothing.

At noon, she was relieved when Alis suggested they take a few of the squires and go to play in the meadow. The day was bright; glazed snow glistened in the fields. Over the top of the forest hung a few ragged clouds, clouds that for some reason made her think of the sunsets over the Ile. She felt sick with the memory.

Alis insisted that they must build a castle of love. When it was finished, they could all climb into it and pretend the squires were knights trying to rescue them. For most of the afternoon, they worked in a frenzy, but when they'd completed the snow castle, there was room for only one person to crawl inside. Heloise scrambled to the top and looked out. Two horsemen were approaching the drawbridge, and she could hear them hailing the gatekeeper.

At the sound of the voices, Alis began to squeal with pleasure. "Jourdain, come here! Jourdain, look at our castle of love!" She laughed happily. "What a fine day. Jourdain's here!"

Ambling toward them, smiling good-naturedly and dodging Alis's snowballs, came a young man with a stocky frame and an old-fashioned face, square, cherubic, his cheeks dusted with freckles. Heloise waited to be introduced, but Alis was too busy rolling up her eyes coquettishly through her lashes. She clung to Jourdain's arm like a thirsty leech.

He looked up at Heloise and grinned with a sheepish shrug.

She grinned back. "Are you another cousin, then?"

He shook his head. "My father's fief adjoins Saint-Gervais. All of us grew up together." He added hurriedly, "I'm surprised to find you here, lady. I've seen you often on the streets of the Ile."

"Oh?" Heloise frowned. "How do you do that when you live in the next fief?" She nodded toward the forest. "You must have very sharp eyes."

Alis answered for him. "He lives in Paris now. Our Jourdain's a scholar." She said it in a mocking, flirtatious tone.

Jourdain leaned over and kissed Alis's cheek, then promptly ignored her. "I have student's lodgings on the Rue Saint-Pierre," he told Heloise. "You should see my landlady, she's a dreadful old witch. But sometimes I stay on the Left Bank with my master. He gets lonely and likes to have someone there in the evenings, and I—"

Heloise cut in. "Tell me something, friend, which master do you study with? If only you knew how I envy you!"

"With Master Abelard, of course." He laughed a little self-consciously.

His laugh pleased her; she liked his voice, by turns grave and then merry as a cricket. "Why do you say 'of course'?"

"Because he's the best teacher in the world. He has more than three thousand students." He laughed again. "What can I say? Believe me, there's no way to describe such a man. He's a prince, a reincarnation of Socrates, a . . ."

Alis turned away with a loud cluck of annoyance. "God's blood, can't you talk about anything but your poxy master!"

"Poxy to you," Jourdain flared, "because your head is empty. I'm very proud that he's my master—and my friend."

Making a face, she snorted at him and ran off to play with Claude. Heloise leaned over the top of the snow castle. Perhaps this trip could not be counted a loss after all; it might even prove to be fun. "Come up," she said to Jourdain.

"No room. Come down."

She slid to the ground and crawled out through the tiny opening. "Your master sounds splendid." She had heard others speak admiringly of Peter Abelard. Even Fulbert, who tended to be critical of other people.

The afternoon shadows were lengthening. The hunting party clattered over the drawbridge, leaving a trail of blood on the hard-packed snow. Those in the meadow followed slowly. In the ward, Heloise's cousin Philip stood by his steaming horse, and as they passed, she was surprised to see him shoot Jourdain a look of venom.

"Still kissing ass for Peter Abelard?" Philip said with a grin.

Jourdain jolted by without replying. Upstairs in the hall, Heloise said, "He doesn't like you."

"No." His voice was quiet and controlled.

"Nor Abelard?"

"No. Philip hates anyone above him."

That night, for the first time since her arrival at Saint-Gervais, Heloise found herself feeling contented. Alis had been right about one thing: the arrival of Jourdain had turned the day splendid. Heloise felt easy with him, and as her tongue loosened, out rolled stories about Sister Madelaine and Ceci, critiques of Lucan and St. Augustine, her fears of marriage to some old, toothless lord, all the misty unsaid debris littering some segment of her mind.

"But don't you want to marry at all?" he asked, obviously curious.

"Not very much." When she saw him staring, she added quickly, "Oh, I suppose. Later. Much later." She laughed. "St. Paul said it's better to marry than to burn."

On the morning after New Year's, they rode back to Paris with Jourdain accompanying them. The sky was overcast, and a sleeting wind kept conversation to a minimum. Heloise had worried about Fulbert's reaction to her friendship with Jourdain, but he did not seem overly concerned one way or another, nor, in the weeks that followed, did he object to Jourdain's visits. At least once a day, the boy appeared at the

Rue des Chantres, sometimes bearing a book for Heloise, or merely to sit in the kitchen and drink a cup of ale with her and Agnes. He had a stock of stories, rumors, and humorous gossip, all of which Agnes adored, and she stuffed his book bag with cakes. For Heloise, his cheerful face brought a predictable bit of fun into her day; his mere presence was like a draft of healthful tonic, good for whatever ailed her.

It was some time before she realized that Jourdain brought with him into Fulbert's house the unseen presence of his master. Since he spent many hours of the day in Abelard's company, both in class and at his lodgings, he was forever chattering about the minutiae of his teacher's personal life: Master Peter threw his servant down the stairs because Galon had bought four-day-old turbot and pocketed the remainder of the shopping money, Master Peter had a cough—could Agnes recommend a soothing posset?—and Heloise had made up a small jug of licorice and anise wine. She was beginning to feel as though she knew Peter Abelard, and in a vague way she did. At least, she knew that he suffered from bad headaches and his undertunics needed mending and that once he'd had a breakdown that sent him back to his home in Brittany for three years. It was some time, however, before it occurred to her that the garrulous Jourdain, with all his infectious tales about his friends, might be a two-way channel.

On a sudden impulse one day, she demanded sharply, "Jourdain, you're always telling us about Master Peter. By any chance do you talk to him about us?"

He flushed and began to stammer. "Uh, well . . . I suppose . . . you might say that. But he's always asking. You don't mind, do you, Heloise?"

She did mind, but was not going to admit it. "I guess not."

"He'd like to meet you."

"Uh-huh." Surely Abelard was merely being kind to poor Jourdain. She had heard that he dined with kings and archbishops. Such a man could not truly be interested in an inconsequential person like herself, a nobody who was also a girl.

Jourdain was smiling earnestly at her. "It's true, Heloise. He did say that. And he asked me to describe you."

"And what did you say?" Immediately she regretted asking; she had no desire to hear herself described.

"That you are not unattractive and—"

Simmering, she swallowed and said, "Gramercy, fair friend, for nothing."

Jourdain bounded to her side, his eyes cloudy. "Come now, lady, can't you tell when I'm teasing? I told him you are comely and brilliant." He turned soft, smiling eyes on her. "I described you just as you are. Please don't be angry."

The next morning while filling Heloise's tub, Petronilla calmly announced, "Jourdain wants to fuck you."

"God forfend, what language!" Many times she had seriously considered reporting Petronilla's shameless outbursts to Agnes or Fulbert, but she always restrained herself in the end. She had no wish to get her into trouble.

Petronilla went on. "It's no secret, you know." Humming, she poured boiling water into the tub. "Anybody with eyes can see. The way he looks at you."

"You're mad. Jourdain is like a cousin. And he's only a boy."

"He has a pizzle, doesn't he?" She grinned, pleased with the irrefutability of her logic.

Suddenly Heloise remembered a time last summer when she had wakened in the middle of the night. She had had to use the chamber pot but, after fumbling about in the dark, realized that Petronilla had forgotten to bring it up. Muzzy with sleep, she groped her way downstairs to use the garden privy, a facility she normally avoided as it housed a large family of water bugs. At the door a noise stopped her; from the direction of the herb beds came the sound of a man's laughter, followed by hoarse panting, and then a girl's voice squealing in a queer way that she had never heard before. The last voice was Petronilla's, that she had been certain of, and she had fled into the house. By morning, she'd forgotten the incident, but now it came back to her.

Petronilla opened her mouth, but Heloise would listen no further and sent her downstairs to her mother. For the rest of the day, she was in a foul mood, and when Jourdain came by just before vespers, she instructed Agnes to tell him that she was unwell. For several days, she managed to avoid him. Then, just when the lewd images sown by Petronilla were fading and she felt able to face him without blushing, he stopped coming. Strangely, three days went by without a visit, something that had not happened since they'd met, and she felt horribly guilty. Twenty times a day she reproached herself; he must feel that she didn't want to see him, he was staying away because she had hurt him. A week or more went by, a week of mounting loneliness, for she missed his bright face, until she resolved to visit his lodging and tell him she was sorry.

When she came down for breakfast the next morning, Agnes handed her a letter sealed with purple wax. "A student left this for you a little while ago."

"What student?"

"Nobody I've ever seen before," Agnes mumbled.

Heloise raced back to her room and tore the seal. Quickly she glanced at the signature, but to her disappointment the scrawl was not Jourdain's. She went back to the beginning and read, "To the Lady Heloise, greetings. My young friend Jourdain has asked me to notify you of his recent illness. To be precise, he was out of his head with fever for several days. He is feeling much improved, but still weak, and I thought it best that he leave the city to recuperate. I have sent him to his friends at Montboissier, and I'm sure he will be back soon, fully recovered. He was concerned that you should know all of this. Farewell. Pierre du Pallet."

Relief flooded over her and she sat down hard on the bed. His feelings had not been hurt; he was only sick. But now he was better. His thoughts had been of her!

It was not until halfway through breakfast that she realized Pierre du Pallet must be Abelard.

All through Lent, the city shivered under below-freezing temperatures. Everyone said it was the coldest spring he could remember, and if the weather didn't break soon, the ground would be too hard for the first planting. Heloise carried her books down to the kitchen, and Agnes set up a small trestle table for her near the hearth. Even so, it was difficult to work, because Agnes was incapable of keeping quiet for more than three consecutive minutes, and if she wasn't jabbering to Heloise, she was screeching at Petronilla.

Near the end of Lent, Queen Adelaide gave birth to a son. The prince was named Philip, after his grandfather, and the Ile reverberated with the pealing and tinkling of bells. To celebrate the new heir, people built bonfires on every corner. Heloise dragged bundles of kindling to the quay and lit one of her own, and she passed out mulberry wine to the half-frozen fishermen who still loitered about the Port Saint-Landry. She longed for Jourdain's return.

Sometime during that cold period, she began to keep a journal of sorts. In a sense, it was a substitute for Jourdain; she had become accustomed to having someone for her confidences, and now there was no one. As much as she loved Fulbert, they were, after all, a generation apart and there was only so much she could tell him. Then too, during this time, she experienced a return of those fantasies that had warmed her childhood at Argenteuil, and these disjointed reveries she jotted into the journal as well. Whereas once her daydreams solely concerned herself, *her* adventures, *her* triumphs, now they began to emerge in a completely different form. She kept imagining another person, a man, and not merely any man but a romantic figure who clearly fell into the category of lover.

The night before Maundy Thursday, she dreamed of this person, and at daybreak, still seeing him clearly, she felt able to write down a fairly detailed description. She hurried down to the kitchen. Agnes was cleaning a duck for dinner and the feathers kept drifting across Heloise's table. They made her want to sneeze. Struggling to keep her mind on the dream, she ignored Agnes's comments about the weather and the high price of ducks, and tried to reconstruct the man on parchment. He was tall and broad-shouldered, with curly black hair and a melting smile that revealed even white teeth. She realized, surprised, that he was not young but in the vicinity of Fulbert's age. What his face might look like in repose she couldn't tell because in her mind she imagined him smiling.

By midmorning, she was deep into a volume of Origen. The kitchen had quieted at last, Agnes having given Petronilla a bucket to scrub the solar tiles and she herself huffing upstairs to air the beds. The room was full of the sound of bubbling broth and the smell of onions and marjoram. She yawned. After a few minutes had passed, she gradually became conscious of another sound, a very faint thumping against the shutter of the garden window. At first she ignored it as only a rattly branch, but the tapping grew crisper and finally shattered her concentration altogether. Sighing, she went around to the garden door and pulled it open. There was no one in sight, no sound but the tinkle of melting icicles. But in the hard morning sunlight she sensed a fluttering movement to her left, and then she saw someone flattened against the wall of the house.

"Heloise, is it you?" Ceci ran toward her. Heloise pulled her over the threshold and closed the door.

"Dear God in heaven, what are you doing here!"

"Heloise, don't be angry."

Exasperated, she dragged Ceci to her with an awkward hug. "Come now, why should I be angry with you? Seeing you startled me, that's all. I don't— Why are you in Paris? Hiding in—" She stared at Ceci's pinched white face, then down at her feet. Out of one slipper poked a bare toe; the other foot was wrapped in rags.

Heart pounding with dread, she led the girl into the kitchen and sat her down next to the hearth. She brought bread and poured a cup of ale. Ceci ignored the ale; she tore off hunks of bread and stuffed them into her mouth with both hands, swallowing them without chewing.

Heloise stared at her. "How many days?"

"Two. Almost two. After nones, day before last." She reached for the ale and drained it wearily. "I would have been here last night but I lost my way. Took the wrong turn near Saint-Lazare. Heloise—"

"I'm listening."

"You've got to help me." Her face was wrinkled with fear. "Please, no one but you can help me."

Heloise tapped her fingers impatiently against the table. "What happened?" She did not have to ask, but she wanted to hear it anyway.

"Lady Alais read me the letter. I'm not going home again. They want me to stay at Argenteuil."

What chilled Heloise was the girl's speech. Everything was said in the same toneless voice. "It—" The word stuck in her throat; she swallowed and gulped it down. "It won't work, you know."

"It must. I won't go back. Surely you can understand that."

"I understand. All I said was it won't work."

"It did for you."

Her face sagged. At last she said, "It was different for me, don't you see? I had someplace to go. People to look after me."

"Heloise!" cried Ceci. "I have you!"

Heloise pretended to pull a knot out of her hair. She could hear Petronilla slamming the bucket against the tiles. There was a stream of soft curses, then silence. Slowly she walked over to Ceci and pulled her head tightly against her hip. She cradled her and stooped down to brush her lips against the dark hair. Rocking back on her heels, she squatted down next to Ceci's stool. "Listen, sweeting, listen well. You think—I don't know what you think, but you're wrong. I can't make miracles."

Ceci was staring off blankly into a corner.

"I'm not the mistress of this house. Are you paying attention? Right now Agnes is upstairs airing the beds. There's a servant just down the hall. In less than an hour my uncle will walk through the front door. How is it possible to hide you? I can't even get you out of this kitchen without somebody noticing." When she glanced at Ceci, she saw that her face wore a queer, flat look, as if someone had applied a coat of paint.

Looking past Heloise, she pointed to a pan of anise cakes cooling on the table. "Can I have one of those?" she asked.

Heloise brought a cake in each hand. They did not speak for several minutes. Then Heloise sighed heavily and said, "All right."

Ceci followed her out the garden door and around the house, down to the Port Saint-Landry, where Heloise left her with a fisherman she knew slightly. She ran back to the house and seated herself next to the hearth. When Agnes came downstairs, she glanced around curiously. "Thought I heard you talking to someone."

"I was reading aloud."

At noon, Fulbert came home. Heloise picked at her duck; once the full enormity of Ceci's act had struck her, her stomach had shrunk to a knot.

In the afternoon, Agnes went out to buy dyes, and Petronilla curled up under the kitchen table and fell asleep. The moment Heloise heard Petronilla snoring, she hurried back to the quay and got Ceci. Quietly they climbed to the third floor, and Heloise opened the door to a room across the landing from hers. She had been in this room only once before. As a bedroom it had stood unused for years, but recently Agnes had begun regarding it as a storeroom for Fulbert's relics, the less important ones that needn't be locked in the cellar. Heloise dragged the dustcover off the feather bed. There was only one thin mattress, but still it was better than sleeping in the fields. She wanted to open the shutters and air the mattress, but she was afraid of attracting attention. The room was choked with dust.

"I'll try to get you more covers," she told Ceci. "But please, you've got to be quiet. Agnes sleeps on the second floor. If she hears noise up here, she'll think it's mice and be up in a second." She added lamely, "Agnes won't tolerate mice in the house."

Ceci nodded, her eyes brilliant with anxiety.

"There's plenty of food in the kitchen. Agnes will never miss it. You won't go hungry." She held her voice even and tried to smile reassuringly.

"What if Agnes comes in here?" Ceci said.

"She only comes to this floor to clean, and there's nothing to clean in here." She was not at all certain of that, but she wasn't going to tell Ceci. Agnes went wherever she pleased in the house—she regarded it as her own—and sooner or later she would open the door. Heloise didn't want to think about it right now. Trying to hide a person in a house where four people lived was impossible. Tomorrow she would decide what must be done about Ceci. If only she had someone to talk to, if only Jourdain were here.

The rest of the afternoon, she scurried cautiously about the house, bringing Ceci quilts, pillows, a chamber pot, clothing, and food. Whenever it appeared as though Agnes or Petronilla might be heading for the third floor, Heloise found an excuse to keep them downstairs. She even emptied her own chamber pot, which made Petronilla give her a quizzical look. In the days that followed, circumstances conspired to keep the house more empty than usual. It was Easter weekend, and Fulbert returned from the cathedral only to sleep. On Easter Eve, the candles in Notre Dame were extinguished and the great paschal candle lit during the all-night vigil. Heloise prayed fervently for a solution to Ceci's problem, but despite her night of prayer, she received no guidance. Perhaps God did not bother to answer because she, Heloise, was in a nervous frenzy. Ceci could not be left alone in that room forever, she would go mad.

The end of it came without warning. On the Tuesday after Easter, leaving mass, she rounded a column in the nave and bumped straight into Fulbert. They chatted a few minutes, and as Heloise turned away, he called her back.

"My fair niece," he said quietly, "who is that child sleeping in the room across from you?"

Her mouth dropped. To her amazement, she heard herself saying coolly, "A friend of mine, Uncle."

"That I took for granted. But which friend and where did she come from? I've not had the honor of an introduction."

Hot with shame, Heloise stared at the ground. "How long have you known?"

"Since Friday, when I went up there for St. Loup's molar. The young lady was asleep."

Heloise rubbed her nose with a fist. She did not look at him. "Forgive me, I'm sorry, Uncle," she said in a small voice. "I was going to tell you, but I didn't know how. Her name is Ceci and—"

"And?"

"—she has run away."

"From where?"

She sighed. "Argenteuil."

Fulbert looked more puzzled than angry. "I see," he murmured.

They stood staring at each other. After a moment, he said, "Go home now. We shall speak about this later."

Outside, she raced alongside the Campus Rosaeus and down to the Port Saint-Landry, dreading to share the news with Ceci. Fulbert was not a cruel man—he was kind and wonderfully indulgent—and he would help Ceci if he could. At the same time, she realized that no matter how kind he might be, he was also a canon of the Church. Under no circumstance could he agree to harbor a convent runaway.

In fairness, she could not blame him.

Ceci did not leave immediately. There were a number of conversations, between Heloise and Fulbert and also between Ceci and Fulbert. In the end, Fulbert offered to write Lady Alais and see if anything could be done. Possibly Ceci's family were unaware of her reluctance to become a nun; once they fully understood the situation, perhaps they would take her home after all. After speaking privately with Ceci, Fulbert said that in his opinion she should not be forced to take the veil against her will: she had no vocation, that was certain. And Fulbert, as Heloise knew, had always been adamant about men or women taking monastic vows if they had no sense of vocation. He said that it disgraced the Church and caused all manner of evildoing.

Heloise wanted to believe that it would be all right. Hours she spent on her knees, at Notre Dame or in her room, begging God to see the justice of Ceci's case, and adding automatically, "Thy will be done." Fulbert, calm and affectionate as ever, did not discourage her hopes. Nor did he encourage them.

"These are hard times," he warned Heloise. "If her kin can't find money for a dower, what choice do they have?" He added, "She could do worse than Argenteuil. There are places like Odette de Pougy where the bellies of the nuns are always swollen."

Weeks passed. Letters slowly moved back and forth between Paris and Argenteuil, and between Argenteuil and Angers. Spring came at last. The chestnut trees in the cloister unfurled green banners, and the students, liberated from their lodging houses and taverns, roamed the Ile with uproarious good spirits and danced, fortissimo, around Maypoles.

On Ascension Day, Heloise woke to see musk roses budding in their garden. For some reason, the roses made her feel guilty; she had not opened a book since Ceci's arrival—that fact she could and did blame on the girl—but then, too, the good weather drove all thoughts of work from her head. For that she could not fault Ceci, and she castigated herself for being a pseudo-scholar. Her lethargy, the shadowy frustration she could not throw off, heightened when she looked ahead. Sister Madelaine had been right, she thought; her studies could be put to no use, now or ever. They must always exist solely for her own selfish pleasure, thus they would forever remain tinged with a certain element of absolute futility. She told herself that she was absurd, for she had everything a girl might want.

At first, Ceci had slept in Heloise's room. But Agnes, having scoured the house from turret to cellar in a fever of spring cleaning, unexpectedly turned her energies to the room across the landing. Fulbert's relics were carefully transported to a second-floor storeroom; buckets of whitewash were dragged up the staircase and the walls freshened to a whiteness that would have done justice to a Lady chapel. Mattresses were beaten and heaped on the bed frame, sheets were rinsed with saffron, and Agnes draped strawberry hangings around the bed. The room transformed, Ceci settled in. She was so happy that she could hardly keep still. Bouncing with both feet on the bed, she shouted, "How kind you are, Agnes! I love this bed, I love Paris, I love everybody!"

Agnes giggled. "You're nothing but a weanling," she said, smiling fondly.

"When I go home, can I take the bed with me?"

Agnes's smile faded. "God's toenails, how could you be carrying a bed to Angers? On your back?" She lifted Ceci off the bed and unfolded a linen sheet. "Off with you now. I have work to do."

"Heloise," said Ceci, tilting her head to one side, "what shall we do today? Quick, think of something wonderful."

"We could—"

"Let's go to a tournament. Oh, Heloise, I've never seen any real knights!"

"There are no tournaments now. Why not a picnic instead? We could take our dinner and eat along the river."

"Just like pilgrims!" Ceci squealed. "Please, Agnes, can we?"

Heloise broke in. "You won't have to prepare a thing, Agnes. We'll do everything ourselves."

Agnes smiled indulgently. "Very well. But don't leave the kitchen a mess."

They ransacked the pantry for tempting morsels and packed them in a basket: a whole roast chicken, salted herring, ham pasties, gobs of dripping Brie, a long loaf of white bread, a skin of raspberry wine, cups, knives, a rough blue and white cloth with napkins to match. At the last minute, Heloise tucked in two *gaufres* from a batch Agnes had baked earlier in the morning.

Petronilla watched their preparations with a sour expression. "Can I come along?" she asked.

"No!" Heloise and Ceci cried in unison, and then Heloise added, "Not today—some other time."

"I saw you take those waffles," muttered Petronilla. "Those are for dinner. I'm going to tell Agnes."

"Tell her," said Heloise brightly, "but you still can't come."

"You've taken the last loaf of bread."

"I'll buy more." She went into the hall and shouted up the staircase, "Agnes! There's no more bread. I'll buy some on my way home."

It was glorious out of doors. They took the river road around the southern rim of the island, down along the towpath, and the sun glimmering through the willow branches dappled patterns of lace in the water. Coming to the Street Before the King's Palace, they gawked at the high stone wall separating the Cité Palace from the rest of the island, and, near a gate, they watched fishmongers selling herrings and mackerels.

"Now," said Heloise, "look carefully. We must find the perfect place for our picnic." After a great deal of debate, they settled in a grassy glade under a willow tree, a spot that looked much the same as any other. Spreading the cloth, they began to lift the food from the basket and positioned the items artistically on the cloth.

Ceci said, "I've never been on a picnic before."

"Nor I." Without bowing her head to pray, Heloise hungrily bit into a ham pasty.

"Do you suppose Lady Alais knows about picnics?" Ceci broke off a chunk of bread and layered it thickly with Brie. Pulling up her skirt over her knees, she lay back and stretched her legs out in the grass. "Wouldn't she die if she could see us now?" The image sent her into a paroxysm of giggles until she began to choke on the bread.

Heloise rolled over onto her stomach and buried her face in a patch of moss. During the last year, she had given little thought to Lady Alais and the others; to be truthful, she had not thought about Argenteuil other than fleetingly until Ceci had appeared at the garden door. And even then her mind had been on Ceci's troubles, rather than on the convent itself. Her memories of it had silted in some remote corner of her mind, memories that she could consider with indifference. Argenteuil had been a way station, an antechamber to her real life, that was all. "How's Madelaine?" she asked quietly.

"Yellow."

"Oh, Ceci."

"Her face. It's turning yellow."

"Is she sick, then?"

Ceci shrugged. "I think so."

Heloise turned toward the girl, sighing slightly. "She's getting old." But Madelaine had always seemed old to her.

"They are all old there," said Ceci, bitterly. "Even the young ones." Awkwardly, she poured wine into a wooden cup, spilling it on the cloth. She passed the cup to Heloise.

Heloise sat up and asked hesitantly, "Why do you hate it so?"

Ceci threw her an indignant glance. She said sharply, "Why did *you* hate it so?"

Heloise did not answer. While they were finishing the last of the wine, she told Ceci about her cousins at Saint-Gervais, about Mabile and her one-eyed husband, about Jourdain, whose father despised him, and about the lovely Alis, who dreamed of a fairy prince and who would, probably, die unwed in her uncle's castle.

When Heloise stopped talking, Ceci said, "So?"

"So—mayhap life outside Argenteuil is not any better than life inside it."

"You don't believe that."

No, she did not believe it. She decided to keep quiet. They had a fight over whether prayers to St. Denis were answered more quickly than those to St. Michael, and then they slept. It was late afternoon when they woke, and bells were ringing vespers. "It's time to go home," said Heloise crisply, "and we must stop at the baker's on the way."

Ants were gorging themselves on the remains of the Brie. Ceci scooped up the cloth, ants and all, and stuffed it into the basket. They walked slowly and turned down the Rue de la Juiverie, then made another turn on Rue de la Pomme. There was a line at the baker's stall, but it seemed to be moving fairly quickly. Ceci stayed outside with the basket, and Heloise queued up behind a woman carrying a trussed goose under her arm. After the nap, she felt drowsy and the roof of her mouth was dry. She should know better than to drink whole wine at midday.

After a few minutes, the line seemed to come to a dead halt. She peered over the head of the woman with the goose. A tall man was standing at the counter, pointing to one loaf and then another, asking question after question.

"Is that white bread?" he demanded. "You're sure. How about that flat loaf over there? What's that made of?"

He seemed utterly unperturbed by the baker's furious glances and by the customers stamping their feet impatiently at his rear.

Out of curiosity, Heloise began to listen more attentively. The man behaved as if he had never seen the inside of a bakery before. Now he was asking the baker for the yeast content of the barley loaves. Smiling involuntarily, Heloise edged out of line and moved around so that she could get a better look at the fellow. He did not appear simple-minded; he was clean-shaven and had shaggy hair, well cut. The profile revealed a handsome face, intense and sensitive. His voice was as silvery as the summer Seine on a moonlit night.

Someone behind her shouted angrily, "By St. Denis's holy farts, pay your money and move your ass!"

He turned around then and bowed deeply in the direction of the irate voice. "Madame," he said, smiling broadly, "it took Our Blessed Savior three days to rise from the tomb and he was the Son of God. The least you can allot me is three minutes to purchase a loaf of bread."

Heloise started to laugh, but the grin froze on her mouth. Paralyzed, she stared at the man's smiling face and then, when he had turned once more to the baker, at his back. She saw him drop a handful of oboles on the metal counter and shove a loaf of white bread under his arm. As he strode by her, she looked squarely into his eyes. His step faltered by half a beat. Smiling sheepishly, he said to her, "That's what comes of being wholly enslaved to one's stomach at regular intervals," and passed on.

Stumbling out of line, she darted after him into the street, only to see his back vanish into a crowd of shoppers.

Ceci ran up to her. "Heloise, you didn't get the bread."

"Did you see that man?" She pointed vaguely toward the Petit Pont. "What—"

Her voice rose feverishly. "The man who just walked out of here. With black hair and a loaf under his arm."

Ceci frowned. "I guess. I don't know. Why?"

"That man is mine."

"Yours? What do you mean—yours? Heloise, what are you talking about?"

"Nothing." Her heart was pounding; she gulped for air. "I didn't mean anything." Slowly she turned and walked back to the end of the line.

5 ❦

JOURDAIN RETURNED as abruptly as he had departed. Two days before St. Barnaby's Day, he was back in the kitchen once more, inviting Heloise to attend a lecture at the palace garden. He was in a fever to be off because Abelard was scheduled to speak first, and if they hurried, they could still hear most of his remarks.

Avoiding the crowds, they sprinted along the towpath beside the river and ran all the way to the Cité Palace. By the time they got there, Heloise had a cramp in her side. Her lungs were burning, and she could only gasp in disappointment. The gates had been thrown back, but the entrance was thronged so tightly with students that not even a lizard could have squeezed through. Milling around outside were hundreds who had obviously arrived too late for admission. She looked at Jourdain despairingly.

"Come on!" Clutching her hand, he made a flying frontal attack on the mass of backs wedged into the entrance. "Make way!" he bellowed. "Make way for the Lady Heloise. Move it, you turd."

Jourdain managed to pummel his way through the solid-packed wall of men, dragging Heloise behind him. Some of them inched aside, more from surprise than from any desire to let them pass; others cursed and retaliated with a volley of elbows and fists. Heloise felt a boot thud into her ankle; unknown fingers pinched her breast.

Inside, it was not much better. Men were sitting and standing on every available inch of space. Jourdain pulled her up to a trellis, but farther he could not go. Breathless, she peered through a thicket of vines at people's backs. Somewhere in the front of the garden a man was speaking, but she could not see him. Her ankle throbbed. Slowly she grew aware of a wet, sticky sensation, and when she looked down, she saw blood rolling into her slipper. Through a haze of pain, the man's voice penetrated her consciousness. It was an extraordinarily compelling voice—commanding, melodic, full of confidence and razzle-dazzle good humor—the voice of a person who knew everything worth knowing.

Glancing at Jourdain, she saw that his face was glazed with a kind of rapturous admiration. She tried hard to pay attention to the content of Abelard's words, but only a phrase now and again sank in; involuntarily her mind kept drifting away on the sound waves of the voice. Abruptly the garden burst into prolonged applause. Beside her, Jourdain was shouting at the top of his voice.

She tugged at his sleeve. "Is it over?" Around them the crowd began to seethe and ripple in the direction of the gate. It looked as though many people were leaving.

Jourdain beamed. "Now, isn't he everything I said? I told you, didn't I?"

"Is it over?" she repeated. "Everyone's leaving."

"Not at all," he insisted. "Three more lectures to come. But Master Peter's are the best attended." He added, "Anyway, now we can sit up close."

"Fine." She smiled.

He turned away and began stretching his neck, looking for something. "Wait here. I'll be right back."

Tides of students were pouring by, all with the same peculiar enraptured look that Jourdain had worn. Heloise clung to an apple tree for fear of being swept out of the garden. Minutes went by and Jourdain did not return. The pain in her ankle had settled into a numb ache. She sat down under the tree and dabbed the blood with the hem of her gown. What a fine mess. The slipper and the gown would be ruined. Agnes always said you must soak bloodstains immediately or they never came out. Agnes, she groaned to herself, Agnes would want to know how she had been injured, and if Heloise told the truth, Fulbert would certainly find out. And he would be hurt or angry or both that she had not asked his permission to come here. Her thoughts spun madly ahead, building catastrophe upon catastrophe.

"Heloise! There you are."

Jourdain was standing over her. She stared up at his face and beyond, past his shoulder, at the face in her dreams. Shivering, she slid her gaze smoothly over the apparition, up and up in an arc until she was looking at the sun sifting through the branches of the apple tree.

"God, you've been hurt!" shouted Jourdain. "Heloise, what happened?"

"It's nothing." She laughed nervously. "Somebody kicked me on the way in, that's all." Gracelessly, she scrambled to her feet.

Behind Jourdain, Abelard said, "Lady, I'm honored to meet you at last."

Heloise turned toward him without meeting his eyes. "Yes, my lord. I've heard a great deal about you as well." With sweating palms she shook the nettles from her skirt and smoothed the fabric over her hips.

Jourdain was glowing, his broad face grinning jubilation at having drawn together his two favorite people. Rather awkwardly, the three of them stood smiling in the early-afternoon sunlight, she and Abelard staring at each other, Jourdain darting his eyes between them. Heloise hugged her arms around her waist; her hands trembled, and she hid them in the folds of her gown. His face took her breath away: it was not only that he was extremely handsome—she had seen beautiful men—rather, it was a face made to be loved—no, adored. Now she could understand why Jourdain, why all these young men in the garden today, worshiped the man; he dazzled like the noonday sun. The magnificent grin, the hypnotic intelligence of the blue eyes, the mouth so elegant and mobile, they shouted to every passerby, "Love me, admire me, possess me if you can!" Unable to face him any longer, she looked away and said coldly, "I suppose you're accustomed to these mob scenes whenever you lecture."

"God's eyes, no," he sighed, "but it seems to be the price of fame." His eyes never left her face. "Men seldom have the option of choosing between anonymity and notoriety. They are thrust upon one."

A kind of careless pride, perhaps complacency, in his voice jarred her into criticism. "One might refuse fame."

"In that case, I trust one would rightly be called a fool."

Jourdain stirred uncomfortably at the turn in the conversation; Abelard gave him a grin and whacked him on the shoulder. "What do you say we get out of here? Let's find some congenial pothouse with a garden. A pitcher of chilled wine to celebrate this occasion?"

"Splendid, but"—Jourdain glanced at Heloise—"my friend came to hear the lectures. And so far she's heard practically nothing."

"No, Jourdain, I'll leave you now. I've had enough for today." Her ankle ached intolerably. Without looking, she knew that it was already swelling. She took a few stumbling steps toward the gate, but the limp could not be hidden.

Abelard reached out to steady her. "Ah, lady, why didn't you tell us? You're in pain. We must take you home."

"Please, I have no wish to inconvenience you. I shall do perfectly well by myself."

"Shhh. Don't be a martyr." He grinned. "Any lady injured at one of my lectures shall have the best service that influence can buy." With that, he strode down a path toward the front of the garden. Heloise began remonstrating with Jourdain, to no avail.

A few minutes later, Abelard returned with a heavy blond man puffing along at his heels. "I don't think anything's broken," Abelard was saying. "Probably only a flesh wound. But we will need a horse, if you would be so kind, my lord."

"Certes, certes," answered the blond man, smiling a sweet, concerned smile at Heloise. "If you can manage to reach the gate, child, I'll have a horse brought around. Careful now. Take my hand."

With King Louis holding one arm and Abelard the other, Heloise was lifted onto a stallion; a palace guardsman, his blue and gold banner snapping the fleur-de-lis, escorted her to the Rue des Chantres and carried her into the house.

Fulbert coughed. He paced from the kitchen door to the herb beds at the rear of the garden. Across the wall, in the close, two drunken students were skirmishing over a skin of wine. Hearing them, Fulbert jerked his head in annoyance and heaved himself on a bench.

"People like that aren't fit company for a niece of mine," he told Heloise. "Why can't you understand—you must not go among them. After what happened today—" He reached for his henap and drained it. Petronilla came up and refilled it; he did not acknowledge her presence.

"Heloise," he said, exasperated, "I don't know how to raise a child."

"I'm not a child." She was sitting under the pear tree, her swollen leg planted in a bucket of salt water. "I'm a woman who disobeyed you, that's all." She thought of apologizing for her offense but decided against it. She had not meant to defy Fulbert; her intentions had been pure.

"You did not disobey me," he corrected. "I never forbade you to go." He drained the henap in one long gulp. "If you had asked me, no doubt I would have given my permission." He turned his face away.

"Still, you are angry with me."

"I'm incapable of anger toward those I love." He smiled, his eyes resting on her gently. "Didn't you know that?"

"No." To hide her embarrassment, she ducked her head and peered down at her ankle. The purplish bruise looked even more grotesque under water. "Why did you leave me at Argenteuil?" she asked quietly.

"I told you. I don't know how to raise children. And you can't imagine what it was like at Saint-Gervais during the crusade. None of those women would have cared about you. They would have treated you like a varlet. At least the nuns—"

"Did they hate my mother?"

Fulbert stared into the henap so long that she thought he was not going to answer the question. She pulled her foot from the water and propped it against the splintered edge of the bucket. The toes were wrinkled and dead-looking.

"I'm trying to decide," Fulbert said. "They didn't hate Hersinde, but they didn't love her, either. She was too pretty. Too perfect."

Heloise dried her foot with a towel and eased on an old slipper. With conscientious soaking, Agnes had promised, the swelling would be gone in three days. Heloise tried to imagine having a mother, a perfect mother who was beautiful and kind. Smiling wryly, she said to Fulbert, "So now you have me and I'm far from perfect."

He looked away. "Tomorrow I must begin to think seriously about your future."

Her chest knotted with dread. "My future?" she repeated faintly. "You promised not to send me away! Who are you going to choose for me? Some horrible old man?"

His head jerked up sharply. "Who said anything about a husband? I'll not give you to another man." His voice was harsh.

She stared at him, and the muscles around her mouth tensed. Uncomfortable, she said at last, "Then what did you mean when you spoke of my future?"

Fulbert shook his head. "I don't know." He rose unsteadily and walked toward her. "You must trust me to find an answer, with God's help."

"Yes." The sun was gone; the garden drowned in shadows, illuminated in flashes by the vague glimmerings of the fireflies, and the river wind brushed her cheek, soft as the plumes of a feather. She said, "I trust you."

"I have spoken with Jourdain. The boy meant well, but it was wrong of him to take you to the palace. In future, he is to come here every day and instruct you in what he has learned from Master Abelard's lectures." He smiled sardonically. "Not that this is a satisfactory solution to the problem."

Heloise burst into relieved laughter. "Oh, but it is. I'll be a secondhand student of Abelard's. Jourdain can be my ears and eyes." She stood and hobbled over to Fulbert. He caught her shoulders and pulled her tightly against his chest so that her mouth was brushing his ear.

"Sweet heart," he whispered, pressing his face into her hair. "Lovedy, my very own sweet girl, my angel."

She did not move. The dark warmth of his arms, the sudden contact with his hard male body, whipped an image of Abelard into her mind. She saw him as clearly as if he were there, and she could not think or speak. After a minute, Fulbert released her and walked into the house without a backward glance.

In the late-afternoon shadows, she sat at the back of the garden with her head pressed against the wall. In the cloister, close behind her, someone was playing a lute and singing. The tune was unfamiliar, but the words she had heard before, perhaps from Jourdain. It was about a queen named Guinevere who falls in love with the bravest knight in Christendom. *Lancelot, my love, my own.* As the words rushed over her, she exhaled a shuddery sigh. *Courteous knight, gentle lover.* The singer paused and repeated the word *lover,* as if he were rolling a jewel on his tongue. Near tears, Heloise waited for him to go on.

Ceci came bounding out of the kitchen door. When she saw Heloise, she ran toward her. Heloise swiveled her eyelids closed and pretended not to see her.

"Heloise."

"Shhh."

"What are you doing?"

"Listening." She jerked her head toward the wall. Ceci slid to the ground beside her. *Dearest angel, I care for nothing but you.* After a long while, the voice stopped and she heard only the sour plink of a lute string. Then there was silence, the wind teasing the leaves.

Ceci asked, "If Arthur was the wisest king in the world, why didn't Guinevere love him?"

Without moving, Heloise opened her eyes and sighed impatiently. "She did love him. Sort of. But Lancelot was her true love."

Ceci leaned her cheek on one hand. She said, obstinate, "If I were Guinevere, I would have run off with Arthur."

"That's stupid. How can you run away with your husband? Besides, true lovers are never married."

"Are you sure?"

"Certainly I'm sure. Then they'd be ordinary like everyone else." She stared up through the branches at a primrose sky and smiled dreamily. "The names of true lovers are written in the stars."

"Who writes their names—God?"

She hesitated a moment. "Yes. God." She closed her eyes.

Jourdain came nearly every day now. Fulbert allowed them to use his private apartments, but when the weather was fine they worked in the garden. Usually at their side sat Ceci, yawning and dreaming, her head bent over the pillowcase she was embroidering. Heloise noticed that the girl had grown unusually withdrawn in recent days. No letters had arrived from Argenteuil in some time, and it almost seemed as though everyone had forgotten about her.

"What are you working on now?" Jourdain asked her.

"The stem of the rose." Ceci held up the fabric.

"Don't you think those leaves are a bit lopsided?" he said playfully. "They look like green worms."

"Oh shut up, will you."

"You mean they're not worms?"

"Jourdain—" She ran into the house, slamming the kitchen door behind her.

Jourdain stood in bewilderment. "What did I say? Surely she knows I'm chaffing her."

"She's not in the mood for it," Heloise told him.

He sat down again and picked up the tablet on which he had scrawled notes from the day's lecture. "Has something happened?"

"That's just it. Nothing has happened." Leaning over his shoulder, she squinted at the tablet. "Holy Mother, I wish you'd learn to write legibly. What's that word?"

"Ezekiel," he said, frowning. "No news is good news."

"Or bad news. Take your choice." She didn't want to think about Ceci. The girl had difficulty sleeping. Hardly a night went by that she did not wake, sobbing and terrified, and slip into Heloise's bed. Horned monsters, she said. Furry black creatures breathing smoke and fire pursued her. It was God coming to eat her alive. Heloise would rock her until she fell back to sleep. She understood the nightmares well enough but could offer small consolation. In the end, Ceci would have to accept God's will, whatever that should prove to be.

Jourdain, glancing now and then at his notes, proceeded to give her an abridgment of Abelard's remarks. She listened dutifully. From the outset, however, it had been apparent to her that this new system would not work. The few nuggets of information that Jourdain passed along were fascinating—she doubted if Abelard could be otherwise—but ultimately unsatisfying. It was like listening to a chanson and hearing only every tenth word. Bored, she interrupted Jourdain as often as possible, attempting, without being obvious, to elicit information about Abelard. "Tell me something," she said. "Where does he come from?"

"Who?"

"Your master."

"Brittany," he answered. "Near Nantes. His father was a knight in the service of the Duke of Brittany."

"Was? Is he dead?"

Jourdain shook his head. "He's a monk now."

"A monk!" she repeated incredulously.

"And his mother has taken the veil." He smiled. "See. Some women want to be nuns."

Heloise said quickly, "She's old. That's a noble way to end one's life." After a moment: "So Master Peter is heir to his father's fief."

"No. Oh no. He gave up his rights." He gave a dry, patient laugh. "You're very curious. What else would you like to know?"

"Nothing," she said, coloring. She added hastily, "I don't mean to pry, but you know him so well. I mean, one hears gossip."

There was a long silence. At last, Heloise said slowly, "I've heard that he has many enemies in the Church."

"A few," Jourdain replied a bit tartly. "You know. Greatness always invites envy. Besides, Master Peter has little patience with fools. I'm afraid that he has crossed swords with a number of high-placed fools in the Church."

She laughed. "Who won?"

"Guess." He patted the bench. "Come sit down or we'll never finish today."

Reluctantly, she sank down beside him. If she stopped interrupting, the lesson would be over sooner. She sat quietly, hands folded in her lap, and waited for Jourdain to finish.

Early on the morning before St. John's Day, two men-at-arms came to the Rue des Chantres and asked to see the canon. By noon, Ceci was packed and gone.

Heloise had slumped next to Ceci on the bed while she erupted in peals of terrible laughter and clawed her cheeks until the blood spurted. Exhausted finally, Ceci had heaved herself to her feet and stumbled down the stairs without speaking. Outside, her face contorted, she crouched in a heap by the side of the road. After a while, the men came out and mounted her on a spare horse. Her eyes gazed ahead, and when they moved off she would not look around or speak a word of farewell.

Heloise had raced after them as far as the Campus Rosaeus, then she walked slowly back to the house and climbed to her turret room. For the rest of that day she stayed there, staring out at the river. As nightfall drew near, she watched the celebrations for St. John's Eve along the Quai-aux-Fleurs. Children were burning piles of rubbish and bones they had collected earlier in the day; students, flown with wine, ran up and down the road brandishing sticks. Darkness was blotting the river when Heloise heard the bedroom door grate. Fulbert stood in the doorway balancing a platter of meat and a henap.

"Starving yourself won't help."

"I'm not hungry."

"Have some—"

"No, thank you."

Fulbert sighed. He placed the food on the floor adjacent to her feet. "Ceci is still immature," he said softly. "When she's older, she will reconcile herself to what is best for everyone concerned. There's no reason for you to reproach yourself."

"Ceci's going to die." Listlessly, Heloise buried her head in her arms.

"You underestimate the resiliency of the human spirit. People don't die because they can't get their way."

"She's going to die without having lived."

Fulbert cocked his eyebrows. "An exaggeration surely. Why, a life spent in the service of God is the most noble life of all."

In the following days, Fulbert did not mention Ceci again, nor did Agnes, who removed the hangings from Ceci's bed and packed them in her cedar coffer. Heloise kept to her room, coming downstairs only for meals and the sessions with Jourdain. Those inhuman, piercing cries of Ceci's had driven from her mind all thoughts of Abelard and philosophy. *Good sir God, why did you punish her? She is only a frightened child.*

Not until after Lammas did the thought of Ceci begin to dull, and then, oddly enough, Heloise felt slightly guilty. As though she had shed too few tears, she began despising in herself the missing piece that made her somewhat indifferent to the suffering of others; and yet perhaps it was not indifference at all but merely fear. Deliberately closing the sluice gate on her thoughts of Ceci, she took up a new work on astronomy that Jourdain had lent her and began reading about astrolabes and quadrants. Toward midafternoon, she was busy computing the angular distance between the earth and Saturn. Thirsty, she called down for Petronilla to bring her a cup of ale. The girl appeared at the bottom of the stairs, swinging her hips haughtily.

"Get it yourself," she yelled up.

"Wait a—"

"Agnes wants me." Petronilla disappeared toward the rear of the house.

Furious, Heloise stamped down the steps. In the kitchen, caldrons of apricots were simmering on the hearth, and Agnes was bustling about, laying out a tray of henaps and platters of cheese and sliced cold fowl.

"God's eyes," she muttered to Agnes. "What's all the fuss about?"

"Oh. It's you, lady. Master wants refreshments right away."

"Uncle is home now? Is something amiss?"

Hurriedly, Agnes sliced a cake and laid the slices on a silver dish. "Canon Martin is here." She stood back and surveyed the tray. "Something very important."

"What?"

Agnes shrugged her shoulders. "How should I know? A privy matter."

Heloise rocked on her heels, thinking. Martin never came to the house at midday. Only to play chess in the evenings or for Sunday dinner. When Agnes handed the tray to Petronilla, Heloise stopped her. "I'll take it in, Agnes. It would be courteous for me to greet the canon."

"Yes, my lady."

Heloise went down the hall. Outside Fulbert's apartments, she paused at the sound of excited voices. She banged on the door with the toe of her shoe.

Fulbert opened. At the sight of her his mouth thinned. "Oh. It's you."

"Uncle." Heloise advanced into the room and set the tray on a trestle. She turned to Martin with a bow. "My lord."

Canon Martin was studying Fulbert's Deluge tapestry as though he had never seen it before. As luxuriously as Fulbert dressed, Martin always outshone him. He wore short, fashionable cloaks and silver spurs. His hair was curled and parted, his freshly shaved skin polished with a pumice stone. He was so fastidiously groomed that he might have been taken for a woman. Summer or winter, Heloise had never seen his chubby hands without gloves. She glanced around the room. "No falcon today, my lord?"

Martin stared into the corner. "Bellebelle is feeling poorly, lady." Neither he nor Fulbert looked at Heloise.

"Sorry to hear it."

There was an awkward silence. Heloise moved to the door. "Good day, my lords." Outside, she paused. The murmur of voices resumed immediately. She heard Martin shout, "Think of the honor! Our own Aristotle!"

Fulbert's reply was jumbled. Heloise pressed her ear against the door. Just as before, Martin's voice rose. ". . . I told Master Peter that . . ."

They were talking about Abelard. Although she caught a word occasionally, she could not distinguish what they were saying.

Quickly she slipped out the front door and ran around to the side of the house by the stable. When she neared Fulbert's window, she dropped into a crouch and crept the rest of the way. That was better. From there the voices were as audible as if she had been in the room. Behind a currant bush she sat cross-legged and pulled her skirt over her knees.

They were speaking of some proposition that Abelard had made to Martin. No, not exactly to Martin. To Fulbert by way of Martin. Apparently Martin considered the request extremely odd. But whatever it was, both men were obviously intrigued.

Martin said, "He promises to pay whatever you ask."

"Why me?"

"He says your house is convenient to the school."

Fulbert snorted. "So is your house, my friend. Why don't you take him in?"

"Master Peter didn't ask me. It's your house he wants to live in."

Sweet Christ! Heloise thought. He wants to live here! It wasn't possible.

There was a long silence. Finally Fulbert said, "What the devil is he—"

Heloise heard Martin give an exasperated grunt. "I've told you all I know. He says that his household problems are hindering his studies. He *says* that his servant robs him blind and the expense of maintaining his own lodgings is more than he can afford. That's what he *says*."

"Surely he is rich enough. All those students."

"Oh, well. I suppose so. Listen, friend, the man is a genius and you've got to understand that these people are cracked."

"Yes, but—"

A hornet whirred above Heloise's head. With her palm she slapped for it and missed. She could well understand why Abelard might be unhappy living with a clodpoll like Galon. The man did not care properly for his master. And he seemed to be a thief as well.

Martin cleared his throat and said, "If you want my advice—"

"I don't," barked Fulbert.

"—my advice, friend, is to take him in. Think of the money."

"Well, yes. There is that to consider. How much is he willing to pay?"

"Whatever sum you think fair."

There was another long silence. A goblet clinked, and someone belched. Heloise waited. She nearly decided that Fulbert had left the room.

At last he said, slowly, as if thinking aloud, "Perhaps something might be arranged. Yes, you may tell the genius that I would be agreeable under certain conditions—"

Heloise gasped in surprise. Fulbert had enunciated the word *genius* with a fleck of contempt. He sounded out of humor today. It did not happen often.

"—I will provide Master Peter with a comfortable room and excellent meals for, let's say, eight deniers a week. But only on one condition."

"Which is?"

"He must devote all, I repeat all, his leisure time to the task of tutoring my niece."

Heloise clapped her hand over her mouth. Fulbert was going to hire Abelard! What had made him think of such a thing?

Martin choked in bewilderment. "Heloise? What does the wise Heloise need with a tutor?"

Fulbert laughed. "Precisely my opinion. She doesn't need one but she thinks she does. I'll not bore you with details. Suffice it to say that Heloise might benefit from Abelard's residence here." He added, "Whether Abelard will benefit is not, of course, my concern. I'm agreeable to his plan so long as he can further my niece's education. You may tell him that."

A stool scraped across the tile floor. Martin was clearing his throat noisily. "Aha, aha, there's something you've overlooked."

"Ummm?"

"Do you, uh, think it's wise?"

Fulbert spoke sharply. "Is what wise? Jesu! Speak openly."

There was a pause, and Martin murmured, "How can I put this delicately? Heloise is a maiden. And Abelard—"

Fulbert broke in. "Abelard is a maiden as well. The man is chaste. As virgin as the day he was born."

"You're certain?"

"Absolutely. I have it on the best authority. Besides, it's a well-known fact that he has no interest in women."

"And your niece?" Martin laughed in a high-pitched voice.

"The damsel has no interest in men. I would put my hand in the fire on it."

They began to talk of other matters: the sheepshearing, which had produced poor yields that summer, the hay harvest, a new tax on salt. Heloise waited a few minutes, making certain they would not return to the subject of Abelard. Then she crawled to the stable and stood up. Humming, she went into the kitchen and helped Agnes stir the apricot conserves.

6

"FULBERT MUSTN'T. He must not."

It was early evening. That day, Jourdain had not arrived at his usual time, and after waiting an hour, Heloise had decided that he must be ill. Finally, at twilight, he had come and sprawled morosely on a bench in the garden. She had never seen him so vexed. Nonetheless, she could not help feeling annoyed with him, and her temper began to rise. "Mustn't, you say! God's death, who are you to say what Fulbert must or must not do! What business is it of yours?"

Jourdain was quiet a moment. Then he began again. "You don't understand—"

"I understand well enough. You're jealous. You want Abelard all to yourself."

Leaning forward, he said edgily, "I love him better than my own kin. But I still believe it's wrong for him to come here. Wherever he goes, trouble has a way of following."

"You know nothing about it."

"I know everything," he snapped. "It's you—you and Fulbert who know nothing."

She walked away from him. Kneeling beside the herb bed, she tore off a stalk of mint. From the corner of her eye, she caught a glimpse of his face, white and pinched. She rubbed the mint spears across her front teeth, pretending to polish them. She did not look at him. "What do you mean—trouble?"

"Forget I said that." His voice continued to sound angry. "He's been talking about you since the Rogation Days. Before he met you."

She closed her eyes, smiling. "What's wrong with that?"

"I'm serious—do you know what Fulbert told him? He is to have complete charge of you." He circled the well and came to stand behind her. "He's to teach you day or night, whichever is more convenient for him. And mark this well. If he finds you idle, he has Fulbert's permission to give you a good beating."

Heloise bit down hard on the mint. "Oh, Jourdain!" She hooted with laughter. "Surely Uncle was joking. He himself has never beaten me. Why would he permit Master Peter to do so?"

Jourdain wheeled and lurched back toward the well. He appeared not to have heard her. "He was amazed by your uncle's simplicity. My dear Heloise, would you like to know what he said?" He snapped his fingers. "He said that if Fulbert had entrusted a tender lamb to a hungry wolf, it would not have surprised him more."

She looked up, uneasy. "He said that?"

"A *hungry* wolf—"

"He called himself a wolf? How extraordinary."

"Think on it."

Petronilla appeared at the kitchen door. "Master wants you," she said to Heloise.

Heloise stood up, slowly, wearily, and spat out the mint. She passed Jourdain without looking at him. "My friend," she said, "you worry without cause." She raked her fingers over his shoulder.

His voice was somber. "What ye sow, ye must reap."

Thoroughly annoyed, she ran into the house. A pox take him! That was the trouble with Jourdain. He was unsophisticated. Of his sincerity and concern she had no doubt. But he was forgetting that Abelard was known as a man of high wit. A lamb and a wolf—it was terribly funny. She was surprised that Jourdain had read into his remark all kinds of nasty meanings.

Summer was over. Allhallows went by and still Abelard did not come. Maybe, Heloise told herself, he had changed his mind. Restless, she would cross the landing to Ceci's old room and sit on the bed. When she learned that Abelard was to have this chamber, she had been surprised. But her uncle said that if Master Peter wished to tutor her at night, they would not disturb the rest of the household.

At last, one afternoon at the beginning of Advent, a cart with Abelard's belongings pulled up to the stable. That night Agnes prepared a feast, saying that this great honor to their house deserved a special celebration, and she carried in the savory dishes fairly waddling with pride. Gilded chicken breasts with rosemary. The dilled veal wrapped in pastry, which Agnes called pomeroy. Pike and dates in a sweet tart. And, later, almond cardamom cakes and a variety of fruits and cheeses.

Heloise forced herself to eat. She sat straight in her chair, glancing across the table at Abelard, who stuffed himself with undisguised gusto and complimented Agnes' culinary genius with every second bite. She looked at his fingernails. They were pink and shapely, more nicely manicured than her own. From time to time he smiled at her, an open smile full of generosity and good humor, and she smiled back shyly. But most of his conversation was directed to Fulbert. Nervously, she kept giving Petronilla her cup to fill, and, as a result, she began yawning before they had finished the Brie.

"My fair niece," said Fulbert, laughing, "I see that your head is nodding into your trencher."

Her cheeks flushed. "God's pardon, Uncle. I've had a tiring day."

"You're sure it's not an excess of wine?"

"No, my lord. I mean, yes, my lord. I'm sure."

She looked across the table to see Abelard wink broadly.

The men began to talk of Melun, where Abelard had taught before he came to Paris. Apparently, he had had a great deal of trouble there with one of his former masters, the famous William of Champeaux, who became jealous and tried to discredit Abelard. This information was new to Heloise, but Fulbert seemed to know all about it. She watched them, not listening very carefully.

She felt hot and her temples throbbed. After a while, she crossed over to the window, where a draft was spearing in around the shutters. Standing with the side of her forehead plastered to the window, she moved her eyes back and forth between Abelard and her uncle. They were deep in some argument about prebends at the cathedral. Abelard was declaring, "As an honorary canon of the chapter, it is my belief . . ." and then her concentration was cut adrift. Soon after, the men stopped talking and rose from the table. They were heading for Fulbert's private apartments when Fulbert called over his shoulder, "You may join us if you wish, kitten."

"No. I'll say good night now." Bilious, she felt the food rolling and heaving in her stomach. "I bid you good sleep, Master Abelard."

Abelard came back into the solar. "Shall we begin the lessons tomorrow evening, then?"

"Splendid," she said, trying to smile. Suddenly she felt as if she needed to be sick.

He stood before her, his head turned away slightly as he spoke. "Let's begin with the place of logic in philosophy. I suggest you read Book One of Boethius. It's a difficult treatise, but do your best."

She nodded silently. Two or three years ago she had read Boethius and had not found him particularly difficult.

He was going on, giving her advice on how to study properly. Each day she was to set aside several hours for reading and make certain to give her undivided attention to the material. It would make life easier, he said, if she took notes as she went along. Once she had finished the assigned pages, she was to write a summary of what she had just read.

Heloise swallowed hard. If only he would stop talking so that she could run to the privy.

He took her hand and held it. Longer, she thought, than was necessary. He said, "And pray, of course. Prayer is the true path to understanding."

"Yes, of course," she replied politely. She bobbed a half curtsy and sprinted toward the kitchen. "Agnes—"

Agnes was standing over a vat, arms immersed to the elbows in hot, soapy water. Turning, she glanced at Heloise's greenish-white face and reached for the closest basin. "God's toenails . . ." She shoved the basin under Heloise's chin and held it with both hands. "Poor lamb, poor sick baby. There, that's better."

Heloise moaned. Her stomach felt as if it was trying to turn itself inside out. After a few minutes, she pushed the basin aside. "Oh, Agnes, I feel very sick—"

Agnes took her upstairs and undressed her. In the darkness, a wet cloth draped across her forehead, Heloise tried to remember everything that had happened since the carter had arrived with Abelard's things. In a little while, she gave up and pulled the coverlet over her chin. When Abelard finally came up, much later, she had been asleep for several hours.

In the morning, her head felt thick. She stayed in bed until midday and then, painfully, got up and washed her hair with rose water. During the afternoon, Petronilla brought a fennel posset and repeated Agnes's instructions to drink it all. Heloise took two sips and promptly gagged. After Petronilla had gone downstairs, she dumped it out the window. She fell back into bed and dozed.

When she woke, the bells from Notre Dame were ringing vespers, and she decided that she felt much better. Guilty now, she raced downstairs to find Fulbert's copy of Boethius. At his writing desk, she flipped through the pages, refreshing her memory and trying to recall whether

Madelaine had ever commented on the assigned passages. Dear God, what a frightful way to begin her lessons with Abelard.

In the solar, Petronilla was laying out the trenchers. Heloise noticed there were only two places. "You've forgotten Master Peter," she told the girl.

"Didn't forget anything," Petronilla grumbled. "He's not eating."

"Not eating," she echoed, and ran into the kitchen. Agnes was busy sifting flour through a sieve. "Isn't Abelard—"

From behind a swirl of flour dust, Agnes peered at her with watery eyes. "Oh, you're up. Feeling better?"

"Much. Where's Master Peter?"

"Dining out." She tied up the flour sack and disappeared into the storeroom. When she returned, she said, "At the archbishop's, I think he said. He left a message for you."

"You didn't tell me!"

"Lady," Agnes replied with irritation, "you've been abed all day." Then: "After compline. He'll return and give you your lesson. If you feel well enough, he said."

She slumped down next to the hearth thinking that it was just as well. More time to think about Boethius, not that there was much to think about. The wind whined against the shutters. From the garden behind her, she could hear the privy door banging and the long creak of a loose board. Probably there would be snow tonight. She felt jumpy.

Agnes said to her, "I'm going to light a candle at Saint-Christofle tonight. Will you come?"

"I don't think so. Agnes—"

"Yes, lady?"

Heloise pushed back her hair and looked at the floor. She frowned. "Everything is different now, isn't it? I mean, with Master Peter here."

Agnes gave her a perplexed smile. "Rubbish," she said briskly. "In heaven's name, everything's the same. Only better. Now you have a teacher. Just like a boy."

It was almost midnight when Abelard returned. Heloise heard his footfall on the steps and opened her door before he had reached the turret landing. "Good evening, my lord."

"Good morning, don't you mean?" Melting snowflakes clung to his cloak. He opened his door and walked in. Briskly he went around lighting candles until the room shone as brightly as day.

Jesu! thought Heloise. Uncle will have apoplexy at the waste of wax.

Without looking at her, he said over his shoulder, "Come in, child. Come in and close the door."

Hesitantly, she did as he said. Her legs like lead, she crossed to the table and seated herself on a stool. Abelard dragged his armchair across the floor and settled opposite her. He smiled and said, "You're still ill."

"Oh no. Not at all. At least not very much."

"Very well, then." Absently, he began to fuss with some papers on the table, turning them over as if hunting for something, then stacking them up once more. He cleared his throat. "Why don't we open our introduction to logic by examining some of its characteristic properties? That is, in its genus, which is philosophy."

She nodded.

"As you will recall from your reading," he went on, "Boethius says that not all knowledge is philosophy. Only that knowledge which concerns the greatest things." He gave a half chuckle. "Obviously, not all wise men are philosophers, but only those whose intelligence is able to penetrate subtle matters."

She squirmed around on her stool; the room was freezing cold. "My lord, I wonder if you would mind lighting the brazier."

"What?"

"The charcoal. It's very cold in here."

"Oh. Oh, certainly." He got up and found a piece of flint. When he'd struck a flame, he returned to the table. "Now then, Boethius distinguishes three species of philosophy. Can you remember what they are?"

She answered promptly. "Speculative. Moral. Rational."

"Very good," he said with a bob of the head. He leaned back in his chair and made a tent with his fingers. "Now can you tell me what they mean?"

Unsure of what sort of answer he desired, she fell silent. She noticed that his fingers were stained with ink. "What do you mean when you say, 'Tell me what they mean'?"

"Lady," he said pleasantly, "Aristotle once said that women are inferior and uncivilized, and must needs be silent. Forget you're a woman and speak up."

Aristotle said that? "Aristotle was a pisshead." She had said it without knowing she was going to, and once having done it, she threw him a challenging grin. To her surprise, he laughed.

"I agree entirely. Nonetheless, Lady Heloise, you must define the meaning of those terms. I have no use for empty words. A man can believe only what he has first understood."

"I see," she shot back fiercely. "Then a man can't believe in God until he has understood him." She was pleased at how neatly she had trapped him.

He started, almost imperceptibly. "Well now. You are very canny indeed." He picked up a quill pen and tapped it nervously against the inkhorn. "I see you have excellent reasoning powers."

"Thank you." By this time, the room was beginning to warm and she felt her body relax. This was going to be fun, like a game almost.

He said sternly, "But you must answer the questions I put to you. Do you understand?"

It amused her to realize that he wanted the standard schoolboy definitions. Memorize and repeat by rote. Any half-wit could do it. "I understand." She slumped her elbows on the table. "Speculative. That which is concerned with speculation on the nature of things. Moral. That which is . . ."

When she had finished, he threw her a sharp glance and said, "Madame, you appear bored." He stirred the pen in the ink.

"No," she said decisively, trying to hide her panic. "Not at all." Immediately she felt terrified of displeasing him; he might discontinue the lessons. In future, she must answer with more enthusiasm.

She noticed that he was drawing something on the corner of a parchment sheet. Two straight vertical lines of equal length. Now he was connecting their middles with a straight horizontal line.

"Go on," he said to her without looking up.

At once she launched into a summary of Boethius's comments on the science of discovering and proving arguments. The room was still except for the rapid rise and fall of her voice and the scratch of Abelard's pen. Outside, snowflakes hurled themselves violently through the fluffy darkness and were snuffed out against the shutters. From time to time, a dog barked mournfully. Abelard bent his head over his drawing.

"I believe," he said at last, "that we needn't go any further this evening. You have an excellent grasp of the material." He added, "Especially for a woman." He threw down the pen.

She felt her eyes filling with tears. Pretending to rub them, she ducked her head and brushed away the moisture. "Thank you, my lord." She twisted on the stool, trying to see around his hand. Now she could make out the capital letter *H*. On its upper vertical he had added a wavy streamer in which he had etched hearts and violets. The pen strokes had almost a pagan flavor to them.

"Tell me what kinds of things you like to read."

"Philosophy, science, mathematics, astronomy. You know, everything."

"Theology?"

"Some."

He pushed the sheet of parchment behind a book. "Romances?" he asked with a grin.

"No." Only because she had never laid hands on one, but she wasn't going to admit that.

He pushed back his chair and walked to the window. "Would you like to know something?" He did not wait for an answer. "You're the first female I've taught. It's not as bad as I expected."

Heloise stared at him and then burst into laughter. "You're the first man who's taught me, and it wasn't as bad as *I* expected."

He walked back toward her and hovered silently at her shoulder like some magnificent moth. Tense, cautious, she could not move or look at him. He said thoughtfully, "There must be a happy conjunction of the planets tonight. I think our lessons shall be a great success." He rested his hand lightly on her shoulder.

"Yes, my lord." She began to fidget.

His voice turned brisk. "It's late now," he announced. "Go to bed."

At the door, he reached for one of her hands and brought it to his lips. He wished her good sleep, he said; they would continue to work on Boethius tomorrow evening. And then he said nothing, and they faced each other, gazing into the other's eyes as if they had been promised this moment before the world began.

Tall scarlet candles all around, great opalized clouds of incense drifting among the marbled pillars. The altar at Notre Dame had been decked for midnight mass, and Heloise knelt on a cushion in the second row, thinking of how expensive the candles must be. God knew how many there were on the altar alone, not counting those in the chandeliers and wall sconces. The flickering patterns mesmerized her, and she sat there, hands clasped tightly in her lap, feeling she could weep for joy. On this night, one thousand one hundred and sixteen years ago, the Divine Child had been born in Bethlehem, and still men knelt solemnly and sang the ancient words of adoration. *Gloria in excelsis Deo.*

She, Heloise, lady of the Rue des Chantres, niece of Fulbert, student of Peter Abelard, would come to this same place every Christmas Eve for the rest of her years on earth, and nothing could possibly go wrong.

Benedicite, omni opera Domini. Eyes lowered, her lips moved rapidly. O all ye works of the Lord, bless ye the Lord.

Afterward, she stood on the cathedral porch waiting for Jourdain to find her in the crowd. People with rosy cheeks were laughing and joking, and admiring each other's furs and embroidered cloaks. Burghers and barons poured forth with their families, and then, preceded by a blasting fanfare of sackbuts, King Louis with Queen Adelaide and their infant son, Philip. In the crowd milling around the king, she noticed Abelard talking to the Count of Dreux. When he saw her, he lifted his hand. The beggars crowded around banging their bowls and scurrying after the half oboles that flew through the air, and squires with flaming torches brought up their masters' horses.

Jourdain, a lute slung over his back, came out and grabbed her arm. "Fair friend, cousin Heloise," he shouted in excitement, "this is Christmas Eve! Do you know what that means?" A few steps behind him followed Abelard.

Heloise smiled, puzzled. "What, my sweet friend?"

"Why, that a girl must give all the boys a kiss in honor of Christmas. It's traditional." He flung himself against her, but she pushed him away shrieking happily.

"Master Peter," she said, laughing, "is that true?"

He replied solemnly, "Absolutely. This is a night for charity, isn't it?"

Her hair swinging against her shoulders, she bent her face and offered Jourdain a pair of frozen lips. He plastered a loud smack on them. They both giggled. "Fair sir," she gasped, not looking at him, "I've never kissed a boy before. Now you must be my betrothed, you know."

"I'm willing," he hurled at her, "but listen here. Mightn't your lord uncle hang me first?"

Heloise laughed at the top of her voice. "You're right. What a pity." She threw back her hair and linked arms with Jourdain and Abelard, the three of them zigzagging over the icy ground toward the Rue des Chantres.

Abelard said, "Dear Jourdain, don't you realize that Canon Fulbert has three loves—relics, Heloise, and money? And the greatest of the three is"—his voice rose dramatically—"money!"

Heloise, laughing uncertainly, made a face at him, but it was Jourdain who growled, quietly, "Wrong. It's Heloise. "

Abelard shrugged and arched his brows cheerfully. "Listen, last week Fulbert offered to sell me some hay from the manger of Baby Jesus."

"Actually," said Heloise, grinning, "that's not a bad buy. Just stay away from St. Michael's sweat. It's rancid." They all laughed together, delighted with themselves, the company, the smoke from the bonfires, with the crowds of stars sliding across the dark sky. In the clear air, the great bells of Notre Dame flung forth glossy sheets of sound. The streets of the Ile teemed with people shouting Noël; the windows of the houses blazed with candlelight, and the moon, white as milk, rode overhead. The whole island looked as if it was going to a fair.

As they neared the Port Saint-Landry, she slid free and ran toward the house, leaping over the drifts that had not been trampled into slush. Could life be more joyous? She had a new silk gown with fashionable double sleeves and red leather slippers embroidered with mayflowers. Already her mouth was watering with thoughts of the feast Agnes had been cooking since dawn, the goose and wild boar and everything people always ate on Christmas Eve. As she reached the door, a mob of students streamed from the Rue des Chantres like new wine bursting from the cask. Spotting Abelard, they began whooping, "Master Peter! Socrates of the Gauls!" The leader of the gang was wearing a woman's dress with a bullock's tail pinned to his buttocks; the others, fox-skin hoods over their heads, carried plows and bladders on sticks. When they saw Abelard and Jourdain heading for Fulbert's house, they began to cry, "Fool plow, Master Peter! Give us oboles or we'll plow your doorstep!"

Breathless, Heloise jerked back against the doorway. "Jourdain," she called, "what the devil—" The boy dressed as a woman raced up to her and waggled his tail obscenely. Jourdain bawled at him to get away. Tripping over his skirt, he somersaulted into a snowdrift. The boys screeched hoarsely and whirled around Abelard in a frenzied dance. Someone shouted, "Quick, Master Peter, some oboles for poor Bessy or we'll plow your door!"

Abelard rubbed his jaw with a benign grin. "Idiots." He drew out a purse and grandly tossed them a handful of coins. "Havo, Arnold! Here's one for you. Get along, boys. Have a drink on me." Yelping like dervishes, they scattered in the streets leading to Saint-Pierre-de-Buef.

Heloise yanked the door and smelled meat roasting. In the solar, thick logs crackled brightly on the hearth, and Agnes had festooned the chamber with holly and pine and bay branches. By the time Fulbert arrived, they had already drunk several cups of hot spiced wine. Even Agnes, between trips to the kitchen, managed to gulp down her share, and she allowed Abelard to swing her in a circle and kiss her resoundingly on both cheeks.

Finally they sat around the white-draped table, Fulbert at the head, Jourdain and Abelard at his right, Heloise across from them. She watched Fulbert ceremoniously carving the boar, which Agnes had decorated with a crown of ivy leaves. And then into her mind nudged a picture of Ceci in her black robes, Ceci whom she thought of rarely, Ceci who seemed now a bothersome child who had died. Trembling, she saw in her mind's eye Christmas Eve at Argenteuil, the church columns decorated with pine and apples, the sweet remembered voices singing the night office, the parchment star that someone always hung atop Lady Alais's lemon tree. The best time of the year at Argenteuil happened to be Christmas, but it was not like this. It lacked—she searched for the word she wanted—froth. And they had no banquets.

Quickly, almost angrily, she pushed away the image of Ceci, and then she forgot everything but the pleasures of the table. When they finished one dish, Petronilla brought out another: venison, goose, lamb dressed with sauces and spices. The wine jug circled the table, the water in the hand basin turned greasy. Heloise yawned and loosened her girdle.

Afterward, they sat drinking Burgundy on cushions before the fire. Fulbert asked Jourdain to bring his lute.

He tugged at his tunic sheepishly. "Gladly, my lord, but—" He looked away in confusion.

"Come, lad. You're not bashful."

"No, sire. But Master Peter sings much better than I—"

"Is that a fact?" Fulbert's eyes widened. He turned to Abelard. "Well, my friend, you must do us honor."

Jourdain darted into the hall and returned with the lute and pick. He thrust them at Abelard, who settled himself on a low stool and cradled the instrument. Tilting his head, he began a song: "*O Fortuna, velut luna—*"

"Oh no!" yelled Heloise and Jourdain gaily in unison. "Too sad!"

Abelard bowed from the waist and grinned at Fulbert. "I defer to the wishes of youth. How about this"—he leaned into the lute and slapped his foot against the tiles—"*Let's away with study . . .*"

Jourdain clapped quickly. "Eya!"

"*—Sweet it is to play.*" The room filled with his voice and the rousing, vigorous rhythms. Heloise listened in awe, transfixed by the richness of his voice. She had never heard a professional troubadour, but she could not imagine any finer than Peter Abelard.

"Let age to books and learning." His laughter rang silvery in the air. *"While youth keeps holiday. Hail Venus! Hail pleasure! Eya!"*

"Bravo! Encore!"

"Admirable!" boomed Fulbert. "By St. Denis, I well remember that drinking song."

"Naturally," Abelard replied, taking a mouthful of Burgundy. "We are of an age, my lord canon."

"Good God, don't remind me." He laughed shortly.

Heloise got up to refill Abelard's cup. When she returned and placed it at his side, she sat cross-legged on a cushion near his feet. Her eyes fixed on emptiness; wine and fatigue plunged her into a delicious stupor. Now he was singing of a shepherdess tending her flock and the lord who tries to woo her. She tried to place it. Cercamon, William the Troubadour? She gave up, unsure. The guttering candles cast vaulted shadows on the walls, and over by the window, his head propped against the arras, Fulbert drowsed, his face half hidden in darkness.

Abelard rested the lute on his knees. He looked down at Heloise. "Enough?"

"No."

"I notice your uncle has fallen asleep. Surely it is time to be abed."

"Never," said Jourdain sleepily.

"It's clear that you have not yet reached twenty. When you're my age, you'll be more sensible." He slid to the floor and stretched out next to Heloise. Drinking, he then handed his cup to her. "Drink, my lady."

She glanced over at Jourdain before laughing dreamily. "Would you make me drunk?" Nervously, she twisted the ends of her girdle, and for a moment she imagined that she heard him whisper distinctly, "I would, lady." But when she looked at him, he was only humming softly. She put her mouth to the cup where it had touched his lips.

After a few minutes, he said to her, "You owe me something."

"Do I? What?"

"Why, a Christmas kiss." He bobbed his head at Jourdain. "Am I not right, lad? Doesn't Lady Heloise owe me a kiss?"

She felt herself coloring and glanced at Jourdain. The boy's head hung low. When he looked up, his eyes were flashing wildly. "Yes," he mumbled grudgingly, "she owes you."

Heloise saw Jourdain turn his head away. Suddenly she felt panicked. "My lord, no. It wouldn't—my uncle—"

He laughed. "Uncle is snoring." He sat up and patted her consolingly on the arm. "Don't look so scared. I'll not force you."

Jourdain leaped to his feet. "It's late, I'd best be going. *Joyeux Noël!*" Before Heloise could stop him, he had gone. The street door crashed noisily.

Abelard rolled languorously on his back and crossed his hands under his head. He stared at the ceiling. "I'm growing old," he sighed.

"You're not old, my lord."

"Old enough to be your father."

"Oh well—"

Abelard grinned. "Old. Would you like to know something? When I was a youth, younger than you, I wanted to be a philosopher. Oh, not merely any philosopher." He laughed sardonically. "No. The *only* philosopher in the world. The best."

"You are."

"Will you believe me if I tell you that it's not enough?"

Heloise could think of nothing to say. She simply did not understand how a man could feel bored being Aristotle or Socrates—or Abelard. Finally she said, "My lord, you could be anything you wished. Archbishop or pope. Anything."

Amusement flickered around his lips. "Is that what you would have me be? Pope?"

She was conscious of him staring at her. "No. I like you exactly as you are."

"You like me, lady?" he asked, his voice so low she almost didn't catch the words.

"Yes."

He studied her face. "But not well enough for a Christmas kiss."

Dumbfounded, she wrenched her head away in embarrassment. "My lord," she stammered, "I didn't say that! Please, I didn't mean to be unkind. It was just that—"

He traced his fingers lazily across the toe of her slipper. "Just what?"

Glancing furtively at Fulbert, she fell silent for a long while, and then, impetuously, she whispered, "Very well. If you like." She jerked her face toward him, mentally preparing herself, and waited. When she glanced at him, she saw that he was looking up at her, scratching his nose, not moving. God's splendor, what was he waiting for!

His eyes met hers. "Well?"

"Why do you wait?" she asked hotly.

"Why, sweet lady, for you to kiss me. Naturally."

What! The man was impossible. She threw back her head and flared indignantly, "See here, Master Peter, you are most discourteous. You must delight in mocking me."

Instantly his arms slid around her waist and yanked her down hard across his chest until her mouth trembled a few inches above his. "Now, sweet lady," he breathed softly. "Now."

She grazed her mouth against him for a moment before twisting away, limp. His palms tightened against the back of her neck and squeezed her forward again. His mouth parted and she felt his tongue stab into her. A tremor streaked through her body. Gasping, she wrenched away and sat up awkwardly, shooting a glance in Fulbert's direction. He had not moved.

She was conscious of Abelard deliberately not looking at her. He stood and stretched, then, as if nothing had happened, reached down for the lute. "Jourdain ran off without this," he said indifferently. "See that you return it tomorrow."

The next morning she was tempted to imagine that she had dreamed it, that the fantastic episode was the product of too much wine.

But it was no good pretending. She remembered everything: her breasts against his chest, the taste of his tongue, the stubbled texture of his chin. And later, jogging the stairs to her room, the wetness between her thighs, which had filled her with shame.

In the days that followed, she was careful to study Abelard's manner, his every inflection and glance. To her relief—and disappointment as well, she had to admit—nothing had changed. At the daily lessons, he expounded on Aristotle and Cicero, and only sometimes, absentmindedly, his hand would graze her shoulder or he would kiss her hand when she bade him good night.

Little by little, she concluded that she had been a silly girl, making something out of absolutely nothing. Yet on New Year's, when the traditional first-gifts were exchanged, Abelard presented her with an ornate mirror of polished steel.

She had never owned a looking glass—they were evil, she had always been told. Stammering a thank you, she turned it over in her hands, careful not to look at her face, and then she blurted ungraciously, "I don't think I want this."

"Take it," he said, expressionless. "Now you can see yourself as I do."

* * *

Abelard pushed Aristotle's *Categories* to the side of the table; with a yawn, he leaned back heavily in the armchair and stretched his legs. "So much for the nature of genus and species." Heloise stood up and made a fitful circle of the room. She stamped to the window and opened the shutters, inhaling deeply. It was still early, the sky a metallic blue. Below, near the Port Saint-Landry, two priests were talking.

"How in heaven's name did you manage to sit still through all those offices at Argenteuil?" he asked.

"Discipline." The river wind was moving in dampness, and she locked the shutters tightly. "Fear of Sister Madelaine's switch."

Behind her, he said, "Anyhow, I can't picture you as a nun."

Her head snapped around. "Indeed! Why not?" Bristling, she came back to the table and ducked her head, looking for her slippers. "I could have been a fine nun. Have you seen my shoes?"

"I don't think you were wearing any." He went on smoothly. "I'm not disputing your efficiency. No doubt you would have made an excellent nun, an abbess most likely. But whether you would have been content is something else."

She raised her head and grinned at him.

"My lady mother is a nun," he said offhandedly.

"I know."

He sounded bemused. "God takes special pleasure in the virtues and achievements of women—in spite of their being the weaker sex."

Sometimes he astonished her. How did he know what God took pleasure in? "Fancy that," she replied, a bit tartly.

With a reproving shake of his head, he said, "Read the great doctors of the Church, read Origen. Or Ambrose or Jerome. All of them showed special concern for women."

"I suppose." She nodded, smiling politely.

Pushing back his chair, he rose and came around to her side of the table. "Didn't God pay the highest honor to women in the person of Mary?" He pulled up a stool and sank down, his knee brushing her thigh.

The warm scent of his body rushed at her. Flustered, she said quickly, "That's right. And Elizabeth, the mother of John the Baptist . . . she prophesied the divinity of Christ." She glanced at him sideways. He was so close that she could smell his soap.

"Ummm," he murmured, folding and unfolding his fingers for no apparent reason. "I dreamed about you last night."

Startled, she jerked her shoulders around facing him. "My lord?"

Jesu, he had dreamed of her! She was itching to know what he could possibly have dreamed, but he was going on, as if he had not spoken about it at all.

"And you recall," he said, "what St. Augustine wrote about the sibyls in *The City of God*. In pagan times, it was women who possessed the gift of prophecy."

Careful to sieve the impatience from her voice, she said hesitantly, "My lord, you were saying before that you dreamed of me. May I ask, what was the dream?"

He turned away from her. After a long silence, he stammered, "It was—nothing of importance."

She stared at his profile. Unthinking, she teased, "Come now, my lord. Why did you bother to mention it then?"

"A slip of the tongue." He fell silent again. After a moment, he said with an air of reluctant precision, "That we were—lying together."

The meaning of his words came slowly. She stiffened and leaped to her feet, heart thumping unnaturally.

"I'm sorry."

"No—"

"I've frightened you."

"No." Nevertheless, she moved away from him. "No. How could you frighten me?"

He got to his feet. They stood warily, facing each other, separated by only a foot or two of tile floor. For a long time neither of them moved or spoke. Then Abelard reached out and touched her cheek with a timidity that she had never before seen in him. She stared at him. He dropped his hand to his side. "I'm sorry," he whispered.

"No—" Impulsively, she caught his hand and locked it into her own. She could feel him trembling, and only then did she realize that he was frightened. Some of her reserve melted, and when he pulled her against him, she made no attempt to resist. Closing her eyes, she felt his hands skim over her hair, her neck, her ears, in a slow, cautious caress. Suddenly she felt absurdly small and helpless.

"Lady, lady—" In a torrent his words rushed out. "My ladylove," he said, and she shivered. Hungrily he kissed her lips, and then her tongue and the soft, moist places inside her mouth. For a long time they stood pressed together. Once, far away, she was conscious of the flames wailing in the brazier.

She felt him lifting her, going toward the bed, and her body went rigid in his arms. He laid her against the fur coverlet and flung himself full length next to her. His hand covered her breast. "Don't," she murmured, rolling away.

"I won't hurt you, sweet," he said. "Just let me—" He pulled her back against him and lay still.

"Kiss me," she whispered. "I like that."

His mouth found hers and stayed there until she pushed him away, breathless and full of sudden anxiety.

"What's wrong?" he said, moving his lips down her throat.

"It's a fearful sin." She saw that he wasn't listening and stopped.

Fumbling at the shoulder of her bliaut, he tugged until she heard the fabric ripping. His hand cupped her breast, and then he was flicking his tongue lightly around her nipple, tracing an unending circle.

"Ah God, don't. It's a—"

"Do you like that?"

Without answering, she pushed the side of her face into the pillow.

"My honey love, my sweet Heloise. It's not my intention to sin."

"I know."

"Lift your head," he murmured shakily. "If we intend no sin, it can't be one. That is my belief."

Oh yes, she thought, that is the core of your philosophy. But does philosophy apply now? She turned her back on him. "I think you may be right. But I also think we're sinning." Her voice trailed away.

"Look at me. Lady, I want to be inside you."

She nosed deeper into the pillow, refusing to glance at him.

"Heloise, I said—"

Muffled: "I heard you."

Even before he had spoken, she knew what he was going to say, and she knew, too, that she was going to do it. She could no more leave this bed without loving him than she could have killed herself. She rolled on her back and stared at the ceiling. When she did not reply or look at him, he seemed to take it for assent. Clumsily, he struggled with her bliaut, first trying to hoist the skirt over her hips, then pulling at the shoulders. She watched him through half-closed eyes, as though his awkward maneuvers were being performed on someone else. At last, he gave up in frustration and merely kissed her stomach through the bunched layers of fabric.

"I'll be cold," she said matter-of-factly.

"You won't be cold. I promise."

After a while, she sat up and stretched the gown over her head. It dropped to the floor, and the undertunic followed. Then she lay down again and stared at him coolly. She saw that he was not looking at her; his eyes were half shut.

Greedily, he crouched over her, moving his mouth across her nipples, down over the milky flesh of her stomach. With the tip of his tongue, he started to stroke the inside of her thighs. Her breath slowed to quivering gasps, and she said, in a small voice, "My legs are melting." She felt the bed spinning away from her and she grew terrified at her loss of control. Suddenly she became aware of her nakedness, of the unknown man bending over her, and she choked with shame.

"Stop," she hissed, jerking his head up to the pillow. "Don't!"

He lay still, one hand thrown lifelessly over his eyes. "Very well," he sighed. "You are quite right. Forgive me."

She looked away, not knowing what to say and waiting for him to go on. His breath was coming in slow, harsh sighs until she thought he must be dozing. Then she realized that he was shaking. She could feel him shaking and sighing. She wrapped her arms around his neck.

"Do you want to lie with me?" She pressed him close, stroking his hair. "Will it make you happy?"

"Lady, lady, ladylove—" Groaning, he wound his arms around her hips.

She would do it if it made him happy. It was not in her power to say no. She whispered aloud, "I love you so much. Oh, you don't know—I'll do anything for you."

He sat up, his mouth working in distress. "Your uncle—"

"Don't speak of him!"

"We must. He's an idiot but he could—"

She broke in. "I know the dangers." She yanked his mouth against her and began to kiss him, at first only to stop his words, later with furious desire. She pulled him on top of her and thrust her tongue deep into his mouth until she felt him shuddering. She wanted to swallow him.

At last he curled his head in the curve of her throat. "Heloise."

"What, my love?"

"Are you sure?" Abelard asked.

"Aye." She kissed the top of his head. "Do you doubt I know my own mind?"

"I want to make certain you won't be sorry tomorrow."

"I won't be sorry," she said, smiling.

They curled together and listened to the night hurtling noisily against the shutters. At last he inched out of her arms and slid to the edge of the bed.

"Don't leave me!" she cried. "Where are you going?"

"Hush." He grinned. "To remove my clothes."

"Oh." Then: "Must you?"

"It's customary, I believe."

Unable to watch, she lurched on her side and waited, repeating over and over to herself in a kind of astonishment, *Then he loves me, he loves me.*

When she heard the mattress creak, she squirmed to face him. There was a flash of pale lemon light from the candle before he jerked the bed hangings. Behind the rosy cloth, shadows plunged as swift and light as fishes. He stretched himself along her body, like a river rushing to meet the sea; her eyes widened at the softness of his skin. Again his mouth pressed against her and his fingertips began drawing wavery lines on her breasts and flanks, propelling her into the whirlwind.

"Your feet feel like ice," she told him, her words slurred.

"Love me," he breathed against her ear.

For a long time, they touched and stroked until they forgot to think at all and gave themselves up to the fire.

7

AT PRIME, while the sky was still a dirty white, she tiptoed barefoot across the landing with her clothes over her arm. On her bed, the coverlet and pillows lay smooth and unwrinkled; she pulled down the covers, slid in, and rolled about vigorously for a few minutes. Then she rose and put on a fresh bliaut and combed her hair. In the looking glass, she inspected her face for changes. There seemed to be none, but the color of her skin was ruddy and flushed. She splashed water on her face and went down to breakfast.

Agnes was standing at the hearth, stirring a kettle and tossing in liberal pinches of cinnamon every now and again. "Good morning, lady," she mumbled, fretful with sleep. "Did you rest well?"

"Thank you, yes."

"Porridge? It's well spiced." She licked the cinnamon from her fingers.

Heloise shook her head. "Bread. And ale. I'm thirsty."

She ate slowly, careful to make appropriately sympathetic replies to Agnes's complaints about the pains in her knees. When she had finished, she went to hunt for a book she had left in the solar. She was climbing the stairs when Abelard's door opened. She stopped and waited. On the second-floor landing, his hand caught her arm. In a loud voice she boomed, "Good morning, my lord."

"How do you, lady?" he asked in a dignified tone.

"Well." She glanced at his face for the first time. "And you?"

He was grinning at her. "I think," he whispered, "that my equipment is broken," and quickly scrambled past her.

She bit her lip to keep from laughing. At the bottom of the steps he wheeled and silently mouthed the word "tonight" up at her. The door banged and he was gone.

In her chamber, she settled herself by the window and opened St. Jerome to the place at which she had stopped yesterday. The sun came out strong, as if it didn't know that it wasn't really spring yet. At midday, she was still sitting there, having turned not a single page. Her cheeks burned with memories; in the silence of her mind she played over and over the scenes of their lovemaking, the words he had whispered to her, what she had answered, until her groin began to throb and she wanted him badly.

She went on re-enacting scenes, arguing, talking to herself. It was clear that she had taken a violent leap into some foreign country. She supposed that a wise girl would have resisted a man who tried to take her maidenhead without marriage—no wonder Sister Madelaine had called her a noodle—but she, *la très sage Héloïse,* could not be wise about Peter Abelard. The only thing that alarmed her was whether or not she had committed some mortal sin. Abelard said no, and she wanted desperately to believe him, but in her heart there were misgivings.

She sighed deeply. Was it God's will that she should love Abelard? Certainly it must be so; he was her destiny, and it seemed fantastic that God should not condone their loving. First this way and then that, she turned her mind in circles, constructing a jumble of syllogisms and letting them melt:

God willed our love.

Our love caused us to lie together.

Therefore, God wills our lying together.

She sighed again, reminding herself that Abelard would do nothing evil or harmful, and it followed that he would be incapable of guiding her into sin. Still, there was Holy Scripture, which said . . . Insoluble dilemmas demanding solutions. What could she hope to settle? She didn't want to think about them now. Later—she would think about them later.

They stood at the window in the half-light. Gently he rested his fingers over hers. "Dearest love," he whispered, "give me your hand. What say you, shall we fly straight out, over the tops of the trees?"

"Above the river," she murmured, "high over the Petit Pont. And then to what country shall we go?"

"Oh, far away." He laughed softly. "Most assuredly far away. Past cities and towns, beyond night and day. We'll follow the fading star until we reach morning."

"We won't set down until we reach the sea sands, hard by a dense forest. Deep in the greenwood we'll come to a glade, the perfect place that has been planned for us—but oh, Abelard, really I care nothing where we go—"

"Shhh." He caught a handful of her hair to kiss. "I'll build you a bower of lilies."

"Roofed with leafy branches."

"Aye. And with the freshest grass for a floor."

"We'll live together in our little kingdom—"

"Forever," he said softly and stroked her head. "My ladylove."

She closed her eyes and leaned very quiet against his shoulder, not thinking. In a little while the great bell of Notre Dame sounded, and she heard him cry, "Oh God, how quickly comes the dawn."

Every night she went to his bed. Sometimes, when they had spent themselves and sprawled in each other's arms, he told her lewd tales about priests taking women behind the altar, and once a hilarious story about a pregnant nun named Rosala who claimed to have been raped 440 times by Jesus. From Ovid he read aloud erotic passages on how to prolong their pleasure; he called her ladylove and teased her about the pretty little garden between her thighs, her oyster, her jewel, her little pink bud. In the spring, they opened the shutters and let the breezes lave over them, and one night he showed her a lute he had just purchased. After that, he wrote poems for her and set them to music, most of them love lyrics but others so bawdy that she could not help squirming with delicious embarrassment.

That year, it did not turn really warm until St. John's Day, and then nearly every day was humid and stifling. She went around the house barefoot, in her undertunic, and still perspiration rolled down between her breasts. In the afternoons, she found a shady spot in the garden, and, even though Abelard had abandoned all pretense of lessons, she continued to read on her own, just in case Fulbert asked. She discovered that she could live quite well on little sleep, but in the great heat of the afternoons she found herself gradually dozing, her book sprawled on the hot pebbles at her feet.

Much of her attention, in one respect or another, was devoted to her body. She badgered Fulbert into colored hose embroidered with gladioli and bliauts in the latest fashion, her knowledge about these matters garnered from Abelard's observations of what the court ladies were wearing. Her lover gave her a gold ring, set with an amethyst, but since she dared not wear it, he bought a Limoges casket with a lock and key and she kept the ring hidden. She also acquired a crisping iron for curling her hair, although Fulbert grumbled about all those crimple-crispings and christy-crosties sending her straight to the gates of hell. She ignored him and sat in the kitchen, Petronilla holding her looking glass, and made herself a headful of ringlets. That hot summer when she was seventeen she felt as though she were the most beautiful woman in Christendom.

About that time, too, Abelard's former servant, Galon, began skulking around their stable. Soon, growing bold, he crept into the garden and banged at the kitchen door, snuffling like an old hound for food. He was a small man, short in the thighs, with a lumpy pudding body and little neck to speak of. He appeared ragged and genuinely hungry, and Heloise felt sorry for him. Agnes, however, called him an able-bodied wastrel who could work if he wished. At first, she grudgingly handed out stale bread, but after that, when he started showing up every day, she slammed the door in his face. Curiously, he never came when his former master was there, although one day, finally, the two men met more or less by chance and Abelard cursed him furiously, calling him "ball-less turd" and threatening to send for the king's bailiff. The end of it was that he gave Galon a purse of deniers and ordered him to stay away. Far from grateful, the man snarled "Pinch-arse" at Abelard and ran off howling.

Afterward, Abelard told Heloise that Galon had once been possessed by demons and that he, Abelard, had arranged for exorcism. The angry words with Galon upset him, and he went to bed with a headache. Heloise covered his brow with a wet cloth and sat on the edge of his bed, not speaking. At midnight, opening his eyes, he reached up and slid his hand under her skirt.

She pushed him away. "Don't. It will make your head worse."

"On the contrary." He grinned. "It will do wonders for my head."

"Surely there are some times when it is best to refrain—"

He broke in. "Undoubtedly. And canon law is quite specific. Wednesdays, Fridays, the eves of feast days, the whole of Lent . . ."

"Nay, by God!" Heloise stared at him. "I don't believe it. Where did you hear this?"

He swung his legs over the side of the bed and began pulling off his shoes. "My dear little girl, everybody knows."

"I'm not little. Listen to me. I swear I've never heard of these prohibitions." She blinked at him in bewilderment.

"That's understandable. Technically you're still a maiden. If you had done things in the usual way, a priest would have told you all about it on your way to the marriage bed."

This was the first time she had heard him mention wedlock, and she shot a quick glance at him. His expression had not altered. She stirred uneasily. "Now listen, in future we must abide by the—"

"You listen. Those rules are absurd. Nobody obeys them."

"Are you sure?"

"Certainly. I wager even your uncle ignores them."

She jerked to her feet. "What do you mean by that!" she roared.

Abelard had not moved. He made a face at her. "I said that I have no doubt Fulbert—"

She threw herself across the bed and grabbed his arm. "You're mad. Uncle is chaste."

"Uncle is *not* chaste. I beg to differ."

"How do you know?" she demanded. "Tell me."

He shrugged. "Common knowledge. Every canon in the chapter knows that Fulbert has been fucking Agnes for years."

"No."

"Yes." His head wagged cheerfully.

Heloise burst into wild laughter. She rolled on the bed in spasms until she began to hiccup. "Agnes!" she howled, wiping her eyes with the hem of her gown. "Agnes and Uncle! God's toenails, what a fool I am!"

"And he gives her a sou every time he fucks her, or so Petronilla told me." Abelard spoke with the impish air of a small boy who had just told some outrageous secret.

"Petronilla told you that!" Suddenly all the pieces dropped into place, and she stopped laughing. What a blind fool she had been all these years. She said to Abelard wearily, "Is anything what it seems?"

He grinned at her. "Flesh is weak." He pulled his tunic over his head and thrust it at her. "Here. Hang this up."

Heloise shook the gown and draped it carefully on a wall peg. She looked at him over her shoulder. "What else don't I know? For God's sake, tell me quickly."

He groaned. "How am I to know what you don't know? Ask me specific questions."

She walked back to the bed and stared down at his naked body, at the soft stick curled between his legs. Suspicion suddenly gnawed at her. "You," she said softly, "were you not chaste before you came to me?" At once she was sorry she had asked.

"Ah, Heloise, sweet heart," he murmured, pulling her over him. "You know I was."

But she could not let go of the doubt. Upon reflection, he had known what to do, and had done it well. Fulbert had said he was a virgin, but Fulbert could have been wrong. "You've had women before me!" she insisted in a hot, querulous voice.

"Think you that I run after harlots!" Abelard flung at her, full of indignation.

"Some noble lady."

"Noble ladies require wooing. I had no time."

"You've never slept with a woman?"

"Never." He tangled his fingers in her hair.

"Swear it by the Blessed Virgin and all the saints."

"I swear."

Relieved, she relaxed against him. But a moment later, she pursed her lips and teased, "Then how came you to be such a marvelous lover, my sweet?"

There was silence. Then he said, quietly, "I didn't say that I had never experienced the pleasures of the flesh. I simply said that I'd never been with a damsel."

She stiffened as if he had struck her. "With whom then?" He did not reply. "Who? Answer me." She waited.

"Men," he replied lazily. "It was nothing."

Heloise lurched upright and stared at him. The sin of Sodom. Nothing, he called it. She opened her mouth to speak and clicked it shut.

"Ladylove, don't look at me like that. It was a long time ago, when I was a student. It's not extraordinary." He laughed softly. "Such things are common for students." He added, "And for canons and for monks. Even for kings. Lady, I could go on but you get the point."

She choked back her shock and replied, "I didn't know." She bit her lips, wondering, trying to picture two naked men coupling, and the idea was . . . amusing. "How do men do it, then?" she asked, earnestly. "I can't imagine—"

He pulled her down gently. "Here, I'll show you."

October storms pounded the Ile. Directly above Heloise's room, the roof began to leak, and when Fulbert summoned a roofer, the man refused to begin work until the rain let up. Agnes positioned a basin under the drip and ordered Petronilla to empty it twice a day. Usually

Heloise wound up doing it herself. She didn't mind, because she now preferred to spend most of the day alone, in her chamber.

Some part of her had irrevocably withdrawn from her uncle's household. She was not exactly sure when this had happened, but she did understand why. After Abelard's revelations about Fulbert and Agnes, she could no longer think of them in the same light. She made excuses for her uncle, but in the end it made no difference. He was the son of a baron—a petty baron, to be sure—but still of noble blood; Agnes was a varlet, and in effect he had taken her as a partner and sired a string of bastards, all mercifully dead save Petronilla. At some deep level within herself, she could appreciate his need to do so.

And yet she raged at Fulbert for his hypocrisy, and at Sister Madelaine, who had told her lies about the purity of the clergy. She had had a glimpse of the naked world, which so confused her that she longed to have back her precious ignorance.

The guilt she had felt about her love for Peter Abelard began to vanish; the dishonesty that she had been obliged to practice for Fulbert's sake ceased to trouble her. Hadn't he deceived her?

The kitchen gossip, the hours of nibbling, drinking, and chatting with Agnes, had gradually stopped. In her room with Abelard's Bible and a dozen other volumes, she hunted for truth. And in these holy works, even, she found a mass of confusion and contradiction. Once, teasingly, she asked Abelard whether it were lawful for a man and woman to marry once they had lain together. Yes, he had answered, quoting St. Augustine. No, she had countered; St. Ambrose likens it to incest. Well —Abelard laughed uneasily—maybe yes and maybe no.

To add to her disillusionment, she found dozens of instances where conflicting statements occurred in the writings of the Church Fathers, in liturgy, and in canon law. If she located a statement saying that Adam was created inside paradise, without too much trouble she could also find another authority claiming the opposite. At first to amuse herself, a while later painstakingly, she compiled lists of these opposing quotations. If saints could not manage to agree, how in the devil were ordinary folk to understand the divine? One night, before she pinched out the candle, she read several of her Yes or No quotations to Abelard.

"Heloise, what is your intention here?" he asked. "To question Revelation? To sow doubt in your own mind?" He enjoyed chewing apart her ideas.

"To understand," she told him.

"To create problems for yourself, you mean."

She was annoyed. "Jourdain says you're forever telling your students to think for themselves. So why have you never told me that!"

"There was no need," he answered matter-of-factly. "And besides, there's no such thing as conflicting authorities." Now he sounded annoyed. "You've probably taken the statements out of context."

Heloise knew that she had not, but he was in one of his arbitrary moods and she had no wish to start an argument. As the months had passed, she had come to better know this man. At times, especially when he was getting a headache, he would be nervous and bad-tempered, and he snapped her head off over nothing; at other times, he was maddeningly preoccupied with himself and appeared to forget her existence. It was a mistake, she had learned quite early, to challenge his opinions and theories.

"Success," he said to her once, "success always puffs up fools with pride." And on another occasion, quoting Corinthians, "Knowledge breeds conceit." She found these remarks startling, because they seemed to imply some kind of self-analysis, carefully quarried insights into his own psyche, but eventually she realized they were no such thing. The wealth and fame and incredible adulation that life had brought him he accepted as something natural and inevitable for one of his talent. Brilliance, he once told her, is not the result of effort: you have it or you don't.

His imperfections were, of course, obvious to her: pride, arrogance, intolerance for those of lesser capabilities, lack of tact. But just as he himself towered over the rest of humanity, so too did his faults loom larger than life. There was something positively grand—indeed, heroic—about his deficiencies, and at the same time something almost endearing. Abelard had the air of a man who completely liked himself, and it was only an ungenerous person who could fail to agree with his self-assessment. To her, he would forever be the laurel-wreathed philosopher-poet-prince, a reincarnation of giants who had trod the earth in ancient days.

The first dry day, she set off on foot for the Rue de la Draperie to buy silk for a veil. After considerable pumping of Abelard, who had recently attended the wedding of King Louis's bastard daughter, Isabella, she had concluded that she looked far from stylish. Fashionable ladies, he had informed her, were now covering their hair. Fulbert had stared when she requested three deniers for a wimple; finally, though, she had got the money without much difficulty.

At a draper's recommended by Agnes, she managed to buy a length of rose silk, very sheer, for less than three deniers; afterward, with the remaining oboles, she bought pigeon pasties from a vendor and began threading her way back toward the cloister. She felt in no hurry to go home. The day was as bright as a bittersweet berry, and the wind whistled briskly among the crisping leaves. Two weeks earlier, before the rains, the trees had cast adrift only a few leaves; now the streets of the Ile were carpeted in shades of vermilion and umber. As she walked along, gazing around at the swarming and arching of black-gowned young men, thoughts of Abelard forced themselves on her. He made this city, she said to herself. Oh, it must have been a fine place before, but not that much different from Bordeaux or Angers, nothing special. Now it was the center of learning in Europe. Why did they come here, these thousands of young men, not only French but students from all over Christendom? To see Peter Abelard. Paris was his city, and she would never think of it in any other way.

At the Rue de la Juiverie, she stopped short. Jourdain was standing in the doorway of a tavern, talking to some students. She watched him covertly for a while. When at last he noticed her, he approached with a clumsy smile. "Fair friend, God's greetings to you."

Heloise had not seen him since early summer, although once, curious, she had sent Petronilla to his lodging, only to learn that he had moved. "Am I your friend?" she asked with a wry smile. "You never visit me." She added, "Where have you been?"

"Here and there," he replied vaguely. "Melun. But you're wrong— I'm still your friend, believe me."

She gave a small sniff of disbelief.

"Truly, Heloise." He smiled at her, and even though his smile seemed warm, it was also unmistakably formal. "Lady, would you like to take a cup of ale with me?"

"But, Jourdain, I can't go into a tavern."

"I could bring it out," he offered.

When he returned with the ale, they sat on a low stone wall belonging to the synagogue and placed the cups between them. At the foot of the wall, in a tangle of weeds, a squirrel was fattening itself on chestnuts. For a while they did not speak, and at last Heloise said awkwardly, "You should have come to see me. I missed you."

Jourdain lifted the cup to his lips and drank. Morose, he put it down slowly, as if the cup weighed a ton, and said, "I couldn't."

Heloise laughed uncertainly. "Why ever not?"

"People are . . . talking," he said, not meeting her eyes. "I've heard stories."

Her smile evaporated. "About what, fair friend?"

A long pause while he foraged for words: "You and Master Peter." He rubbed his knuckles across his lower lip. "They say—I mean they claim—that you are his leman."

Her ears began to tingle. She grabbed her cup and drained it. Jourdain's gaze was pinned to his knees. Defiant, Heloise squared her jaw. "Bibble-babble. People always talk about something. I—"

"Master Peter has changed. He comes to class half asleep and repeats the same lectures he gave last year. His students laugh at him."

She jerked toward him, boiling. "Sons of dogs! How dare they? Why don't you fight them?"

He paid no attention to her. "Master Peter appears to spend his time writing love songs. All of them about women. Pardon me, *a* woman."

Heloise pretended that she hadn't heard the latter. "Yes, he writes beautiful lyrics, the finest in France."

"Oh, yes. Every tavern and boardinghouse in Paris is ringing with them. *Ah God, Ah God, the dawn! it comes so soon.*" He spat the words with waspish bitterness. *"Ah, would to God that night must never end."*

She colored deeply, seared to hear those familiar words on a stranger's lips. Leaning back, she glanced at Jourdain from the corner of her eye. She heard him say, "Is it true? Are you his leman?"

Calm and direct, she stared at him. "Yes."

He sighed fretfully and scrambled down from the wall. Turning to face her, he said with conviction, "He doesn't love you."

"How would you know whether or not he loves me!" She was aghast that he had dared judge Abelard's love. "You have no right to say that."

"I'm sorry. It's true."

"Don't be absurd."

"Heloise, he planned to seduce you. He had it all worked out months ahead of time. Why do you think he wanted to live at Fulbert's? It was only to—"

"You lie!" she screamed at him, leaping off the wall and plumping both feet in the dirt. "He loves me!"

She saw him examining her, detected the gleam of pity, and her eyes began to fill with tears of rage. She wanted to strike him. Her voice shook. "You know nothing, nothing at all, do you hear me? Mayhap he didn't love me before he came to Fulbert's. But he loves me now. That I know as truly as if the Blessed Virgin had told me." She stopped to catch her breath. "And I love him. More than my life! I would rather be his whore than the empress of Augustus!" Wheeling away from him, her eyes overflowing, she lurched into the crowd of shoppers. Dimly, somewhere behind her, she heard Jourdain calling her name. She ran on.

At the corner of Rue des Oubloiiers, he grabbed her with both hands and swung her around violently. "Lady! Listen to me."

"Go away," she mumbled, obstinate. She shook him off and hurried on.

"Heloise, please." He trotted along at her side. "I can see that you love him. Mayhap I'm wrong about his feelings for you. Would to God I'm wrong. I should never have spoken as I did."

The bells of Saint-Christofle were clattering vespers. Heloise felt mortally tired. It was an effort to speak to him. "Forget it," she said. "You meant well enough."

"Forgive me, lady. I was most discourteous."

She answered impatiently. "Amen. I said I have taken no offense. Listen, Jourdain. As you very well know, he is the grandest of men and I—I am only . . . a grain of salt."

His face was impassive. "Friend, I understand. But I beg you, be careful. Think of yourself."

She shrugged. "I? What can I do now? I can only think of him."

Jourdain asked, "And marriage? Has he spoken to you of marriage?"

"My dear Jourdain," Heloise said gently, "you are dreaming. You know that he cannot marry."

"Well, he might. There is actually nothing to forbid it."

"Except custom," she interrupted. "A married philosopher! Pah!" They walked on silently. "Besides, I have no wish to be a wife. You know that."

Outside Notre Dame, they said farewell. She hoped that he would go quickly, but at the last moment he kept thinking of something more to say. He warned her that half the streets in Paris were ringing with her name and urged her to protect her reputation. He begged her to make sure Master Peter got more sleep. He promised to visit her soon.

"Very well," she said several times. "Very well."

Years later, she was to remember that afternoon, but not because of her meeting with Jourdain. What he said she forgot almost immediately. On her way home, a few hundred yards from the Rue des Chantres, she saw a horseman ride down a small girl, a child no larger than a mite. She sprawled perfectly still in the mud and dung, her neck twisted like a chicken's, her mouth open in a silent scream. But she had not screamed, Heloise remembered that clearly. She couldn't explain why the girl's death affected her so profoundly, as such accidents were not uncommon in the crowded streets of Ile. Perhaps it was that nobody came to claim the tiny corpse, perhaps some ancient terror of her own. Finally, some women laid the body at the side of the road, as if they would now put her out of harm's reach. Shivering, Heloise kept vigil for a time. Then it grew dark and she went home.

Three weeks later, Thibaut the Lecher descended on the house in the Rue des Chantres. If it had been Thibaut alone this might not have been so frightful, but he brought with him from Saint-Gervais a sizable entourage: his eldest son, Philip, his squires, varlets, grooms, hounds, even his falcons. Hola, Heloise said to herself, this is going to be bad.

With so many extra people, the house quickly seemed to shrink to half its normal size. Moreover, within hours of their arrival the place began to take on an uncanny resemblance to Saint-Gervais, and even Agnes complained of the fleas, the sourish smell of unwashed bodies, the noisy drinking, and, particularly, the dogs, who had never been taught the habit of defecating out of doors. As a result, Heloise was forever groaning aloud and stepping over piles of dung.

That year, both the harvest and the slaughter had been exceptionally good, and Thibaut generously wished to share the fruits of blood month with his brother. Enormous haunches of beef, as well as pigs, ducklings, rabbits, and kids, were unloaded from the sumpters and carted into the kitchen. Frantically, Agnes began salting down the meat for use throughout the winter, and she also made pig jelly, blood pudding, minced beef and raisin tarts, and several other dishes Heloise had never heard of. In any case, the men of Saint-Gervais were great eaters, and the spit kept turning from dawn to midnight.

The eve of Martinmas was a fast day, and they ate nothing but bread and cheese. But on the day of the saint's feast, Fulbert invited Canon Martin and Abelard, and they all sat down to a bountiful meal. As head of the household, Fulbert carved the meats and made sure the goblets remained filled.

As the meal went on, the men began to loosen their girdles, and their voices grew more excited from the wine.

"God, I'll never forget it," said Thibaut, starting on another story about the crusade. "Three blackamoors, dark as the devil's belly. They were guarding the door and standing in blood up to their ankles, and when they saw my sword—" Thibaut had been little more than a boy when he went to the Holy Land with his father and elder brothers, but one might think that he had taken Jerusalem single-handed. Certainly he never tired of recounting his adventures. Heloise honestly couldn't tell whether or not his stories were true.

"And I daresay you took on all three blacks at once," Abelard said mildly, chewing on a capon's wing. To Heloise, his remark sounded merely conversational, but her cousin Philip apparently interpreted it as an insult.

"At least my father fought for Christ!" he said, bristling. "Not like some—"

"Soft, fair nephew," said Fulbert. "Master Peter meant no offense. He was only asking your father a question."

"I mislike this fine gentleman's questions," Philip muttered thickly. He was a handsome youth of twenty, or would have been handsome if not for his wolfish expression. Heloise decided, for the second time, that she disliked him.

There was a heavy silence, and then Canon Martin hurriedly changed the subject. The men began to talk of Louis the Fat and his perpetual quarrels with King Henry of England. "The king," said Thibaut, "is far too trusting. He treats Henry Beauclerc as a man of honor, when everyone knows the Normans are shifty dogs. Look at the battle of Gisors, when they—"

Heloise yawned. Across the table, Abelard stirred restlessly. He did not appear to be following the conversation. As she knew, the subject of war bored him, and she had no doubt that he would have hated being a knight. Suddenly, however, she heard his voice ring out above Thibaut's.

"King Louis is a good siege fighter," said Abelard, "but I tell you this. When it comes to military strategy, he's as brainless as a woodcock. At the battle of Gisors, he should have taken care to—"

Thibaut, who had expressed virtually the identical opinion a few minutes earlier, threw him an angry look. "I'm the king's man!" he shouted at Abelard. "I won't listen to anyone speaking evil of my liege lord!"

"God's pardon, sir, but I'm the king's friend. I've said nothing that he would not admit about himself. I repeat, he has yet a great deal to learn about the art of war."

"Indeed, sir," bellowed Martin. "As I recall, Louis fought bravely enough in the Vexin."

"I did not say—" Abelard growled. The table trembled on the brink of a quarrel.

"Calm yourselves," called Fulbert from the end of the table, but no one listened.

In a cutting tone, Philip said to Abelard, "Yes, and what would a clerk know about fighting? I wager you've never been near a battle."

There was an embarrassed silence around the table. Abelard smiled tightly. "It is clear that you have no high opinion of clerks, my friend."

"True," Philip answered curtly.

"I pray you. Why?"

"I've yet to meet one who didn't think a lot of himself." He grinned maliciously. "Or else was a nancy."

Abelard went white. "You bastard!"

Instantly pushing back from the table, Philip staggered to his feet and whipped a dagger from his belt. "Milksop! Coward!"

Abelard stood to face him. He shouted, "Liar! If I had a sword, I would prove you a worthless piece of shit!"

The men scuffled to their feet, knocking over chairs; the trestle swayed wildly. Goblets rattled, and a bowl of pears landed in Heloise's lap. In the midst of the uproar, she continued to sit, rigid, on her stool.

"Nephew," Fulbert implored over the noise, "for the love of God, you are discourteous to Master Abelard. You must beg his pardon."

"By St. Denis, never!" Philip cried. "I spit on him. He dared to insult my lord father." His face was clenched with rage.

Heloise watched Abelard turn from the table and go straight for the hall. Knees shaking, she levered herself from her stool and bolted after him, clutching his arm as he fumbled with the latch of the street door. "Abelard," she said uncertainly, "wait."

Eyes blank, he tore his arm from her grasp and threw open the door. Bitter air rushed at her.

"Abelard, please. Where are you going?"

"To some friendly pothouse. Your barbarous kin are not to my taste."

"Sweetest love, wait. It's cold." She sucked in her breath and stationed herself in the doorway. "I'll get your cloak."

"Get out of my way."

She struggled to keep the tears from her voice. "Won't you take your cloak, please? You'll catch a fever."

"Gramercy, lady mother," he snapped with a savagery that stung her. "I have no need of a wet nurse." He thrust her aside roughly.

One hand on the door, she lunged at his sleeve. He backed away and struck her, slamming her shoulders against the wooden door. Dazed, she watched him disappear in the direction of the cloister.

After a while, she made her face expressionless and went back to the solar. The men were still going on about the quarrel, everyone laying the blame on either Peter Abelard or Philip. Mostly on Abelard. Agitated, Fulbert said to her, "Where did he go?"

"Out."

Canon Martin was attempting to smooth things over, his meaty face sagging with distress. "Oh dear, oh dear God. That's what comes of too much Cypriot wine."

Thibaut grunted loudly. "God's mouth, what's wrong with the man? Methinks he takes offense too easily. Surely he could see Philip was only jesting."

Philip grinned snottily.

Gradually the confusion began to die down, and the men returned to the table. Heloise, just inside the door, stood nervously on one leg and looked for an opportunity to bid them good night.

"Never mind," Martin was saying to Thibaut. "Master Peter is not himself lately."

Fulbert squinted at him. "What do you mean by that? I've noticed nothing."

Martin puffed himself up. "Why, brother canon," he said in a slushy voice, "the whole chapter is talking. Where have you been? Master Peter is bewitched, they say."

"Indeed."

"He's turned lazy. I mean, he's lost all interest in study and won't even prepare lectures anymore. They say"—he lowered his voice—"they say, and I'm only repeating gossip, that he runs after women."

"Women!" Fulbert echoed in surprise. "Master Peter runs after women! Preposterous!"

Martin shrugged and said helplessly, "Well, I'm just repeating what I've heard. Mayhap it's not true, but everybody has noticed a change. It's something of a mystery."

Fulbert filled his henap and glanced over Thibaut's head at Heloise, still standing in the doorway. He called abruptly, "Fair niece, come here." Heloise walked to his chair demurely. He pulled her into his lap and folded his arms about her waist. "Pussy, have you noticed Master Peter behaving oddly?"

She took a quick breath. "No, my lord."

"You're certain? He's not skipped lessons or skimped on the instruction?"

"No."

Fulbert shot a satisfied glance at Martin, as if to say his friend was quite wrong. To Heloise he said, "Tell us what you're studying now."

"Theology, my lord. The Bible, St. Jerome, St.—" She wriggled out of his arms and jumped to her feet. "Uncle, may I bid you good night now?"

He stretched her close and pecked at her cheek. "God give you good rest, child."

In the hallway, she could hear Fulbert's voice. He was still talking about Abelard. "—and there is no doubt in my mind that he's a strict master. If my little one doesn't recite her lessons properly, he punishes her. Why, I know for a certainty that he has struck her, because once I heard her cry out—"

The back of Heloise's neck prickled.

8 ❦

"THEY'VE GONE NOW," Abelard said. "There's nothing to fear." He gave one final glance around the lecture hall and blew out the lamp.

They stepped outside into the cloister and turned west. The night air was raw, and Heloise could feel him shivering. All day he had walked around without his cloak; tonight she would prepare him a wine posset and stir in some anise, so that he should not take ill. Abruptly she slowed to a halt. "I'd better leave you now," she told him.

"Why?" He glanced at her, surprised. "Aren't you coming home?"

"I don't think," she murmured vaguely, "that we should be seen together."

"Lady, it's pitch-black. Nobody will see us. Come on."

Heloise pulled her cloak around her face and trotted after him. "Uncle told Martin that he heard me cry out in the night."

"Did he?"

"He assumed that you were punishing me."

"Of course. If I were him, that's exactly what I would assume." He laughed, very low, and took her arm. "My ladylove, you must remember to bury your face in the pillow when you—"

She grabbed roughly at his arm. "If he finds out, he might—"

"He won't find out."

"You don't know!" Heloise whispered harshly.

They were skirting the western edge of the cloister with its rambling border of canons' houses. As they passed a lighted window, she glanced at Abelard's face. There were lines of exhaustion around his mouth. Oh God, he looked so tired. She said steadily, "Uncle is not a stupid man."

"No." He frowned. "But that's not the point. I know of two reasons why he will never suspect."

"Two?"

"It's not easy to think ill of those we love most, and he loves you dearly. That's one."

"And—"

"I have a well-known reputation for chastity." For a while, neither of them spoke. They reached the gate leading to Fulbert's stable, and then walked around to the front of the house. Abelard finally added, "Even if someone told him about us, he wouldn't believe him."

Abelard opened the door, and they went in. The solar was dark, but Heloise could see candles smoking through Fulbert's half-opened door. She went in to kiss him good night. When she returned to the hall, Abelard was waiting for her, and he followed her up the dark steps, his hands bouncing lightly on her hips.

Heloise said nothing; she opened her door and went to light a candle. In the hall, Abelard was fumbling with his door latch. "Come over when you're ready," he called in a loud whisper.

When she had hung up her cloak, she walked slowly back toward the door. "Abelard—"

"Yes."

"I'm not coming." She expelled her breath sharply and licked her lips.

He slid out of the shadows and stood in the doorway, staring at her. Then he stepped inside her room and closed the door behind him. "Don't be silly. My sweet lady, you're being very foolish."

She nodded. "All the same, I'm not coming to you again."

"May I ask why?"

She hesitated. "I love you."

"I know. Is that a logical reason for not lying with me?" He moved to the bed and carefully sat down on the edge. In the haze of light from the candle, his eyes smoldered with bewilderment and resentment.

Heloise said blandly, "I'm afraid that I will destroy you." In her ears, the words sounded ridiculous. Overdramatic. "I'm—" Without saying anything more, she went to the brazier and reached down to light the charcoal.

Abelard was watching her intently. "Go on," he prompted.

"You won't understand."

"I'll try."

"I'm not good for you." Her words began to tumble out. "Ever since we became lovers, you've been utterly bored by the school. There's no time to study because we make love all night. Even Jourdain says that your lectures lack inspiration—you repeat yourself. He says the students snicker. And all of this is my fault!"

Abelard shook his head. "Dearest, no. You're raving."

"Wait—I haven't finished!"

"Heloise, hush. Listen to me. Do you imagine I could give you up?" Slowly she swayed to the bed and sank down beside him.

"I promise to give more time to my lectures." His voice was low with fear. "But don't turn away from me."

She closed her arms around his head and squeezed him to her. For a long time, she rocked him against her breast as if to suckle him. His mouth rested above her nipple; she could feel his breath through the fabric. Slowly she rolled back across the bed, dragging him with her. Against her thigh she was conscious of him hardening slightly. Quickly she rolled out and sat up; she tugged his tunic over his thighs. Oh God, she loved him, she loved to roll his name on her tongue, "Ab-eh-lard, Abelard," saying it to herself as one might repeat the name of a deity. She treasured every breath that came from his lungs, every inch of his body, every hair, every muscle, and she loved the private, familiar part of him that none saw but her. So adorably formed, so sweet. Cupping her hand under his scrotum, she lowered her mouth. Her hair spread out in ripples over her face, like the cascading of a golden fan.

Moaning, his fingers tightened around her neck. Very gently she wrinkled back the frills of flesh and sucked lusciously, like an adder in a honeycomb.

"Oh God!" he cried out hoarsely, and she looked up to catch a glimpse of his face, naked with a kind of holy ecstasy. They lay, at last, with their tongues in each other's mouth. Hotly, she felt him press his body into her.

With a soft explosion, the candle guttered and sent the room black. Through the shutters, a shaft of moonlight silvered a thin horizontal ribbon across the bed. She stirred voluptuously under him, drawing the coverlet around his shoulders.

He grinned down at her. "And you were never going to lie with me again."

During the next few weeks, she and Abelard reorganized their daily routine so as to live more nearly like normal people. Sometimes, now, Heloise left him shortly after matins and crossed the hall to sleep in her own bed. She insisted that he prepare new lectures for his classes and that he also set aside two hours a day for his own studies. The tension that had electrified their lives began to dissolve so that a new feeling of relaxation and companionship became possible.

All during Epiphany a play based on the Book of Daniel was being performed in the porch of Notre Dame. Fulbert, having already viewed the work, pronounced it suitable for an unwed girl and promised to escort Heloise. But at the last moment he pleaded a pressing appointment, summoning Jourdain to accompany her in his place.

The piquancy of the rhythms, the courtly procession with its banners and immense orange gonfalons, the piercing shrieks of the trumpets and vielles, all welded together into a pageant that left the audience in a mood of wild intoxication. Afterward, Heloise and Jourdain reeled home chanting the *Te Deum* and growling at each other like the silly lion-actors who had shuffled on the porch steps.

Heloise invited Jourdain into the house for a hot drink. From the hallway, she noticed Fulbert and Abelard talking together in the solar. Both men were smiling quite amiably, but something about the set of Abelard's mouth made her feel uneasy. She sent Jourdain home and went into the parlor.

"Fair niece," Fulbert said, "we've just been talking of a matter that concerns you."

She advanced toward him, reassured by the warmth of his smile. Without looking at Abelard, she said eagerly, "What a marvelous play, Uncle! Thank you for allowing me to go."

"Yes, yes." He brushed aside her words with an impatient wave of his hand. "There is something I must speak to you about—"

She stared at him expectantly. From the corner of her eye, she could see Abelard gazing at the arras with apparent casualness. He seemed almost bored.

Fulbert cleared his throat several times. "It has come to my— An extremely unsavory fact has come to my attention. That is to say"—he cleared his throat again—"it seems there is gossip in the Ile—" He trailed off and stopped.

"Gossip?" Heloise felt herself stiffen. She gripped her wrists together behind her back.

Fulbert grunted. "Filthy whispers about Master Abelard's residence in my house! Why now? That's what I don't understand. He's been here more than a year. If there was anything untoward about his living here, I should think there would have been talk last year. No, but *now* some people with nasty minds suddenly start to—" He rattled on, complaining about the small-mindedness of the burghers, the depravity of the students, the way certain pernicious wretches, immoral themselves, saw evil in the most innocent events. And so forth.

Heloise kept shooting half glances at Abelard. He was nodding his head in agreement, punctuating Fulbert's tirade with sympathetic murmurs of "shocking" and "absolutely." She did not enjoy watching his performance, although she did have to admire his skill. She supposed that she should follow his lead but wasn't sure what to say.

"Are we barbarians?" Fulbert demanded of no one in particular.

"Mark me, my dear Fulbert," Abelard broke in with a jab of his finger. "Great minds of every age are smeared by the rabble. Consider the case of Socrates—"

"Quite right," sighed Fulbert. "Against the highest peaks, the storms will break."

Watching them, Heloise thought that all along Abelard had read her uncle correctly; of course he refused to believe any evil about either of them. Whether this counted in his favor, or whether he deserved contempt for his stupidity, she didn't want to ask herself right now. She had long given up fretting about her own crime in deceiving a man who loved her and had never treated her with anything but kindness; for her behavior there could be no excuses, nor did she attempt to make any. All she could think of now was that, apparently, everything was going to come out all right. "Uncle," she broke in cautiously, ignoring Abelard's signal to remain silent. "Uncle, what has all this to do with me?"

Fulbert stood to throw another log on the hearth. Laughing nervously, he said over his shoulder, "Never mind, little one. Monstrous filth, bibble-babble, that's all. I wouldn't repeat it before a maiden."

Suddenly Heloise's hands began to shake. She sat down on a chest under the window and curled them under her skirt. She wondered who had been Fulbert's informant. "God help me, I'm not a child anymore."

"Keep quiet, lady," Abelard said between his teeth. "There's no need to be so inquisitive. Your lord uncle and I have discussed the situation and made our decision."

Heloise looked from Abelard to Fulbert. Both of their faces appeared calm. For one wild moment she believed the crisis had passed.

Fulbert smiled at her. "I think," he said, "it would be best if Master Peter found himself another residence."

"Leave?" Heloise staggered to her feet.

"It would be prudent. Under the circumstances."

Very pale, Heloise turned to Abelard. He was gazing into the corner. She kept her eyes on him and cried to Fulbert, "Uncle! You can't!"

"Hush, child."

"My lessons!"

"Aaah, Heloise, you have no more need of lessons. Master Peter admits as much himself. Don't you, my dear Abelard?"

Abelard nodded grimly. He turned to look at Heloise. "Your uncle is far too diplomatic, lady. My presence here is bringing dishonor upon your name—"

"And what of your—"

"—and that cannot be tolerated. The only solution is my going."

"I don't care about my name!" Heloise gasped, unthinking.

"Lady!" Abelard roared, striding toward her. He gripped her elbow so hard that she almost cried aloud. "This childish petulance is unworthy of you."

Uncertain, she wrenched her arm away and stepped back. Fulbert was watching her, shaking his head miserably like a man who wishes himself elsewhere. At last, controlling herself, she said, "God's pardon, Uncle. I forgot myself." Her breath was coming quickly. "Of course. You're quite right. Master Peter must find other lodgings."

Fulbert started to wring his hands. "Dear God, the best-laid plans— don't fret, little one. No harm has been done. I hope."

Her legs were trembling so that she could barely control them. Carefully she walked past Abelard and dropped on a stool before the hearth. Life without him was beyond envisioning. Beyond, even, bearability. How, she shrieked inside, how could God have permitted such an appalling error? She said, calmly, "And you, Master Peter? Surely this will be a great inconvenience."

He smiled thinly at her. "Don't vex yourself, lady. There are hundreds of lodging houses in Paris." He threw a cool grin at Fulbert. "Although none that can match Agnes's cooking."

A log falling in the hearth ricocheted a trail of sparks onto the tile floor. Heloise kicked a burning ember into the fire. Outside, very close to the window, she heard feathery footfalls and an unknown mouth whistling a cheerful tune; she recognized it as one of the melodies from the Daniel play.

Fulbert started telling Abelard about a Canon Victor, who had doubled his prebend income in less than two years. When he had finished with Canon Victor's business acumen, he began to talk about an abbot named Bernard of Clairvaux, who had founded a new Cistercian monastery in Champagne, saying that this Bernard was a fanatic who made his monks eat boiled leaves. Abelard's eyes grazed past her head and focused pointedly on Fulbert; he told an amusing story about the monk Suger, who was Louis the Fat's favorite confidant and who slept on silk sheets. It was all very cordial. Both men appeared to have forgotten the discussion. Heloise got up and went off down the hall to the kitchen. Agnes was on her knees scrubbing the floor.

"Is there any raisin wine?" Heloise asked her.

"In the pantry."

"Agnes—"

Agnes lifted her head and stared. "What's wrong, lamb?"

"Nothing."

"Tell Agnes."

"Master Peter is leaving." She rocked backward and forward against the wall, her hands flapping loosely at her hips.

Awkwardly, Agnes wobbled to her feet and dropped the rag into the bucket. She walked over and laid a wet hand on Heloise's hair. "Well, mayhap it's for the best," she sighed. "You've been working too hard."

Heloise turned her face to the wall.

It had never occurred to her that she and Abelard would not go on and on, playing at being a couple in Fulbert's turret. As the months had slipped by safely and he had become almost a member of their family, the likelihood of his leaving had become more remote. Somewhere at the back of her mind, she had acknowledged the possibility of irremediable change, just as she understood that a person might be struck by lightning or trampled by a horse. But these annihilations, acts of God as they were, happened to other people. It was not wise to dwell on calamity, or it would, unerringly, seek one out.

Now everything had gone askew. By the following Monday, Abelard was gone, his books, his armchair with the carved arms, transferred to one of the hives of lodging houses on the other side of Notre Dame. The room across the landing stood vacant, peopled only by cobweb memories, and Heloise could not bring herself to open the door and look in.

He did not come back. The endless days slithered on around her, and finally it was Jourdain who came to see her. She half expected him to make some reproach, but he looked at her as if nothing had happened. "I've been to visit my friend Peter of Montboissier," he told her evenly. "You know, the one who's a monk at Cluny."

Jourdain seemed in no hurry to finish chronicling his journey to Cluny.

After what seemed like an eternity, he sat down on a chest and fell silent. "I have a message from Abelard," he said, studying her intently. "But first I must ask you something."

She widened her eyes expectantly.

"Do you wish to see him again?"

"How can you ask?" Heloise cried in a low voice. "I've been in hell, can't you see that?"

"I thought mayhap you wished to end it now."

Jourdain did not look at her, and finally she had to remind him about the message. Then he fumbled laboriously in his girdle and brought out a letter sealed with purple wax. When he saw that she would not open it in his presence, he made some excuse to say farewell.

Upstairs, she forced her fingers calm so as to avoid ripping the parchment. The letter said little. Nothing personal. Only that she was to meet him the following day at Master Adam's classroom on the Petit Pont. He wrote that Jourdain would call for her at sext and take her home afterward.

The lecture room used by Master Adam, Adam du Petit Pont his students called him, was on the second floor of a house halfway across the bridge. A goldsmith owned the building and practiced his trade on the street floor; above, connected by rickety stairs, was the room Adam rented for his classes. At noon on Tuesday the chamber stood cold and silent. Straw littered the plank floor, as well as cushions that students had left behind.

They coupled quickly, without speaking.

Afterward, she found Jourdain downstairs against a shopfront, whistling softly. He suggested that she might rethink what she was doing. Without becoming angry, she assured him that nobody was forcing her to do anything. On the way home, he talked about the weather, and she said nothing.

Quickly, she and Abelard settled into a curious pattern of letters (delivered by a resigned Jourdain), meetings in the temporary refuge of deserted classrooms, and, from time to time, predawn visits to his room, although the latter Abelard considered unsafe. Heloise failed to understand his apprehension. At his room, at least, nobody could break in on them; they could take off their clothes and hold each other. It was amazing, though, how many opportunities they invented for meeting, sometimes every day, at the very least three times a week. Heloise closed her eyes to the risks, although sometimes she wondered idly what Fulbert would do if he found them out. But this was not a thought she wished to dwell upon for very long.

Days when she did not see him had to be lived somehow. Agnes was making bliauts for Petronilla. Dyes had been purchased, red and a brilliant green, and the linen colored in a vat of boiling water near the stable. Then Agnes stretched the cloth over her dress patterns and cut out backs and fronts and sleeves. This sort of preparation for Petronilla's wardrobe was unusual, and there was, of course, a practical reason for it. The girl was sixteen and should have been married long ago, but Agnes, loath to give up her only source of household help, had postponed the day as long as possible. Now, still reluctant, she had an opportunity to betroth her daughter to the son of a fishmonger from the Greve. Even though Agnes had offered to part with 120 sous for a dowry—more than the man deserved, she said—the fishmonger nonetheless wished to have a look at Petronilla before closing the deal. Hence the new bliauts.

Heloise helped with the sewing. She flashed the needle back and forth through the fabric, listening idly to Agnes humming and Petronilla prating incessantly about her unknown boy. She couldn't stop talking: he would love her, she knew, he'd buy her a feather bed and ribbons for her hair. She tried, without success, to imagine what he might look like. It didn't much matter because she loved him already. Agnes laughed. "Idiot!" she said.

Petronilla, it suddenly occurred to Heloise, would soon be sleeping with a man she loved. And she, Heloise, would rot away with Agnes and Fulbert in this sterile house.

Just before dawn, she snapped herself awake, as if some internal bell had chimed in her head. She was asleep in her undertunic and for a moment could not remember why. Then she did. The room swelled with blackness, but she could not risk lighting a candle. She fumbled for the gown she had purposely laid across the end of the bed the previous evening.

When she had dressed, she opened her door a crack and listened. The house rustled with silence. It was too early for Agnes to be up yet. Halfway down the stairs, she remembered her uncombed hair. Well, she was not going back now; she pulled her shawl over her head and felt her way down, pausing briefly on the second floor to make sure there was no chink of light under Agnes's door.

She smiled to herself. Abelard wouldn't mind her scraggly hair; he liked to tease her, saying it was foolish to dress at all. She should throw on a cloak and nobody would know she was naked.

The Ile was uncannily quiet this morning, its obsessive rhythms stilled for a few hours. The deserted streets, left to an armada of rats, wore a shut-down look: no street vendors shrilling their wares, only overturned crates and a few people stumbling toward the cathedral. It was dangerous, of course, for a woman to walk the streets of Paris before daylight. Not long ago, she'd heard about a girl who had been raped by an apothecary's prentice, but the girl had been abroad at midnight, which was asking for trouble. Surely, Heloise thought, all the rapists were abed at this hour. Nonetheless, she walked quickly, but not too quickly lest someone recognize her and report back to Fulbert. Even in the thick half-light, she could feel that it was starting to be spring. In a few minutes, the sun would burst out and the March day would be mild.

For almost two weeks, she had not seen Abelard, in part because something unexpected and quite absurd had happened to her. At the advanced age of eighteen, she had begun having her monthly flux for the first time. That she may have been abnormal all these years had never troubled her, although Agnes would question her periodically and shake her head, and Abelard, even, had commented on this unusual situation, saying that it was unhealthy when a woman was not regularly purged of her superfluous humors. Since Heloise had felt perfectly well in every other respect, she had not paid much attention to either of them.

Then, one night in February, on the heels of so many other misfortunes, she had noticed stains on her undertunics. Later, Agnes had shown her how to wash the rags and fold them for use the next month. But in her opinion the whole thing was literally a bloody nuisance. She would not go to Abelard at this time, even though he had insisted it didn't matter; it mattered to her. She stayed home for several days, and after that Abelard had accompanied Louis the Fat on a royal hunting trip to the forest near Compiègne. It had been a long time, too long.

As she passed Notre Dame, she slowed down. Usually she slipped in to say a fast prayer to Our Lady, because this was a procedure Abelard advised, a kind of alibi in case she was seen. But this morning she felt too full of urgency to bother.

At the corner of Rue Notre Dame, she jumped back to avoid a horseman. Abelard lived in a house on a side street west of the cathedral. Compared to his quarters at Fulbert's, this new place was cramped and hopelessly ugly, full of badly made cupboards and a stool missing a leg. One of the good things, the only good thing, about the room was that his window fronted on an alley. Obviously she could not enter through the main door of the house, but it was easy to climb in his window without being seen.

Two monks were heading toward her; she ducked into the alley and began to run. An upended barrel was standing beneath Abelard's window. She thought, Some night a thief will decide to pinch that barrel and I'll be in a pretty fix. She climbed up and gave the shutters a gentle push. Slinging one leg over the sill, she peered in to find Abelard grinning at her from the untidy bed, his hands crossed behind his head.

"What took you so long?" he said, laughing. "I've been waiting since lauds."

She slid to the floor and threw her shawl at his head. "Sweet, I've been waiting since Monday before last." She stayed at the window enjoying the look of him, his flawless head disheveled with sleep, the fragility of his mouth.

He said to her, teasing, "Are you through being a woman for this month?"

Heloise wrinkled her nose at him. "What a bother. Why did God have to build me this way?"

"God knows what he's doing." He raised his arm and hurled the shawl back at her. It sailed past her shoulder and dropped over the windowsill.

"Ah, Abelard, look what you've done." She leaned her head out and saw the shawl draped over the barrel like a tablecloth. The sky had begun to whiten, and a pink streak was splashed across the sky over Notre Dame. The day was going to turn out glorious.

"Leave it," she heard him call. "You can collect it on your way out."

"I'd better—"

"God's blood, come here!"

Hearing the urgency in his voice, she smiled mischievously. Straightening, without turning around, she clucked at him in a playful tone, "Forsooth, my lord. What's your big hurry? Haven't you heard that ladies need to be wooed a while?" She could go to him, or she could wait. If she waited, he would be wilder. This morning she wanted him wild.

He was beginning to sound cross. "Heloise, come here or I'll beat you."

"Beat me." Slowly she unwound her girdle and let it slide to the floor.

"I'll rape you."

"Ummm," she sighed happily, still not looking at him. In her mind's eye, she could picture him behind her, his blue eyes gritty with desire.

"Heloise," he called, softly. "Come here. I have something for you."

Sinuously she lifted her bliaut to the waist and began to raise her arms. "What?" She made her voice innocent.

"Something you'll like."

She struggled to keep from laughing out loud. The gown fell at her feet. She stood in her undertunic, shivering a little at the thought of him looking at her. The game was making her groin ache deliciously. Kicking off her shoes, she thought, In a minute. She would end it in one more minute. "What do you have for me? Breakfast?"

"Not exactly, sweeting." He paused, and she could hear the laughter brim in his voice. "But you may taste it if you like."

She giggled as she pulled off her undertunic and flung it into the corner. "Tell me," she whispered, hugging her arms across her nipples. "I won't come unless you tell me what you have for me."

"Heloise!" he yelled. She heard him thump a threatening fist against the bedboard. "Come here."

She wanted him to say something bawdy; it always made her blood race hotly when she heard that dignified voice utter outrageous things. "Tell me," she insisted.

"The biggest erection in all of the Ile!" he rumbled.

She turned and ran to him. He sprawled her down among the covers and gave her bottom a stinging slap. "Shameless minx. Making me say wanton things." His fingers began to pluck her like a lute, now gentle, now savage. "Aren't you ashamed of yourself?"

She shook her head, letting him do as he liked. "I'm not ashamed of anything." Abruptly a thought thrust its way into her mind. "Sweet, wait," she told him impulsively. "I did do a terrible thing."

He lay still and looked down at her, smiling. "Did you?"

She whispered, "I gave myself pleasure. Last Friday."

Abelard grinned. "Is that all?" He moved his body over her, laughing at her. "As I recall, the penance is six days' fast on bread and water."

"I don't care!" She closed her eyes and locked herself around him. She felt him plunging wildly inside her. "My stallion, my own bawdy boy—"

He was talking quickly against her ear. "Do you like that, angel? Ah God, how I've missed you. Heloise, ladylove. It's torture without you. Do you like that!"

She didn't answer. Heat rushed up all over her skin in a thin layer of dew. After a while, his honeyed voice deepened, chanting almost incoherently the familiar words and phrases, the exquisite litany she knew as well as the paternoster. She clung to his neck and waited for it to happen.

A cool draft brushed across the soles of her feet. Heloise sighed and opened her eyes. Over Abelard's shoulder, she saw framed in the sunlit window a man's head and upper body. He was watching them.

She screamed.

Fulbert said, "Fair niece, it's time to go home."

9 🌿

"I'VE ALREADY TOLD YOU WHY."

"That's nonsense," Fulbert said in a flat voice. "There's no need to protect him."

"It's as I've told you," Heloise murmured. She threw down the embroidery frame and stood up. Leaning back crooked in his chair, Fulbert lifted a henap to his lips and scrutinized her coolly over the rim.

An uneasy silence reverberated through the house, as if someone had died. The ordinary after-supper sounds, the clanging of caldrons, the splashing water, the whine of commands, were strangely muted. All day long, Agnes had said little to Heloise, except half-audible grunts; tonight even Petronilla scurried around with eyes glued to the floor.

Heloise walked to the window and jabbed at the shutters. The last stain of lilac had faded from the sky. At the corner, near the quay, the watchman had lit his cresset. He was talking to two women who lived farther down the street; the current of their voices moved lazily to Heloise in the dusk.

She watched the women's shadows glide past the house. One of them was complaining about a toothache. She closed the shutters and yawned, then turned back to Fulbert. "There is nothing more to say."

He scratched his chin. "It's getting late," he said benevolently. "Quickly, now. Tell me what happened."

She anchored herself motionless in the middle of the room. There was no use talking to him. She had said everything that could be said, but it had not penetrated. He was beyond hearing. She had expected him to beat her, but he had not—only repeated his wearying questions over and over without listening to her replies.

"Heloise." He was sipping the Macon in jagged gulps. "Did he force you?"

"No. I told you. It didn't happen that way."

"Beast." He sat like an effigy. "The dirty beast violated you. You should have told me."

"I love him."

"Yes. So you've said." He added, acidly, "I've heard all I want to hear about your love."

Heloise stared down at her slippers. "Free will," she said, painfully hoarse. "God gave us free will. I chose to lie with him."

"He forced you to submit to his filthy deeds."

"I wanted to lie with him—because I love him."

"The dirty Breton Judas came into my house like a fox. He ate my food, slept in my turret—" His voice grew ragged, a lot less careful than before, but he did not seem to notice. "He stole my little one and fouled her with his poison."

"Uncle—"

"Honor has no meaning for that cunning whoreson. My innocent child—mutilated and dishonored by his filth. God's curse on him!" The venomous words rushing out made him sound weak, almost childlike, and invited her contempt.

Heloise avoided looking at him. "No," she whispered. "I'm not a saint."

"I trusted him. He dared sit at my table and lie to me!"

"You trusted *me*," she said quickly, deliberately meeting his eyes. "*I* sat at your table and lied." The words stuck in her throat like a sob.

Fulbert ignored her. He was clenching the henap below his chin. On his index finger gleamed an enormous ruby. "By the wounds of Christ, he shall learn what it means to dishonor the house of Saint-Gervais." His lips had turned gray; for a moment, his scowl seemed almost maniacal. "You shall not go unavenged, that I swear to you."

"No." Heloise staggered to the hearth and stooped for her embroidery, her hands twitching. On no account must Abelard be made to suffer. Barely above a whisper, she said, "For the love of God, don't say that. I can't stand it."

"Better that he should have murdered you," Fulbert cried scornfully. He put down the goblet with a little click. "How can you show your face on the streets again!"

"Stop." She pressed her hand over her mouth, trying to control her shuddering. "Uncle, please, listen. His love has raised me above all the women in this city."

"You think he loves you!" he shouted. "A man like that, who makes a common whore out of a noblewoman. Think you that is love!"

She wheeled on him. "I *am* a whore. His whore." Then: "But I tell you this, I'm proud of it."

Fulbert ground his teeth audibly. He spat out the words, "I don't believe you."

The room was glutted with the stench of sorrow and fear. The fear was hers. From beyond the shutters cracked the jingle of metal on metal. The watchman was dragging the chain across the Rue des Chantres. Fulbert jerked to his feet and moved slowly, like a man walking under water, toward his apartments. Without looking back, he went in and closed the door. Heloise stood staring. She could go now; it was ended. The standing candle was drawing fleecy shadows on the door; beyond, she could hear sounds. For several minutes she forced herself to listen to him crying, great dry, weary sobs. Then he stopped abruptly.

She went to the kitchen. Agnes flicked a glance at her before turning back to the caldron she had been scouring. Heloise took a goblet from the cupboard and poured unwatered wine up to its brim. Unsteadily, she lifted the goblet and drained it. She set down the goblet and refilled it.

Behind her, Agnes croaked, "Lady—"

Heloise twisted around. "Leave me alone."

"You'll be drunk."

"I don't care!" She wanted to be drunk, as if by being drunk she would not have to think.

Agnes did not look at her. In a tight voice, she said, "Tomorrow we must find a priest. Some church on the Right Bank. Where we're not known. If you say you were raped—"

"Agnes! I was not raped."

"—he might give you a light penance. Or we'll slip him a purse of deniers. You'll receive absolution."

Was this the way it was going to end, then? Heloise thought wearily. A priest, a few coins, and the history of their love would be wiped off the skein of time and space as surely as if it had never been. "I don't want to be absolved," she said quietly.

Agnes crossed herself. "Lady, you blaspheme—"

"I have no regrets," Heloise said sharply. Leaving her untouched goblet on the table, she went up to bed.

She had come too far now along a tangled path to go back and retrace her route; she could only stop, and remain rooted where she stood. Further meetings with Abelard would be impossible, for even if he somehow found a way, she did not dare go to him. If Fulbert found them together a second time, she realized that he might harm Abelard. She snuffed the candle.

Sometime after lauds she awakened, sweating. In the darkness, she swooped her feet over the side of the bed and crouched on the icy floor, her hands clasped under her forehead. Our Blessed Lady, Queen of Heaven, Mother of Our Lord Jesus Christ. I have sinned. *Mea culpa, mea maxima culpa.* I have acted like a bitch in heat. I have betrayed the trust of those who love me. I have dishonored my house. *I lack all shame!* Lady of God, you who know what it is to love, I ask no pity for myself. Let my soul be branded forever, but intercede for me: Allow no harm to befall my beloved.

It was over. It was like a death, but she would live on, unfortunately; she would read Aristotle, walk circumspectly to mass with Agnes, eat meals in the solar with her uncle. On the street, she would, sooner or later, encounter him, and she would be obliged to bow and smile. She would say, "God's greetings, my lord," and other meaningless pleasantries and then walk on. More than that could never be. Gazing down the corridor of time, she saw neither hope nor escape. And she saw, too, something far worse, the slow reality of a truth too bitter for tears; in time, Abelard would forget her.

At first, Fulbert forbade her to leave the house, a prohibition that left her wholly indifferent as there was no place she desired to go. But he couldn't keep her locked up indefinitely, and some days later she began going out with Agnes. She was surprised to find that the sun still rose at dawn and died after supper.

In the fourth week of Lent, Jourdain came to the garden door one afternoon, and Agnes reluctantly admitted him. In plain terms, however, she let him know that it was against her better judgment, saying that she would not permit him to stir up trouble.

"Trouble," Heloise repeated dully when Agnes had left them alone in the kitchen. "The trouble is past." She laughed shortly.

"Trouble comes in threes," Jourdain replied cheerfully. He cut himself a piece of bread and spread butter on it.

"Oh, marvelous." Heloise pulled up a stool and sat opposite.

"Lady, you look pale. Are you ill?"

"No. No." Then: "Tell me quickly. Have you seen him?"

Jourdain shrugged. "Of course. Every day."

"Well?" Her voice snapped impatiently. "Christ's blood, tell me. Why has he sent no letters?"

"Ummm, this butter is delicious." He dabbed a whitish gob on the crust and stuffed it into his mouth. "He thought the danger too great for you," he said, chewing.

Heloise grunted. Fulbert had calmed down considerably in that he no longer referred to Abelard as "dirty beast"; for that matter, he rarely mentioned his name, but Heloise had no illusions on that score. Fulbert was, she had discovered, a man of uncertain temper and she had no wish to provoke him unduly. Left alone, he might forget his threats of revenge; he was, after all, a civilized lord. With a knife she chipped away a shard of crust and ate the crumbs. "How is he?"

Jourdain licked the butter from his fingers. Petronilla came in for a bucket, stared at them, and left. He said, expressionless, "Worse than you look, believe me. He suffers pitifully from the headaches."

She turned away, tears welling up in her eyes. "Oh God, God." Later: "Does he speak of me?"

"Of nothing else," he said. "Friend, may I give you some advice? As your friend."

Heloise blew her nose on her sleeve.

"It would be better if you tried to put him out of your mind."

"How can I do that?"

They fell silent. After a few minutes, Heloise said, "You're quite right." Somewhere within herself, she must embalm and entomb Abelard. Sooner or later. Outside in the garden, birds were twittering. Suddenly she felt a desperate need to know how much Abelard had revealed to Jourdain. "Did he, uh, tell you how Uncle came to discover us?"

"A little." He shrugged. "That Fulbert came to his lodging and you were there."

Heloise stood up. "We were in bed."

His eyes widened.

She looked away hastily, afraid that she had shocked him. "Uncle was—it was hideous. You can imagine. Uncle has spoken of revenge."

Jourdain patted her arm. "He's just talking."

"I know." But in her heart she felt far from reassured. There seemed to be an immense stone sitting on her breast, and at times she felt in danger of suffocating. Weeks earlier, she had been positive she would die, or, more likely, that God would strike her dead. Certainly she felt deathly sick and often had trouble getting out of bed in the mornings. It was no joy to get up and think of the blank hours stretching before her, hours to be filled somehow before it was time to sleep again. Finally, queasy, she would rise and pull on her clothes without much thought about what she wore. In the mornings, she wandered aimlessly about the kitchen, the garden, the solar, and lacked even the orientation to bathe or comb her hair. Later, if she went out walking with Agnes, she took no delight in the shops, or in the crowds busy with their errands on the narrow streets of the Ile. Suddenly it was just another city, full of earsplitting noises and sickening smells. And then, too, she could not help suspecting that everyone knew of her shame—Abelard's leman caught like a laundress with her skirt thrown over her head, Abelard's *former* leman. And if anyone looked twice at her, she bent her head and walked a little more quickly.

Improbably enough, a feeling of acute numbness gradually overtook her, perhaps a result of having purged herself of emotional debris, perhaps merely the narcotic of resignation. Then, once again, she felt able to read, a sort of indulgence conferred by God, and she opened Plato's work on freedom. One passage in particular plucked at her attention: it said that man, a creature of the divine Creator, may order his life so as to live wisely and justly, or he may do precisely the opposite. When appetites seize control of him, when his passions refuse to obey the dictates of his reason, then man becomes dysfunctional. He contorts the divine harmony of the universe. It seemed to her an exotic idea. Goodness comes, Plato said, when one has met evil and overcome it, or has made a choice and chosen wisely. Had the cool, ordered mind of Plato made correct choices, or had he ever ceased to function, as she had? Had Plato loved? Known desire?

And then she looked into Aristotle and found the place where he said, "Virtue is a disposition, or habit, involving deliberate purpose or choice."

The implication seemed clear enough to her. Did blind fate, inevitable and predetermined, rule one's life? Or was she able to choose, to determine her own fate? She did not know, but the latter seemed more reasonable. One day she would have to begin life again. Abelard had gone, but there was nothing to be gained by wallowing in an ooze of self-pity; she was eighteen, and she determined to stop shuffling about the house like a wilted cabbage.

So full of resolution, she continued, nonetheless, to do nothing.

On Palm Sunday, Petronilla's betrothed came across the river to spend the afternoon. Richwin, his name was, and he turned out to be a bearded colt with big teeth and a tunic that smelled, not unreasonably, of fish. Fumbling in his purse, he brought out a colored egg and thrust it at his future wife without raising his eyes. After that, he completely lost his tongue and did little but sigh and scratch. Petronilla had put on her red dress and rouged her cheeks; she talked enough for both of them, calling him "mouse" and "my fair falcon" until Heloise had to smile.

All during Easter Week it rained—warm, silver showers that promised tufted trees and the budding of violets and daffodils, blossom by blossom. Soon the curving meadows on the Left Bank would spring into rainbow prisms, and students would dance their frenzied *caroles* on the hillsides. Spring surprised Heloise; it seemed wildly out of place in the ruins of her life.

Agnes was teaching her to spin, and several hours a day she sat, cauterized, in the solar and worked unhurried fingers to the hum of the wheel and the rain, watching the movement of the flax and trying to think of nothing. At the end of April, despite the liquid mud of the roads, Fulbert rode down to Melun to visit his farms, and the house seemed vast and empty. He had a new purple cloak plumed with vair, and he had kissed her goodbye warmly, promising to bring her a present. "Some trifle," he called it.

Two mornings later, she woke and vomited into her chamber pot. Agnes prepared an anise posset, and by sext the nausea had subsided. The next morning it happened again, and the next and the one following. She had no appetite and lost most of what she did manage to get down; Agnes called it a bad case of indigestion and fed her ground cloves and cooked pears until they choked her.

Sitting in her bath one afternoon, she recalled having had mild sieges of nausea the previous month, after Lady Day it must have been, but then she had been feeling far too miserable to worry about an upset stomach. Now a thought rushed into her mind and stuck there: She had not passed blood for a while, how long she could not remember. Quickly she began to count backwards, and when that proved inadequate, she computed on her fingers. In the end, her best reckoning told her that she had not had a monthly flux since Lent began. She made it two months, more or less. Hastily she stood up in the water and examined her belly. Slightly bloated. Overripe but still flat. Before the afternoon was out, she made up her mind that she was going to have a child.

There was no one to consult, of course, no woman anyway. In the end, she dispatched Petronilla to track down Jourdain, and when he could not be found at his lodging house, she sent her out again to search the taverns west of the cloister. Finally, after supper, he turned up at the garden door looking slightly quizzical and out of wind. His breath smelled of sour ale.

Hurrying around the stable, she dragged him down toward the river, shushing him and refusing to say a word until they were some distance from the house. At the quay, he slapped his feet in the mud and refused to go farther. "Lady, friend, enough! What ails you?"

Clutching his soiled tunic with both hands, she threw back her head and laughed. "Jourdain, I'm going to have a child. His child, friend! His child."

"Oh Christ," he groaned under his breath.

"Can you believe it? A little babe, his and mine. Oh God, Jourdain, do you think it will be a boy? I hope so. No, a girl is fine. God grant that it's a boy! So sweet and soft, just like him. Jourdain . . ." She waited for him to answer.

In the coppery light, he blinked at her, moving his eyes impassively across her face. He said, "When?"

"Christmas. Or New Year's. Sometime around then." She laughed.

"Are you sure?"

"Well, no." She laughed again, delightedly. "It's impossible to figure the exact day."

He broke in. "I mean, are you sure you're with child?"

"I'm sure." She turned away with a smile and peered down at the water licking the embankment. A breeze flurried the wrinkled surface into deep shadowed pools. Down by the dock, torches winked nervously from a clump of boats. She heard Jourdain clear his throat and say, "Lady . . ." and when she turned back to him, she saw, much to her annoyance, that his face was grooved with a scowl of indecision. "Mark me, lady," he said slowly, "there are ways to get out of this, you know."

Instantly alert, she said, "What do you mean?"

He stammered slightly. "Things women drink. Let's say, potions." Hunching his shoulders, he stared into the water. "To make the babe go away."

"How do you know that?" she cried angrily.

He shrugged. "I've heard."

She looked away, her eyes enormous with rage. He disgusted her. What did he take her for? A fool, a murderess who would extinguish the seed of Peter Abelard in some excrement-smeared privy? She began to wish that she had not told him.

Brushing past her, Jourdain walked a few steps up the quay. From the shadows, he said softly, "Don't be angry with me. I'm sorry. Heloise, I said I'm sorry. But he may not want the child. Did you ever think of that?"

No, she had not thought of it; such an idea was unthinkable and only a man could have said it. "He'll want it," she said, with barely opened lips. "Don't be stupid."

Without speaking, he began to walk back toward the house, and she followed. The river breeze smelled of moss and whiffs of baking bread. Her thoughts kept turning to the babe growing inside her, and a few minutes later she'd almost forgotten her anger at Jourdain. "When do you think my belly will show?" she asked him eagerly.

"And how do you think I would know that!" He laughed, uncertain.

"Don't you have married sisters?"

"Well, yes, but—I know nothing about it."

Transported by her happiness, she could not stop chattering. She forgot that he was a man, and babbled on about morning nausea and her prayers to Our Lady, and did he think having a baby would be terribly painful. And when he fell silent or only replied with little grunts, she did not deign to notice and went on marveling. As they neared the stable, he only gestured toward the house and said, "Soft, lady. Fulbert might hear."

"He's away. But you're right, friend. I must put a guard on my tongue now, that's for certain." She sighed. "Although I would greatly love to tell the whole Ile."

Abruptly the garden door slammed, and she heard Agnes calling, "Lady, lady!" She sounded agitated.

"Here!" Heloise lifted her voice. "With Jourdain."

He murmured, finally, "Tell me this. What do you plan to do?"

"Do?"

He motioned toward the house. "Well, you can't very well stay here."

"Certainly not." It was impossible to say what she would do. She hadn't had time to consider the consequences of her pregnancy. "Why I— As a matter of fact, I was going to write Abelard. He'll know what I should do. Stay here!"

"Lady, I—"

Before he could offer an objection, she dived into the house and took the steps two at a time. In her room, dizzy, she lit a candle and started to scrawl a note to Abelard. There was no time to think about wording or style. She was going to have a child, she wrote. It was a miracle. She overflowed with joy and gratitude to God. She loved him. He should tell her what she must do now. That was all. She had no proper wax to seal it, so she folded the parchment into a small square.

Outside, behind the house, Jourdain was slouching against the privy. He tucked the wad of parchment into his girdle and stared at Heloise. "What did you tell him?"

"I told him—what I told you." All of a sudden, she flung her arms around his neck and smiled mistily. "Oh, Jourdain, I'm so happy!"

Matins rasped coarsely from Notre Dame, but not until an hour later did Jourdain come with the horse. The moon kept sliding in and out from behind a flurry of low-lying clouds, so that sometimes Heloise worried that the yard would be too full of light. Under her window, she heard something bump softly in the brush. Peering down, she could distinguish a shadow.

"Ssss."

She rapped a light signal on the edge of the shutter and turned from the window. The room was pitch-black—nothing to look at for a last time even had she wished. She left and felt her way down the staircase.

The warm night was full of rose scent and the twanging of gnats. A shape slid out of the dense shadows at the shoulder of the house. Shivering, she groped for Jourdain's arm. "Where's the horse?" she whispered.

"Up the road. Where did you put your things?"

"In the stable."

When she had steered him to the bundles, he began to grumble under his breath. "I said a few things."

"That's what I brought. A few things."

"Shit! What the devil do you have here!"

She didn't answer. Her life, she thought to herself, or all of it she wished to keep. A Limoges casket, an amethyst ring, a looking glass, a rose wimple, and several gowns. The other, much larger parcels contained the work she had done on the Yes or No quotations and a fair number of books. She felt guilty about taking Fulbert's copies of Plato and Aristotle. But not that guilty.

A horse was tied to a tree this side of the Quai-aux-Fleurs. In the ghost light, it was too dark to tell its color; as long as it had four good legs, she didn't much care. Jourdain swung her up behind the saddle; he mounted.

"Am I going to ride pillion all the way to Brittany?" She laughed softly.

"Don't be silly. We're not even taking this one. Master Peter bought two fine stallions."

"Jourdain, I can't ride a stallion." She didn't even know if she remembered how to ride a mare.

"You'll get the feel of it."

They set off down the river road with its rotting Roman wall, the Seine spreading away to the left, the cadenced hoofs drumming past the silent Hospital of St. Mary. The mill wheels, unceasing, groaned with a furry sound. Jourdain swung the horse onto the Petit Pont. At the south end of the bridge, they had to pass guards at the tower gate.

"Who goes?" one of them called out.

"Lambert d'Ardres. I crossed over a half hour ago."

"Who's that with you?"

Heloise ducked her head against Jourdain's shoulder.

"A friend."

In the torchlight, she could feel the guards staring at her, sense the grins racing in their voices.

"Nice," one of them shouted to Jourdain.

The gate scudded open, and they clattered onto the Left Bank. Inhaling deeply, Heloise could feel herself relax. Slightly. She still felt as if she were standing on a windy precipice; if she thought about what she was doing, she would plummet into the void. "How far to the house?" she asked Jourdain in an even voice.

"Not far."

They had turned off the cobbled Orleans road and were jogging west toward Saint-Germain-des-Prés. In this quarter, there was a lot of new construction she had not seen before—ugly modern houses that looked forlornly the same. Some now called this area the Latin Quarter because so many students congregated here. "I'm glad he's left the Ile," Heloise said. "Is his place nice?"

"You'll see. Solar with a fireplace. Behind that, a large sleeping room."

"Fleas?"

"Not many."

She stared at the darkened houses as they passed; in a few windows she could distinguish tendrils of yellow light. Students studying late, she guessed. "He must get a servant to cook for him."

"I think Galon's coming back."

"Can't he do better than that?"

Jourdain clucked in disgust. "Nobody can tell him what to do, you know that." He slowed the horse before turning into an alley alongside an imposing shingled house. He dismounted and reached for her. She didn't move.

"What's wrong?"

The moon was out now. "Nothing," she said, sighing. "Nerves." For three months she had hungered for the sight of him; now it was almost like going to meet a stranger.

"Come on," Jourdain said softly and pulled her to the ground.

Inside the entrance was a vestibule with a staircase leading straight up. Halfway, Heloise paused to lift her head. Abelard was standing on the landing. She stopped dead. He unfurled his arms and she staggered swiftly toward them, her eyes flooding with unshed tears.

"Ladylove," Abelard whispered. He folded her up tightly against his chest, rocking backward and forward. After a while, he released her and lifted her face with one hand. He began to stroke her cheek.

The breath came back into Heloise. She couldn't take her eyes off his face, he looked tired to her. Behind her on the steps, she could hear Jourdain breathing.

Abelard nodded, motioning them through a door at the side of the landing. The solar was richly furnished, as Jourdain had implied. There was a tiled fireplace at one end of the room, Abelard's majestic arm chair behind a writing table, windows fronting on the street. The windows were inset with thick glass. Heloise walked over to take a look; she had never seen glass before, except in church.

"No trouble?" Abelard asked Jourdain. "Agnes still sleeping like a babe?"

"No trouble."

"And the guards at the Chastelet?"

"I gave a false name. All they know is a man went over to the Ile and came back with a woman. It happens fifty times a night."

"There'll be questions later, you know."

"I know."

Heloise turned and looked at them. There was an awkward silence, and then Jourdain moved toward the door.

Abelard said to him, "Stay."

He shook his head. "I have to water the horses and take care of Heloise's things. If you need anything, call." His footsteps thumped softly on the stairs.

Abelard turned slowly. She tensed, conscious of her heartbeats. "Come to me, darling," he said in a husky voice. She did as she was bidden and stood before him. In the dreamy stillness, he moved his hands calmly, silently, over her hair, her face, throat; rapt as a blind man, he touched the backs of her hands, her arms, her breasts, and then, tenderly, her belly. When he had rememorized her, he pulled Heloise close and gave her his open mouth, long, shuddering kisses that sucked out the quick of her being. She felt emptied.

Somewhere, softly, the sleepy night was pricked by a horse coughing. Taking her by the hand, he led her into the inner chamber and began to undress her methodically. Heloise stood quite still. "Jourdain . . ." she said anxiously.

"Jourdain will wait." He smiled. Naked in the rosy flickering of the candlelight, they knelt facing each other on the coverlet. "God is full of mercy," he said, reaching for her. "You're mine now. Part of me."

"I've always been part of you," she murmured, but he wasn't listening. Shutting out everything, they rocked together, nearly insensible, conscious of only their one body, and the sounds of their loving dusted the corners of the chamber.

Later, from the crook of his arm, she saw tears drying on his cheeks. "Abelard," she said, after a long while, "don't you think we should get up?"

"Yes." He made no move to stir.

"I think it's going to be a boy."

"Indeed." He grinned. "If you say so."

"Do you care what it is? I mean, be honest."

"Honestly, no. All I care about is that you'll be safe."

She pulled away and sat up. "Oh, now I'll be safe. Nothing can go wrong now." She stood and went to look for her undertunic. A wave of dizziness overtook her, and she collapsed awkwardly on a stool.

"Lady?" Abelard said, swinging off the bed.

"I'm all right." There was so much to say and no time left. Suddenly she began to cry miserably.

"Lady, lady . . ." Abelard held her head between his palms. "Everything's going to be fine. You'll be happy at Le Pallet, and my sister will love you as I do. And after Lammas, I'll come to you. Don't be afraid."

"I'm not." She didn't want to worry him. She had no fear of the future, since everything had been decided at last. Only these last moments were unbearable, the reality of unreality. Seeing him and leaving, the best and the worst.

She clamped down on herself and mopped her face on her shift. Abelard dressed and went to the window. She heard him talking quietly to Jourdain in the alley, the uneven ticktack of their voices floating to her ears like a dream. Over his shoulder, he called to her, "Wait—don't put your bliaut on."

"Why—"

From a chest, he brought a black bundle and thrust it at her. "Here."

"What's this?" She frowned. She shook the fabric loose and saw that it was a nun's habit. Breaking into laughter, she said, "Where did you get this hideous thing!"

"Put it on," he ordered. "I have the veil here someplace."

"But, sweeting, I don't want to wear this—"

He rested his hands on his hips and glared at her. "God's eyes, don't argue with me."

She didn't want to put it on. It was ugly. "Why must I?" She grimaced, thinking of Ceci.

"Because it's a long way to Brittany, and the roads aren't safe. Nobody bothers a nun."

"I'll be with Jourdain."

"Yes, and people at the inns might remember you and Jourdain. Nobody will remember a nun with her escort. If anybody asks, say you're joining the order at Fontevrault."

Sighing, she began to pull the habit over her undertunic. She supposed that he was right. When Fulbert began looking for her, as he was sure to do, he would never think of inquiring for a nun. She heard Jourdain come into the solar; Abelard went out and they started talking together. Heloise draped the veil over her hair and fastened it. She knew that she looked ugly. And wasn't it a sacrilege to disguise yourself as a woman of God? She sighed again. She would burn it the moment they reached Le Pallet.

When she came into the solar, Abelard glanced at her, pleased. Jourdain stared, neutral. She grinned at him. "No nasty comments, please."

"I didn't say a word," he murmured, and turned back to Abelard. "It's going to be prime in less than two hours."

"There's an inn near Corbeil—the Three Pigeons, I think. Stop there tonight."

"And stay on the Roman road?"

"Straight through to Orleans."

"No fords?"

"No. At Orleans, you follow the Loire."

"I know. Meung. Beaugency. Right along the river."

"Right. Be careful before you hit Tours."

"My lord?"

"That's a bad stretch of road. I've run into bandits in those parts. But there's a good inn the other side of the town. Marvelous *vin rose.*"

"And the ferry?"

"At Angers." Abelard frowned. "But you'd better go on to Nantes and cross there. You'll have to double back a few miles, but it won't matter."

"And from Nantes? Then how far?"

"A dozen miles east. On the road to Poitiers."

Jourdain rocked back on his heels. "I don't foresee any problems."

"I gave you enough money?"

"More than enough."

"Good. Now listen to me. The Bretons can be testy bastards. Don't get into any fights. And watch your purse."

Jourdain shifted his feet and nodded impatiently.

"And for Christ's sake, be careful who you talk to. We don't want to leave a mile-wide trail."

Abelard took Heloise's arm. They went downstairs. It was still dark, but a murky color of dark. She heard him ask Jourdain, "You have a sword?"

"And a knife."

"Good." He stalked over to the horses, a chestnut and a brown stallion, and looked surprised at the size of the packs lashed to their sides. "Lady," he said, laughing, "you don't believe in traveling light, do you? What's all this?"

"Books," she told him, shivering. "And something that I'm writing."

He pulled her to him. "Perchance you'll write a book someday," he said softly. His fingers tightened around her waist.

"Perchance." Deliberately, she numbed herself.

He hoisted her onto the chestnut and handed up the reins. Behind her, she heard Jourdain mounting. Abelard buried his head against her hip.

"Heloise."

She leaned over and kissed the top of his head. After a moment, he raised up and backed away. In a cracked voice, he said, "Good journey. Jourdain, be careful. Now go quickly!"

They began to move off into the night. Heloise called out softly,

"God in heaven keep you, my love." She looked over her shoulder, but his face was hidden by shadows.

They doubled back toward the Orleans road and turned south. Water trickled down the sides of her nose, yet she had no sensation of weeping. When the rivulets reached the corners of her mouth, she licked away the salt and swallowed. Ahead, Jourdain rode in silence. They rattled briskly between fields of vineyards, past some tumbledown buildings that had once been Roman baths. Jourdain glanced at her over his shoulder. She nudged the chestnut stallion and drew up even with him. He reached out and handed her a wafer. Smiling at him, she took a bite but had a hard time getting it down.

"You'll feel better," he said. "By and by." His tone was hearty, unnatural.

"I know," she said in a small voice. Abruptly a cry ripped from her throat. "Oh God, Jourdain, I wish I were dead!"

He shook his head. "People don't die from love." A few seconds later, quietly, "Most people I know wouldn't sacrifice their lives for love, either."

"I would."

He said blandly, "That's the difference between you and—most people I know."

She knew that his face was bitter, but she hadn't the strength to argue with him. The road began tilting sharply upward. Over to her left, there were torches atwinkle in the abbey of Sainte-Geneviève. When they reached the crest of the hill, she asked Jourdain to rein in.

"Why?"

"I want to look."

"There's nothing to see."

She pulled up the stallion and moved it around. Down below, the Ile slept in its thinning gray mist. A few lights blinked like fireflies; she could see, indistinctly, the slender spires of the Cité Palace and the smudged contours of the topmost bell tower on Notre Dame. There was nothing to see.

They rode on.

10 🌿

LE PALLET WAS A SMALL fortified castle perched on the slope of a hill, some dozen miles southeast of Nantes. Above the castle, the hill tapered to a summit capped by a fine grove of pines; below, on the far side of the hill, droned the river Sanguèze, which local chroniclers claimed had been named after the savage battles between the Bretons and Angles centuries earlier.

If once the Sanguèze had gushed with blood, Heloise could find nothing of violence in the landscape now. The scenery was as unpretentious as a cup of cool, clear water. Under an open sky, the land fanned away into the distance with nothing to jostle the eye but fields of vines, clusters of poplars and oaks and flapping willows, cattle grazing peacefully in the ragged meadow grass. Nothing, she thought, could happen there.

As baronial fortresses went, Le Pallet had to be regarded as outmoded. Nearly two hundred and fifty years old, it had been continually occupied by a succession of owners, some of whom had found it necessary to withstand expeditions of Scandinavian barbarians who had come in their long-prowed dragon ships and ravaged the countryside. But now it had been fifteen years or more since the castle had withstood a siege, that during a paltry private war between two local barons, and certainly no one had suffered the least inconvenience. Recent innovations in fortifications as a result of the crusade had rendered unformidable such strongholds as Le Pallet. It was now a well-run farm and little more.

Despite Heloise's confident farewells to Abelard, she had arrived there with tangled emotions: joy, hope, considerable apprehension. Abelard had assured her of a loving reception from his kin, but by now she knew both Abelard and human nature well enough to realize that this might not be the case. She was, she warned herself, the pregnant mistress of their famous brother, and, from what Jourdain had said of the family's piety, they might very well hold her lack of chastity against her. In the end, as these things have a way of doing, nothing turned out as she had anticipated. Secretly she had expected—a bit unreasonably, she knew—a castle full of Abelard facsimiles, that is to say, brilliant, good-looking men and women, as if the womb of Abelard's mother could only produce geniuses, and what she found were ordinary people, well-meaning and unsophisticated.

For that matter, very few of Abelard's family remained at the castle. Some years earlier, Berengarius and Lucia had retreated into their respective abbeys, and by now the children too had scattered: Porcarius and Dagobert to Nantes, where the former had become a canon, the latter a knight in the service of the Duke of Brittany; Radulphus, dead of dysentery, to a grave under the pine grove on the hill. Abelard's middle brother, Dagobert, preferred to live at the duke's palace, and he returned to Le Pallet only three or four times a year, on which occasions he invariably impregnated his wife if she were not already carrying a child. If it had once troubled Alienor that she saw her husband infrequently, this was no longer true, and she had come to regard his periodic visits as a seasonal annoyance that must be borne philosophically, like the sudden storm that leaves in its wake a torn roof to be mended.

Since Berengarius's departure, Le Pallet had become, in effect, the property of Abelard's sister, Denise, and her husband, William. A petty knight, a younger son with no prospects whatsoever, William had responded to this rise in his fortunes with a gratitude that bordered on the touching; he stewarded Berengarius's fief as if the land had been his own and toiled harder than any peasant. Denise, a small, slightly plump woman, was by no means happy with her hardworking spouse, but it took Heloise many months to realize this. Her first impression of the castle was a blur of children, for with Denise's surviving eight and Alienor's thirteen, the hall and ward echoed from prime to matins with the sound of excited voices and always, it seemed, with the squalling of one infant or another. Depending upon one's capacity for noise and affection for children, it was either a juvenile utopia or the worst sort of chaos.

Unwilling to make any such judgment at the outset, Heloise decided to reserve opinion and observe, although as the months passed, after Jourdain had gone and she had made friends with some of the children, she was obliged to conclude that the only word for Le Pallet was bedlam. Happy bedlam, but bedlam nonetheless. This was, she often reminded herself, the place where she would be spending the remainder of her life. It was, after all, the real world, just as Saint-Gervais was also the normal world of dogs and children, horses and halls with their smoke-blackened walls. She had never existed in this world, neither Argenteuil nor the Rue des Chantres falling into any such category, and she embarked on a self-conducted campaign of adjustment. And when she sometimes awakened in the night with a queer hunger, only a dream perhaps, for her turret chamber in Fulbert's house, she hastily walled up the memories.

Living at Le Pallet, she decided, was just like sitting in a warm tub; it clipped the senses utterly so that the weeks and months slipped by with the greased passage of buttery soap. Perhaps, though, it was only the condition of pregnancy. She felt like doing nothing, and no one required anything of her, although she volunteered her services with the chores without being asked. At first, Denise and William seemed to approach her on tiptoe, as if she were some countess who had inexplicably stumbled through their gate for her lying-in. This partial awe in which they held her created, of course, barriers, and by autumn Heloise still had not become fully intimate with the members of the household. This did not bother her as much as it might have under other circumstances; she felt strangely lethargic, half there and half someplace other, but where she could not say.

Nothing troubled her excessively, except the news from Paris. It was very bad. Abelard had not come at Lammas as he had promised, only letters from both him and Jourdain describing more or less the same situation: that Fulbert had reacted to her disappearance with a grief and fury so spectacular that it bordered on insanity. It had to be seen, Abelard wrote, to be believed.

Her uncle roved the Ile and the Left Bank, knocking on doors and pleading with goodwives to tell him if they had seen his niece. Canon Martin and others had been sent bearing threats to cut Abelard's throat if he did not return Heloise, and when it finally became apparent that she was not with him, Fulbert took his complaints to Louis the Fat, accusing Master Peter of debauching and kidnaping his niece. He hired men to guard Abelard's house and to follow him day and night, and for this reason Abelard had not dared journey to Brittany in the summer. Only after classes had resumed in the fall did he explain the situation to King Louis, asking him to inform Fulbert that further search was futile, that Heloise, pregnant, had gone to Le Pallet.

Her uncle's uppermost thoughts were of vengeance, but what could he do? If he were to kill or injure Abelard, some retribution might fall on Heloise among the barbaric Bretons. Nevertheless, Jourdain reassuringly wrote to her, Abelard was very much on guard against assault, and he had taken the precaution of hiring a bodyguard who accompanied him to class and slept outside his door at night. Fulbert had not, Jourdain added, the courage to harm Abelard now.

Heloise could do nothing—but worry.

By the end of August, her belly was beginning to unfurl and she could feel the floating and fluttering of butterfly wings, a sensation that the women of the castle quickly demoted from the realm of the poetic to a prosaic observation: The babe was kicking.

The day before Michaelmas, Alienor gave birth to a stillborn son, and then, a week later, Denise followed with a live daughter, whom she christened Agnes. Neither of these occurrences created a ripple in the daily life of the castle, where gestation and parturition were as unremarkable as the passing of the seasons. Two days after Agnes's birth, Denise was out of bed, jangling the keys she wore on her girdle and screeching at the servingwomen for having neglected their chores.

"Lazy wretches," she grumbled to Heloise. "When I'm in childbed, they take it for a holiday."

Heloise watched as she opened her bliaut and guided the infant's mouth to her nipple. She looked at the color of Agnes's face; it was a queer reddish purple. She looked as if she had been boiled. "Does it hurt badly?" she asked impulsively.

"What? Giving suck?" Denise gave her a blank look. "Of course not."

"No, I meant having it." After listening to Alienor's shrieks, she had steeled herself when Denise's time had come. But Denise had done little more than whimper.

"It hurts," she said. Seeing the dismayed look on Heloise's face, she quickly added, "But not always. It depends. Don't think about it."

"I can't help thinking about it." Denise's second youngest child crawled between her feet. She hoisted Agatha into her lap and bounced her. The child, giggling, clawed with plump fingers at her plaits.

"Don't worry. Alienor's an excellent midwife."

Heloise hesitated, then said, "Alienor told me that I'm too old to have a first babe. Is that right?"

Denise smoothed her free hand wearily across her forehead. That single gesture reminded Heloise of Abelard, that and the thick dark hair; otherwise she would never have taken them for brother and sister. Denise answered reluctantly, "Well, eighteen is old. But I wouldn't worry. Just pray it comes out alive."

There was an inflection of mild rebuke in her last words, and Heloise fell silent. Although Denise invariably spoke to her in tones sweet as honey, she sensed a trace of something sharp behind them. She bit her lower lip and lowered Agathe to the floor. The child let out a howl, which Heloise ignored; she had wet through her napkin and left a damp patch on Heloise's skirt. After a moment: "How old were you when you married William?"

"Thirteen."

Heloise smiled. "How very young to be in love."

"In love? Believe me, I wasn't in love." Denise lifted the infant to her shoulder and rubbed her back. "I cried for a week. My lady mother kept threatening to beat me if I didn't stop weeping."

"You didn't want to marry?"

Denise corrected her matter-of-factly. "Didn't want to marry William."

"Why ever not? He's a worthy man."

"And poor." Denise laughed.

"What difference does that make?" Heloise said softly. "A man's worth depends on his merits, not on wealth or power."

"Oh, I suppose." She stood up and laid the infant in a basket of unmended clothes near the hearth. "But it's better to have a rich worthy man than a poor one."

Watching Denise's face, she felt a crackle of revulsion at the woman's mercenary attitude. What kind of marriage could Denise have? Keeping her voice neutral, she said, "Don't you think that a woman who marries for money is offering herself for sale?"

Denise straightened with a glare that she quickly amended. She said, rather carelessly, "Rich, poor. Who had a choice? I was given to a poor man, that's all."

"Yes, but—"

"Lady, it's all very well for you to talk." Denise's lips quivered with annoyance. "You have a rich man."

Struggling to keep from shouting, she deliberately folded her arms over her stomach. "Abelard isn't rich."

Denise's eyes rounded, disbelieving. "What are you talking about?" she snorted. "Mayhap he's not rich to you, but I call him rich."

Heloise looked beyond her, at Agathe poking a finger into her sister's mouth. Her temples were beginning to pound. She should have known better than to start this discussion with Denise. Now she could only try to maneuver herself out of it before any great damage was done. Finally she said, "Of course you're right."

Denise stood before the hearth, face flushed, hands clamped on her hips. This was the first time that Heloise could recall seeing her hands idle. She was staring down at her feet, as if some question were forming in her mind. Whatever it was, Heloise didn't want to hear. Smiling, she hoisted herself to her feet and started to walk away. Over her shoulder, she could hear Denise calling her name. She turned back, bracing herself slightly. The rushes crunched under her feet.

"I was wondering—" Denise cleared her throat. "In the letters I've had from my lord brother, there was no mention of when he plans to visit us."

Stiffening, Heloise said quickly, "Nor in mine."

"Christmas, do you think?"

"Mayhap. I don't know."

Denise rubbed her hands together frettully. "I hope you don't mind my asking. But preparations must be made for the wedding, and if I know in advance I—"

"Wedding?" The lone word heaved itself involuntarily out of Heloise's mouth and hung in the air between them.

Abruptly, Denise began talking of slaughtering and baking, of special decorations for the chapel, and of how many casks of wine she would distribute to the varlets. She planned to invite the surrounding countryside and perhaps, she said, the duke.

Replies washed up to the end of Heloise's tongue, and she kept swallowing them down. When Denise paused for breath, she said quietly, "There isn't going to be a wedding."

Denise looked at her. "What did you say?"

"I said we're not getting married."

She laughed uncertainly. After a moment, she said, "I don't understand."

"It's very simple. We don't wish to marry." She went past Denise and stood so close to the hearth that her hands felt fried.

A flaming log collapsed with a spattering of hisses. Denise jerked her chin toward Heloise. "But surely you want your child to—"

Impatient, Heloise cut her off. "There is no great dishonor in illegitimacy. But the child has nothing to do with it."

Denise said, as if she had not been listening closely, "You mean, my brother does not wish to marry you."

Heloise shook her head politely. "I've never discussed the subject with your brother. I'm only saying that I do not wish it."

"Why?"

She might have made an attempt to explain herself to Denise, but abandoned the idea as futile in advance. As one shouts a message into a gale wind, expecting it to be instantly lost, she said tautly, "The title of mistress is sweeter to me than wife."

Denise burst out with a wordless gasp. Then she said severely, "If you think of yourself as a concubine, you can't expect people to respect you."

"I know what I am," she said with a certain amount of grit in her voice. "What people think of me is not something I lose sleep over." She looked over to see Denise absolutely motionless, watching her with barely veiled contempt.

"My lord brother," she told Heloise, "is an honorable man. He will marry you." She clapped her hands together for emphasis. "Yes! There will be a wedding."

Mildly, Heloise said, "I will refuse."

"Refuse?" echoed Denise, wagging her head fiercely. "Lady, you have some outlandish ideas." She stalked through the hall in the direction of the kitchen. From the hall, Heloise could hear her racketing at the cook about some fowls he had forgotten to pluck for dinner.

The pains started early on Christmas Eve. They were mild, and she saw no reason to mention them yet. Shortly before midnight, everyone filed into the ward and walked to the chapel through deepening soft snow. It was a fine night. The snow silenced the sound of footsteps, and above a fleet of stars gentled down the sky. Inside the chapel, Denise was marshaling the children into formation—the smallest ones in front, Justin must not sit next to Maria because they whispered, and so forth.

The priest began mass. It was cold in the chapel, but Heloise's palms were sweating. The pains in her belly grew more insistent. After a while, she could not concentrate on the Latin words and tried to think of something else. Before the first snowfall, a peddler had come to the castle, his saddlebags stocked with a surprising assortment of goods, and she had purchased an ivory toothpick for Abelard. Now she began making a mental list of the peddler's wares: pins and needles, gloves, linen handkerchiefs with embroidered flowers, ribbons, tweezers—her mind began jumping around, and she gave up. She said a prayer, urging God to make the babe a boy. A little while later, she canceled the request. Thy will be done, she said, and asked forgiveness for her sins.

Back in the hall, she took her place at the trestle. When William heaped her plate with goose and capon, her stomach swam with nausea. Between contractions she smiled politely at Alienor's eldest son and answered his questions about Socrates. The boy was beginning to annoy her; he was asking questions only to hear himself talk. It was hot and smoky in the hall, and she gripped the edge of the trestle until her knuckles whitened.

Alienor came around the table and stood behind her. She said quietly, "You should go upstairs now."

"Later."

"When did it start?"

"After vespers."

Alienor's narrow face twisted into disapproval. "Don't be a fool. Go up and lie down."

Upstairs, she crawled under a fur and lay like a child with her knees drawn up. Below in the hall, they were singing and clapping, and somebody was banging a spoon against a kettle. She wondered when Alienor would come up and how long this whole thing might take. Hours, possibly. She dozed for a while, and when she awoke, she could feel Alienor and Denise next to the bed.

"When will it be over?" she asked without opening her eyes.

Denise laughed. "That's what they all ask the first time."

Heloise opened her eyes. Half a dozen women scurried around the bed, some of them trying to look busy but the rest merely staring. Anger gagged her. "Get out!" she whispered hoarsely. "Leave me alone." Nobody moved. She shut her eyelids tight, swallowed up by a wave of unspeakable pain. Suddenly she was afraid that she would die.

Alienor sat on the side of the bed and unclenched Heloise's fists.

"It's worse when you tense your body," she said. "Try to relax."

"I can't."

"Relax between pains."

"All right." She gulped a deep breath and forced her body limp. Several times she opened her eyes and looked at the women. None of them seemed to be upset, or even terribly concerned. After a while, she forgot the women, forgot her vows to be brave. Some time later, a long way off, she could hear someone screaming and understood vaguely that it was herself.

The sun was just coming up when the baby was born. Alienor

brought it in a blanket and laid it next to Heloise, and then, almost as an afterthought, she told Heloise it was a boy.

"Ah, yes," said Heloise and plunged into sleep.

All day long, there was a great coming and going at Le Pallet. The castle's tenants and their families brought the Christmas rents—firewood, bread, hens, home-brewed ale. In return, Denise gave them Christmas dinner, mainly the food they had provided. Bonfires crackled in the ward, and everyone gathered noisily around the flames, talking, singing, some dancing. At noon they were allowed to enter the hall with their cups and trenchers, and the kitchen varlets carried out enormous platters of cheese, stewed hen, bacon with mustard, and loaves of white bread. And as much ale as they could drink.

Washed and combed and propped against the pillows, Heloise held the baby gingerly in the crook of her arm. She could not take her eyes off him. Again and again she tentatively inspected his fuzz of light hair, the tiny fingers, the pearly rose mouth. The dark-blue eyes staring back into her own seemed otherworldly, as if his body were there but the rest of him with the angels. There was an expression around his eyes and mouth that awed her.

All afternoon, people had been climbing the ladder to look at the new babe, and Heloise had smiled at the visitors and accepted their clucking and aahing. Finally, Denise came up with a plate of bread and cheese, her face red from the heat of the kitchen.

She said, "You can hold him tight. He won't break."

"Denise, he smiled at me a little while ago."

She laughed indulgently. "Silly. New babies don't smile." She leaned over to stare into his face. "A fine boy. He looks just like you."

Heloise pursed her lips indignantly. "Certainly not. He looks like Abelard."

Denise straightened with a grin. "If you say so." She set down the plate on the bed near Heloise's elbow. "See, it wasn't so bad now, was it?"

"I guess not." It was bad, she thought.

"Next time you won't be frightened. You're a good breeder and you have plenty of milk. Count your blessings."

"Yes." She turned her head away slightly. No doubt Denise was right, but she didn't like people reminding her about counting her blessings, as though she were a child who couldn't think for herself. Denise was a good person, but her manner of speaking irritated Heloise. Next time indeed. There would be no next time, Heloise thought.

"You're going to call him Peter, aren't you?"

"No."

"What do you mean, no? Who else would you name him after?" Denise sat down hard on the bed.

"I think I'll name him Astrolabe." She smiled down into the baby's face.

"Astro—what?"

"Astrolabe."

"I beg your pardon," Denise said coldly, "but I've never heard of any person called Astrolabe."

Heloise reached down and popped a piece of cheese into her mouth. "An astrolabe," she said patiently, "is used by astronomers to chart the movement of the planets."

"I'm sorry. I don't understand."

"It's like the sextant that navigators use at sea. Only it's to chart the heavens."

"You're going to name him for a machine?" She looked down in amazement.

Heloise said, expressionless, "If you want to put it like that, yes."

Denise's eyes needled into her. "I don't like the name."

"That's obvious."

"People will laugh at him."

"No they won't." She hoisted the child into both arms and began to rock him.

Denise slid off the bed and started out. Then she turned and came back to stare at them. "Nobody in our family has ever been named after a machine. And I can tell you this, lady. My lord brother will be furious." She looked really angry.

Heloise said softly, "Please, Denise. I'm very happy. Don't spoil everything."

Denise grunted. "It's a stupid name."

Heloise slid Astrolabe under the coverlet. She said to Denise, "It's not inappropriate. He was born on Christmas."

"Hmmm," said Denise, unconvinced. "You might as well call him Star of Bethlehem."

"I'll take it under consideration." Heloise grinned, but Denise did not even flicker a smile.

* * *

Denise complained about the baby's name until Heloise's churching, but by that time everyone in the castle was calling him Astrolabe, and she finally gave up. Winter closed in around Le Pallet. It snowed off and on all through the month of January; the temperature remained frigid and the road to Nantes impassable. No letters came into Le Pallet, and none went out.

During the time, Heloise did not open a book. Every other day she wrote to Abelard, and occasionally to Jourdain, until she had used up the castle's supply of parchment. The letters she kept locked in her Limoges box against the day when the road thawed and someone could take them into Nantes for the Paris courier. The rest of her time was spent with Astrolabe. He was too young to really play with; about all she could do was watch him, and cuddle and kiss and fondle, and this she did incessantly until Alienor warned her that he would grow up dreadfully spoiled. She should not pick him up every time he cried, Alienor instructed, nor was it necessary to give him the breast twenty times a day. Heloise smiled sweetly. Sometimes she brought Astrolabe's truckle bed down to the hearth and rocked him giddily until he laughed out loud and his plump cheeks dimpled with pleasure. And when he lay still, his mouth budded a delicate pink, she talked to him and told stories about Ulysses and Jason. The castle women laughed and shook their heads.

"Lady." Denise grinned. "Wait a bit. He can't understand you."

"Of course he can. He just can't answer yet."

Denise shook her head. "And all that attention is going to make him high-strung. Mark me, by the time he's walking, he'll be a real devil."

Heloise thrust out her chin. "What kind of woman are you? He's my son, and I'll love him as much as I please. I don't tell you how to raise your children, do I?" Her voice trembled.

Denise stiffened and went off in a huff.

At the beginning of Lent, Dagobert came from Nantes to hunt with a party of the duke's courtiers. In his saddlebag he had a bundle of letters for Heloise. The one from Jourdain she shoved aside to read last. Abelard's she made herself read slowly, like a starveling trying to make a crust of bread last. After a few pages, she forgot about going slow and skimmed the pages to find out when he was coming. Astrolabe began to howl, wanting to be picked up. She ignored him. In the last letter, she found what she was searching for. As soon as the weather broke, he wrote, when the roads improved, he was setting out for Le Pallet.

Which, of course, told her nothing useful. How did she know what the roads near Paris were like?

She paced the floor near her bed, suddenly sick with missing him. The self-control she had clamped on herself as month had passed into month, the deliberate putting him out of her mind, began to spin away from her. She wanted him with a physical hunger that made her stomach churn.

After a while, she sat down and calmly read all the letters. That made her feel better. He had, he wrote, been to see Fulbert. The two of them had spent the evening together and everything had been arranged. Heloise was not to worry, because her uncle bore them no ill will. Abelard repeated the sentence "Everything has been arranged" several times, once underlining it for emphasis. But precisely what he and Fulbert had arranged he did not reveal. If Fulbert would allow her to return to Paris with Astrolabe, she would kiss the ground under his feet. That must be what Abelard meant. She could not stay at Le Pallet, that much she had decided even before Astrolabe had come. Already half of her mind was dead, and if she remained, the rest would slowly rot from disuse. She longed for the Ile and for the stampeding students shouting in Latin, for her uncle's quiet turret chamber with the only sounds those of parchment pages turning and the scratch of her pen.

She sighed. With Astrolabe, there would be no such quiet in her uncle's house. Perhaps he would not allow her to come, after all. He had no love for infants. Hadn't he sent her to Argenteuil as a babe? On the other hand, he had not, apparently, objected to Agnes's babes, and of course Petronilla had been raised there. She lay down on her bed and turned over the problem in her mind. If he would not have her and her child at the Rue des Chantres, then she would find other lodgings. One room, that was all she needed for herself and Astrolabe. The solution was simple enough, and she chided herself for having fretted over nothing. She went downstairs to tell Denise about Abelard's visit.

That night, getting into bed, she found Jourdain's letter, and again she was seized by anxiety. Visiting Melun at Christmas, he had ridden over to Saint-Gervais once. He did not wish to worry her unduly, but she should stand warned that Thibaut and Philip had talked a great deal about Abelard and Heloise, and the talk had been ugly. Threats of cutting Abelard's throat and throwing him into the Seine. Of course, Jourdain allowed, it could be talk for talk's sake. Yet he felt, as her friend, that she would like to know.

She did not want to know, not today. Leave it to Jourdain to spoil things, she said to herself wearily. Trying to reassure herself, she told herself that all this had taken place at Christmas; since then, Abelard had made up with Fulbert. Her nerves on edge, she had a hard time falling asleep.

The next day, she washed her hair with rose water and manicured her nails. Over her head she pinned her silk wimple. Every time she heard a horse on the drawbridge, she ran to the window slit, until Alienor, smiling, said to her, "A tended kettle never boils," and everybody laughed.

After that the children teased her. When she was suckling Astrolabe or taking a bath, they would run to her and cry, "Lady, lady, your lord's here!" and scamper away giggling. As the days passed, however, and Abelard failed to appear, she stopped wearing the wimple and running to the window at the sound of hoofbeats. Alienor was right about the tended kettle.

The week following, Dagobert and his friends went back to Nantes. The castle quieted, and Heloise began embroidering a shift for Astrolabe. She had debated about what sort of picture he might like and finally decided on a jongleur playing a lute. She went up to the sleeping chamber to get some green thread from her chest. Sitting on the edge of her bed, she wound the threads around her fingers indecisively. Perhaps she should make the jongleur's cap red. Behind her back, the hanging tapestry began swaying, and she heard the shuffle of feet. "Lady aunt," huffed Agathe, "Beelar come."

Heloise did not bother to glance around. "You mustn't tell lies. God will punish you." She would use green for the cap and give it a bright-red plume.

The child trundled around the end of the bed and slapped a grubby hand on Heloise's knee. "No lie," she lisped. "Gathe no lie."

"Good morning, lady," Abelard said gravely.

Heloise snapped her neck around. He was standing inside the tapestry, smiling. She pushed off the bed and stood up, staring without speaking. He came around next to her and held her so tightly that her bones cracked.

Heloise kissed him on the mouth and cheeks and hair. He had not shaved. She looked over his shoulder at the child blinking up at them. "Agathe, go down to the hall now." The girl moved away, reluctantly. "That's a good girl." She said to Abelard, "Have you seen him?"

"Who?" He sank on the bed and swung her down next to him.

"Astrolabe."

"No—I just rode into the ward a minute ago."

"You must see him."

"Later. I want to look at you."

"He's adorable."

"You look marvelous. By God, this country air must agree with you."

Heloise smiled, pretending not to be disappointed at his lack of interest in the babe. "The only air that agrees with me," she said softly, "is the air where you are." She brushed a hair from his cloak.

"I've missed you," Abelard said abruptly.

"Is that all you have to say?"

"No." Abelard grinned at her. "Not all." He reached for her.

"Did you go to him," she asked, "or did he come to you?"

"I went to him." Abelard pulled his cloak against the gusts of spring wind and looked up. The sky seethed with torn gray clouds. There was rain coming. He yawned. "Poor bastard."

Heloise sat down on Radulphus's gravestone. From the top of the hill, she could see a peasant woman following her ox along the road. "He might have killed you."

"No chance. Ah, lady, you should see him. He looks like an old man."

"He's not old."

"He drags through the close with his head bowed. You can't help but pity him."

"Yes." She turned away, inhaling the briny fragrance of pine, wishing that she could feel pity but feeling nothing. She could not imagine Fulbert as Abelard described him. Then: "I'm surprised he let you set foot in the house."

"Agnes let me in."

"What did he say to you?"

"Nothing. He was as mild as a lamb."

"A lamb?" Heloise frowned.

"I swear it."

"Then he was putting on an act for your benefit."

On a bed of pine needles, Abelard squatted on his haunches and glowered at her. "Don't be ridiculous. You weren't there. How could you know?"

"Tell me what you said," she demanded. "Then we'll talk about me being ridiculous. Well, tell me."

"Oh, that," he said, seemingly careless. "Naturally I took all the blame on myself. Called it deceit and the basest treachery. I–" He shrugged one shoulder. "You know."

Watching his face, Heloise waited for him to continue. "And naturally he agreed," she prompted. "What else?"

"That's all."

"Hah! Come, my lord–"

Abelard spoke briskly. "I reminded him that I had done what any man in love would do. That, er, since the beginning of the human race, women have brought the noblest men to ruin."

She turned away, furious to the bottom of her heart. "Gramercy."

"Heloise." He stood up. "Don't be foolish. I had to use words he would understand."

"Oh. Did he?"

Abelard smiled. "Completely. I begged his forgiveness and promised to make any amends he thought proper."

Heloise disliked his careless tone. She lounged against Radulphus's stone and gazed dully over the furrowed fields below. Fringing the fields, the poplars were thrusting forth leaves. In Paris, the chestnuts would soon be in bloom. "And what did Uncle suggest?"

"To make a long story short–"

"Don't. I want the long story."

"He said his house had been irrevocably dishonored and there was nothing I could do to wipe out the stain. And I said yes there was"–he paused and shrugged–"I could marry you."

She staggered to her feet, catching a pine branch to steady herself.

"I wronged him. I'll make it right. All I asked was that the marriage be kept secret, so as not to damage my reputation." Abelard grinned. "You should have seen his face. That was more than he ever hoped for."

She had to bite her lips to keep from screaming. "And what did he say?" she asked softly.

Abelard wrinkled his forehead. "Why, what would he say? He was overjoyed. We drank a cup together to seal our reconciliation."

"Do you believe him!" she cried.

"Yes. Don't you?"

"No."

"He kissed me."

"Judas kiss. The easier to betray you."

"Well, lady," he muttered thickly, "I don't understand you. I've solved this entire mess. I've humbled myself before your idiot uncle and yet you have no word of thanks for me."

"God's pardon, sir, you've solved nothing. Because I'm not going to marry you."

He stared at her. At last he said, rather sharply, "Oh?"

"You might have consulted me before you went to the bother of humbling yourself. You could have saved yourself the trouble." She was beginning to shout. "Oh, you and Uncle, you mighty male protectors, you arrangers of people's lives! Have I no say in all this?"

Smiling slightly, he reached for her hand. "You are right to be angry. I should have told you first. Now, what say you, lady? Will you be my wife?"

She said, "I will not," and held her breath.

Abelard's face flushed crimson. He dropped her hand and took a step backward. "You chaffer me wickedly, ladylove. I've no sense of humor in this matter." His voice was dangerously quiet.

She went to him and folded her arms around his shoulders. A huge drop of rain pelted her forehead. "Sweet heart," she whispered in a coaxing way.

"You should not have said that."

"I know." She clung to him. "But all the same, I won't marry you."

"Isn't my name honorable enough for you?" His voice was dulled with hurt.

"Honor. Don't speak of honor. What honor could there be in a marriage that would dishonor you and humiliate both of us?" Water splattered her hair and nose. "Nature creates philosophers for all mankind, not for a single woman. Think of what people would say—what a sorry scandal that would be!"

"Never mind what people will say—"

She put her hands on her hips. "Why don't you admit it? Marriage would disgrace you."

"Lady, you keep talking about disgrace and dishonor. Let me remind you that nothing prevents me from marrying." He turned his back on her and stood gazing out at the horizon darkened with black clouds.

"St. Paul said—"

"Don't quote St. Paul at me!"

"If you don't care about the words of the Apostles, at least you might listen to what the philosophers have said. Theophrastus, Jerome, Cicero. They wrote about the endless annoyances of marriage in considerable detail."

"Lady, can I—"

"You can't devote your attention to both a wife and philosophy—St. Jerome. Have you forgotten?"

"All right. There are difficulties." He twisted around to face her. "I admit that the idea of a married philosopher is extraordinary."

"Unique, you mean."

"Very well, unique. But what of it? *Fortes fortuna juvat*. The extraordinary doesn't scare me. There's a first time for everything."

"Do you want to be a philosopher or not?" she cried.

"Now, what do you mean, do I *want* to be? I *am*." He stopped and looked at her unhappily.

"You have absolutely no idea of what married life is really like."

"Eh?" he said coldly. "I think I have a fair idea."

"No you don't. It's—undignified."

He threw back his head and began to laugh. "Sweeting—" He reached for her arm, but she flung him off. Backing away, she started to scramble down the slope, wet brambles catching at her skirt. "Sweeting, come back." When she refused to stop, he plunged after her, yelling her name.

The next day, Abelard rode off to Nantes.

Heloise knelt to pray in the chapel. God must guide her now, give her a sign about what to do. Halfway through the Credo, her mind strayed to Abelard swaggering in his saddle that morning. He looked like a knight about to enter a tournament. Dashing and refreshed. That had surprised her. They had argued most of the night.

She thought, He's the most stubborn man. For all his protestations, he knew nothing about family life and wouldn't listen when she tried to explain. Look around you, she had finally yelled, do you want to live like this? And he had assured her that he had no intention of living like his kin at Le Pallet; it would be different for them.

Again she started the Credo, and this time managed to finish it. Then she asked God whether she should marry. More accurately, she told God she should not marry and asked for his confirmation. Then she curled her fingers tightly and prayed to the Blessed Virgin, asking her intercession. She thought, Uncle is shrewd. Even if Abelard had offered to marry her openly, Fulbert would not have truly forgiven him. And certainly not for a secret marriage. How would that expunge the dishonor to Saint-Gervais? It would not, and she couldn't understand how Abelard failed to recognize this. All at once, she remembered Fulbert's expression that morning he had found them in bed. No, it had been a Judas kiss.

She stood up and went back to the ward, careful to avoid the puddles from yesterday's rain. When Abelard returned, late that night, he began talking comfortably about their marriage, as if it were all settled. The next week, they would ride back to Paris, as Fulbert had requested, and be wed in a secret ceremony. Then she would live at her uncle's house, as before. If anyone remarked upon her absence, she could say that she had been living at Saint-Gervais.

She thought wearily, How can a whole year be erased? She said aloud, "And what of the babe?"

"He can stay here."

"But I don't want to leave him."

"In June we'll come back to get him. That's only three months."

"And then?" she asked fretfully, looking down.

"I'll find a nice house near Paris. There are some lovely villages beyond Sainte-Geneviève. You and the boy can live quietly."

"Where will you be?"

He gave her a sour look. "God, with you of course. But I'll keep my rooms in the Latin Quarter for studying."

She almost laughed aloud. What kind of secret marriage was that going to be? Within a week, the whole of Paris would know where Master Abelard spent his nights. She thought, For a teacher of logic, this man is surely befuddled. She said to him, "Good. I'm glad you have it so nicely planned. But you're returning to the Ile without me."

"Sweet Christ, lady! Don't you listen?"

"It's you who don't listen. I said I wasn't going to marry you." People in the hall were beginning to stare at them. She turned away swiftly and went upstairs. After undressing, she blew out the candle and slid into bed. A while later, he came up and began bumping around in the dark. When he pitched himself under the covers, she pretended to be asleep.

He stretched out next to her, not touching. "Heloise."

"What?"

"Nothing."

She said quietly, "Mark me. This secret marriage isn't going to satisfy my uncle. I doubt if anything will. He hates you." Minutes passed. She could hear Abelard breathing by her side.

At last he spoke. "Why don't you love me?"

"I love you more than my life." She squeezed her face against his shoulder and began to weep, deep, shuddering sobs that shivered down the length of her body.

Abelard gathered her up and rocked her gently. He pulled the coverlet over her neck.

"I love you, Heloise," he said. "I love you."

11 ❦

AFTER MATINS, they were permitted to enter the abbey church at Saint-Victor, Abelard having made arrangements with the prior. A white-haired porter unlocked the door and led them through the nave to a chapel behind the altar. Abelard pressed some coins into the old man's hand, and he hobbled off without speaking.

Heloise went to the front of the chapel, where a row of candles smoked. The place smelled of mold and incense. In the shadows behind her, Abelard's footsteps clattered on the stone. He came up and took her hand, and they knelt side by side.

"Heloise."

"What?"

"Relax. We'll be all right."

She smiled faintly. "You're so trusting."

"That's right. I trust Our Lord to forgive sins. *Deus misereatur.*"

"God I trust. It's Uncle who worries me." They had been through this many times before.

"Pray for him," Abelard suggested.

She bowed her head and folded her hands over her nose. Ever since they had returned to the Ile, the muscles in her shoulders had been tensed hard as stone. Earlier tonight, after supper, she had soaked herself in a steaming tub, hoping for relief. But after she dressed, the muscles began screaming again. She unclasped her hands and reached around to touch her shoulder. Knots.

Even though it was spring outside, the chapel felt dank and chilly. She had so longed to see Paris again—willows budding along the towpaths, the *talemeliers* with their baskets of hot pasties. But since their arrival three days ago, she had not gone out of the house. At the thought of the crusty pasties, her mouth began to water; she could taste them. She wanted a cheese pasty. Or eel. After the wedding she would go out, whether Uncle liked it or not.

Abelard sat perfectly still, his eyes glued shut as if he were alone in the chapel. Heloise had seen him only once since they returned, a brief formal meeting with Fulbert watching them, and they had talked of little but plans for the wedding. Heloise remembered the expression on Fulbert's face these past days; it never varied. He appeared unconcerned, listless. When she had begged his forgiveness, he had smiled phlegmatically, as if her plea was of no interest at all. His thoughts were elsewhere.

Earlier today, she had gone to his apartment and deliberately brought up the subject of the secret marriage. Would it really satisfy him, she had asked? Would he consider it sufficient reparation?

Fulbert nodded toward his writing table and pointed to a book. "Have you seen that new translation of Lucan? You must. I think it's much finer than the old one."

Heloise remembered staring at him, startled. He did not look wretched, as Abelard had described him, only older and crankier. His face was thin, the carved cheekbones more prominent. Otherwise she could see no change in him. Perhaps he was growing deaf. She had replied, finally, "I'll have a look at it tomorrow," and returned to her room.

A draft coursed through the chapel. She glanced briefly at Abelard's head, a gray shadow at her shoulder. She thought again of the pasties. Then she blotted her mind clear and began to pray. She asked forgiveness for the pain she had caused her uncle, for the lust that had led her into sin, and she asked God's blessing on her union with Abelard. Settling on her heels, she went back as far as she could remember. I told Lady Alais that Ceci stole three sticky buns, and Ceci was punished. *Mea culpa.* I called Sister Madelaine an old bitch. *Mea culpa.* I bore hatred in my heart against my cousin Philip and Petronilla and Denise and Alienor and Alienor's boy Fulk. I lied to Uncle about . . .

Later, deep in the night, she heard the monks filing into the church and then voices grating the night office. She stared at the damp walls, remembering Ceci in exile at Argenteuil. But the image failed to upset her. Today was her wedding day. Ceci wanted this; she didn't. After lauds, she tried to go back to her prayers but could think of nothing more to say.

After a while, she raised her head. Her knees and the front of her legs ached. She saw Abelard watching her.

He asked, "Feel all right?"

"I don't know."

"What's wrong?"

She thought, Everything. Her breasts, full of milk, were sore. "I don't know. Nothing." Then: "It's not right."

"What's not right?"

"Everybody acts like they're at a wake. God's splendor, weddings should be gay."

Abelard sighed. "I would have liked a jongleur or two. I remember a fine wedding at Montboissier. They decorated the streets with tapestries and burned spices in the squares."

"They had jongleurs?"

"A good many," Abelard said. "And acrobats. And a mime who did bird calls."

Heloise swallowed. "What did they have to eat?" she demanded.

"The usual."

"I don't know what the usual is."

"Oh. Venison, boar, peacock. And spiced wine."

"Sweets?"

He laughed. "Certainly. All sorts of confections and wafers. Oranges, too, I think."

They fell silent. Knees creaking, Heloise stood up and stretched her arms over her head. "There was a nun at Argenteuil," she said dreamily. "When I was a little girl. I can't remember her name because she left. Or died. I don't know . . ."

"Yes."

She went to the slitted window and peered out. The dawn had not begun to come up yet. "She told me about her sister's wedding. What her sister wore."

Abelard grunted.

"A red silk tunic trimmed with vair. Over it, a velvet cloak embroidered with gold thread and a mantle edged with lace—and she had slippers worked with gold."

In spite of herself, she felt like crying. It was foolish, she knew. For all her gibbering about never wanting to marry, now that the time had come, she felt deprived at not having new clothes and jongleurs. Childish, she thought.

Abelard called softly, "Are you distressed?"

"Of course not."

"Of course not." He snorted gruffly. "Come over here. My dear love, we don't need shoes and oranges. We have—"

"I know." She sat down next to him and pulled her shawl tightly around her chest. Looking down at the floor, she thought of Astrolabe in his truckle bed. She thought of Denise, who barely attended her own babes, and of Astrolabe wondering where his mother had gone to. She wished that they had brought him to Paris. He might have stayed with her in the turret room, bundled under the furs, and they would have slept with their bodies touching, his tiny fat one and her very long one. She closed her eyes. Sweet darling. Dearest little bunny.

Abelard got to his feet and went to the door of the chapel. She heard him talking with someone. Shortly he came back and told her the priest had come, and they must speak with him. In the church, the priest was holding an open book and a gold ring. He began asking questions in a low voice. Were they of age? Did they swear they were not within the forbidden degree of consanguinity? Did their parents consent? And so forth.

Jourdain appeared at Abelard's shoulder. When Heloise crossed to him and clasped his hands, he shot her a shaky grin. A few minutes later, the others arrived—Fulbert, Agnes, Canon Martin. Beaming, Abelard walked over and, one by one, kissed them. Fulbert, his face a mask, smiled pleasantly at Heloise.

The priest took them into the chapel and waited while Agnes, sallow-faced, pinned a red silk veil over Heloise's hair. She and Abelard went to the altar and stood before the priest. He began to talk about the Flood and how the Lord had saved all the married creatures, and then he told them that if the Blessed Virgin had not been married, God would not have been born from her womb. Heloise glanced at Abelard and saw him smiling slightly. He looked happy. Her palms began to sweat.

The priest was blessing the ring. He handed it to Abelard, who took her left hand and slipped on the ring, first on one finger and then a second, saying each time, "In the name of the Father and of the Son and of the Holy Ghost." Agnes was weeping softly. Heloise's fingers were clammy, and the ring stuck slightly when Abelard tried to pull it off. Finally he fitted the band on her third finger. "With this ring I thee wed," he whispered, so low that the priest asked him to repeat it. Heloise wondered how Abelard had known about the three fingers; the priest must have told him.

After mass, the priest gave Abelard the kiss of peace, and Abelard transferred it to her. He took her arm, and they started out of the chapel, through the nave of the church to the portico. Outside, it was still gray and moist, and mist nudged the tops of the abbey buildings. Martin went to get the horses.

"Oh, Uncle," Heloise said, "we could all go back home and have some wine."

Fulbert frowned slightly and looked at Abelard. Heloise glanced at Jourdain, who shrugged and turned away.

Abelard said, "I don't think— I have a class soon." He looked annoyed.

Dazed, Heloise mounted and flexed her fingers around the reins. She looked at the gold ring and then at the unsmiling mouths of the wedding guests. Suddenly she felt enraged. She had not been angry before, but now she wanted to slash all those dead, grim eyes, stab and smash until they ran away screaming and left her alone with Abelard. All their yammering about the honor of Saint-Gervais. What difference did it make, she thought, what did she care about their honor? Making her face show nothing, she raised her arm at Abelard in a weary salute. Fulbert spurred his stallion, and they moved down the road leading to the Rue de Garlande.

Fulbert's house remained unchanged: Agnes scrubbed and baked, and promptly at noon the canon sat down to dinner and reached for his silver henap. On Sundays, Martin came to see him, and they sat by the fire in Fulbert's apartment and bickered over the chessboard. One Friday evening, Petronilla and her new husband visited Agnes, this apparently not a usual event, because Agnes put on a new shift and made walnut cake for the occasion. Petronilla was pregnant—five or six months, she said—and all she talked about was birthing and babies. Heloise stood listening, and when Petronilla asked about her confinement, she supplied all the details she could recall. Petronilla patted her arm familiarly once and referred to them as both married women; starting inwardly, Heloise drew back. Agnes changed the subject in a hurry.

It had rained during the night, and by the time she reached the Latin Quarter, her bliaut was spattered with mud. Along the Rue de la Huchette, most of the shops were still shuttered and the dawn light opaqued the houses a dirty pink. Glancing around, she paused outside an apothecary shop and tried to get her bearings. Possibly she had misjudged the distance from the Petit Pont to Abelard's house. It had been dark, that night last year, and she had been on horseback.

Slowly more people began moving up and down the street—goodwives towing children and shopping baskets, yawning students in wrinkled black gowns. A vendor, half asleep, called limply, "Good Champagne cheeses, good cheese of Brie." At the next square she stopped, hopelessly confused. More than likely she had passed Abelard's house without knowing it. A grocer was setting out baskets of onions. Behind him, in the doorway, squatted a monkey with a crumpled sign around its neck. *Requiescat in pace.* She watched the monkey for a while; at last, she went up to the grocer and asked if he knew where Peter Abelard lived.

The man grinned and looked her up and down. Waving in the direction from which she had come, he told her to look for a green door, across the road from the Bloody Saracen pothouse. Jogging, Heloise retraced her steps until she found the house. Across the road, she stopped under a hawthorn tree and scanned the second-story windows of the house. Presently a man with tousled red hair opened the shutters and leaned over the sill. Galon. She was surprised that Abelard still kept him.

Beneath the tree it was damp, and when the wind stirred the leaves, a shower of drops sprinkled her hair. A few minutes later, Galon emerged carrying a bowl, and crossed to the Bloody Saracen. When she saw him enter the tavern, she ran across the road and ducked into the green door.

On the second-floor landing, she took a breath and shoved lightly against the door. It was unlatched. She tiptoed through the empty solar and into the bedroom where Abelard lay sleeping. For a long time she sat very still on the edge of the bed and watched him, her mind at ease.

He half opened his eyes and squinted blindly past her face. Motionless, he scowled. "You look like Heloise."

"I am Heloise." After a moment: "Good morning, my friend. Did you sleep well?"

Startled, he sat up with a jerk and gripped her arms. "Lady, how did you get in here?"

"Walked in." She grinned happily. "You should lock your door. Any maiden could walk in here and rape you."

"You look very pretty."

"Thank you."

He flung both hands around her waist and cuddled his head against her breast. "Where's Galon?"

"At the Bloody Saracen. I thought you had a bodyguard to protect you."

"From what?" He kissed her. "I let him go. Take off your clothes."

"Would you care for breakfast first?" she said. "A cup of ale?"

"Not now." She began to wriggle out of her gown. "My stomach can't digest ale in the morning anymore. I take a little clabbered milk and bread."

She slid under the coverlet and wrapped her legs around his. She hoped that he wasn't ill. It must be his age, she thought. Even Fulbert had trouble with digestion, and Agnes was always preparing special possets. Abelard pulled her on top of him, and she straddled his thighs, guiding his stick into the center of her. His fingers tightened over her buttocks, stroking, kneading, pressing her forward. She worked her pelvis slowly, all the while inspecting his face. Poor sweet heart. There were bags under his eyes, if she wasn't mistaken. He needed looking after. Below her, he lay with his eyes widened, his breath coming in tiny gasps. "Oh God." From the adjoining room, she heard the door bang and the sound of a bowl being squeaked along a trestle top. She felt Abelard explode inside her, the spasms bursting in rapid succession. A moment later, she slid off him, her belly sticky with sweat.

"Stay here," he said in a muffled voice.

"Galon's back."

"Lady, forgive."

She blinked. "What for?"

"You had no pleasure."

"Oh, I did." She dismissed his words with a wave. "Anyway, that position—I can't do it that way."

"You used to."

She laughed lightly. "Out of practice, I guess. Shall I get your breakfast now?"

She threw on her undershift and swung open the door to the solar. When Galon saw her, he started violently and stared. She forced herself to meet his gaze. "Good morning," she said stiffly. "My lord would like his milk now."

Pointing dumbly to a covered bowl, he swayed to his feet.

Motioning him back, she took the bowl and a half loaf of bread. In the bedroom, Abelard was sitting up against the pillows. She gave him the sweet-smelling milk, undressed, and rolled back clumsily into bed.

Watching him eat, she thought of Fulbert's sly references to Abelard in recent days. He would be talking about something, a quarrel in chapter meeting, a new edict of the king's—it could be anything—and then he would say with a half grin, "Now if only my famous son-in-law were there," or "I wonder what my esteemed kinsman would have to say about that." It angered her beyond measure, but there was no complaint she could make to him. Abelard was Fulbert's kinsman now, that much could not be denied despite the secret marriage. Abelard finished the milk and handed the bowl to her. She placed it on the floor next to the bed.

"Have some bread, sweeting," he said.

"I'm not hungry," she said. She had better tell Abelard what was going on, but he wouldn't like it. It would worry him, even if he pretended otherwise. She forced a smile. "Something funny I must tell you."

Next to her, he sat chewing on the bread, dusting the coverlet with crumbs.

"Uncle is being miserly. He wants you to pay him for my room and board."

"Indeed."

"He says I'm married now, and he shouldn't have to support me."

Abelard nodded. "Quite right. I should have thought of that." He yawned and said again, "He's right."

Slowly, wearily, Heloise said all at once, "Beloved, I don't want to upset you, but I don't think our secret is a secret. Petronilla knows we're married. I guess Agnes told her, and Jourdain says that one of your students mentioned it. I can't understand—"

He cut her off sharply. "Which student?"

"Jourdain didn't tell me his name. Someone in your theology classes."

Abelard looked irritable, as if she were being unnecessarily concerned. "My dear girl, you shouldn't let these things bother you."

"But—"

"No one has said anything to me. And if they do, I shall calmly answer, 'Sire, you are in error.' And change the subject. Simple."

He lied so coolly. She didn't know whether to admire him or be angry. She said, "All right. But that wasn't my point."

"What was your point, sweet heart?" He opened his arms and drew her close.

Heloise looked away. She understood how Petronilla had found out, but not the student. That was what scared her. If one student knew, it would soon be common gossip in every pothouse in the Ile. Probably it was already. She might have anticipated this happening—in fact, she remembered thinking it at Le Pallet when Abelard first mentioned being married secretly. Except that he had almost convinced her it would work. She was going to remind him but changed her mind. Aloud she said, "When are we going back to get Astrolabe?"

"June," he said, kissing her hair. "As soon as classes end."

"You must find us a place to live."

"There's plenty of time." With his fingertips, he began to stroke the inside of her thighs. "Patience, ladylove. You hate living with Fulbert. But no more than I hate being here with Galon."

Yawning, she pressed her hips hungrily against his thigh. Another month, she thought, six weeks at the most. Then it will be all right. She felt him hardening. "Don't you have to be somewhere?" She laughed softly. "Like in class?"

"It can wait," he whispered against her mouth.

"I'd like to stay here all day."

Knowing the end of her residence at Fulbert's to be in sight, Heloise suddenly found herself brimming with energy. Nerves unjangled for the first time in months, she returned to her compilation of the conflicting Yes and No quotations and soon realized she had collected nearly a hundred examples. Carefully, she copied them onto good parchment, and in several places wrote glosses in the margin. Her mind active, the days passed quickly.

During Whitsuntide, when she had been married about two months, her uncle began to behave with uncharacteristic gaiety, almost as he had in the days when she had first come to the Rue des Chantres from Argenteuil. Only more so. He made jokes, somewhat nervously, and spoke in a hearty tone and called her puss and sweet girl. Perhaps it was the Maytime holiday, because nobody did much work all that week, and the weather was unusually mild and sweet. He's got May fever, Heloise told herself, smiling, and she could not blame him for she had it herself. Even Abelard sent her a love letter, a poem actually, and enclosed a bunch of pressed violets.

They saw each other from time to time, furtive meetings at Abelard's lodgings, and exchanged letters frequently. Jourdain, as always, could be depended upon to act as courier. Abelard had been looking at cottages south of the river, a mile or so beyond Saint-Victor. One in particular he described in some detail in one of his letters, as it had caught his fancy. It had been a bailiff's house, when that section belonged to the estate of a wealthy knight, and somebody had taken care to panel the solar with hand-carved pine. The floors were inset with blue and white tiles, and the house had plenty of windows to let in the sunlight. A se-

rene, pleasant place for her to study, Abelard had written enthusiastically, and he promised to take her out there some Sunday, so that
she might inspect it herself.

In the last days of Whitsuntide, Fulbert announced that he was going
to entertain, something she knew he had not done all the months she
had been away, and he invited more than two dozen friends and colleagues—canons from Notre Dame, merchants and their wives, barons
who owed him money, even a few masters from the school whom he
knew only casually. It was to be a garden affair. Cressets would be hung
in the trees and a jongleur engaged to sit behind a bush and provide
tasteful selections on the lute.

Fulbert himself carefully drew up a list of melodies he wished performed and asked Heloise for her opinion. None of the selections were
her favorites; for example, he had not included anything by William the
Troubadour, and to her dismay, halfway down the list were several
songs of Abelard's. Nonetheless, she smiled prettily and pretended to
approve of his choices. For a change, it would be pleasant to hear
music, any music. Scratching his head, Fulbert said to her absently,
"Ah, I see that my memory is failing. I forgot to invite Master Peter.
How discourteous of me."

"Uncle!" Heloise snapped. "Why do you say such things? He could
not possibly come."

"Why not?" inquired Fulbert, full of innocence.

"You know very well why not," she answered impatiently.

"Mayhap your husband is ashamed of his in-laws. I admit we are not
counts or dukes but—"

"I don't care to discuss it. Holy Virgin, you know why he can't
come."

The day of the party, Fulbert went around the house humming. It
was touching, in a queer way. Agnes had been cooking furiously—tarts,
wafers, a row of cakes, as well as platters of cold ham, fowl, and
cheese. The best goblets were polished, the good wine brought up from
the cellar, and Agnes had hired two small boys, one to act as page and
the other to look after the guests' horses. Never had Heloise known either Agnes or Fulbert to take such care with an affair. The excitement
in the house proved contagious. Heloise found her old crisping iron and
curled her hair, and she wore a new lavender bliaut trimmed with gold
braid. Abelard had bought it for her; it was of the finest linen and, she
guessed, quite expensive. Certainly she had never before owned a gown
so elegant.

At dusk, the guests began to arrive. The garden was filled with the fragrance of roses and the heavier perfumes of pine and lily worn by the men. Heloise took a goblet of chilled wine and went around to greet people. A draper whom she knew slightly was standing under the pear tree with his wife, a thin woman whose expensive satin gown was obviously meant to advertise her husband's business. When the merchant saw Heloise coming, he turned away from his lady and took Heloise's hands. He said, "My lady, I've not had the pleasure of seeing you in some time."

"No," Heloise said. "I've been away. But now I'm happy to be back." She heard herself rattling on, mouthing clichés. "The Ile is so beautiful in the spring."

"The winters in Brittany are dreadful," he said. "I've not been there myself, but everyone says so."

She swallowed quickly. "Pardon, my lord?"

"Brittany. Did you not find the winter cruel?"

"You're mistaken," she said. "I was at Saint-Gervais."

The man frowned and scratched his chin. He opened his mouth, wordlessly. His wife reappeared at his elbow, and Heloise hastily moved away.

She sent the page to refill her goblet and sat down near the jongleur. He smiled at her and said, "Shall I play Master Peter's songs now, lady?"

"Why, I don't care," she said, flushing. "Play what you were told to play."

At first she listened to the music, dreary stuff in her opinion, Fulbert's church-music taste, but after fifteen or twenty minutes a group of canons came over and began speaking in Latin. One of them knew a few words of Greek and wanted to show off. The men started to discuss Aristotle's *Ethics,* about which they were totally ignorant. She had to be careful not to let on. Men. Even if they knew nothing, it didn't prevent them from talking. One of them said, smiling, "Lady, it's clear you're the protégé of Master Peter."

"Aye, I was his student for a while. But certainly not his protégé."

The canon answered with a smirk. "There is nothing more pleasant than discussing philosophy with a philosopher. Except perhaps discussing love with a philosopher. Tell us your opinion, lady."

Heloise took a long drink from her goblet, and said that since she had never discussed love with a philosopher, she was in no position to comment.

Martin, who had come up to the edge of the group around Heloise, gave her a cheerful smile. He nodded to the canon who had been talking about Abelard and said, "There you are, Garin. I told you Lady Heloise is discreet."

The man cocked his head, grinning at Heloise. "Your secret is safe with us, lady."

"I don't know what you mean." She stood up, her arms hanging stiffly at her sides. Her head was beginning to ache.

"Come on," said Martin, laughing. "There's no reason to pretend. You're among friends."

The jongleur began playing Abelard's most popular love song, the one in which a lover cries passionately that the dawn comes too soon. At first he ran through only the melody, then he began to sing the words. People stopped talking; the garden grew hushed. When he had finished, a few clapped and Fulbert called to the jongleur, "Splendid. Well done." He turned to somebody behind Martin and said in a loud voice, "An appropriate piece, don't you think? Now that our families are joined."

Heloise started violently. There was an embarrassed silence, and somebody coughed. She looked around and caught the eye of the draper. Shaking his head, he winked at her. "I thought you were chaffing me earlier. Let me be the first to give my congratulations, lady."

"About what?" she asked, tight-lipped, trying to maintain her composure.

Fulbert circled around to face Heloise. "My niece is a modest girl," he said. "Of course the marriage is secret, and we all understand the reasons for that. It would never do if the information were made public." Wily as a snake, he kept his eyes on Heloise. "But, between friends, there is no harm in admitting that Master Peter and Lady Heloise are wed."

Heloise reddened. "That's a lie!"

Fulbert threw her a reproachful glance. "God will punish you for lying."

"I'm not married."

He said to the draper, "Brother, she has a child by Abelard."

"You fool, keep quiet!" Involuntarily, she stepped toward Fulbert, shaking her fist as if she would throttle him.

"You're overwrought." Fulbert laughed harshly. To the guests who were standing with open mouths, he repeated, "Pay no attention. She's overwrought."

Heloise stared at him, rigid with anger. Fulbert motioned the jongleur to resume playing. He turned to a trestle and snatched up a slice of roast fowl. Over his shoulder, he said to Canon Garin, "She's married, I swear it. Ask Martin. Is that not so, Martin? You witnessed the marriage."

Martin nodded agreeably. Happy to be the center of attention, he began describing the ceremony and said that Master Peter had hurried off to class afterward. He went on talking, ignoring Heloise as if she were a hundred miles away.

"*Damn you,*" she lashed out. "May God damn your soul for all eternity."

Martin's mouth dropped, and he fell silent. Fulbert said to her pleasantly, "I'm warning you."

She took a deep breath, sucking in rage. Her eyes full of tears, she shouted ferociously at him, "*Liar!*"

His hand made a fist and shot toward her. She made no attempt to back away. The blow chopped her on the side of her jaw. Blindly, she spun around and ran into the house.

An hour later, after the last of the guests had departed, Heloise heard him climbing the stairs toward her chamber. She stood up and waited, her throat clogged with nausea and loathing. When he opened the door, she gave him a look so laden with hatred that he flinched. Flustered, he said, "Niece, you acted badly tonight."

"You promised to keep it a secret."

"I promised nothing." He put down the candleholder on her writing table and turned. "And I do not like to be called a liar before my friends. You have picked up very bad manners from that Breton dog. Pardon, my distinguished Breton-dog kinsman."

"I hate you," she whispered.

"Shut up. I saved you from whoredom. You would have ended as Master Abelard's discarded cunt."

She ran past him toward the door. He reached out, clutching at the sleeve of her gown. "In future, you will obey me," he wheezed. "When I tell somebody you're married, you will hold your tongue. Understand?"

"No." She pulled away and heard the sleeve rip. "No. I won't obey you."

With an open hand, he slapped her across the mouth. She braced herself. The second blow bumped the side of her head. Her ear ringing, she grabbed his hand and bit it. With both hands, he drove his fists into her face; she felt something crack on her face, her mouth filling with blood. Suddenly she bounced on her back and thudded against the bed. Fulbert stood over her. Sucking in her breath, she raised up both feet and kicked blindly at his stomach. Gasping, he fell back into a crouch. "Bitch!" He panted. He plunged toward her, gripping her by the shoulder to hold her still. Again and again he knocked her across the chest and belly and legs until she felt her flesh give way. Limp, she wrapped her arms around her head. In her mouth she kept tasting blood. Fulbert stood up, and she heard him walking toward the door. She lay quietly, not thinking. Some time later, perhaps only a few minutes—she did not know—she swayed to her feet. Throwing a shawl over her head, she hurtled out of her room and down the stairs. Outside, in the Rue des Chantres, she began to run toward the river.

When Galon opened the door, he screamed. Over his shoulder, Heloise saw Abelard sitting at his writing table, his face ashy. She grabbed the edge of the door and stumbled toward him.

He caught her by the arm. "In the name of Jesus!" he gasped.

Her lungs were on fire. It was hot in the room. She wiped her mouth, and the hand came back sticky. "Fulbert—" She began to babble incoherently, spilling out Fulbert's betrayal.

"God, God. Your face. Heloise, look what he's done to your face!" He sat her in his armchair. Shouting at Galon to bring water and towels, he held her, cuddled her close like a baby.

"Don't." She pushed him away, her body a sheet of pain. "You'll ruin your tunic."

Abelard shook his head slowly. Very low, he said, "I'll kill him." He took a basin from Galon and gently began to wash the wounds on her face and head. Her right eye was almost swollen shut. He stripped off the filthy lavender gown; when he saw the mottled purple welts running the length of her torso, he burst into sobs.

"Don't, beloved."

"The dog!"

"Please. You won't send me back there."

"For the love of God," Abelard cried, "do you think I would! I won't let you out of my sight."

Heloise shook her head. "He won't come here."

He picked her up and carried her into the bedchamber, calling for

Galon to bring wine. "Be still now. He might have killed you." Heloise lay against the pillows watching him. "I'll not let you out of my sight," he repeated bitterly.

"Sweet, don't be foolish. How can you do that?"

He kissed her. "I don't know. I'll think of something." After a moment: "It's not safe here." He raised the cup to her lips.

Opening her mouth a crack, Heloise sipped the wine painfully; it stung her cut lips. Her eyelids drooping, she could hear Abelard's voice mumbling and Galon padding around behind him.

"Argenteuil," Abelard said suddenly. "You would be safe at Argenteuil."

Heloise forced her eyes wide open and strained to sit up. "I don't want to go to Argenteuil," she said hoarsely.

"Just for a few weeks. Until classes are over. Then we'll leave for Brittany."

"How can I go anywhere looking like this? I look terrible!"

"Shhh. Rest now." He pushed her back. "I'll send a message to Abbess—what is her name?"

"Alais."

"Abbess Alais. I'll write and explain. When your face is healed, I'll take you there myself."

"I don't think—" Heloise felt herself falling asleep.

12 ❧

SHE WAITED in the reception hall for more than an hour, quietly fanning herself with the side of her hand. *Perhaps Lady Alais won't have me,* Heloise thought. But she knew it was not true. There was no sound from the little passageway leading to the abbess's apartments. She rose and listened for Abelard's voice. Nothing. The hall looked shabby, as if no one had sat in there for months. The floor rushes needed changing, and when Heloise had leaned her arm against the trestle, it had come back dusty. She blotted perspiration from her face, and remembered her surprise as they had ridden up the road to Argenteuil. It looked small, as if some sorceress had shrunk the buildings and outer walls. The paint on the gatehouse was peeling, but maybe it had always been that way and she had never noticed.

Restless, she paced up and down by the window. In the shadeless courtyard there was a knight with his horse and squire. She watched the knight walk slowly to the portress's lodge and shout something into the doorway. A nun came out, but it was not the same portress Heloise remembered—Matilda had been her name. The silence made Heloise uncomfortable, and she wondered if it were time for nones yet. A bell, anything, to break the awful stillness. At nones the nuns would come running from all parts of the convent and file into the church for the afternoon office. She caught herself waiting for something to happen, forgetting that nothing much ever happened there. Well, she told herself, it will only be for a few weeks, and it is cooler here than back in the Ile. That was something to thank God for.

Abruptly, she heard a padding noise and then the click-click of rosary beads. She looked up, curious to see who was making so much noise. Sister Madelaine stood in the doorway squinting at her, her face as yellow as a withered turnip. After a minute's hesitation, Heloise ran to her, fell on one knee, and kissed her dry hand. Above her head, she heard Madelaine whisper, "I knew you'd be back."

She got up. "I'm only visiting," she said, smiling.

Madelaine turned away from her and went over to a bench under the window. She sank down wearily and stared at Heloise.

Heloise coughed and said tentatively, "I'm wed now."

"So I hear."

"I have a son."

"I've heard."

Heloise forced her mouth into a grin, with difficulty. "Is that all you can say? Aren't you pleased to see me?"

Madelaine stared at her steadily without replying.

Heloise looked around the room. When her eyes came back to Madelaine, the prioress was still watching her. "Stop looking at me like that."

Madelaine shrugged. "You're back," she repeated testily.

"I'm not back. I told you."

"You caught yourself a great lord."

Heloise flushed.

"And yet you're back. Why?"

"Only for a few weeks. And then we're going to Brittany. To get our babe."

"You didn't answer my question. Why are you here?"

Heloise compressed her lips.

"Hah! You're in some kind of trouble."

"I don't want to—" Heloise stopped. She crossed to a bench at the opposite end of the parlor and slouched down. "My—husband thought I would be comfortable here." She had almost said "safe" but thought better of it. She didn't want to tell Madelaine about the trouble with Fulbert.

"Your husband"—Madelaine spat the word "husband"—"is a rich, celebrated man."

"Yes."

"With many friends."

"Many."

"Then why did he bring you back here? To get rid of you."

"This is a foolish conversation. You don't understand."

"Think I'm stupid, don't you?" Madelaine snapped.

Heloise said nothing. Sweat was making her back itch.

"Paris is a wicked city."

"Sister Madelaine, I don't want to talk to you now. Please leave me alone."

Madelaine rose quickly; she left without looking back. Heloise went over to the window and leaned out, her throat gritty with thirst. The knight and his squire had gone. The yard was an empty oblong of pink heat.

As the abbess's door opened, Heloise got to her feet. Abelard and Lady Alais were coming down the passageway, Abelard grinning and the abbess laughing flirtatiously and crinkling her nose at him. Neither of them looked at Heloise. They were talking about King Louis and his friend Suger, and the abbess was patting Abelard's arm, saying, "Wonderful, my lord. If it wouldn't be too much trouble. Bless you." Heloise decided that Abelard must have promised to secure some royal favor for the convent. She shifted her weight from one foot to the other, waiting for them to finish. God, she thought, Lady Alais is acting like a schoolgirl. She ought to be ashamed.

With a grand flourish, Abelard bent over the abbess's right hand and kissed her ring tenderly. She glowed at him, her dimples winking, while they exchanged the kiss of peace. Then she turned vaguely in Heloise's direction.

"Child," she called loudly, "you are welcome here."

"Thank you, lady."

The abbess turned and went back into her apartment. The door slammed after her. Heloise went to Abelard and wrapped her arms around him. She pressed her nose against his cheek. "What did she say?"

"Well. What do you think? She said you might stay."

"Did you tell her about Uncle?"

Abelard backed away. "Certainly. Walk with me to the stables."

"You're leaving already?"

"I'm dining with the Count of Dreux this evening. On second thought, you'd better stay here. Lady Alais will be sending someone for you."

She sighed, thinking of Paris, and kissed him on the cheek. "All right. I might as well get it over with."

"Hunh?"

"I mean, seeing them all again." She pointed vaguely in the direction of the cloister. "You'd better go."

"I'll come next week, sweeting. Saturday, if I can. Or Sunday. Heloise . . ."

"What, love?"

"You'll be all right?" He sounded anxious.

She answered with a grin, "I'll be fine." She watched him cross the courtyard.

After a while, a novice came in and motioned to her. The girl, who was about twelve and pretty in a pinched way, looked familiar. Following her, Heloise saw that she limped. The abbess's favorite, but she had grown up. Over her shoulder, the girl said, "I'm Astrane. You remember, lady."

"I remember. How do you?"

"Very well," she answered politely.

Astrane led her into the cloister and along the vaulted south walk. They passed the chapter house and, at the corner, turned and started up the east walk. Three schoolgirls were sitting on a stone bench near the fountain, sewing; they stared at Heloise solemnly.

Heloise said to Astrane, "Where are we going?"

"Wardrobe."

"Why?"

"Lady Alais said so."

Inside, the nun in charge of wardrobe greeted Heloise with a smile. She began looking her up and down, measuring her with her eyes. "You're quite tall," she observed critically.

Heloise felt her irritation rise, but she said nothing. The nun turned away and started to rummage in one of the dozen great chests that practically filled the room. She mumbled, "I might have to rip out a hem."

Annoyed, Heloise said, "What are you talking about?" Behind her back, she could hear the lame girl shuffling her feet.

The nun pulled her head out of the chest. "Most of the gowns would be too short for you."

Startled, she growled, "I don't need a gown. I have one."

Clutching a black novice robe, the woman got to her feet with a pleased smile. As if she had not heard Heloise, she said happily, "This looks plenty long. We can try it."

Suddenly Heloise began to laugh dryly. "Hold on now, Sister. Just a minute. You've made a mistake."

Frowning, the nun glanced at Heloise and then at Astrane, who lingered in the doorway.

"I'm not a new novice," Heloise reassured the woman. "I'm a guest." She added, "A paying guest."

Astrane said loudly, "Lady abbess said you're to have a novice gown."

Heloise stared at her. "Whatever for?" The girl frowned again, her lips pressed. "I won't wear it. This is ridiculous."

The three of them stood watching each other. Finally Astrane wheeled and dragged out the door. Heloise said to the wardrober, who was still holding the gown, "Put it away. There's been a misunderstanding."

Doubtful, the woman shook her head. Slowly she shook out the gown and hung it on a peg. It was clear that she did not believe Heloise. She sat down at the trestle, threaded a needle, and began hemming a towel. Heloise stood near the door, her hands folded behind her back. A few minutes later, she could see Astrane hurrying down the walk, and behind her, frowning, trotted Lady Alais.

Heloise waited until the abbess drew near, and then she said lightly, "Please tell her I am not a novice. I wear my own clothes."

Lady Alais stepped inside and put her arm awkwardly around Heloise's waist. "Yes, yes," she said soothingly. "But you are to wear it just the same. Lord Abelard said so."

Heloise shook herself loose. "Don't be silly. I mean, I'm sorry, lady—but he could not have said such a thing. I'm only going to be here three weeks. Four at the most."

"I know." The abbess snatched Heloise's arm and pulled her outside on the walk. Leaning up to her ear, she whispered, "I know, but Master Abelard and I discussed this. He told me in confidence that considering the—er—situation he is in, that is—" She began to stammer slightly. "That is to say, if people believe you have become a novice, they certainly can't think you are the wife of Master Abelard. See?"

"No." Heloise stared fiercely ahead, her fingers clenched. It was as if the abbess had struck her. She repeated angrily, "No."

"Rumors will cease once it becomes known you are wearing a habit." She smiled earnestly. "Then you can leave quietly and no one will know."

Heloise glanced down at her, thoughts reeling, and then she scowled. "It's a terrible idea." Although the habit would convince people that she had been speaking truth about the marriage, Fulbert, not she, would seem the liar.

"Child. Listen to me. It's your lord's wish that you wear the habit while you're here. Won't you obey?" The abbess smiled coaxingly.

Heloise thought. She would do whatever Abelard desired. But he should have told her first. Finally, she nodded at Lady Alais. She was not going to make herself unhappy over a piece of cloth.

* * *

She felt light-headed. In the cloister, the potted lemon tree still flourished, and she walked over to it and sniffed the leaves. The tree was considerably taller than she recalled. Of course, she told herself, everything and everybody around here has grown or aged or died. She didn't know what she had expected. The bell for nones chimed, and women in black began streaming along the walks in the direction of the church. Heloise moved into the shadow of the lemon tree and watched them, detached. She kept waiting for some obvious sensation to strike her, like depression or scorn, even the clench of fear she usually experienced when she thought of Argenteuil. She felt nothing. In the yellow light, the black figures looked like some queer silhouette design on a frieze.

A thin woman with puffy eyes detached herself from the tail of the line and came slowly down the path toward her. She was looking past Heloise, as if she had her eyes on something just to the right of the lemon tree. Heloise smiled inwardly; the nun's veil was hanging crooked, her sharp little face smudged with dirt. Such things had never happened when Heloise lived here. Lady Alais must be getting lax about discipline.

Skirts rustling, the nun came to within three feet of her and stopped; she muttered in her throat. Something about the sound of the woman's gurgle made Heloise's heart beat faster. Her right hand pressed against her collarbone, she thrust out her neck and peered uncertainly into the grimy face. "Ceci?" Heloise stretched out her hands. But the nun stood motionless, gaping. "Ceci, it's me. Don't you remember me?"

With a sob, Ceci rushed at her. "I knew it," she moaned against Heloise's shoulder. "I prayed every day. God answered. I knew you'd come ba—"

"Shhh. Calm yourself."

"Madelaine said you'd never be back."

"Hush now. She was right."

"No, you've come."

Already Heloise could feel her muscles tensing in annoyance, the effect Ceci always had on her sooner or later. This time, apparently, sooner. She was such a child. Except that now she no longer looked like one. She had the face of a mature woman, a woman older than her age. "Holy Mother, why don't you listen!"

"Don't curse in the cloister."

"I'm not cursing." Lowering her voice, she said, "I'm married. But I need a place to stay for a few weeks, and my husband brought me here. It's only till July. So stop saying I'm back. All right?"

Ceci drew back. "Oh. Married, you say?" She smiled crookedly.

"That's right."

"You have a husband."

"And a child. A son. He's six months old."

"What's his name?"

"Astrolabe."

Ceci laughed.

"What's funny?"

"Astrolabe." She laughed again. "That's just like you. Nobody but you could pick a name like that."

Heloise grinned. She spit on the sleeve of her gown and dabbed at Ceci's face. "Doesn't anybody wash around here? You're filthy."

Every morning, Heloise visited the schoolroom. It smelled of ink and wax and old parchment. As she had done as a child, she sat at a carrel by the window and gossiped with Madelaine, sometimes filling the ink-horns and laying out the tablets before the others arrived. Now, of course, there were new boarders, those noble young ladies whose fees helped Argenteuil eke out its resources. At most convents, the curriculum was weak: grammar, singing, needlework, a little Latin. Writing was discouraged lest it lead to clandestine love letters. Argenteuil was not most convents, however, and Madelaine would not tolerate laziness among her students.

Now there were eight boarders, as well as the lame novice Astrane, who, Madelaine said, showed potential. Heloise was surprised, because the child seemed to her the epitome of stupid subservience, a pretty emptyhead always groveling at the abbess's heels and cleaning up parrot droppings. But Madelaine said no—appearances sometimes lie, and Astrane had a fairly good memory.

Sitting with Madelaine one morning, Heloise suddenly had a thought. Something had seemed missing in the convent, and now she remembered. The abbess's parrot, Baby. She wondered what had happened to the bird.

"Oh. That," Madelaine said. After her initial testiness, she had warmed and obviously was enjoying Heloise's visits. "Somebody poisoned the bloody thing. Help me correct these lessons." She handed Heloise a stack of wax tablets.

Heloise glanced at the neat script on the top tablet. "How would anyone here have access to poison? Mayhap the bird died of natural causes." She ran her eyes down the composition and decided that it had a nice style. "Whose is this?" she asked Madelaine.

"Astrane's. Quick mind. Wicked heart."

"Oh, come." Heloise laughed. "That little thing have a wicked heart. Oh, I see. You're trying to tell me she poisoned Baby?"

"No," she said. "Not Astrane. Somebody else."

"Who, then?"

Madelaine shrugged. "I have a good idea. But no proof."

Heloise began to laugh. "Somebody who hates the abbess?" she prompted, her eyes on Madelaine's face.

Madelaine turned away with a grin. "I'm not saying." She began dragging stools to the center of the room and aligning them in rows.

"Here," said Heloise, taking a stool from her. "Let me do that. You shouldn't exert yourself." Madelaine was ill, she knew. Her face had a yellowish cast, even the whites of her eyes had turned a sickly yellow, and Heloise noticed that she ate practically nothing. "Can't you get someone to help you around here?"

"Bah! I have more work to do than ever. When Baby died, Lady Alais mourned for two weeks. Never came out of her apartment. You should have seen the accounts after that."

"I thought you did the accounts."

"Oh, of course." She sucked her wrinkled cheeks into a grimace. "But she is supposed to administer this place, not I."

After that conversation with the prioress, Heloise went to the schoolroom several times a day. She took over the Latin and mathematics classes, which delighted the children since, unlike Madelaine, she was kind and cheerful and spurred them to work harder. In the evenings, after vespers, she worked on the convent's accounts and wrote whatever official letters required composing. Madelaine did not object, and that made Heloise feel useful. She was surprised to discover that she enjoyed teaching children, and she thought a lot about Astrolabe and made plans in her mind as to how she would instruct him when the time came.

Madelaine did not mention again the subject of Heloise's marriage, or the fact that her visit to Argenteuil would be temporary. Heloise was content to leave the subject alone, and sometimes she went out of her way to avoid talking about her life outside the convent. But one Friday afternoon just before St. John's Day, while she was in the schoolroom writing a letter to Abelard, Madelaine said mildly, "That husband of yours. Is he as brilliant as everyone says?"

Heloise looked up. The children had acted badly in church that morning, making noise and giggling, and they were being punished with an extra-long singing lesson. The room was empty. "He is. He's brilliant and handsome, and he writes verse and he plays the—"

"Verse?" Madelaine frowned. "Tell me something. Did he teach you anything of worth?"

Heloise nodded. "I was his private pupil for a while."

"That isn't what I asked you. Did he teach you anything you didn't know already?"

Heloise hesitated. "Well"—she cleared her throat—"honestly?"

"Honestly."

"No. Not much."

Madelaine grunted in satisfaction. "Didn't think so."

Guilty over having made that admission, Heloise went back to her letter. She wrote, "You would be horrified at the food they serve here. I'm dying for a cheese pasty and a cup of good Burgundy—and for you, beloved." She put down the quill. It was not Abelard's fault the lessons had failed. They had been too interested in each other's bodies. She sensed Madelaine staring at her, as if she were reading her thoughts, and her face colored pink. Across the carrel, she heard Madelaine saying, "I was wrong."

She looked up. "About what?"

Madelaine tugged at her veil. "Your destiny was not the Church." She sighed deeply and gave a little sniff. "And you have no vocation anyway."

Heloise stared.

Abelard said, "God, the time drags," and kicked at the pebbles with his shoe. The air was a hot blue. Clots of white clouds floated across the roof. In the abbess's private garden, into which she invited only distinguished guests and merchants who wished to contribute money, there was the gentle whir of bumblebees and the jetting of the fountain. Heloise looked over her shoulder toward the abbess's apartment. "It drags more here than in the Ile. I think Lady Alais naps the whole afternoon."

Abelard followed her gaze with a yawn. "I could use a nap. Do you think she would lend us her bed?"

"Abelard!" She was genuinely shocked. "That is very wicked."

He grinned at her. "She's extremely accommodating in every other respect."

"She thinks you're charming."

"Well, of course."

"You did that deliberately," Heloise said in a mock-accusing tone. "To charm her, I mean."

Abelard stood up and walked down the path to the fountain. "I want her to treat you like a countess." He splashed water on his face and came back to the bench beside her. The breeze blew a lock of hair over his forehead. She reached up to brush it back. He caught her wrist tightly and pressed his mouth to her fingers.

Nervous, she twisted around toward the abbess's window. Inside, by the open shutter, she saw Astrane watching them. "Don't," she whispered, "someone can see us."

He dropped her hand. Abruptly, he said, "I had a letter from William."

"Oh, Abelard, what does he say about Astrolabe?"

"Healthy and growing."

"Is that all?" Heloise asked impatiently.

"I think he said the boy is crawling." He went on talking, about Le Pallet and then about plans for their journey. They would travel in easy stages—there was no hurry—and they could have a holiday and enjoy the countryside. He knew of several good inns in the Loire Valley. On their way home, they might take a boat up the Loire. "It will be fun for the babe," he said, smiling.

Happiness filled her eyes with tears. She so wanted a holiday, a real one such as other people had. And to be alone with Abelard and their son—her family—that would be heavenly. She moved close to him, the side of her hand touching his thigh.

He said softly, "How is your pretty little garden?"

A little shiver ran down her body. "Shhh."

"I dream of it." His voice lowered to a whisper. "The day I come to take you out of here, we'll go directly to the nearest inn."

Her eyes roved hungrily over his face. Groaning, she leaned toward him. "Please. Don't."

Impulsively, he stood and jerked her to her feet. "Isn't there some unused corner in this place?"

"You must be mad to think of such a thing!"

Yet minutes later she was leading him into the darkened refectory. The tables were bare, the shutters closed against the afternoon sun.

Blindly they stumbled into a shadowy corner. She closed her eyes, grinding her hips against him.

"Ladylove," he breathed against her tongue.

Afterward she opened her eyes to meet his, but her gaze slid past him to a statue of Our Blessed Lady. "Abelard," she said, shaken, "we've done a terrible thing."

His eyes followed hers to the Virgin, and he shrugged lightly.

"God will punish us," she insisted.

"Don't be silly." He kissed her on the nose.

From what she had seen of Ceci, Heloise realized that the girl had not reconciled herself to Argenteuil. According to Sister Madelaine, Sister Cecilia was a troublemaker, and scarcely a week went by that she did not break one rule or another, and was, of course, punished. After three years, she could not be trusted to take responsibility for any duty at the convent, and the work she was given to do under the cellaress's supervision she invariably managed to botch. Worse, said Madelaine, Sister Cecilia was in the habit of slipping into the guest quarters and mingling with the pilgrims and knights.

Ceci was bitter and unhappy. Constantly she told Heloise so, whimpering resentfully that Heloise had everything—intelligence, beauty, a rich husband and a child, everything—while nothing exciting had ever happened to her. It was not fair, she cried. Heloise warned that defiance would only cause her further grief and eventually Lady Alais would be forced to expel her. And what would become of her then? She would have to beg her bread on the highroads. She must change her attitude.

"Shit," answered Ceci savagely, her eyes smoky with anger.

"You're not supposed to say words like that."

"You do."

"I'm not a nun," Heloise told her. "And you're not allowed to talk to me. I'm a guest. Sister Judith warned you not to speak with guests."

"I don't care." She turned her face away. A moment later: "Tell me about your lord. He wrote love songs, didn't he? Were they sad or happy?"

Heloise said, "Both." She was reluctant to talk about it for fear of putting ideas in Ceci's head. She should be thinking about the lives of the saints, not love. "I can help you with those medicines you're to mix. Sister Blanche said you should finish them this morning."

"If you wish." Her expression softened. "They give me stupid tasks to do."

Heloise spoke patiently. "No task is stupid, especially mixing herbs for the infirmary. That's very important." She put her arm around Ceci's shoulder.

In the afternoon, Heloise wrote a receipt for Lady Alais, who had just received a generous bequest from the father of a novice. While she was drying the ink, a lay sister came in and said there was a visitor waiting at the gatehouse. Her eyes downcast modestly, she added in a whisper, "A man."

"Young or old?" It could not be Abelard again, although it might.

"Young," the sister replied.

Jourdain was leaning against the water trough, talking to a sun-blackened pilgrim. When he saw Heloise, he waved and grinned. "Lady," he cried excitedly, "this fellow has been to Compostela. Look —he has a scallop shell!"

For a while they stood in the courtyard, questioning the pilgrim and admiring his scallop badge, the sign of a successful pilgrimage to Saint-James. Heloise took Jourdain's arm. They strolled in the direction of the guest parlor. "Fair friend," she said, laughing, "you'll not be content until you've undertaken some great pilgrimage."

"Aye," he sighed. "The Holy Land. That, please God, is where I'd like to go."

"Oh, it's too dangerous. You might be killed."

He shrugged. At the cloister gate, he paused and tried to peer through the grating. The portress on duty gave him a warning glare. Jourdain backed off with a wave and threw a denier in the alms box. He said to Heloise, "It's very pretty in there. Serene, you know."

"Hah." She snorted. The parlor was crowded with merchants unbundling their wares. A peddler was displaying an assortment of combs, assuring someone that the teeth were guaranteed to last a lifetime. Heloise found two stools and brought them to the window. She sat opposite Jourdain, smiling happily at his freckled face.

With a grin, he dived into a pouch hanging from his girdle and brought out a parcel. He handed it to her with a flourish.

Heloise placed the parcel on her lap while she unwrapped it. She whooped, "Holy Mother, aren't you a sweet heart!" and stared down delightedly at the assortment of cakes and pies. "How did you know what I wanted?"

Jourdain laughed. "Go ahead. Eat."

Eagerly she stuffed a sinnel cake into her mouth, hardly bothering to chew. "Ooooh. Delicious! Is it obvious that I'm a pig?"

"Fairly. Don't they feed guests decently here?"

"Don't know." She took a bite from a beef and raisin pie and held it out to Jourdain. "I've been eating in the refectory. Two meat dishes a meal, but badly cooked."

"You got spoiled in Paris."

"I know. I could indulge my cravings for sweets." She glanced at him. "How's my lord?"

"Well. He bought new horses for the journey. Costly, they were. I think the price of animals has gone up since last fall."

Heloise hitched forward with a smile. "I hope he's got me a gentle one. Remember that creature I had last time—"

"Ummm."

Jourdain was silent a minute, his face turned toward the window. Heloise thought he looked exhausted; there were pouches under his eyes.

He turned back sharply. "Thibaut's in Paris."

"Oh." Heloise stopped chewing, surprised.

"Thibaut and Philip. I ran into Philip. In a tavern near the bishop's palace."

Heloise frowned, remembering the enmity between Jourdain and her cousin. "What did he say?"

"Who, Philip?" Jourdain shrugged. "He was drunk."

"He's a nasty bastard. God forgive me, he's my own blood, but it's true."

"He said my lady friend finally got what she deserved."

She stirred uncomfortably. "Your—he was talking about me?"

"Apparently," said Jourdain slowly, "apparently he thinks you're going to take the veil. He said Abelard married you and then put you in a convent. An easy way to get rid of you."

The comb peddler, smiling, appeared at Heloise's elbow, holding out a comb in each hand. She waved him away. "Count on Philip to jump to conclusions."

"Heloise." He groaned. "That's what everybody thinks." He pointed emphatically at her habit. "God's teeth, what else did you expect?"

"Well," Heloise said. She gave a short laugh. "No matter. Let them think what they like." She stood, brushed the crumbs from her lap, and sat again. "Next week classes are over and we're off to Brittany."

Jourdain nodded slowly. Abruptly, he said, "I'm—I'm leaving the Ile."

"Melun?" She wrapped up the rest of the cakes, thinking of how she could sneak them to Ceci.

"Champagne," he told her hurriedly. "I was thinking of taking service with the count."

Her eyes opening wide, Heloise said, "Oh, Jourdain! You're not going to leave Abelard."

He turned his face to the window. "Lady, one can't be a student forever, you know."

"I know," she said, "but—listen, friend, you have a fief of your own."

"It's not mine yet. The Count of Champagne's service is very prestigious. Someday I might become bailiff, or keeper of the fair. I have a good education." His voice rose hotly.

For a long while, Heloise argued with him, but he would not listen. She had her future all planned out, he told her. Why should she object if he did likewise? He was twenty-two and he could not trail after Master Peter's skirts forever.

13 ❧

JULY CAME, day after day of fierce sun cooking the limestone walls. The grass in the cloister began to brown, and the cellaress had the novices dribble buckets of water over it. From the highroad, someone dragged in a pilgrim suffering from sunstroke. He died the next day, and the abbess ordered the body to be buried immediately—in this weather, you couldn't keep anything.

That night Heloise dreamed about Abelard. They were lying in a meadow. Her head rested on a pillow of violets. The day was hot, and he pulled off her bliaut, tossing it into the air. Far away, she heard someone screaming her name, but she ignored it; she held Abelard tighter. At breakfast, she glanced around at the dark bowed heads and felt a gurgle of shame, as if she had transgressed one of St. Benedict's Rules. Moments later, she'd forgotten it and was laughing deliciously to herself. Abelard. A few more days.

In the schoolroom, she read to the children from a treatise called *On Beasts and Other Things,* a book she had loved in her childhood. She told them about the habits of animals, and how stags live nine hundred years, and how doves can look at themselves with their right eyes and at God with their left.

After the lesson, Sister Judith came and took the children away for their catechism. The morning was hot, drowsy. Heloise wandered around the cloister. With departure imminent, she found herself viewing the convent with an emotion close to affection—these past few days, the singing of the offices brought tears to her eyes; at night the bells rocked her to sleep and she woke happy. Under her breath she sang, thinking of the rolling countryside along the Loire, the good rose wines that the innkeepers chilled in their wells and served in earthen goblets. She walked through the cloister, past the lavatory, and out through the postern gate, toward the river.

An hour later, hungry, she trudged slowly back to the convent. They would be ringing the refectory bell soon. Coming in the postern door, she saw the portress's assistant bouncing toward her.

"Lady," she called breathlessly, "I've been seeking you everywhere. There's a man asking for you in the yard."

Heloise's heart began to pound. Could Abelard have come for her already? But he had said Friday or Saturday. She said, "I'm coming right now," and trotted behind the nun toward the cloister gate.

In the yard, she craned her neck from side to side. Near the gatehouse there was a clump of people, the usual beggars waiting for alms, pilgrims, a caravan of merchants. She headed toward them. The portress's assistant picked at her sleeve and pointed to a man slouching alone in the corner near his horse. Despite the heat, he was wearing a hooded cape that covered most of his face. Disappointed not to find Abelard, she started slowly toward him, the heat of the cobbles burning through her slippers. "Brother, did you want to see me?"

"Heloise," Jourdain said, throwing off the hood.

She smiled, surprised. "Friend—I—did not expect you."

Jourdain looked over his shoulder at the travelers milling around the portress's lodge. Moving toward a bush near the wall, he beckoned Heloise to follow. She ran after him. "What news from the Ile?" she asked excitedly. "Have you seen Abelard?"

Jourdain did not answer.

"When is he coming for me?"

Jourdain said haltingly, "I have a message for you." Then he fell silent again. He leaned against the wall, looking down at his boots.

She smiled quizzically. "What's the matter with you? Aren't you going to tell what it is?"

Silence. Now, for the first time, she noticed his face. He looked pale and frightened. "Friend, what is it—"

He murmured at last, "Master Peter has been hurt."

She stepped back, shocked, not wanting to believe him. "Hurt? What kind of a jest— Who hurt him?"

He was watching her through narrowed eyes. "Your cousin Philip . . . Thibaut . . ." Her hands began to sweat. "They did him—an injury."

"What do you mean?" she asked carefully. "What kind of an injury?"

"I told you." He clamped his lips.

She flung both arms straight at him, as if to shake him. "For the love of Christ, speak! What is it?"

He said, expressionless, "They castrated him."

She looked down at her hands.

"Castrated. Gelded." He began talking wildly. "Those sons of dogs, they gelded him. Like an unclean beast—"

The sound of Jourdain's voice echoed hazily in her ears. The sun beat on the nape of her neck. Face still lowered, she stared down at the ground. In the mud crevice between two stone cobbles was wedged a rusty nail, and a line of ants skibbled madly up and over it. Heloise raised her head and looked at Jourdain. He had stopped talking and was watching her. To his right, a dozen strides along the wall, the portress was yelling at a pilgrim and scratching the side of her head through her wimple. The pilgrim nodded angrily at Sister Martha. Some of them tried to stay longer than two nights, even though they knew it was against the rules. Some people always tried to take advantage.

"Friend," Jourdain said.

She rocked backward a step and steadied the soles of her feet against the cobbles. The heat slithered brightly around her head. Any time now, they would be ringing the bell for dinner. Some kind of fish soup. She had smelled it cooking before she went to the river. Her arms ached. She saw Sister Martha coming toward her.

Sister Blanche crossed herself and said "Name of God" twice. She would not permit Heloise to leave the infirmary, and when Heloise tried to force her way past her, she took away her clothes and locked them in a cupboard. Under no circumstances would she allow a patient to go roaming around the courtyard. She pushed Heloise back into bed. Heloise should not assume her husband was dead, there was no reason to jump to conclusions, and in fact the young man from the Ile had distinctly said Abelard was not dead. Sister Blanche sent a novice to fetch Lady Alais. The abbess, her face white, stood above Heloise's bed without speaking, and then she walked to the doorway and talked quietly with Sister Blanche. After she had gone, Sister Blanche had Heloise bled.

In the darkness, later, she opened her eyes. She lay rigid, holding the terrible images at the edge of her mind. The thoughts were there, but she would not permit them full life. She remembered Jourdain sobbing in the yard, but she had not. It was long ago. At her core, something felt obliterated.

Not that evening, but the one following, Sister Blanche unlocked her clothes and said she might see Jourdain in the abbess's garden. She sent two heavyset nuns with Heloise in case of a fainting attack.

At the entrance to the garden, Heloise paused a moment. Jourdain saw her and lurched forward. "Friend—"

"He's dead." She mouthed the words without speaking.

"No."

She shook her head sluggishly, disbelieving.

"Lady, he's alive. I swear. He's not going to die."

She stood still. Tears began to trickle thinly down her face, and she brushed at them with the back of her hand.

"Galon has been caught," he said. "They castrated and blinded him." He dropped on a bench and stared at his knees. "And your cousin Philip as well. Thibaut got away."

Heloise blinked. Galon? What did Galon have to do with it? She could not understand why Abelard's servant had been punished; he did not even know her kin.

"I was there earlier. At supper. I left him before compline. They bribed Galon to open the door after Abelard was asleep." He fell silent, shuffling his feet against the pebbles.

Heloise waited, her fists clenched. Fulbert did this. Jourdain had not mentioned Fulbert's name. She heard the sisters from the infirmary whispering beyond the garden gate. It was beginning to grow dark.

Jourdain went on rapidly. "The following morning the whole city was gathered before his house. People were weeping and groaning. Thousands. God, I have never seen anything like it. Indescribable." He flung back his head. "Traffic was halted all the way to the Petit Pont."

She nodded. Something gagged in her throat. She swallowed and thought, Judas.

"The schools closed," Jourdain was saying. "They made Galon tell everything. He said that your uncle—"

Heloise stared at him.

"—your uncle plotted the whole thing. Oh, he's denied it. Swore he knew nothing about it. He spent the night in the cathedral. There were witnesses. Lady, are you listening?"

She bobbed her head once, her mind screaming.

"The king's bailiff tried to enter the close and take him. But the bishop refused him. Violation of clerical immunity. The bishop's court will try him. I wish to Christ—" He broke off.

At last she spoke. "Was I born to be the cause of such a crime?" Her voice sounded far away.

"Don't talk stupidly."

Heloise walked slowly toward the shadows by the gate, not listening. "God is cruel. We were both to blame. He alone was punished."

"Please," Jourdain answered severely. "You don't know what you're saying." He rose and followed her.

The stallion raced steadily. Heloise sat behind Jourdain, her arms curled tightly around his waist. The road to Paris was dark and misty and the moon had gone. For a long while, they passed no one, but Jourdain told her that was good. Usually the only people abroad at night were evildoers—whores and cutpurses. As they pounded by Montmartre, she could see over his shoulder streaky tints of light in the hollow below. They went on. Torches flamed from the walls of the stockade. They reached the Saint-Merri gate, paid their toll, and entered. Coming to the Chastelet, Jourdain slowed the horse to a walk and mumbled something, but Heloise did not catch the words.

"What did you say?"

His voice was unsteady. "Master Peter."

"Yes."

"You must expect to find him changed."

Then the thoughts that she had held off for the past two days, for sanity's sake, swam around her. Closing her eyes, she slumped against Jourdain's back and sobbed in small, retching cries. Jerking away, she flung her head over the horse's side and vomited into the black road. Jourdain put his hand on her shoulder.

Bonfires smoked in the road outside Abelard's house. The crowds were still there, perhaps a hundred or more people choked around the fires or stretched out like shapeless parcels on the ground. A pasty vendor was doing brisk business, and wineskins littered the road. Jourdain cursed under his breath. By the side of the house, he reined in and pulled Heloise to the ground. They ran for the door.

Upstairs, a fat man with large, soft eyes answered Jourdain's knock. Heloise heard them whispering and Jourdain calling the man Hilarius. She stood with her back to the door, breathing heavily. The fat man went to the bedroom door and opened it with an efficient air. He went in. Heloise remembered Abelard talking of him. He had written a play about Lazarus. Two youths, students, sprawled near the window, playing tables; they glanced up at Heloise and then turned back to their game.

When Hilarius came out, Heloise reeled toward him. Looking at Jourdain, he shook his head and pulled the door tight behind him. Heloise's mouth was dry. She hurled herself toward the door, but Hilarius caught her wrist. "Lady, please. Jourdain, tell her."

She glanced at Jourdain, unreasonably furious at him.

He said, "He won't see you. Heloise, listen, mayhap tomorrow he'll feel differently."

She gave Hilarius a burning stare, and he stepped away from the door. She went in. There was no light in the room except a small rushlight next to the bed. The shutters were clamped, the air clotted with the smell of herbs and aromatic oil. She caught a quick glimpse of the side of Abelard's face before he wrenched his whole body toward the wall. She moved forward a step, breathing the pressure of his silence.

"Get out." His voice was slurred, feverish.

Not answering, she stared at the back of his head and ventured an other step.

"Let me alone," he spat weakly.

His voice, webbed and ugly, struck her in the middle of the chest. Quietly rooted in place, she continued to observe him, felt the weight of his pain. "I love you," she said, very softly.

Abelard did not answer. She waited, watching the rushlight spin delicate patterns against the wall. At last, he said wearily, "Go away."

Heloise backed off to the window and stood looking out, her arms crossed over her breasts. She did not turn. After a while, she sat down on a chest, still not looking at him. There was no sound from the bed, and she thought he must be dozing.

Suddenly she heard him whisper, "A eunuch is an abomination to the Lord."

Her knees went to water; if she had been standing, she would have fallen. She prayed that he would fall asleep, but the prayer was hollow, mechanical, and she knew that God did not listen anyway. He had done this; why should he listen to her now? She got up and went out for a cup of herb wine. Jourdain was asleep on the floor; the other men stared at her. She took the wine to Abelard and sat on the side of his bed, thinking that the room needed airing. The sheets should be changed. She watched Abelard drinking, never once looking at her. His lips were cracked with fever. When he had finished, she took the cup away and lay down on the floor near the bed. After all movement from the bed had stopped and she heard only his even breathing, she slept without knowing.

In the morning, the crowd gathered in the road grew considerably larger. Many were Abelard's students, boys who worshiped him; others came because they had nothing better to do and wanted a little excitement. The Bloody Saracen was bursting with customers, and those who could not squeeze into the tavern were patronizing a wineseller who had set up for business near Abelard's stoop and who was charging what the traffic would bear. Heloise sent Hilarius down to ask the people to leave. From the window, she heard him shouting and pleading. He came back up, but when Heloise looked down a few minutes later, nobody had gone, and for that matter the size of the crowd had swollen.

She washed her face and unplaited her hair, then replaited it. There was nothing she could do about the filthy, sweaty gown. She said to Hilarius, "The wound. Is it bad?"

"Clean." Hilarius cut a piece of linen into thin strips for bandages. "They brought a surgeon with them."

Heloise turned, surprised. Jourdain had not mentioned a doctor.

"A Spanish doctor, I'm told. They wanted to take no chances with Master Peter dying."

She covered her mouth with her knuckles, willing her stomach to stop heaving. Hilarius meant well, she knew, and he wanted to talk. Out in the road, people were yelling. She went over to lean against the shutters, watching them mill around aimlessly. Hilarius was saying, "The surgeon used a bronze clamp. Surgical instrument. Nothing new, I'm told. A medical student told me—"

Heloise nodded. Hilarius, folding bandages, went on talking. He told her how the penis was drawn through an oval ring, and when the clamp was closed, the scrotum and testes were removed with a rapid slash of a knife, leaving the penis intact; the wound was then cauterized and sutured. His friend, the medical student, had described the operation in detail to him. When she did not reply, he came to her, belly quivering under his black gown. "Lady, if it is any consolation to you, it could have been worse. He might have been butchered and left for dead. We must thank God for that."

"Mayhap," she answered. No, she had nothing for which to thank God. In a little while, she excused herself and went downstairs to the street. She walked around and quietly asked people to go home. Master Peter was ill, he needed complete quiet to recover, and if they stayed he might sicken and die. She waited calmly on the stoop, staring at them, watching them move slowly down the Rue de la Huchette. When only a dozen or so remained, she turned and went in. In the vestibule, a woman opened the door of the ground-floor flat and caught Heloise's arm. She introduced herself as Master Abelard's landlady.

"Lady Heloise," she said, her eyes big, "how is my lord this morning?"

"Sleeping."

"God help me, lady, I blame myself. I can't sleep in this heat. I heard people climbing the stairs in the middle of the night. But you know Master Abelard—people coming and going at all hours."

Heloise nodded impatiently.

"The next thing I heard were screams. It turned my blood to ice, I can tell you that. Lady—"

Heloise cut her off. "Please—" She put a foot on the bottom step.

The woman said, "Lady, a favor. A lock of your hair, please. As a token."

Drawing in a rough breath, Heloise ran up the stairs. Hilarius was standing in the middle of the room looking uncomfortably at the half-opened bedroom door. Inside, Abelard was cursing someone. Jourdain came out and carefully closed the door.

"He must feel better." Jourdain grinned wanly. "He's swearing."

She found a broom, went in, and threw back the shutters. Abelard, propped up, was sipping from a bowl of milk.

"Good morning, my lord," she said with as much cheer as she could. "It's a beautiful clear day. I think it will be cooler today."

He did not answer or glance at her.

Starting near the bed, Heloise began sweeping the old rushes toward the middle of the room. "Where do you keep your linen? Fresh sheets will make you feel better."

"Let me be."

"I'm your wife," she said mildly and went on sweeping. When she had made a pile of rushes near the door, she leaned the broom against the wall. Seeing his bowl empty, she took it from him. "Good. Milk will help you regain your strength."

His eyes were dazed. "Go home," he muttered.

She wondered what home he was talking about. Fulbert's? Argenteuil? It occurred to her that at the present she had no such place as home. "I'm going to stew a fowl later," she said. "You should drink the broth. It will calm the fever. In no time you'll—"

"What for?" he whispered scornfully. "How can I show my face in public? So that everyone can point at me, every tongue deride me, a monstrous spectacle to everyone I meet?"

"No," she said. "The whole Ile weeps for you."

He paid no attention. "Eunuchs are stinking, unclean. Forbidden to enter a church. Even castrated animals were rejected for sacrifice."

"Abelard—"

He began quoting Leviticus to her. " 'Ye shall not present to the Lord any animal if its testicles have been bruised or crushed, torn or cut.' "

"Animals aren't sacrificed anymore."

" 'No man whose testicles have been crushed or whose organ has been severed—' "

"Stop it!"

" '—shall become a member of the assembly of the Lord.' God, God!"

"An ancient law," she replied evenly. "Outmoded. It does not apply today." When he did not reply, she added impulsively, "Dearest, you can't hide for the rest of your life."

"Hold your tongue." He flung himself against the headboard. "Don't tell me about the rest of my life. What do you know about it? I shall hang myself."

Wooden, Heloise went back to the solar. She said to Jourdain, "You must find a place for me to stay. And, friend, this afternoon I'll be needing your horse."

She tied Jourdain's stallion by the Port Saint-Landry and walked up to the house. Two men-at-arms were sprawled on Fulbert's stoop playing dice. Bishop's men. She went around behind the stable and into the garden. On a rope strung between the privy and a branch of the pear tree were hanging a row of half-dried towels. Heloise ducked under the towels and quietly opened the kitchen door. In the empty passageway, she stopped and listened. Low voices were coming from the solar, and she could hear an occasional clink of platters and goblets. Fulbert must be having a late dinner. On tiptoe, she edged her way to the stairs and started up.

The turret room was the same. Her clothes were all hanging neatly on the wall pegs. She opened the chest under the window. Abelard's letters, tied with a cord, had not been touched. She sat on the bed, wondering if Agnes had come in to clean. Nothing appeared to have been changed, except that the bloodstained coverlet had been replaced.

She began packing. The gowns she folded and laid inside her winter cloak, and then she tied them into a bundle. Her comb and Limoges box and the letters she wrapped in a shawl. When there was nothing more that she wanted, she pulled a bundle under each arm and kicked open the turret door.

At the bottom of the stairs, Agnes stood staring, her eyes round with fear. Heloise walked around her and dropped the bundles by the front door. She turned. "Where is he?" she asked, low.

Agnes motioned in the direction of the solar. Fulbert was calling, "Agnes, who's there?"

Heloise went in to him. When Fulbert saw her, he set his goblet down hard on the trestle. Wine spilled, making a purple blotch on the cloth. He sat as still as a statue.

Heloise said, "Assassin."

"Why, niece." He laughed nervously. "I don't know what you're talking about."

It was stifling in the room. The windows were open, but no air stirred. Behind her, Heloise could feel Agnes breathing. Fulbert remained silent. "Assassin," she repeated.

"Now, now," Fulbert said, clearing his throat, "he's not dead. Nobody killed him."

"You killed me."

"Surely—"

"You killed everything that made my life worthwhile." Her voice rose to a quiet explosion. "It is me you have murdered!" She waited until she could control herself.

"There," he said soothingly, the way a man speaks to a hysterical child. "I had nothing to do with the crime."

She laughed hollowly. "Liar." After a pause: "I curse you and the whole house of Saint-Gervais."

"God will punish you," Fulbert told her sharply. He shifted uneasily in his chair.

"God damn you. God damn you to hell everlasting."

He stared at her. "God is just. Vengeance is mine, saith the Lord. He punished Master Abelard, and he will punish you for blaspheming against his holy name. Abelard ruined our house. Is that nothing to you? My nephew unmanned, blinded. What of him? My brother hunted down like a dog. Who will look after the fief now?" He rose from the trestle, shaking. "He has done us harm, don't deny it."

Heloise turned her back on him and walked to the hall. She stooped for the bundles. When Agnes came up to open the door, Heloise did not look at her. She stepped over the guards on the stoop and dragged toward the Port Saint-Landry.

Jourdain found her an inn near the Petit Pont. A half dozen beds were wedged into the tiny chamber, and Heloise had to share hers with the wife of a wine merchant from Bordeaux and with uncountable vermin. Jourdain said the inn was respectable, but still, downstairs in the public dining hall, men drank and diced around the oaken trestles. In the garden at the rear, prostitutes crept in after dark, and Heloise could hear their smooth laughter. The whole place was dirty and smelled of stale wine and bad cooking.

Abelard's wound was healing, and now he spent the days in his armchair in the solar. Outside, the crowds had gone, the Rue de la Huchette returned to its normal traffic of sumpter beasts and rumbling carts, although patrons of the Bloody Saracen still stared at Abelard's windows and discussed the crime over bowls of ale. Every morning, Heloise took a basket and did the marketing, and then she came back to cook Abelard's meals—simple soups and stews. More complicated dishes were beyond her. Abelard did not ask her to do this; on the other hand, he offered no objections either. He spoke little to her, some days barely acknowledging her presence. His uncut hair grown shaggy on his neck, he sat, with bent head, quietly thinking, reading the Bible, occasionally playing tables with Jourdain or Hilarius.

At the window, Heloise made her face betray none of the unrestrained rage and pity that occupied her thoughts at the inn, and she examined Abelard from the corner of her eye when she thought he was not looking. His whole person seemed vastly altered: his head and shoulders slumped as if the ligaments in his neck and spine had disconnected. The face was sealed, the dazzling grin and reckless arrogance that had once lit him and shown like a beacon to all he met—this was gone. And without it his face, in repose, looked almost ordinary. This absence of arrogance was what most frightened Heloise; it was the psychic glue that had held him together, and now he seemed to be another person. For hours, he maintained the same position, turning the pages of Scripture slowly, suspended alone in some other world.

She did not intrude. Soon he would awake and life would go on. It had to. If he appeared indrawn, indifferent, at least he had calmed and he no longer railed at her to go away. They would have to leave the Ile for a while; in her mind she had it planned. The sensible thing would be to live quietly at Le Pallet with their son. She was ready to leave, weary of the inn and these rooms of sickness and horror.

Once he said to her, "Heloise," not loud, and when she ran to him, he repeated her name. "Heloise."

"Oh, my love, my love," she murmured, and held his head.

He caught her left hand, kissing the fingers. He said nothing more, released her, and went back to his Bible. Heloise eased her way to the window stool again and stared into the road.

Suddenly he called, "Have you been attending mass?"

"No."

He leaned forward in his chair. "Why not?"

Cautiously, she answered, "I can't." Then: "God is unjust."

Shaking his head, he murmured, "Oh no. God's justice is all too apparent." He smiled slightly. "His judgment struck me where I had sinned. And isn't it justice that the reprisals were taken by the man I betrayed? Oh, it's absolutely perfect justice."

Shocked, she leaped up to face him. "No, my lord. I accuse God of the greatest cruelty. For us, he reversed the laws of equity. What adulterous women bring upon their lovers, your own wife brought on you."

Abelard did not reply, and when she glanced at him, she saw that he had returned to his reading. He did not look up again. She went back to the inn and allowed herself to weep.

Lammas Day came in a torrent of thundershowers. The Ile cooled off for a day and a night, but then the heat returned, more oppressive than ever. Heloise took a chill, which immediately settled in her chest. Her lungs filled with phlegm so that she was constantly coughing and spitting up greenish gobs. Jourdain ordered her to stay in bed, and he instructed the innkeeper to bring a poultice for her chest. The illness, inconsequential as it was, threw her into even deeper misery. It had not occurred to her that Abelard would take the attitude he apparently had; his humble acceptance of the castration, so utterly uncharacteristic, frightened her. She huddled on her bed, staring into emptiness, wheezing. Her mind spilled over with stray thoughts, flotsam-and-jetsam bits from twenty years of reading. Was it women's lot to ruin great men? Plenty of examples. It was the first woman, in the beginning, who had lured man from paradise; she who had been created as man's helpmate became the instrument of his downfall. And what of Delilah and Bathsheba and Job's wife, who had urged him to curse God? But she, Heloise, was not like those women, no consent of hers had been responsible for the crime.

Her chest racked by coughs, she wept and flung herself against the pillow. Why did she bother to defend herself, as if she were innocent? It was all words. She had committed too many sins to pretend freedom from guilt now. Long ago she had yielded to the pleasures of the flesh, long ago she deserved punishment. An evil beginning assures a bad end, she told herself; she should have expected it.

Abelard's reputation would be smeared, how badly she didn't want to guess, and certainly his life had been ruined. Those facts could not be altered by her or anyone. A thousand times she told herself that she would spend the rest of her life trying to make reparation to him. That, at least, she might do.

All through the early days of August, she waited for Abelard to announce their departure. He had written to Denise; she knew that because Jourdain had delivered a letter to the Nantes courier, but Jourdain did not know its contents. Heloise herself wrote a kind of letter to Astrolabe. She drew a picture of lords and ladies at a garden party, drinking, laughing gaily. In the background, she sketched a castle with ornate spires and gables, and she drew blue and yellow flowers and an enormous mouse chasing a small dog. Her skill as an artist left a great deal to be desired, and even the theme was not original—she had once seen something like it in a book of hours. Her babe. How big he would be now. Soon he would be walking and then running. It had been so long since they had left Le Pallet—four months; no, nearly five. It was not good for a mother to leave her babe; she would not, she swore fiercely, be parted from her angel again.

Gradually her coughing subsided, and she returned to the Rue de la Huchette. Now visitors began coming to see Abelard—abbots, priests, an emissary from the bishop. Once King Louis's monk friend, Suger, came, and he spent several hours shut up with Abelard in the bedchamber. Time crawled. Hilarius taught her to play tables. They sat whispering over the dice, discussing Hilarius's secondhand information about the aftereffects of castration. Eunuchs, castrati, harem boys, philosophers like Origen who had castrated themselves. She supposed it unseemly for a lady to discuss such matters with a man, but she didn't care and Hilarius was eager to share his information. Several times she had noticed, with a nervous shock of excitement, that Abelard had a slight erection. Did this mean that he was not completely dysfunctional? But to that question Hilarius had no ready answer. "We must wait to see God's will," he would say.

Heloise attempted a pigeon pie, but it came out soggy, and she threw it away. She scrubbed the solar floor and covered it with rushes, and this drew criticism from Jourdain. "A noble lady shouldn't behave like a servant," he told her with a grimace of disapproval. "Master Peter must hire someone to clean."

"No," she said. "I want to care for him myself."

He shot back in a whisper, "Lady, it's plain to me what you are thinking. But it's not your fault that all this happened."

"No? Whose then?"

He muttered, "Why, your kin. They are mad dogs."

Heloise looked away without replying. Abelard came into the solar and seated himself in his chair. Resting his elbows on the carved arms, he turned a weak smile on them. "The two of you look peaked," he said. "You could use sun and fresh air."

"My lord," answered Jourdain quickly, "you could use the same."

Abelard nodded agreeably. "I suppose." He did not appear to be offended by Jourdain's suggestion but obviously had no interest in pursuing the subject. "Lad, I won't be needing you for the rest of the day. Go find some cheerful pothouse and relax."

Jourdain looked surprised. "My lord," he began to protest.

"Go on," Abelard said. He waved him out the door.

Hands on hips, Heloise waited by the hearth, wondering if she should cut up the hare she had bought for tomorrow's stew. After the disaster with the pigeon pie, there would be little for Abelard's meal that evening.

"Heloise."

"Do you feel like having hare for supper? I don't know. It's so hot. Mayhap a light supper of fruit and cheese would be better."

"Heloise."

A fleck of nervousness in his voice, a certain jagged quality, made her look up sharply. His face was grave. "Come. Sit down. Over here." With his foot he nudged a stool toward her.

She sat facing him.

"You've had the patience of Job these past weeks."

"My lord, I—"

"It's true. The patience of Job. And you've been wondering when I will put on my clothing—"

She smiled uneasily.

"—and get off my haunches and leave these stinking rooms."

"Something like that," she admitted. "You can't stay like this forever."

Abelard said, "No. I can't." He paused. "Nor can I walk through the streets of the Ile and return to my former life. There's no place for me here."

"Then we must leave at once for—"

He was going on, as if she had not spoken. "Lady, it is my intention to take religious vows and enter the abbey of Saint-Denis. There are other abbeys, but I think Saint-Denis would be best. Abbot Adam is willing to have me, and King Louis is especially eager for me to associate myself with the royal abbey."

All the while he had been talking, Heloise had held herself rigid, her mind frozen around the words "religious vows." The rest of it she had barely heard. "No," she shouted angrily, "I won't listen! You have no vocation. It's only shame speaking, not any devout wish for conversion. If it's shelter you want, it needn't be in a monastery. We'll go to Le Pallet." She stopped. "You're a philosopher," she added in a more careful tone, "not a monk."

There was a lengthy silence. Abelard rubbed his forefinger back and forth over his upper lip. "I *was* a philosopher. Now it is my desire to become a monk. My motives may be suspect, but my resolve is firm. I will not change my mind, that I can tell you."

"And I tell you I won't let you."

"The Lord's hand touched me for an express purpose, I believe. To free me from the temptations of the flesh and worldly distractions. No more will I pursue fame and wealth."

He can be talked out of this, Heloise thought. Once they got to Le Pallet, he would hold his son and remember that he had responsibilities; he could not hide like a criminal. She leaned toward him and said, "These decisions shouldn't be made hastily. Even Abbot Adam will tell you that. You must allow yourself time to consider. Six months from now you may feel differently."

He was staring into the corner, shaking his head slowly. "Lady. This is painful for me. Don't make it worse."

She leaped up from the stool. Her bliaut soaked in perspiration, she poured two goblets of wine and brought them back. It seemed, curiously, as if all this had happened to her before. Someone had gone away suddenly, and she had beat her hands against some wooden object and screamed, pleading with them to stay, but they had not listened. She couldn't remember where or when this had happened, only the cold fear, then and now, gnawing her stomach. She gulped a mouthful of wine.

"Heloise."

She looked down at her feet. The sunlight streaking through the window had lightened the rushes to a pale golden green. Trying to think of something to say, she whispered finally, "Have you no thought for me or your son?"

Abelard said, "Our marriage is over. I can give you no pleasure now."

"I don't care if you can never lie with me again. All I want is you, yourself. It's all I've ever wanted. You know that."

"God's eyes, stop it!" he shouted, covering his eyes with one arm.

"Abelard. Don't leave me." She went to him and cupped his hand in hers. She told him there were other alternatives besides a monastery. No matter how he felt now, there was no reason why he could not wait a while and then return to teaching. His reputation as a philosopher was too eminent to be seriously diminished by the crime. He was her husband, she was his wife—he was alive, and a long life of happiness together was still possible. Clinging to him, she pounded him gently with words, always seeking the one magical phrase that would turn him back from despair. The bars of sunlight across the trestle began to fade. Abelard stood and tramped to the window. He kept his back to her.

She said, "At Le Pallet, you said you couldn't bear to be parted from me—that was why we had to marry. I tell you that I can't conceive of a life without you. Surely you understand that."

After a long silence, he nodded. "I understand." Heloise waited, her eyes steady on his back. She took a sip of the wine. It was warm and made her feel sickish.

Abelard said, "We needn't be separated. I—" He said something more, but his words were so faint that she did not catch them.

Heloise squinted. "I didn't hear you."

"We might enter religion together," he said, his voice almost inaudible. He was still looking out the window.

For a moment, she thought that she had misunderstood him. He must have said something else. If she didn't answer, he would turn to her and repeat himself, and then she would hear his actual words. He couldn't have—

Abelard turned. She sat down hard, her eyes enormous with astonishment. "You can't—" Her hands groped blindly for the wine goblet.

Abelard said quickly, "It's the only thing to do, the best thing for both of us. I can't leave you alone. I must see that you're cared for."

She heard him rattling on. Swallowed up by the shock of the idea, she did not really listen. No, she thought. *I want to live.*

"You'll see. In the long run, it will be best for everyone. Even for Astrolabe. Denise will raise him. He'll be happy. You and I can serve God."

She thought, I don't want to serve God. It is you I wish to serve.

"Heloise, speak to me."

She said cautiously, "Why do you ask this of me?"

He hesitated. "You're my wife. At Argenteuil you'll be safe."

"Safe from what?" she exploded.

He looked away.

"Do you think I'll bed with someone else?"

"You're young. Someday you will—"

She licked her lips. "God in heaven, is that what you think? Do you know me so little that you think I'll crawl into another man's bed?" She lunged forward and grabbed his arm. "You think me wanton?"

"Lady, listen."

"Answer me! Is that what you are thinking?"

"Your blood is hot," he fired back.

Tears burning at her lashes, she bolted for the door. Halfway down the stairs, she heard him shouting her name. She was out on the open street, running, horses and carts and people streaming past in a steady blur. Her heart thudded painfully in her chest. She looked over her shoulder, but no one was following her. Absurd hope. She allowed her legs to slow down. He had not been out of his rooms since the assault; he would not come looking for her. She walked slowly the rest of the way to the inn.

Heloise flopped across the sagging bed, something thundering against her ribs until she felt as if her chest would split open. Panic. Rage. She had heard of people strangling on their own angry breath, and with each breath she willed that it should be the last. It began to grow dark. Men-at-arms came into the garden below, talking of a tournament at Le Mans and boasting of the ransoms they had collected, and then compline rang and they went to bed.

After a while, from habit, Heloise groped to the side of the bed and knelt. Prayer was not her intention. There was nothing to pray for; no help would come. This person who had been Peter Abelard, who was now someone she barely recognized, this man she loved would vanish behind the walls of Saint-Denis, and no prayers of hers could prevent it.

For herself, all roads to safety were barred, on earth as in heaven. All roads, she thought, but the one leading to Argenteuil. Oh Lord, she thought dully, how terrible are thy works, and no more would she address to him.

The night stillness was broken by the watchman's staff tapping rhythmically against the cobbles. Heloise heard him call, "Pray for the dead!" and then he moved down the street.

She got into bed. In the morning, she would find Jourdain and ask him to take her to Argenteuil. It was quiet there. On her rock, she could think what to do.

14 🌿

BY THE TIME they reached Argenteuil, she and Jourdain had stopped speaking. Her throat felt raw from yelling, and she imagined his must be the same.

When they rode into the yard, the portress looked up in astonishment. Heloise waved stiffly and slid down before Jourdain had reined the horse to a halt.

"Mark me," Jourdain muttered, dropping beside her.

Heloise cut him off harshly. "I have marked you. All the way from Paris. Jesu, what more is there to say?"

He grunted. "All I ask of you— Mark me, I'm pleading with you. Friend, use logic. Be reasonable."

She shrugged and laughed. "In a reasonable world, there would be incentive for making reasonable decisions. This is not a reasonable world."

Jourdain glowered at her. "It's the only world we've got."

"Well, it's not good enough." At the stricken look on his face, she thumped his shoulder with a fist. "Ah, friend, I told you. I've made no decision yet. Mayhap I'll take your advice. Let's part in peace."

He smiled sourly and resumed lecturing her.

The sound of his voice enraged her, as did the sight of the banner atop the gatehouse and the snapping of the wind against her ears. "Enough!" she roared, and walked quickly toward the cloister gate without looking back. Dancing toward her, one foot twitching along the cobbles, came Astrane.

"Lady, what happened!" Astrane gasped.

Heloise did not reply.

By nightfall, the convent heaved with gossip about Heloise and Master Peter Abelard, and Heloise could turn neither one direction nor another without noticing a whispering novice or nun. She was not surprised at their interest in the matter, since they had little else to occupy their minds. She watched them watching her. The whole thing bored her. They were alive and she was dead: what difference that they took her blood and nerves and brain in their voyeuristic hands and passed judgment. At dinner, she ate two helpings of fish and listened to the weekly reader droning a passage from Corinthians. Everything tasted and sounded blurred, as if she were wearing a band of linen around her senses. Abelard will not have me, she thought wildly. He has chosen death for himself; he has chosen it for me. Because he loves me.

There was no question of her not understanding all this. To keep from losing her, he was willing to bury her. She wondered what she would do in his place. No, she did not think she would feel compelled to bury him. The reader stopped suddenly and everyone else rose from the trestles. Dark and brooding, Ceci's eyes followed her as she left the refectory. Heloise looked back over her shoulder, and Ceci plunged to her side.

"Heloise," she said, "don't."

Heloise nodded. "I didn't seek your advice," she said mildly.

"Leave here tonight. Jourdain is still at the guesthouse. I saw him. He'll take you home." She was babbling.

"Home?" Heloise laughed. "Where's that?"

"Jourdain will marry you. He told me."

"I have a husband. Did you forget?"

Abruptly, Ceci's face wrinkled into tears. She pawed convulsively at Heloise's sleeve.

"Let go." She dipped around the corner of the cloister and lurched down the west walk. Entering the schoolroom, she pulled a stool to Madelaine's table and sank down.

Sister Madelaine put down her quill with a click. "That young man. Jourdain. He loves you."

"Oh," she said, surprised to hear Madelaine use the word *love*. "Him. Mayhap."

Madelaine's eyes fixed on her face. "More than your Master Abelard."

She turned away, uncomfortable, and tried to strain the anger from her voice. She said evenly, "Sister, you talk foolishly. You do not know my lord. Or Jourdain." Or anything about love, she added silently.

For a week, she lay in the infirmary, too exhausted for grief. Gray circles ringed her eyes. When Sister Blanche brought soup, Heloise turned her head toward the wall. On the eighth day, Sister Blanche's assistants tried to pour broth down Heloise's throat. From a stool by the side of the bed, Sister Madelaine crouched like a wizened yellow bird and studied her. Each time she opened her eyes, Madelaine hissed, "Fool."

"Go away."

"Idiot. It's not so easy to die. Besides, I won't let you." She gestured to the sisters with the broth. Heloise jerked away, feet and arms flailing. One of the nuns caught her by the jaw and wrenched. A little of the hot liquid sloshed over her tongue. The rest of it she spat at Madelaine.

The prioress grinned. "Good." She winked at Sister Blanche.

On the tenth day, Heloise rose and dressed. Her bliaut hung like a sack over her bony shoulders. Feeble, she said to Sister Blanche, "Is that boy still here?"

"What boy?"

"You know. The one who brought me here."

The infirmarian shrugged. "I can find out. Do you want to see him?"

"No. Ask him—ask him if he has a message for me. From Paris. That's all."

There would be no message, she was certain of that. A long time ago —two weeks, a century—she had had a husband and infant son. Little by little, her mind had been letting them go. Possessing them no longer seemed so desperately important; nothing seemed important.

She went into the cloister and sat on a bench near the lemon tree. Around her, September leaves drifted into the grass. Throughout the morning, she watched the nuns passing in and out of the cloister, whispering, arguing, carrying piles of linen and manuscripts. Busy with their duties, they seemed happy. Or at least content. Once, with effort, Heloise got up and walked the few steps to the lemon tree. Then she dragged back and sank down again. No strength remained to her—no strength to fight—but somewhere she must find strength to do one last thing. Very well, she thought, very well. Thy will be done. You know that I never wanted anything but Abelard, not wealth or power or marriage or possessions, only my beloved. You have denied me the one thing I love above all else; I will deny you the one thing you love. My heart and soul. Those belong to Abelard. The rest of me, the part that does not matter, you may have. He heard; she knew that he heard.

Sext rang. She went to find Lady Alais.

* * *

"Here is the law." The abbess read from the Rule. "If you can observe it, enter. If you cannot, you are free to depart."

"I can."

"Do you truly seek God?"

"I do."

"Are you zealous for the work of God?"

"Yes."

The abbess looked up. "The journey to God is made by hard and rugged ways."

Heloise returned her gaze calmly.

The abbess went on reading. "According to the law of the Rule, from this day forward you may not leave the convent." She paused. "Nor withdraw your neck from under the yoke of the Rule. Do you understand?"

"I do," said Heloise.

Lady Alais spoke of other things, but they were unimportant and Heloise did not listen.

The cloister had emptied but for the birds. Sister Madelaine led her down the east walk and into the side entrance of the abbey church. The sanctuary was crammed with a blur of people and candles, and the air stank of sweetish incense. Heloise tried not to focus. Her palm against Madelaine's began to sweat. They walked to the back of the nave and crossed to the center aisle. Madelaine said they would wait there until Bishop Gilbert gave the signal. Ahead and to her left, somebody was crying. Deliberately, she turned her head away, staring at nothingness. The sounds of the whimpering grated on her ears.

"Sister," she said to Madelaine, "somebody is bawling. Can't you make them stop?"

"Shhh—pay no mind. Stand up straight."

For a while, they stayed there, not speaking. Madelaine sent a novice up to notify the bishop that they were ready. Nuns were swarming around the altar as Sister Judith arranged them into lines. The ultimate ritual. Heloise had watched it dozens of times. As a child, she could hardly sleep for excitement on the nights before a novice was to be received into the order. There was Sister Marie, who had cried for her lord father, and Sister Custance, who had forgotten to wear an undershift and was sent back to the dormitory to dress properly. Or was it Sister Marie who'd neglected her undershift? It was all a jumble now. Sister Custance was dead anyway. She'd had beautiful breasts, rose-tipped and saucy. But she had bled to death one Advent—Heloise thought it must have been the sixth year she had been at Argenteuil.

Behind her, the door to the porch opened on a shaft of cool air. The door closed noisily. Someone came forward and stopped behind her right shoulder. From the corner of her eye, she realized that it was Abelard. Heloise glanced at him quickly. He looked well, his cheeks clean-shaven and ruddy from the crisp fall weather. She remembered the blue cloak. The fine soft wool had come from England, and it had been very dear. All in a rush, she realized that he was still wearing his usual clothes. Which meant that he had not taken his vows yet. He had waited for her to leave the world first. She turned away without looking into his eyes.

Abelard pulled a bundle from under his cloak and stepped around to Sister Madelaine's side.

The prioress looked annoyed. "What is this, sire?" she muttered.

"Lady Heloise's personal belongings."

Madelaine frowned. "I can't take them now, my lord. You must leave them with the wardrober."

"Very well, Sister." Abelard backed away and came around to Heloise once more. He held the bundle awkwardly under one arm and finally placed it on the floor near his feet.

Heloise stared at the altar. She heard Abelard breathing heavily behind her. Pivoting her head for a moment, she had a glimpse of his white face, and she heard him say low, "Lady."

Madelaine grabbed her hand. "It's time."

Nodding, Heloise turned to face Abelard again. Into her mind suddenly slammed a passage from Lucan, Cornelia's famous lament. She began to recite rapidly, " 'O noble husband, too great for me to wed, was it my fate to bend that lofty head?' " She felt Madelaine's hand stiffen in disapproval. " 'What prompted me to marry you and bring about your fall?' " Abelard's eyes widened in shock, and he looked away. " 'Now claim your due and see me gladly pay.' "

Madelaine jerked her forward, and they strode quickly, almost running, to the altar. When they reached Gilbert, Madelaine released her and went to join Lady Alais. The bishop began to pray.

Candle wax hissed and sputtered. "Let the petition be presented," the bishop announced. Sister Madelaine came up with a parchment scroll, which she handed to Heloise. Heloise offered it to the bishop, who unrolled the petition and gave it a perfunctory glance.

"Is this written in your own hand or by another at your request?"

"My own hand."

"This is your signature?"

"It is."

"Place it upon the altar with your own hand."

She nosed forward and dropped the scroll. Kneeling, she intoned, "Receive me, O Lord, according to your word, and I shall live. Let me not be confounded in my hope."

Behind her back, the refrain rose from the nuns. "Glory be to the Father."

Rising, Heloise faced the bishop. "I renounce my parents, my brothers, my friends, my possessions, and the vain and empty glory of this world." She glanced toward the nave, but she could not see Abelard. "And I renounce also my own will for the will of God, and accept all the hardships of the monastic life."

Slowly, deliberately, she walked to the far end of the line of nuns and stopped. Pitching to her knees, she prostrated herself at Sister Angelica's feet. "Pray for me," she said. Rising, she moved on to the next sister, prostrated herself, and repeated the words. Halfway down the line, her sore knees stopped aching and she began to move through the motions mechanically. Her legs and neck had no more feeling than a stick of wood. In the roar of the silence, she began to think about the package Abelard had brought. Personal belongings, he had told Madelaine. She remembered the things she had packed that last time at the Rue des Chantres. The Limoges box containing her rings and Abelard's letters, ribbons and a crisping iron and her little mirror. She wanted to laugh wildly. What would the wardrober do with those miserable remnants of a life? She glanced to her right. A dozen more pairs of shoes. She bent quickly and touched her forehead to the ground. "Pray for me." The blue tiles on the kitchen floor in Fulbert's house, the garlic and sage hanging from the rafters. Pasties soft as butter. Lutes and men laughing and the warm, safe fragrance of roses curling up to her turret window. Feather beds and sheets that rocked her in lavender, all these she renounced. "Pray for me." Creaking, she rose at last and walked to the altar.

Sister Madelaine and Sister Judith, carrying the habit and veil, came to stand beside her. They scooped her bliaut over her head. Shivering, she stood exposed in her shift. The black robes fell blindly over her eyes, the hands tugged and pulled, and then it was done. After blessing the veil, Gilbert moved toward her. Heloise snatched the veil from his hands and clamped it on her head. The bishop scowled. Leaning toward her, he said, "Repeat after me. I offer myself—"

"I offer myself—"

"To the Omnipotent God—"

"To the Omnipotent God and to the Virgin Mary for the salvation of my soul." She breathed noisily. "And so shall I remain in this holy life all my days until my final breath."

"Amen." Gilbert turned away, in a great hurry to get somewhere.

Later, Heloise stood just inside the cloister gate and stared into the courtyard. Abelard was saddling his stallion and beside him, already mounted, was Jourdain. With a shock, she remembered that she had not thought of Jourdain during the ceremony. She wondered where he had been standing; she should have said goodbye. Rocking forward on the balls of her feet, she pressed her face to the iron grille. Jourdain was backing his horse away from Abelard. His mouth was moving, but he was too far away for Heloise to make out words. She saw him swerve toward the gate and leave.

Abelard stood beside the stallion. After a while, he hoisted himself into the saddle and wrapped the cloak around his neck like a blanket. He was staring at his knees, the reins held limply in his hands. At last, straightening his spine, he edged the stallion to the gate. He did not look back.

For a long time, Heloise stood there. The air had turned damp. She stared at the cobbles where Abelard had sat on his horse, trying to imagine the black stallion and the blue cloak. Heavily, she turned away. There would be rain before evening.

The next day, she sent letters to Abelard and Astrolabe, cheerful lying letters that cost her a great deal to write. In her mind she had decided that Argenteuil would be tolerable if she could correspond with the persons she loved. She waited for replies until Christmas before concluding that the letters had been lost. Sister Madelaine, her temper uncertain, warned that they were a waste of time and parchment, and furthermore Heloise had broken the Rule by neglecting to show the letters to Lady Alais for approval. Angry, Heloise replied that she had no intention of submitting her mail to the abbess, and if Madelaine wished to report the offense in chapter meeting, she should feel free to do so. After that, the prioress stopped objecting and Heloise wrote again to Abelard, this time sending the letter to the abbey of Saint-Denis.

"He won't answer," Madelaine insisted. "He's finished with you. Why don't you stop beating a dead mule?"

"I wish you would mind your own business. You know very well that letters can go astray."

"That's true, but—"

"Especially in winter."

"Especially," Madelaine grunted.

"But the one I sent to Saint-Denis will not. I gave it to the abbot's courier when he last brought messages for Lady Alais. I put it in his hand myself." She glared at Madelaine, challenging her to continue.

"Oh well. In that case."

"There is no possibility of his not receiving it."

Madelaine's mouth curled into a grin. "Oh, I'm not saying he won't get the letter. I said don't expect a reply."

Heloise flinched with hurt. "Why do you hate me?"

"I don't hate you." The prioress looked surprised. "What a notion."

Sister Madelaine's health was deteriorating, although she had good periods when she spent ten hours a day at her table with accounts and correspondence. At other times, however, she seemed on the brink of wasting away, and then Sister Blanche would insist that she move into the infirmary and be nursed with fortifying broths and meat dishes. Heloise took over the ledgers and conducted the children's classes. Astrane, cold as ice, assisted her.

Christmas was bad. Night after night, Heloise suffered from sleeplessness; rather, she rested well enough during the early part of the evening, but after getting up for the night office, she could not fall back to sleep. Thoughts racing in circles, she worried herself sick about her husband and son. Or she fretted over the laziness and inefficiency of the nuns. Lady Alais, in her opinion, was one of the worst offenders because, as abbess, she should be setting an example for her flock. Instead, she pushed nearly all the administrative duties onto Sister Madelaine and concerned herself exclusively with courting aged, wealthy barons who might wish to make donations for the good of their souls. These efforts, Heloise had to admit, were not entirely unsuccessful, and it was true that in the past year Argenteuil had collected several bequests and two extremely wealthy novices. Still. There was more to being an abbess than accumulating bequests. And now, during the season of the Lord's Nativity, Lady Alais suddenly burned with a passion for travel. On the pretext of making a Christmas pilgrimage to Vézelay, she had set off for her home in Burgundy, where her niece was being married to a third cousin of the duke. By Epiphany she still had not returned, and Astrane said, uncharitably but no doubt truthfully, that they should count themselves fortunate if they saw her before Candlemas.

One morning after chapter meeting, Heloise went to the river and stood stock-still on the rock. The wind scudding off the water was fierce, and she did not linger long. In the distance, across the bend in the river, she could see the roofs of Saint-Denis looming against the cloudless sky. It comforted her a little to know that beneath one of those roofs lived Abelard. He was not so far away, after all, very close really.

After vespers, the portress's girl came to tell her that a Lord Jourdain was waiting in the guest parlor. Heloise bounded to her feet and then, with an effort to control her steps, she sedately followed the girl out the cloister gate, cursing her slowness.

He stood before the hearth, his cloak bundled clumsily about his waist. The first thing she noticed was that he had put on weight, the second that he had aged. She had always thought of him as a boy, but he certainly was not that now. Probably he had not been a boy for some time, but she had failed to notice.

"Sister Heloise, friend—" He came forward, his eyes gleaming gently.

Blinking away tears, she kissed him on both cheeks. "Ah, ah," was all she could say. They stood awkwardly before the fire, shifting from one foot to the other and murmuring stiff remarks about the weather and each other's health.

She had to bite her tongue to keep from asking about Abelard. Finally she said, "Tell me, what is happening in the world?" Her arms were trembling.

Jourdain sighed. "He took his vows three days after you."

"Three?" She swallowed. "You mean he has been at Saint-Denis since September?"

"Of course."

"Please, Jourdain. Forgive me for asking questions."

"I forgive you." He grinned.

"How does my Lord? Have you seen him? Did he speak of me?"

"Whoa, lady. I saw him yesterday. He asked me to— Look, Heloise, I have something for you."

Unwinding his cloak, he drew out an untidy ball of white fur. Heloise began to laugh. "I have no use for furs here," she said, and then she saw the fluffy mound twitch. "Why, it's a—"

"It's asleep. Little mite."

"Oh, Jourdain," she gasped. "Oh look, it's a sweet little thing."

"It is that."

Taking the dog from him, she cradled it in the crook of her arm. It opened black eyes and gazed up at her. She stared, transfixed. It nuzzled its nose against her breast and then closed its eyes again. "Poor little thing is tired." Heloise bent to kiss the dog's head. "It's a babe."

"Two weeks, I think. Lady, something you would like to know—"

Smiling happily, she looked up.

Jourdain said, "The dog is from Master Peter."

"Oh." She closed her eyes and opened them. "Oh, Jourdain, he thinks of me." Helpless with happiness, she sank down on a bench and let the tears gush out of her eyes. She lifted the dog to her wet face and pressed her lips to its nose, paws, ears. "Jourdain, you don't know—"

"I know," he said softly. "Lady, it's good to see you smile." He sat down next to her and scratched behind the dog's right ear.

"Jourdain, is my lord well?"

"Completely recovered."

"And happy?"

"It appeared so."

"Did he sound cheerful?"

"I suppose."

She turned impatient. "What does that mean? 'I suppose.' I'm sorry. I only meant is he his old self? You know."

Hesitantly, Jourdain answered, "Lady, that is too much to expect. And remember, he's a monk now. All I can tell you is that he smiled and even made a few jests."

"About what?" For an hour, she pumped him about the smallest details of his visit to Saint-Denis, and when there was no more to learn, she fell silent and stroked the puppy. It sat up, wobbly-legged, and looked around. "What shall I name him?"

"Her," Jourdain corrected. "It's a she."

"All right. She. I think I shall name her Aristotle."

Jourdain hooted. "Lady. I said the dog is a female."

"Well, I don't care. I would name her for a great philosopher, so she must be called Aristotle. Or Plato."

"Aristotle. She doesn't look like a Plato."

"That's what I thought." Heloise giggled. She set the dog on the ground. It waddled a few steps, looked around indecisively, and squatted, leaving a sizable puddle. "Oh, look at that!" she cried in amazement. "How cunning."

"Heloise, you are silly. It's not a toy."

They laughed together. Aristotle snorted twice and began to root furiously among the rushes.

"I have another bit of news," Jourdain said. "Your uncle."

"Tell me."

"Condemned and banished. The bishop's court took away his canonry and all his prebends. Everything. He can never return to Paris."

She turned her face away, trying to think of something to say. "Where has he gone?"

"One of his farms near Melun. With Agnes. He won't suffer much. More's the pity."

Heloise slid off the bench and went to get the dog. "He shall roast in the flames of hell for all eternity. That is for certain."

Jourdain nodded. He said slowly, "Lady, I must leave you now. It's growing late. I—I don't know when we shall meet again. I leave for Troyes."

"Jourdain."

"The Count of Champagne has taken me into his service. It's all arranged."

"Of course. I remember." She went to him, the dog resting on her hip, and gripped his hand. "God give you peace."

They talked for a few minutes longer, and then Jourdain was gone. Heloise cuddled Aristotle in her arms, took a big breath, and stamped toward the cloister gate. The sky was black and starry. She had missed supper, but it did not matter. Cutting through the cloister, she hurried down the north walk in the direction of the kitchen. Cook must give her a bowl of milk for Aristotle.

15 🌿

MADELAINE SAT MOTIONLESS at her table, parchment piled at her elbow. Her eyes were sunk deep in their sockets.

"You can expect no help from Sister Astrane today," Madelaine murmured wearily. "She's ill."

"I heard."

"Lady abbess is in a fret. With Astrane in bed, who will take the pouch to Saint-Denis?"

Heloise's scalp prickled under the wimple. She said lightly, "One of the lay brothers from the farmyard." Every Tuesday, Astrane delivered official correspondence to the abbey, and, as the abbess's pet, she was the only nun at Argenteuil to regularly leave the convent. Once, in desperation, Heloise had asked her to inquire about Abelard. Astrane had given her a look of such disgust that Heloise had flinched and turned away. She never asked again.

Sister Madelaine was shaking her head. "There will be documents to sign in the abbess's name. I must go myself." She glanced at Heloise. "Or send someone literate."

Heloise said nothing. Madelaine was in no condition to travel; she could barely stumble from the dormitory to the schoolroom. The prioress began to fumble with a stack of bills. After ten minutes of grumbling, she scratched her chin and told Heloise that she might go.

"I must be crazy," Madelaine muttered.

"God's pardon, Sister," stammered Heloise, "but I am perfectly capable of conducting the business satisfactorily."

"That wasn't what I meant."

"Well, what did you mean?"

"Don't do anything to disgrace us. Promise me."

"Thank you," she said, flushing, "for your confidence."

In the late morning, it began to drizzle, and by the time Heloise reached the abbey of Saint-Denis, the rain had settled into a steady downpour. Her veil hung like a sodden rag about her shoulders. The royal abbey was constructed very much like Argenteuil, but it was vastly larger. Over five hundred monks were in residence. One of them was Brother Peter Abelard. Heloise dismissed the lay brother who had ridden her there and presented herself to the porter. Soon a monk came and led her through a maze of passageways to Abbot Adam's offices. She was ordered to wait on a bench until one of the abbot's assistants could see her.

Clasping the leather pouch to her stomach, Heloise tucked her skirt around her ankles and pretended to keep her eyes demurely on the floor. Somewhere within these walls, he was reading or writing. Or praying. She wanted to scream his name aloud. From the corner of her eye, she inspected every monk who passed. The door leading to the abbot's secretariat opened and closed regularly. From inside came a steady hum of voices. Two merchants brushed by, looked at her with curiosity, and sat on a bench near the window.

"Sweet Jesu," she heard one of them say. "An afternoon's wait just to collect fifty livres." His companion laughed.

Heloise wanted to be sick. Our Father who art in heaven, she thought. Just once. Let me see him once more. That wasn't very much to ask. God, why did you bring me here if I can't see him? In everything you taunt me.

Somebody called her name.

She rose and shot forward into the offices. The room, stifling, smelled of ink. A dozen monks sat at tables. Coins clinked. Heloise sat down tentatively before a hook-nosed monk who did not look at her. He took the pouch and dumped its contents on the table. With ink-stained fingers, he carefully examined each piece of parchment and laid it to one side. Abruptly, he glanced up. He said, "The miller at Aventin-sur-Seine owed you two hogsheads of wheat on St. John's Day. One is listed."

"He brought only one," Heloise said slowly. "He promised the other at Lammas."

The monk scowled. "See that you collect it."

"Yes, my lord."

He picked up the empty pouch and shook it. "Lady abbess owes twenty-six livres interest on her loan from the bishop. Where is it?"

Heloise reddened. "I know nothing about it. I'm sorry."

"Now, listen to this. The bishop will tolerate no further excuses from Abbess Alais. Tell her that."

"Yes, my lord. I'll tell her."

He gave her a sheaf of receipts to sign, and then he filled up the pouch with mail. When she was finished, he said, perfunctorily, without meeting her eyes, "God be with you, Sister."

"God be with you, Brother." Outside in the reception hall, she tried to remember how to get back to the courtyard. Her head was pounding. She had not known that Lady Alais had borrowed from the bishop. That was foolish. And to renege on the interest was equally stupid. Heloise turned down a passageway and saw a sullen sky ahead. When she realized that the passage opened into the cloister, she wheeled and hastily retraced her steps. Stalking toward her was a tall monk surrounded by a cluster of chattering novices. Something about the set of his shoulders made her tense up. A smile began to form at the corners of her mouth. Abelard's eyes met hers and slid past the side of her head. Suddenly he was behind her, and she could hear him saying, "St. Augustine, you know, was of two minds on that point."

The stone walls heaved around her. Blindly, she lifted one foot and then the other, not caring where they took her. He had pretended not to know her; he had looked at her as if she were a stranger. She walked on until she came out into the yard. The cobbles, slippery from the rain, made her stumble. The cathedral bells began to roar nones.

"I must get home," she thought. "Ceci will have forgotten to feed the dog."

The road through the forest oozed with mud; the trees formed a dripping canopy over her head. *Why did you do that? O God, cruel to me in everything. O merciless dispenser of mercy.* A little while later, she told herself that God had spoken to her through Ceci earlier that day. Ceci had told her that Abelard had not loved her—she must forget him. She had not believed it, but now God had forced her to see with her own eyes. She began to weep.

When she reached Argenteuil, it was beginning to rain again, a sticky drizzle. Her mood black, she went up to the dormitory and changed into a clean habit. Later, in the schoolroom, she found Madelaine reading the Bible. "Did Sister Cecilia remember to feed Aristotle?"

"Yes."

"Good." She licked her lips. "Lady Alais is in trouble at Saint-Denis."

Madelaine screwed up her mouth and began to laugh. "My sweet child," she said finally, "Lady Alais has been in trouble for twenty-five years."

* * *

After matins, she woke from a dream, still tightly wrapped in a feeling of intense warmth and softness. Drowsy, she squirmed to her stomach, trying to hold on to it, whatever it was. Aristotle, curled beside her ankles, twitched his tail restlessly. Under the covers, she grazed her fingers under the curve of her breast and up over one nipple. She tried to remember what the dream had been about, but it was gone. She knew what it was. Something wanted to explode inside her. If she could fall back to sleep quickly, the sensation would pass without the necessity of her doing anything about it.

Hastily, she wrenched her hands away from her breasts and clenched them under the pillow. She hated her body, which insisted on torturing her during the nights. Wide-awake now, she tried to think of something else, but only pictures of Abelard in his black gown came to her, and him she could not bear to consider. The only way she could permit him into her thoughts was to think of him as dead. She tested the idea: her beloved was and now he is not. *Abelard is dead.* In a way, she wished it were true, so that she might grieve for him, as one normally did for the dead. No comfort there, though. She had seen him surrounded by young men, watched his arms and legs swing toward her, heard him speak of St. Augustine. Thinking about him now, she decided that he looked happy. Or at least he did not appear unhappy. He still walked like a king.

Two beds away, someone coughed. Heloise reached down, fumbled for the dog, and tucked the curly body under her chin. She nuzzled her face against Aristotle's nose.

"Sweet heart," she whispered, "my sweet little love." In the dark, Aristotle licked her throat. Heloise closed her eyes.

Queen Adelaide gave birth to a second son. In honor of the new prince, who had been christened Louis after his father, Sainte-Marie of Argenteuil conducted a special thanksgiving mass. A silver chalice, made in the crafts workshop, was sent to the Cité Palace, with a letter promising that the nuns would include Prince Louis in their prayers. Heloise composed the letter and copied it on a good grade of parchment.

She no longer hoped for letters from Abelard or Denise, although during that autumn she did receive her first piece of correspondence, a message from Jourdain. As if apologetic for his long silence, he wrote sheets and sheets describing the court at Troyes, the marvelous poets and minstrels, and one entire page devoted to his friend Peter of Mont-boissier, who had recently been elected abbot of Cluny at the astonishing age of twenty-seven. Even though Jourdain wrote little about himself, the cheerfulness of the letter lifted Heloise's spirits in that it re-established her link to the outside world. To hear news, to know that people still sang and laughed and were amused, shivered a thrill through her. She read and reread the pages, always finding some item that she had passed over during previous readings. For days she dwelt on Peter of Montboissier. How young to be an abbot—he must be as unusual as Jourdain had always insisted. And he was a cheerful young man, Jourdain wrote, gay of heart and full of love for life. How a person could be gay in a monastery was hard for Heloise to imagine, but she decided that she would make an attempt to emulate Abbot Peter of Cluny. Some days it worked, but it was a matter of constantly reminding herself.

Just when she was successfully managing to put Abelard out of her mind for days at a time, word of him reached her ears in a roundabout way. On a visit to Saint-Denis, Astrane learned that Abelard had left the abbey and was now teaching at a priory near the city of Provins in Champagne. He had been, Astrane revealed to Lady Alais, requested to leave.

Cornering Astrane near the abbess's apartment, Heloise stretched out her arms and refused to allow the girl to pass. "Why did he go?" she demanded. "I want to know everything you heard."

Astrane sniffed. "I don't carry tales, Sister."

"You've already carried this one. Now I want the details. Why did he leave?" Heloise lowered her arms.

"Truly, I know nothing," Astrane muttered. "He was at odds with the abbot. And others."

"About what, in God's name?"

"He said the monks were lewd and filthy-minded. You know, worldly. He complained to the abbot of their foul morals."

Heloise gasped. That did not sound like Abelard. "Foul morals," she repeated. "Is that true?"

"How do I know?" Astrane shrugged. "But Brother Abelard charged thusly."

"And Abbot Adam? What did he say to all of this?"

"Don't ask me." Her eyes were icy blue points. "But they say that he called Master Abelard an odious burden to Saint-Denis. In any case, the abbot has sent him away." She smirked. "Everybody disliked him. They say."

She limped away, and Heloise let her go. A few weeks later, Madelaine told her that Abelard's new priory was called Maisoncelles-en-Brie. He had set up a school there, and students were flocking from all over Europe. Heloise, realizing that Madelaine had made a special effort to obtain this information, asked no further questions. It was enough, in a sense, to know that Abelard must be content. He was a born teacher. Now he would have his admiring young men again and, she hoped, the self-assurance that had made him so glorious. She merely said to Madelaine, "These charges of immorality made against Saint-Denis, are they true?"

Madelaine's eyes flickered. "Mayhap," she answered, and left the room.

Heloise was to remember Madelaine's admission, because the first scandal at Argenteuil occurred shortly afterward. A novice named Isabella was surprised behind the altar with a kitchen scullion, one of the lads who had worked for Cook since he could walk and who was now about thirteen. It was said that Isabella's skirts had been around her waist when she and the boy were caught, but Isabella swore on relics that she had not known the boy carnally. Lady Alais took the easy way out, merely switching Isabella and dismissing the kitchen boy. The matter might have ended there with nobody the wiser, but it did not. The morning after the boy had been sent away, Isabella hanged herself. The body was discovered hanging from a limb in the apple orchard. Plainly, there was no way that Lady Alais could conceal this unfortunate tragedy from the bishop, who threatened an investigation of the abbess's affairs. The promised inquiries did not come, however, and gradually the prospect of danger receded.

Of course, the incident was not forgotten, and the nuns chewed over Isabella's escapades for a long time. Heloise closed her ears, fornication being a subject that she dared not think about lest she drown in her own longings. Throughout November, while Sister Madelaine sickened in the infirmary and Lady Alais remained incommunicado for days at a stretch in her apartment, Heloise tried to put the convent's financial affairs in order. The window shutters in the schoolroom had blown out during a storm weeks earlier, but the abbess had not bothered to have them repaired. At Madelaine's table, Heloise flexed her numbed fingers and wished for a charcoal brazier. Even Aristotle, with her coat of fleecy curls, shivered under her skirts. Heloise's task appeared hopeless, as the abbess had borrowed and mortgaged and run the institution deeply into debt. She could see that no help, or even cooperation, would be forthcoming from Lady Alais. Confronted with figures documenting her poor judgment, she merely smiled fuzzily and sighed. Often Heloise smelled wine on her breath.

On a Friday morning, angry that Astrane had not yet appeared, Heloise went to the abbess's apartment to fetch her. Most of the time, Astrane was willing to drill the children in Latin and rhetoric, and Heloise had come to rely upon her. The cloister stood deserted, and the wind hissed along the north walk. Heloise was tempted to run, but she settled for a fast trot and hoped no one would notice. In the passageway leading to the abbess's chambers, it was not much warmer than out of doors. The reception parlor was empty, but the door to the apartment stood ajar. Abruptly, Astrane's voice bellowed hoarsely, "I'm sick of this. Don't touch me."

"Sweet," Lady Alais wheezed. "Sweet, I meant nothing."

Heloise, who had been about to knock, stopped her arm in midair and rocked back on her heels. She had never heard anyone shout at Lady Alais, and that was what Astrane was doing. Uneasy, she ducked back against the wall.

"You stink like a swineherd," Astrane croaked with a short laugh. A goblet crashed to the floor. "Get up."

Her face burning, Heloise stood rooted to the spot. Astrane had always been bad-tempered, but no one had ever spoken to the abbess with such disrespect.

The voice of Lady Alais rose to a sickening whine. "Come back to bed. I won't touch you, I promise."

"No. Get dressed."

"Ah, sweet. I just want to hold you."

Astrane began to mutter. "Disgusting old pig. You make me want to vomit."

"Please, lovey."

The pleading, slurred and groggy, made Heloise recoil. She sidled back a step, frantically wondering how she could get away without being heard. It sounded as if Lady Alais were crying.

She whimpered, "You used to love me. Why don't you love me?" Astrane was silent. "Come, it shall feel so lovely. And then I'll get dressed. I promise."

"You promised me an embroidered shift, and you never gave it."

"Why, pussy, I was going to give it today. You shall have your pretty shift. You know that I would do anything for you." Lady Alais's voice trailed slowly away, toward an inner room. "Come, puss, you needn't take off your habit."

Feet shuffled, and then it was quiet. Heloise, nauseated, nosed into the cloister and gasped at the icy air. Two of her pupils were chasing Aristotle with a dead rat. One of them, shrieking, threw the rat at Aristotle's feet.

"Hie!" Heloise called crossly. "Don't do that." Aristotle grabbed the rat and shook it. "She could get sick from that filthy thing."

She scooped up the dog and carried her into the schoolroom. God in heaven, Lady Alais and Astrane. Once Abelard had told her that nuns coupled with each other, but she had laughed at him. "Mayhap in evil convents," she had retorted, "but such things never happen at Argenteuil." She slumped against Madelaine's table and tried to remember what else Abelard had said, but her brain refused to work. All she could think of was the abbess and Astrane, in bed with their tongues in each other. The insides of her thighs throbbed. She rushed to her feet and began to march nervously up and down the room, willing the disturbing images from her head. Nothing had prepared her for this. The worst was Lady Alais's pitiful voice, wheedling, begging a girl thirty-five years her junior. God's eyes, Lady Alais would burn in hell for this. She must have seduced Astrane as a child. Heloise rubbed her hands together, scalded by the thought. Yes, Lady Alais had done a wicked thing. Astrane had been a mere babe when the abbess got her, a crippled little maiden whose parents had sent her away. Surely she could not be blamed.

Grimly, she pushed back from the table and hurried to the infirmary.

Madelaine sprawled against the pillows, reading.

"Sister, how do you feel this morning?" Heloise pulled up a stool and sat down. Now that she had come, she wondered if it would be wise to tell Madelaine. The old woman deserved peace.

"The same," said Madelaine. "No better, no worse." She laid the volume of St. Jerome on the coverlet and studied Heloise's face. "You look tired."

"No. No."

Madelaine pointed to the open book. "St. Jerome writes that the concept of reincarnation was widely accepted among the early Christians. Strange."

"Origen mentions reincarnation," Heloise said. "He thought that certain scriptural passages could only be explained in that light."

Madelaine leaned forward, grinning a little. "Then in my next life I wish to return as pope."

"Naturally." Heloise grinned back. "And I shall be the queen of France." The grin died, and she glanced around to make sure the infirmarian was out of earshot. She gritted her teeth. "Sister, something bad has happened." She did not know how to start.

Madelaine barked impatiently. "Well, hurry up and say it. Bad news can't wait."

"I—I went to Lady Alais's apartment. The door was half open. I—"

"Come on," Madelaine said.

"Astrane was with her. I overheard them talking." She threw Madelaine an anguished look. "I couldn't help it, Sister. The door was open."

Madelaine said nothing.

"Do I make myself clear?"

"Perfectly." Madelaine's voice whistled.

"What should I do?" Heloise cried.

"Nothing."

"You knew of this?"

"Aye."

The breath went out of Heloise. "Sister Madelaine."

"Do nothing," Madelaine murmured. "Forget everything you heard."

"But I can't." She swelled with anger at Madelaine. "What's the matter with you, Sister? This is—"

"Heloise. I order you. Now go back to the schoolroom."

Heloise stood, knees trembling. "I don't see why I should obey you. It is against every law of heaven and earth. I don't see why."

"You will. Someday."

"You must hear him," Ceci was saying. "I swear, he sings like a nightingale."

Heloise sat on a bench in the chapter house, blowing her nose. If only she could stop her running nose and eyes, she might be able to enjoy Christmas. It seemed bad luck that she should be sniffling during the only real season of festivity at the convent. She said to Ceci, "We've never had jongleurs before."

"Lady Alais said we could go."

"Lady abbess is not herself lately." She had been surprised when the abbess announced the minstrel's presence in the guesthouse and gave permission for the nuns to attend his performances.

"Besides," Ceci added, "Sister Judith told me they used to have minstrels at Christmas. In King Philip's time. So it's nothing new."

Heloise grunted. She did not believe it wise for Ceci to be exposed to minstrels. Repeatedly, the girl had been punished for mingling with visitors who stopped at the convent. Many of the travelers were pious pilgrims, but the portress did not interview each person she admitted, and some of them were rough and coarse. Once Ceci had picked up a lewd jest from an English knight and, failing to understand its implications, had innocently repeated it in the dormitory. On that occasion, she had been punished with a two-week fast.

"Please, Heloise"—she clutched Heloise's wrist—"there's no harm in it. And he's leaving tonight."

It was one of those crystal nights with a blizzard of stars flickering high overhead. A bonfire sputtered near the porch of the gatehouse. The crowd stamped about restlessly while the minstrel tuned his lute. He was young, no more than a pretty boy. His green velvet cloak was of a good cut, and over his straw-colored curls he had pulled a cap with some kind of exotic feather. He had an air of breeding.

Ceci nudged her. "Raimon was trained at the court of Eble of Ventadour," she whispered.

"How do you know?"

"He told me." Her voice had a cocky edge that Heloise disliked.

Heloise swiveled her head in exasperation. "Ceci, when did you—"

"Shhh." She patted Heloise's arm.

By the light of the fire, the jongleur rolled his pick across the lute strings. He began with a Provençal poem about Raymond of Saint-Gilles and Bohemond and the great crusade. Adventure. The siege of Antioch, the capture of Jerusalem. Ida, margravine of Austria. More adventure. Without realizing it, Heloise began to smile. Afterward, the crowd clapped and whistled, and somebody shouted, "Let's have *Chanson de Roland,* boy."

The jongleur ignored the request, apparently preferring to make his own selections. He broke into a merry little tune, "I rose up yestermorn, before the sun was shining bright . . ." His voice was husky and sweet, and he played tolerably well. Before long, the crowd, conquered, was clapping in rhythm and tapping feet on the freezing cobbles. Ceci, weaving back and forth, hummed gently. A well-dressed matron called to the jongleur, "Can you play something of Abelard's?"

Heloise lurched against Ceci's shoulder, but the girl did not notice.
The jongleur bowed gallantly. "Madame," he shouted, "I can play
anything you like of Abelard's. Name it."

"The 'Dawn Song.' " She smiled provocatively.

Snapping her eyes shut, Heloise listened and let the tears roll from
under her lashes.

Ceci poked her. "Heloise, isn't that pretty? Raimon says that Abelard's songs are so popular that even villeins sing them."

"Shhh."

When the compline bell rang, the nuns began to walk rapidly toward
the cloister gate. The jongleur drank a few sips from a wineskin and
started a sad, slow *canso*. Ceci stood stock-still until Heloise tugged at
her sleeve.

"I'm coming in a little while," she protested.

"You're coming now." It was an effort to make her voice firm.

"Heloise, please."

"Holy Mother, what's the matter with you? Are you crazy?"

Ceci nodded. "All right." Her voice was sullen.

The evening office: Psalm 3 and after it Psalm 94, chanted simply.
They did the Ambrosian hymn, followed by six additional psalms with
antiphons, and then Lady Alais read three lessons. It went on, inter-
minably. Heloise moved her lips automatically, her mind on Abelard
and the turret room in the Rue des Chantres.

Afterward, she went to bed and lay awake until matins, Aristotle
curled under her arm. At the far end of the dormitory, a group of sisters
were sitting on Sister Blanche's bed, chattering and drinking wine. The
jongleur had made everyone giddy; suddenly, keeping the rules did not
seem very important. Half intending to reprimand them, Heloise got up
and went over. Before she reached them, she had changed her mind. It
was none of her business. Sister Blanche, not a worldly woman, had
been a nun for thirty years and infirmarian more than twenty. If she
wanted to drink wine in the dorter at Christmas, she knew very well the
penance for such an infraction. Heloise felt that discipline had grown
very lax at Argenteuil, with Madelaine dying and Lady Alais tipsy
much of the time.

The nuns were talking about jongleurs they had seen, or heard of,
and debating the virtues of their favorite troubadour poets. Heloise
stood by them for a while, sipping the wine when it passed to her. When
the conversation turned to love, she left. Passing Ceci's bed, she noticed

that it was empty. Shivery, she dived under the covers and hugged Aristotle, who had not stirred. Finally, she dozed.

In the morning, nose still dripping, she paid her daily call on Madelaine before shambling to the schoolroom for classes. At midmorning, she sent one of the children to fetch more handkerchiefs from the wardrober. She felt badly, but her nose was only half the problem. She knew why. Today was the eve of Christmas, her son's natal day. He would be three today. No, she corrected herself, actually he was born on Christmas Day. But her pains had begun on the previous evening and in her mind she ran it all together. She wondered if he missed her. Probably he thought of Denise as his mother. Something in her gut flopped over.

The children were running around, smacking each other and pulling hair. She bundled them off to Sister Judith for their embroidery lesson and settled down at Madelaine's table. There were letters to answer. A baron from Compiègne wished to enroll his daughter as a novice. Would Argenteuil be willing to accept a small gift of money now and, on his death, a sizable donation to cover the installation of a rose window in the abbey church?

Heloise did not see how Lady Alais could refuse the offer, even though she knew that this particular baron had an evil reputation; he had been at odds with the Church for years and once had been excommunicated for pillaging a church in Normandy. Tainted money, she thought. No matter. Lady Alais would take his daughter. Heloise tossed the letter aside, remembering Astrolabe. What would become of him with no mother or father? She could not imagine Denise reading Plato or Seneca to him.

Astrane hobbled in, looking sour. She was carrying a tablet and stylus. Heloise forced a pleasant smile. She had had a hard time feeling comfortable around Astrane since she had discovered her relationship with the abbess. "God's greetings, Sister."

Astrane mumbled in her throat. "Sister Heloise," she said, scanning the tablet, "the sacristan informs me that Sister Cecilia has not reported for work this morning." Quickly, she darted a sharp gaze around the room, as if Heloise might be concealing Ceci in a cupboard.

"Isn't this her day in the infirmary?"

"I've looked there." She rapped the stylus against the tablet. "And Sister Marguerite missed chapter meeting. And Sister—"

Heloise cut her off. "I've seen no one but Sister Madelaine and the children since we broke fast."

* * *

That night, the nuns sipped spiced wine and ate almond cakes, their traditional holiday treats, and went to midnight mass. Argenteuil celebrated Christ's birth with three masses—midnight, dawn, and Christmas Day. In Heloise's opinion, the proper for midnight mass with its five chants, along with the eight great "O" antiphons sung at vespers during Advent, was some of the most moving church music ever written. Abelard once told her that it dated from the tenth century, but recently she had found evidence that it went back much farther, probably to the reign of Pope Vitalian in the seventh century.

In the cloister, Heloise joined the line snaking into the church. Behind her, somebody laughed. "I like snow for Christmas—it doesn't feel like Christmas without snow." Heloise bundled her hands into her sleeves. She wondered if Astrane had finally caught Ceci napping. It would mean another punishment, because Astrane went strictly by the rule book.

The church was full. People stood in the aisles and sat in the transept. As Heloise passed Lady Alais, the abbess grabbed her arm.

"Sister," she whispered, "would you mind waiting after mass. I wish to speak with you."

Heloise took her place in the choir stalls. It was hard to concentrate. She kept thinking of Christmas at Notre Dame and Agnes's roast goose, Christmas mass in Brittany with her belly cramping and the muffled snow coming down flake by flake. *Dominus dixit ad me.* Why did Denise never reply? She wondered if Denise hated her, and decided that she must. *The Lord said to me: Thou art my son, this day have I begotten thee. Gloria patri et filio.*

The introit completed, they began the gradual. Abelard, that first Christmas after he moved into Fulbert's house. She remembered that they had walked home from Notre Dame, all smiles, and Jourdain had been with them and he had kissed her. Happy times, she thought, too lovely to last. That jongleur—Raimon was what Ceci had called him—that jongleur sang well, but nobody could sing Abelard's songs as well as Abelard. Nobody but the angels. *In splendoribus sanctorum. In the splendor of saints, from the womb before the day-star have I begotten thee.* Thoughts of Abelard and his songs seethed in her mind. *Ah God, ah God, how quickly comes the dawn.* Oh, how quickly came the end of their loving. *Gloria patri et filio.* The nuns rose and filed from the choir.

Near the door, Heloise dropped out of line and waited for Lady Alais. When the last of the women had disappeared up the dorter stairs, the abbess approached. Her face looked grim. Tonight she was sober.

"Child," she said, "Sister Heloise, what precisely do you know about the whereabouts of Sister Cecilia?"

"Well—nothing, my lady. I've not seen her today."

"No one has seen her today."

"Oh." Heloise stood motionless, a sick pounding beginning in her temples.

"When did you see her last? And where?" The abbess sighed impatiently. "Think carefully."

Heloise knew that Ceci had not been in her bed after compline. Had she attended matins? Heloise tried to remember. "She was in the yard last night, listening to the jongleur. And then we came to compline together."

"And after that?" Lady Alais still looked grim.

"I've not seen her since. Don't worry, my lady. She must be here. Where could she have gone?" Suddenly the jongleur's feathered cap battered into her head. Ceci knew a lot about him. He had come from Ventadour. She leaned toward Lady Alais and feigned unconcern. "Sister Cecilia is mischievous, you know that."

Lady Alais looked away. After a silence, she said to Heloise, "Tomorrow after chapter meeting—we must search the entire convent and grounds. Every corner, every inch. Do you hear?"

"Yes, my lady." Heloise knew it would be a waste of time. By now Ceci must be leagues away, riding pillion behind a jongleur in a green cloak. She followed Lady Alais into the cloister, her hands shaking.

In the early spring after Ceci had been gone several months, Madelaine finally died. Heloise was elected prioress, a foregone decision since she had been handling Madelaine's duties for nearly two years. There were halfhearted grumbles, of course, some of the elderly sisters declaring that Heloise was far too young for such a high position. But her experience could not be denied.

Once, Heloise went to the woods, to a place where she recalled that violets and lilies grew, and she picked a nosegay to lay below Madelaine's cross. After that, she made a habit of bringing flowers every Sunday morning, for no other reason than that it made her feel better. With neither Madelaine nor Ceci there, she felt stripped. She told herself that she had never loved either of them that much, Madelaine the stern taskmaster, Ceci the malcontent. She hoped that Ceci was happy now, wherever she might be, and she prayed for Madelaine's soul. Still, she cried. It was no use trying to deny that everybody she had cared about had left her—Abelard, her son, and now the prioress and Ceci. And Fulbert. Once she had cared about him. She wondered if he were still alive, he and Agnes together in their farmhouse.

On Maundy Thursday, she received a thick letter from Jourdain and suddenly realized that he had not entered her mind for months. Instead of opening the packet immediately, she slid it into her girdle, and in the late afternoon she went to the rock. She was unsure why she put off reading the letter, except that pleasures came so infrequently that she liked to prolong them. If only Abelard had written to her, she would have been the happiest woman in the world. What he wrote would not have mattered, even if he had scribbled the alphabet. Merely to know that he remembered her would have been enough.

Wreaths of clouds drifted away toward Saint-Denis. Out on the Seine burst a shaft of sunlight, gauzy and radiant, staining the surface a hazy gold, and Heloise could see the sky reflected in the water. There was something ghostly, deceptive, about the way the light fell at Argenteuil—silently it softened and rounded the contours of objects so that one seemed to be gazing at the world through a mist of diaphanous fabric. She kept seeing a small, unhappy girl, dreaming, and she thought bitterly, Well, I have no illusions now.

Aristotle sprinted headlong down the embankment and sniffed cautiously at the water. When a frog croaked, she began to yap furiously. Laughing, Heloise shouted, "Go get it, beastie! Go on!" The dog looked at her uncertainly. "Aaah, what kind of a fighter are you?" She hoisted her onto her hip and climbed up the rock. "Sit. Aristotle, sit."

After a dozen repetitions, Aristotle gave in, reluctantly. She hunkered on her hindquarters and stared out at the water. "Good girl, good Aristotle." The dog rarely left Heloise's heels and even tried to follow her into church for the offices. Since this was strictly forbidden, Heloise usually tied her up. She was a plump little creature, probably because Heloise overfed her.

Smiling, Heloise nudged her with a toe. "Hullo, sweeting. A long fast is what you need. That's right—a fast." She took out the letter, breaking its seal with her thumbnail. The first part was devoted to Count Thibaut and some insult he had received from Count Ralph of Vermandois, who was King Louis's cousin. Since Heloise knew nothing of the feud, she could make little sense of its significance. If there was any. Jourdain sometimes liked to include trivia if they were sufficiently titillating. More gossip: William the Troubadour had installed a leman in his palace at Poitiers. His wife had withdrawn to Fontevrault Abbey, where she died of a broken heart. Heloise laughed skeptically. Jourdain could be terribly melodramatic. Broken heart indeed. No doubt the duchess had some bad fish.

At the bottom of the sheet, her eye caught the words "Master Peter." She skipped over the Duchess of Aquitaine and got to Abelard. Jourdain explained that he had written a book on the nature of God—*Discourse on the Trinity*. According to Jourdain, who said he had read the treatise several times, it was a distinguished piece of writing. Still.

When Heloise read the word "still," she sensed trouble. Apprehensive, she skimmed the page. Names of churchmen: Roscelin, Alberic of Rheims, Lotulph of Lombardy. The latter two, she recalled, had been fellow students when Abelard had studied at Laon under Anselm. They had been jealous of him. Why was Jourdain being so poky in getting to the point? She knew there must be one. On the next sheet there was a defense of Abelard's book—he was only trying to combine Christianity with human reason. His students demanded explanations.

"My dear friend," Jourdain went on, "Master Peter intended to say nothing heretical, nothing that is not already implied in the Church's teachings. But he has never been cautious, as you well know."

She knew. Spine stiffened, she raced on. These two enemies, Alberic and Lotulph, charged that Abelard had preached and written that there are three Gods. They had denounced him as a heretic.

"Oh God," Heloise moaned aloud. "When will you have done torturing this man? Leave him be, for pity's sake."

"Dear Heloise, he is summoned to a Church council at Soissons, in July I think, and ordered to bring his book with him. I see no cause for worry, friend; there are few who can debate with Peter Abelard and win. Besides, he wrote me that if there is anything in the tract that dissents from the faith, he will readily correct it." He had written Jourdain? Jealousy stabbed at her. "Set your mind at ease. There is nothing in the book to condemn him."

There was more. The *White Ship*, King Henry's royal vessel, had been wrecked off Barfleur, slammed into the rocks by a drunken helmsman—Prince William had drowned and now there was no heir to the throne of England. She folded the letter and tucked it into her sleeve. To accuse Abelard of heresy was utterly mad. These enemies of his must be very stupid men. Pulling Aristotle onto her lap, she sighed and closed her eyes.

16 ❧

THE NEW ABBOT OF Saint-Denis was short and fat, like a gargoyle with its chin encased in lard, and the top of his tonsured head barely reached Heloise's shoulder. His silk vestments were embroidered with stiff gold thread, and on each of his fingers flashed a precious stone. When the portress announced the arrival of Abbot Suger's retinue, Heloise had accompanied Lady Alais into the courtyard. The abbot's splendid livery, the gilded spurs and fringed saddles, rivaled anything that a king might own. Heloise stared with intense curiosity at the little man. She had seen him once, when he had come to visit Abelard after the castration. In the bedchamber of Abelard's quarters, she had served them goblets of wine, but Suger had not bothered to glance at her, as if she were a varlet. "God's greetings, my lady abbess," Suger said briskly. "A fine house you have here. Venerable. It was once a house for men, you know."

Lady Alais made a deep bow and sank to her knees. "Why, no, I—no, my lord. I didn't know." She went on, stammering, "Of course it has been owned by Saint-Denis for centuries, but Theodrada, er, the daughter of Charlemagne—"

Suger broke in tightly. "I know who Theodrada was." He stretched forth a chubby hand. For a moment, the abbess stared in confusion, unsure which ring to kiss, and finally settled on an enormous garnet. Standing, she gave the abbot one of her dimpled smiles, wrinkled up her nose, and fluttered her lashes helplessly. At fifty-five, Lady Alais was no longer adorable, the fact of which she was unaware.

Abbot Suger paid no attention to the dimples. "I hope you've made no elaborate preparations for my visit," he said, waving his escort to come forward. His rings flashed in the sunlight.

"Why, no, my lord," Lady Alais squeaked. She turned away and led him over the bleached cobbles toward the cloister gate. Groaning to herself, Heloise followed. For a week, the convent had been in a frenzy preparing for this day, and a sumptuous dinner would be served in the dining hall reserved for royalty and other distinguished guests. Kids had been roasting since dawn.

"This morning," he said sharply, "I will inspect the buildings, the tenant farms, and the vineyards. Later we shall review the convent's financial affairs."

"Yes, my lord."

"And of course I shall wish to view the sacred tunic and any other relics you own."

"Certainly, my lord abbot. We have the collarbone of St.–" Her voice trailed off; the abbot had turned his attention to his secretary, who was whispering into his ear.

The yard glistened under a hard blue sky. It was spring again, the universal season for pilgrimages, and the roadsides were choked with daisies and lemon cuckooflowers. Already visitors were coming in a steady trickle, and in a few weeks there would be hordes, palmers who had spent the winter grayness crowded around their hearths and shivering in dim garrets, now liberated, feet propelling them toward Saint-Denis, Compostela, Rocamadour. Mouths to feed, Heloise thought, and she wondered how Argenteuil would manage until the first harvest came in. If the squat little Abbot Suger could suggest solutions for their money problems, she would count this a blessed day. But she doubted it. The abbess was trotting to keep up with Suger, and Heloise took her elbow, steadying the old woman as she stumbled over the crannies between the cobbles. For a fat man, who virtually waddled, the abbot moved fast. Wheeling around, he suddenly said to Lady Alais, "Is that meat I smell cooking?"

She nodded.

He arched his brows. "During Lent, madame? Meat during Lent?"

"Oh. Well, in your honor, my lord. I thought—"

Suger grunted. Without saying anything more, he turned his back on the abbess again and began talking to his secretary. Heloise recalled that the abbot, a lover of luxury, wore undertunics of the finest wool and slept under fur coverlets and sheets of the most costly linen. Undoubtedly he would eat the kid when it appeared on his trencher. Lady Alais's mouth was crinkled into a wad of distress, and she kept rubbing her hands together as if scrubbing them. Heloise thought, I would not like to stand in her shoes today.

All that morning, as he had promised, Suger toured the convent and spoke with cellaress, infirmarian, and others, making comments when something displeased him. Mostly he found fault. This did not sit well with Sister Angelica and Sister Blanche, because, even though Lady Alais may have been guilty of laxity, they believed themselves performing their duties with the utmost efficiency, and by sext nearly everyone was smiling at Suger through clenched teeth. After he had poked his nose into every corner of the grounds, he called the nuns together in the chapter house and announced that anyone who had a complaint was obliged to stand up and voice it. This procedure was standard in all convents when the bishop made his annual inspection, and usually the nuns had plenty of petty gripes. Today every mouth was clamped shut. Heloise had never heard the chapter house so utterly silent.

After dinner, Suger closeted himself with Lady Alais in the abbess's quarters. In midafternoon, an anxious-looking Astrane appeared at the door of the schoolroom. Heloise, reading, jumped to her feet.

Astrane said, "My lady wants you."

"Is it bad?"

She shrugged. "He won't be happy until he crucifies her."

In the abbess's parlor, Suger sprawled in a high-backed chair, a sheet of parchment dangling from his right hand. Behind hovered the secretary, who occasionally handed him a paper or stooped to whisper into his ear. A goblet of wine waited on the trestle.

Lady Alais, her face pale, motioned Heloise to a stool in the corner; Astrane stayed by the door. Suger gave no indication that he noticed their arrival. He was speaking rapidly, now and then glancing down at the parchment sheet, which appeared to be some kind of dossier. He read a name aloud. "Isabella, daughter of Henry of Gramat. Novice." Lady Alais nodded. He said, "What about her?"

"She took her life."

"Where is she interred?"

Confused, Lady Alais cleared her throat. "Why, in the cemetery, my lord."

"A harlot in the abbey cemetery?"

"But my lord, no offense was proved. The girl was deranged."

Suger sniffed. "Suicide is a mortal sin. Dig up the grave and bury her outside the walls."

"Yes, my lord."

Suger contemplated the list again. "Custance, daughter of Estienne of Nangis."

"Died young," offered the abbess quickly.

"Of what cause?"

"A bloody flux."

Heloise remembered Sister Custance, the one with the voluptuous body. That was right, she had bled like a river, right through the straw pallet in the dorter, before someone had carried her to the infirmary. She had been young and extremely pretty. Heloise waited for Suger to go on to the next name, but he had swiveled in his chair and was listening to his secretary.

He jerked back to Lady Alais, face cold. "Abortion or miscarriage?" he asked dryly.

"I—" The abbess colored dark red. "My lord, nothing like that."

"My records show otherwise."

"There was some talk at the time," the abbess admitted. She looked away nervously. "But—"

The abbot took a mouthful of wine. "Very well. Let us go on. We can return to Sister Custance later." He consulted his list. "Sister Ida, daughter of William of Vézelay. What information can you give me concerning her?"

Lady Alais straightened her spine. "A priest raped her," she said without hesitation.

"Oh?"

"Father Jacques, as I recall." She glared at Suger. "During confession, and the poor girl—"

Suger didn't give her a chance. Leaning forward, he talked over her voice. "In the year of Our Lord 1094, there was a sister named Genevieve, bastard of the abbess of Notre Dame Sainte-Eulalie."

"Ten ninety-four," repeated the abbess carefully. "That was a long time ago."

"Come now. Were you not abbess at that time?"

"Yes, my lord." Paler than before, she began to chew the thumbnail of her left hand.

"Sister Genevieve gave birth to three brats in this convent." His eyes, unwavering, were stuck to the abbess's face.

She stared at him dumbly. "Surely not, my lord. I would remember that."

Suger took a long drink and set down the goblet with a crash. "Let us say your memory leaves a great deal to be desired. But somehow I had a feeling you would not remember that name." He actually smiled.

"I'm sorry, my lord."

Heloise hardly dared breathe. From the corner of her eye, she glanced at Astrane, who was staring openmouthed at the floor. Ten ninety-four. Surely the abbot could not go back in time much further than that; surely he would have to complete this interrogation soon. She licked her lips, waiting. She looked at the secretary with his smooth expression and ink-stained cassock. Suddenly she heard Suger bark, "Sister Cecilia, daughter of Baldwin of Larris." Astonished, Heloise tried to keep her face a blank. God's eyes, how did Suger know about Ceci? Lady Alais had not reported Ceci's disappearance. Heloise had argued against concealment, but Lady Alais always said that she would wait a few more months—perhaps Sister Cecilia would return. Still, Heloise was stunned. There was no way that Abbot Suger could have learned about Ceci, but, incredibly, he had. She heard him repeat Ceci's name.

Lady Alais said, "Missing," and snapped shut her mouth.

Heloise watched the secretary scribble on a tablet. "Missing," echoed Suger. "Under what circumstances?"

"I don't know, my lord. She vanished one night."

"When was that?"

"Christmas." The abbess's voice quivered.

"Christmas of what year? Brother Richwin, are you writing this down?"

Heloise had a feeling that Suger already knew the answer. It was several minutes before the abbess replied. At last she said, "Eleven twenty."

Suger said calmly, "My dear lady abbess, I make that three years ago."

"Two," she corrected him. "Two years and three months."

"Very well. May I inquire why Sister Cecilia's disappearance was not reported to Saint-Denis?"

"What do you mean?" the abbess asked, in exaggerated bewilderment. "It was reported."

"No," Suger murmured, "it was not. Not at the time it occurred. Nor at any time up to the present."

"Mayhap the letter was lost or mislaid."

"Mayhap," said the abbot, agreeable. "Mayhap not. The fact remains that a runaway occurred without notification of your superiors. Or, I might add, without notification of the nun's kin. This is a serious omission. But, of course, as you stated, sometimes your memory serves you ill, lady. Perchance it slipped your mind."

Lady Alais bristled. "Such matters are handled by the prioress. Sister

Madelaine was quite ill then. She died a few months later. It may have slipped her mind. No doubt that is what happened."

Suger seemed to accept her excuse. Folding the list, he handed it over his shoulder. The secretary gave him the wax tablet on which he had been writing. Suger studied it, nodded, and then handed it back. He raised his eyes to Lady Alais. "Speaking of prioresses—" He paused. "I understand that the chapter has elected Master Abelard's leman to the office."

Lady Alais swayed on her stool. "My lord, no—"

"No?" He lifted his brows. "You say no? I have it down here."

An explosion of venom spurted into Heloise's throat. Yes, she screamed silently, I was his leman—and proud of it. The man was devilish. No fault could be found with her election, but he seemed determined to make trouble.

Lady Alais cried, "I meant, no, she was not his leman. She was Master Peter's wife, my lord."

"Leman first, wife second. Bore a brat out of wedlock. Once a whore, always a whore."

Flesh crawling, Heloise waited for Lady Alais to inform Suger of her presence in the room. But the abbess seemed to have forgotten.

"My lord abbot," she said, "Sister Heloise was best qualified for the office. She was Sister Madelaine's assistant, and she had been performing the duties prior to Sister Madelaine's death. My lord, she is quite efficient." Gulping for air, she added lamely, "There is no question of any illegality concerning her election."

"I was questioning the propriety of such an election," Suger snapped. "How many dissenting votes?"

Lady Alais moved her hands convulsively. Her face was blank.

Heloise cleared her throat. Rising, she took one step forward and said, "Eight, my lady," and stepped back.

Suger swung to face her. For a moment he stared flatly, and then turned back to Lady Alais, who was blotting perspiration from her forehead. "Who's that?" he demanded.

"Sister Heloise. Our prioress."

"I see." Suger's face registered no expression. He called to Heloise, "Come forward."

She went to him, knelt, and kissed his ring. The limp, stubby fingers smelled of garlic. Hands of a peasant, she thought. Which was exactly what he had once been. The son of a tenant farmer who had tilled the land for Saint-Denis and somehow had managed to get his bright lad enrolled as a novice at the abbey. There Suger had made friends with the son of King Philip, a chubby boy like himself, and thanks to his life-long intimacy with Louis the Fat, he had risen to become second man in the kingdom. Heloise got up and faced him.

"So," Suger said to her. "Sister Heloise. *La très sage Héloïse?*" His glance was full of hostile curiosity.

She did not reply, but continued to stare at him. He hadn't even the good breeding to look embarrassed. Wash a hound and comb him, hound he is and hound he remaineth.

"You have not collected reap silver from your tenants this spring." It was an accusation.

"As you know, my lord, there has been famine. Our tenants have no money. I commuted the reap silver, and instead they will provide physical labor and cut our grain in June." This decision she had made reluctantly, but in the end she had seen no alternative.

"You could have taken their property. Kettles, stools."

"We do not wish to do to others what we would not have done to ourselves."

Suger grunted. He rubbed his nostrils with his right forefinger, gazing at her over his hand. "Manure," he said.

"Pardon, my lord?"

"Your tenants on the east fields are neglecting to put their sheep in the convent's pens at night. You will have no manure."

"Most of them own no sheep, my lord. This winter they were obliged to slaughter their stock." When he did not reply, Heloise went on. "In lieu of the manure, they will catch eels for us and I think—"

Suger was not listening. Sliding to his feet, he ambled to the window. "It's getting late," he said over his shoulder. He waved a dismissal, and his secretary began to gather papers from the trestle. A moment later, he had reached the door, Astrane bowing low as the two men passed.

From the reception hall, he called to the abbess, "You will attend me in the yard, lady. In a quarter of an hour." Their footsteps died away.

When the door had closed, Lady Alais slipped off the stool and huddled on the floor. "Astrane, a henap." Astrane went to fetch the wine. "And don't water it," the abbess moaned.

Heloise went out, her shoulders throbbing with tension. Lady Alais was foolish to begin drinking now, with the farewells still to be said. Suger might smell the wine on her breath. Heloise sighed and rounded the corner of the abbess's garden. The sky over the chestnut trees had paled to lavender. She pulled up short. Ahead, on the walk leading to the cloister, Suger and his secretary were standing, talking. Suddenly an idea began to form in her mind. Deliberately, before she lost her nerve, she strode up to the men and looked pointedly at the abbot. He ignored her.

She coughed. "My lord abbot Suger, may I speak with you, please?" Surprised, Suger took a step toward her.

In a rush she said, "Forgive my impertinence but—have you news of Master Abelard? How fares he at Saint-Médard? Is he in good health?" At the council of Soissons, Abelard had been condemned. The Church had ordered him to thrust his book into the fire, and afterwards he had been compelled to recite the Athanasian Creed, as if he were some stupid schoolboy. He had been committed to the abbey of Saint-Médard, a house for the perverse and licentious. Since then, Heloise had been able to learn nothing of him, although not for lack of effort.

Suger's eyes had narrowed into points of contempt. He did not speak.

"Please, my lord. You were Abelard's friend once."

"I am still his friend."

Heloise stared him down, searching his face for clues. He said, "You should not concern yourself with worldly matters, Sister. This is unseemly behavior."

"For pity's sake," cried Heloise, "just tell me if he's alive at Saint-Médard."

Suger thrust his hands into his sleeves. Abruptly, he said, "He is no longer living there—not for the past year." He nodded to his secretary and started to walk away, his short legs pumping.

Heloise went after them. "But, my lord, where is he?"

Over his shoulder, Suger hissed, "Champagne."

"In an abbey, my lord? Where in Champagne?" She was close to tears.

Suger spun around, his face scarlet with rage. Under his breath, he said, "Sister Heloise, if it were not for you, Peter Abelard would be a whole man today. Now begone."

Heloise did not stir. He was a little man. She was not afraid of him. "My lord, I—"

"Get you gone!"

She stumbled away, wanting to weep because an instant earlier, while Suger had been shouting at her, she had tried to visualize Abelard's face. And could not.

*　*　*

Lent ended. On the day after Easter, Lady Alais departed on a pilgrimage to Compostela for, as she put it, the good of her soul and her nerves. Heloise, as prioress, was left in charge. Although she was reluctant to admit it, Argenteuil seemed to function better without the abbess, probably because Heloise was quick to make decisions and Lady Alais put them off as long as possible. Still, money worries continued, and their stores fell to a distressing low. Nobody went hungry, but meat appeared on the trestles only once a week.

Astrane was furious because Lady Alais had not taken her along. Instead, the abbess had selected a novice, Sarazanne, to accompany her as maid. Sarazanne was a complete pudding brain, but unfailingly cheerful, so Heloise understood the reason for her choice. Astrane sulked. For some reason, her displeasure at Lady Alais turned itself, once the abbess had gone, on Heloise, and she began to dispute Heloise's orders. Once, shrill-tempered, she called Heloise a whore.

Heloise shrugged. "If I was a whore," she said, unperturbed, "it was by choice. Now I am prioress of this house and your superior. Get to work, Sister."

She heard from Jourdain in the early summer, the letter spiraling her spirits. Abelard was now living near Troyes, and Jourdain had visited him during Lent. Apparently Abelard had not stayed long at Saint-Médard, but had returned to Saint-Denis, where he immediately became embroiled in a dispute. Jourdain believed the trouble of his own making, because he had insisted that St. Denis, the abbey's patron, was not the same person as Dionysius the Areopagite, as everyone at the abbey believed. Already in disfavor with the brethren for his persistent criticism of their morals, he then found a new tempest of fury unleashed against him. As Jourdain pointed out, Abelard would have been wise to keep quiet.

Heloise was surprised to learn that Abelard had been rescued, so to speak, by Abbot Suger, who gave him a dispensation so that Abelard could teach and live without being connected to any monastery. He had gone to Champagne, where Count Thibaut had given him sanctuary, and in the end a wealthy baron had presented Abelard a gift of land on the banks of the Arduzon River. It took Jourdain several pages to describe the details of this complicated transaction, and, reading between the lines, Heloise got the impression that he had been instrumental in arranging things. There, on the banks of the Arduzon, living with one clerk, Abelard had built a chapel of reeds and thatch, and he had dedicated it to the Holy Ghost. He called it the Paraclete, the Comforter who had brought him solace during his misfortunes.

Ever since the Church had condemned Abelard at Soissons, Heloise had worried incessantly about his mental state; she feared for his sanity. And sometimes she had railed against God for continuing to send one disaster after another to her beloved. Let be, she would shout in her prayers, let be! But of course he had not paid the smallest morsel of attention, and that was understandable. Now she took Jourdain's news as a good omen. Abelard's newly acquired property was deserted, a lonely stretch of wilderness along the riverbank. But it was also peaceful, Jourdain pointed out, and it provided Abelard the solitude he desired. He was reading; he was happier than Jourdain had seen him for years.

Her fears having proved groundless, Heloise grew calmer. In June, after sheepshearing, she devised a new system of accounting that allowed her to make substantial reductions in Lady Alais's debt to the bishop, going in person to present the plan to the clerks at Saint-Denis. On her return, she found waiting in Lady Alais's reception hall a peasant woman, Jehane, the widow of an Argenteuil tenant farmer.

Jehane fidgeted and took a long time in getting around to the purpose of her visit. Nervously, she kept peering into the passageway and out the window, until Heloise finally took her into the abbess's parlor and gave her a bowl of water. When she finally did begin to talk, Heloise had difficulty making sense of her story. A beggar had come to the door of her hut. When Jehane told her food was scarce and there was no money for alms, the beggar pushed her way in and refused to leave. She had insisted that Jehane visit the convent and speak to Sister Heloise. Sister would come with money, and everything would be all right.

Jehane sighed angrily. "She made me swear that I wouldn't bother Lady Abbess. The message is for you, my lady."

Heloise shrugged. "But what can I do? Tell her that bread and alms are distributed every morning. She must come to the yard."

"She doesn't want to. She wants you to come to her." Jehane shook her head in annoyance. "Please, lady. She won't go. What am I to do with her?"

"Is she crazy, do you think?"

"Can't tell. Mayhap."

Slipping a few coppers into her girdle, Heloise whistled for Aristotle, and tramped behind Jehane into the yard and out into the south field along the river. The smell of wild parsnips hazed the air; the dog danced in circles around her feet. Poor baby, she thought, she doesn't get a good run very often. Nor do I, she thought, smiling to herself. Lately she had spent so much time with her ledgers that she had forgotten to visit the rock.

Jehane's wattle hut looked like every other cottage on Argenteuil's land, except hers had no door. Probably she had used it for firewood last winter and never bothered to replace it. Fifty yards distant, under a tree, sat a thickset woman in a red tunic. Jehane nodded. Heloise started toward the tree. Halfway, Aristotle let out a squeal, hurtled over the ground as if shot from a catapult, and slammed herself into the woman's lap. Heloise stopped and stared. Aristotle never bothered with strangers. The woman must be a witch if she could cast that powerful a spell on a dog.

Cautiously, she approached. "Bad girl. Aristotle, come here."

The woman in the red gown set Aristotle on the ground. Awkwardly, she hobbled to her feet and thrust forward her arms. "Heloise, Heloise—"

Heloise's skin exploded in goose bumps. "Oh dear God!" she cried. She ran to Ceci, tears flooding from her eyes, and neither of them could speak.

"Ceci," Heloise said, "you've come back."

Ceci laughed. "That's exactly what I said when you came back. I said, 'Heloise, you've come back.' You know, I prayed for your return. Did you pray for mine? Did you, Heloise?"

Heloise leaned against the tree trunk and studied Ceci. She saw a plump woman in a shabby tunic, her face grimed with dust and her hair done up in two matted plaits. And then she noticed, for the first time, that Ceci was not fat but pregnant. Near term, too. "No," she said, forcing a smile, "no, I didn't pray for you to come back. I prayed you would find happiness wherever you were."

"Oh, well. That." Ceci grimaced and shook her head. "It was not God's will that I should be happy. But gramercy for your prayers, sweeting."

"What happened to Raimon?" Heloise gulped.

"Left me. In an inn near Pamplona." Her voice was quite calm and matter-of-fact.

"Pamplona! God's eyes, you've been across the Pyrenees?"

"Farther than that," Ceci said proudly. "Oh, I've traveled. Heloise, I went to Compostela. Oh, you should see it—there's a *botafumeiro* swinging from this big pulley on the ceiling, and the incense—"

"Whoa!" Heloise laughed. "Slow down." She led her toward Jehane's hut and made her sit down. All the way Ceci babbled—Rouen, Limoges,

Gascony, she had been everywhere. Raimon had bought her silk gowns and he had taught her Moorish dances, so that she could dance while he played. People put more oboles in the bowl when a jongleur is accompanied by a dancer, did Heloise know that? She had little silver bells for her ankles, but she had been forced to sell them along the road.

"Ceci," said Heloise, "you didn't travel from Pamplona alone, did you?"

"Certainly not. I came with pilgrims. They were very kind to me."

"Still, that was dangerous. What if you'd had the babe on the road?"

Jehane brought bowls of water. They drank. "What if—what if—I don't think about what if." Ceci clicked her teeth impatiently. "Oh, Heloise, please don't look at me like that. I'm sorry. I know I'm a burden to you." She stood and swayed a dozen steps. Aristotle followed. She picked up the dog and kissed her nose. "Adorable, you're adorable."

Heloise's shoulders sagged. "Ceci," she said, weary. She took a step toward her.

"If you can spare a few deniers," Ceci said, "I'll be on my way."

"Don't be stupid." The perspiration was rolling down her nose. Soon they would be ringing the bell for vespers and she wouldn't be there. Forcing herself to think clearly, she said, "When is the babe coming?"

Ceci shrugged. "I don't know. Soon mayhap."

"From the size of your belly, it looks very soon. You need a place to stay."

"Where? I can't go over there." She waved in the direction of the convent. "Lady Alais would have an attack of apoplexy."

Heloise pressed her fingers to her temples. "Lady Alais is away. But even so, I daren't let you come back." Suddenly she thought of Suger and his list. "Listen, you can stay here."

"Jehane doesn't like me."

Heloise watched Ceci's face. For all her bravado, she was scared. "Don't argue. If I give her money, she'll like you. Once the babe comes, we can decide what to do. Let's worry about one thing at a time. All right, Ceci?"

"All right."

Ceci's daughter was born at the end of the month. She lived three days, turned blue, and died. Ceci wanted a priest, so that the babe's soul would not be damned, but Heloise could not risk it. She found a small wooden box in the storeroom, and they wrapped the little girl's body in a towel. After dark, they dug a grave in the woods.

In a gust of weeping, Ceci stood over the freshly dug earth. Heloise took her hand. It was cold. Ceci said, "Do you know her name? Heloise. I called her Heloise."

"Thank you."

After a long while, Ceci dropped to the ground and kissed the dirt. She stood and darted away into the trees. Grabbing the shovel, Heloise ran after her. "Ceci—"

"Her soul is damned."

"Surely not," Heloise murmured. "An innocent babe—"

Among the trees, there was a breathless silence, as if every leaf, every branch were lying under a spell. Nothing was moving. They came out alongside a field of sharp-edged wheat glistening in the moonlight and made their way toward Argenteuil.

Ceci said quietly, "The Lord has punished me."

"Be quiet now. Try not to think about it."

Her voice vibrating, Ceci cried, "God has punished me for poisoning Baby."

"Holy Mother, you poisoned your babe!"

"No, no. The parrot. Remember? Lady Alais had this bird. I poisoned it."

Unsure whether to be angry or laugh, Heloise said severely, "Pox take the parrot. Ceci, you are a bride of Christ's. Did it ever occur to you that God might be punishing you for running off with a jongleur?"

She shook her head. "I hurt nobody by going. But Lady Alais loved Baby and I killed her. God has smitten me by killing my babe. An eye for an eye."

"Well," Heloise said after a while, "the Lord does not judge twice on the same offense. Your tablet is clean now."

The following week, as Heloise had instructed, Ceci presented herself at the convent gatehouse, asking for sanctuary and claiming that her absence had been the result of a spell cast by river fairies. Three-quarters of the nuns accepted the story without hesitation; the rest called her a liar and a harlot and protested against her readmission to the community. If Lady Alais had been present, the furor would have continued for some time. But Heloise squashed all dissent by simply declaring the case closed: Ceci, the unfortunate victim of spirits, now delivered by God's mercy back to their gate, should be welcomed as a lost sheep restored to the flock. Amen. As for her own sin in concocting such a lie, she would worry about that later.

After mass, she knelt at the grille to say her *confiteor*. A half dozen candles smoked on the altar. It was cool in the church, far more comfortable than in the schoolroom, and she longed to remain there all day. The flames of hell were hot, or so it was said. She began.

"Father, I have sinned. The sins of the flesh—I dream about them. The pleasures I shared with my beloved—they please me still. I can't drive them from my thoughts."

Behind the grille, Father Garin stirred restlessly. He had heard it before. Countless times.

"Father, during the celebration of mass, when my prayers should be pure, lewd visions fill my mind. Father, my thoughts are on wantonness." *O God, God, free me from these torments. . . . O my God, who searches our hearts and loins, you know everything. I do not ask for absolution. I pray thee. Miserable creature that I am, make haste to help me.*

Father Garin coughed. Heloise could hear him mumbling.

"Do you repent?" he asked dully.

She didn't answer. *Abelard, my lord and my darling . . .* Her mind retained the will to sin, her body burned with its old desires.

Father Garin went on. "My daughter in Christ, you must repent and do penance. I cannot grant you absolution otherwise."

After a while Heloise got to her feet and went out the side door to the cloister. Sister Marie's bracket hound, huffing, was trying to bury a bone in the herb bed, and he had rooted up a yard of mint and sprayed dirt over the walk. A strong odor of lemon rolled slowly toward Heloise's nostrils. She crossed to the abbess's tree and began to count the hard yellow balls.

It was during dinner when Abbot Suger arrived, unannounced. All morning, the sky had been gray and thunder crackled uneasily on the far bank of the Seine. Breathless, Heloise plowed through the cloister, wondering what the devil Suger could want, and hurried into the abbess's parlor. Suger came toward her. "Where is Lady Alais?" he demanded. "I didn't ask for you."

"On pilgrimage," Heloise said. She hoped that he would not ask when Lady Alais was expected to return, because she had no idea. She made herself look at Suger's face, just to show the man that he could

not intimidate her. He did not seem concerned with the abbess's whereabouts, or so it appeared to Heloise.

"You are harboring a harlot," he said. "I want explanations."

Heloise went taut. She said, "God's pardon, my lord. I don't understand what you mean."

"Sister Cecilia."

"Sister Cecilia has returned to us." She clenched her fingers behind
her back. "God be praised."

Walking to the window, Suger stood gazing out at the abbess's plum
trees. Without looking at Heloise, he said sarcastically, "By whose
leave, Sister, have you admitted a wanton into the house of God?"

"My own, my lord." She added quickly, "The sister was sick, sire.
No doubt some spell—"

He shrugged aside her words. Turning, he said, "I'm not an idiot,
Sister. Tell me no tales about fairies and spells." Thunder cracked over
the roof, and a second later lightning speared close to the shutters, but
Suger seemed oblivious. He went on talking. "Sister Cecilia departed
this house on December twenty-four in the year of Our Lord 1120 with
a Bordelais minstrel, one Raimon Gerlai. She returned on June thirteen
of the present year bearing the fruit of her wickedness in her womb.
Approximately June twenty-eight she dropped a brat, which she stran-
gled and buried secretly. Five days ago she—"

Heloise's head jerked up. "My lord," she protested, "you must be
misinformed." Inwardly she was gasping. It seemed beyond belief that
Suger could have obtained this information. "Sister Cecilia is renowned
for her piety."

Suger pulled a gold toothpick from his girdle and slowly began to ro-
tate it along the crack between his front teeth. "Did you interrogate the
sister as to her whereabouts?"

"Yes, my lord. She can't remember."

"That won't do."

He went on steadily, demanding to know if she had beaten Ceci and
why she had been so naïve as to accept her word. Heloise, half listening, raced her mind desperately. Clearly Suger had an informant living
within the convent—there was no other way for him to know so much
and so quickly—but who?

"Expel her from your midst," Suger was saying. "One diseased sheep
contaminates the entire flock."

"My lord, St. Benedict said that if a brother leaves the monastery
and wishes to return, let him promise to reform and let him be received

in the lowest place as a test of his humility. We have dealt with Sister Cecilia according to the Rule. I can't expel her."

After a moment, he said, "Are you defying me?"

"No, my lord."

Suger's face showed no emotion. "Let me tell you something, Lady Prioress. I intend to close this house of harlotry, this brothel, this abbey of bawds. I will turn the lot of you into the road to beg your daily bread or fill your bellies by fornication. That is a vow, Sister, and I keep my vows. Remember that."

"Yes, my lord."

Heloise froze to the ground, and Suger continued to stare up at her, the only sound in the parlor the scratching of the toothpick against his teeth.

Ceci stayed. Despite Heloise's efforts to discover the identity of Suger's spy, she had no success, and while she did not totally dismiss the mystery, weightier matters eventually pushed it aside. Between Michaelmas and Advent, she accepted eight new novices, two of them with generous dowries, and she also instituted a policy of accepting permanent paying guests. The latter was standard practice at some convents, but, traditionally, Argenteuil had never done so. The reason was not clear to Heloise, because, even though nunneries had difficulty controlling the worldly habits of guests and it was often fatal for discipline, the laywomen did bring much needed income into the community. Taking no chances, she screened applicants carefully and finally accepted three wealthy widows, elderly women who seemed sufficiently weary of life.

By the time Lady Alais came back, the widows were happily installed, and it was almost impossible to distinguish them from the sisters. The abbess offered no objections—indeed, she made no attempt to resume her supervisory duties as abbess. She did not turn over her authority to Heloise; she simply stopped exercising it and kept out of the way as much as possible. She had brought back a new parrot and, of course, Sarazanne, who shared the abbess's private quarters. Astrane never went near Lady Alais now.

Travelers who stopped at Argenteuil that winter brought news of war approaching—the German emperor was threatening to invade France. He was assembling his forces on the borders of Champagne. No, the king of England, who had married his daughter to the emperor, was planning to invade Anjou. It was all very contradictory and confusing, and Heloise waited to see what would happen. At the end of Lent, the road passing Argenteuil clattered with men-at-arms and war-horses heading east, Louis the Fat having called for a muster of his vassals on the plains of Rheims. Heloise climbed to the top story of the gatehouse to watch them ride by. In the distance, she could see them coming up the highroad, standards thrashing in the wind, baggage wagons piled high with lances and sacks of grain. An army of clanking iron. Rheims was in the north, a long way from the Arduzon River. Still, her stomach wobbled.

She came down to the yard and looked around for the portress. Sister Martha had died before Lady's Day, and in her place Heloise had appointed her deputy, Sister Esclarmonde. The office of portress required a special kind of personality, tough and dedicated. She did not sleep in the dormitory, but at her lodge by the gate, where she could be ready to admit, or reject, all comers. Passing into the yard, Heloise noticed Esclarmonde speaking to a bearded knight. Grinning, he stretched one arm toward her.

"Sister Heloise," he murmured.

She blinked; a grin split her face and she spun toward him, eyes brimming with laughter. "Jourdain, I didn't recognize you."

"Have I changed so much?"

He was perhaps heavier in the chest, and the beard gave his face maturity, but he still grinned in the same toothy, earnest way. "No. But how splendid you look."

Jourdain smiled. "As a trusted minister of Count Thibaut's, I must dress for the role. Don't you think?"

"Naturally." She gazed into his face. "Oh, Jourdain, I'm so happy to see you."

He nodded. They kept staring, as if they had forgotten how to move or walk, and Sister Esclarmonde left them. Words and sounds came back to Heloise, her pretty cousin shrieking against the afternoon wind, the snow crunching under her feet. *What a fine day! Jourdain is here!* She took his hand and led him toward the abbess's garden.

"How long will you stay, friend?"

"Not long. I carry the count's messages to King Louis. I should be on the Paris road right now." He smiled. "But how could I pass close to Argenteuil without seeing you?"

Heloise sent a novice to fetch wine and bread. "Will there be war?" she asked anxiously.

"Aye, mayhap," he replied. "There has been no real fighting in a long while. The barons are eager to break a few lances. You know."

Neither of them spoke for a while. The novice brought a tray of cheese and bread and a jug of wine, and Jourdain ate. He said, "How is the dog? What did you call her—Aristotle?"

She laughed. "Splendid. My pretty baby. She is like a child to me, since I have no other." She tried to keep her voice light.

He regarded her gravely. "And your son? What news of him?"

"None." She tried to think of something more to add, but there was nothing. The pain of his loss had dulled, although it remained with her constantly, like a chronic toothache. Shrugging, she repeated, "None."

"That is wrong of Denise," he sighed. "And bad for the boy as well. He has two living parents. Denise should bring him to visit you."

"Ah, Jourdain, you know she will never do that."

"Heloise."

"Yes, yes." Uncomfortable, she was on the verge of changing the subject when he asked suddenly, "Have you found peace here, my friend?"

The question startled her. "Do you mean have I made peace with God?"

"Forgive me. That was a stupid question."

She hesitated, but only for an instant. "I am here for love of Abelard and none other. That has not changed."

"Heloise!" Jourdain was dumbfounded. "Surely you owe loyalty to God first. For certain God sees everywhere. I—you must know that you're endangering your soul."

"I know," she said very softly, "I know."

Leaning forward, Heloise said to him tremulously, "Listen, Jourdain, there is not much time. I pray you—Jourdain, he never loved me, did he?"

"Of course he did." But it was obvious that his response was automatic. She watched his face and knew that he wanted to spare her.

"I don't think so," she insisted. "Everyone says he didn't love me."

Jourdain took her hand. "This is what I think. I think he did love you and I think he still loves you. But in his own way." He looked away. "It is not your way."

She didn't believe him. If Abelard had written only once, she would have believed in the truth of Jourdain's words.

His gaze wandered over the garden, the fountain, the cherry trees straining to bud, the carefully tended beds of costmary and Our Lady's bedstraw. "Do you know what his students call him now?" he said, smiling. "*Rhinoceros indomitus.*"

In spite of herself, she laughed. "The rhinoceros that can't be tamed? But wait a bit—what students?"

"Thousands. I think Paris must be empty."

"But where do they live?" she asked, bewildered. "There are no houses. You said it's a wilderness."

"Was. They've built themselves huts along the riverbank. The place looks like a good-sized city. Really. You should see it."

"I can't imagine—how do they live?"

"On herbs and coarse bread. And they sleep on mattresses of thatch and straw."

Heloise got to her feet, excited, and began to pace up and down. "It's just like the old days, isn't it?"

"They look after him," Jourdain was going on. "He'd built a small chapel of thatch. Well, some of the students are rebuilding it from stone and wood."

She felt easier; he was all right then, still the philosopher of all philosophers. Sext began to chime. Jourdain stood and stretched, and slowly they began strolling toward the courtyard.

Waving his hand in a circle, he drawled, "How peaceful it is here. Surely that is something to be thankful for."

"Appearances deceive. A spy lives in our midst."

He grinned quizzically. "Come now."

Heloise jerked her head at him. "Tell me something, friend. What do you know of Abbot Suger?"

"Why—what everyone knows, I suppose. He's shrewd and ambitious —and powerful."

"Is he evil?"

"Evil?" He paused to think. "I don't know—why do you ask?"

"He has threatened to close Argenteuil."

"On what grounds?" Jourdain snorted. "Bah!"

"Oh, Jourdain. He's gone back into the archives and found old cases. I don't think he has proof of course, but—" She remembered Ceci. She should have told Jourdain, but it was too late now. A groom was bringing up his horse. Swiftly she said, "Suger hates me. He calls me Abelard's leman."

Jourdain scowled. "Probably he hates all women. But I know one thing. The abbot is just about the only true friend that Abelard has in the Church." He grinned at her. "Suger was just blowing hot air. How can he close Argenteuil? God's blood, it's been here two hundred years."

"Three hundred. Or more."

"Well." He laughed heartily. "You see."

The troops had passed on. The yard echoed with bursts of excited laughter: people jostling and yelling, and a knot of beggars clamoring for their dinner. A lay sister appeared carrying two enormous baskets of bread. Sister Esclarmonde, hands on hips, was surveying the yard with haughty indulgence, as if saying to them, *Don't kill each other. Your bellies will be filled.* Heloise stood there trying to shake off her sense of dread. She said quietly, "Jourdain, sooner or later, he means to destroy us. And I think it will be sooner."

She was wrong. It took the abbot of Saint-Denis five years to fulfill his vow.

17 ❧

"LADY VIRGIN! HOLY ALAIS!"

Heloise glared at the parrot. This bird, also called Baby, was a good deal smarter than its predecessor, and Lady Alais had taught it a few words, which it usually managed to scramble.

"Holy Lady! Virgin Alais!" It inched along the window bench, leaving a trail of droppings. Heloise made a mental note to avoid sitting there. From the abbess's bedchamber came the muffled rustling of clothes being pulled on. She went to the half-open door and tapped lightly, so that the abbess would understand she was still waiting. "My lady," she called, "this matter is of some urgency. But if you would liefer I came back later—"

Lady Alais came out, her eyes pouchy with sleep, and she flicked her gaze around the floor. "Where's beastie?"

"I left her in the schoolroom."

"Why?"

Heloise bit back her irritation. "My lady, you know her barking upsets Baby. Lady, please. I beg you, attend me. This is extremely important." She bore down on the word "extremely."

Yawning, Lady Alais sat down at the trestle and took a long gulp of ale. She raised her head, a spasm of weariness brushing her face, and said to Heloise, "Proceed then."

"Have you had any private communications from Abbot Suger?"

Lady Alais gave her a puzzled look.

"Any personal messages?"

"Why, child," the abbess answered, "you read all my correspondence." She turned toward Baby and puckered her lips into a kiss.

"I know that. But has there been anything that perchance you forgot to show me? Anything at all. Think."

The abbess frowned. She didn't like to be bothered with matters that required thinking. At last she said, "Nothing I can recall."

"Have you had any letters from the bishop? From Pope Honorius?"

"Merciful Mother, why would the pope write to me?" Lady Alais turned away, apparently losing interest in the conversation.

Heloise remained silent for a moment. Abbot Suger was an underhanded son of a dog, that fact she had understood for several years now. But she had not imagined that he would initiate eviction proceedings against Argenteuil without some kind of formal warning. Or without allowing the nuns to defend themselves. She crossed to the trestle and sat down opposite the abbess.

Heloise pulled a sheet of parchment from her sleeve and laid it flat between them. "I have here an announcement of a synod council to be convened in Paris on the second day of February. It is to be held at the abbey of Saint-Germain-des-Prés."

Lady Alais broke in, smiling. "The second. That's Thursday, isn't it? My, my, is it February already?"

"Yes, lady. Or it will be tomorrow. Please, lady, permit me to continue." She did not wait for the abbess to reply but hurried on, making sure to speak slowly and precisely so that Lady Alais would grasp the situation. "Now. The purpose of the council is to consider the question of reforming the monastic rule in several abbeys where zeal is thought to have waned. I am quoting, lady. Are you following me?" She looked up sharply.

"Certainly," Lady Alais said.

"Now follows a list of the abbeys to be considered. There are six, seven, eight of them down here. The second on the list is Sainte-Marie of Argenteuil."

Lady Alais's smile dried up. "There must be a mistake," she snapped.

"No mistake." Out of patience, she slid the sheet across and pointed. Lady Alais peered for a second and then slammed the paper back at Heloise. "Now—"

"Stop saying 'now' constantly!"

"Yes, my lady. Now we get to the interesting part of this announcement. It goes on to state that a claim has been presented by Abbot Suger, to the effect that our lands and buildings belong to the abbey of Saint-Denis—and that we are, er, trespassing."

Lady Alais stared at her. "The abbot must be daft," she said slowly. "Charlemagne gave this abbey to his daughter. It says so in our cartulary. There is no question of its belonging to Saint-Denis."

Heloise held out the paper. "This announcement says that Suger will present documentary evidence to prove that Argenteuil was founded in the reign of King Pepin as a priory of Saint-Denis's." She had sat up until matins last night with a tallow candle, going through chests of dusty archives. Suger lied. Argenteuil had been founded a century earlier than Pepin, in the reign of King Clothair, by a nobleman, Hermenricus, and his wife, Numma, and—Suger was correct about one thing—they had presented the land to Saint-Denis. Probably men had inhabited the premises then. But under Charlemagne, it was declared autonomous and turned into a nunnery for his daughter. There had been some talk of its reverting to Saint-Denis after Theodrada's death, but this had never taken place. Argentcuil had been handed down, from abbess to abbess, for over three hundred years.

The abbess had screwed her face into a scowl. "The abbot can prove nothing," she said firmly.

"I agree." Heloise paused. "Unless he produces a forgery."

"Don't be silly," she murmured. "It is a mistake, that's all."

"Lady, don't you think it's strange—Abbot Suger has made these charges, but the synod has not asked us to refute them." For that matter, the announcement had not arrived until the previous day, stuffed in carelessly among other Church circulars in the pouch from Saint-Denis. Since it was dated January 5, obviously the letter must have been delayed at Saint-Denis—deliberately, she suspected. She said to the abbess, "We should have been given an opportunity to answer."

Lady Alais stood and took a crust of bread to Baby. Squawking furiously, the bird tore it from her fingers. "Baby hungry?" she crooned, tilting back her head. "Baby wants breadie? Child, what is the use of answering such ridiculous charges? No doubt the Church realizes that."

"Listen, my lady. There is still time. You could go to Paris and—"

"I?" The abbess seemed shocked. "I, go to a synod meeting? Among all those men?"

Heloise put the letter away. "I merely thought—"

"Besides, I was not invited. No, child. You'll see. Next week we shall get a letter apologizing for this mistake. Mark me, nothing will come of it." She hoisted Baby to her shoulder. "Do you know whether Sister Marie has finished the silk cushion she is sewing for me? She promised it several days ago."

"I don't know, lady. I'll remind her." She rose and moved swiftly toward the door, anxious to get away. Through her mind flashed a picture of Suger, standing in that very room, questioning her about Ceci. It had happened so long ago that she had gradually discounted his threats. I underestimated the abbot, she thought angrily. Not that taking him at his word would have prevented this.

In the cloister, snow was melting and the walks were covered with rivulets of slush. God's elbows, she hated the winters; she should have entered some house in Provence or Toulouse. Along the east walk, a shower of droplets cascading from the roof splattered against her forehead. Ducking back, she slowed her steps and finally shuffled to a complete stop. To be sure, Abbot Suger hated her. But would he expel ninety-three women from a religious retreat for that reason? It seemed absurd—surely no sane person would consider such a step. And then too he had continued to help Abelard. Three years earlier, when attacks on his writings had made further residence at the Paraclete impossible, had not Suger arranged for him to be elected abbot of Saint-Gildas-de-Rhuys?

She leaned up against a stone capital and traced her fingers over the acanthus-leaf carvings at its base. These walls and pillars had seen thousands of women live and die, and events had not always been peaceful, either. She laughed softly, remembering that last night she had come upon a notation in the archives that had cheered her. In the ninth century, during some war or other, an army of Normans had swept the countryside and stormed the walls of Argenteuil. The abbess, one Ertrude, had led her daughters in hurling boiling oil on the besiegers, and the Normans had fled. Unfortunately, Lady Alais was no Ertrude.

Sighing, she started across the cloister toward the cellaress's quarters. She had enough to do today without worrying about Suger and his trumped-up documents.

Ceci hurried out of the refectory door with an armful of laundry. When she caught sight of Heloise, she ran to her and grabbed her arm. "What did she say?" she cried.

Heloise shrugged. "Shhh. Nothing much. She thinks it's a mistake." "She didn't swoon?"

"I told you. She's not terribly concerned. She says nothing will happen."

Ceci, solemn, studied her face. "Do you think she's right, Heloise?" "I don't know."

Every day, Heloise taught Latin, totted up her accounts, and waited for news from Paris. The fiercest part of the winter had passed. Without mishap, the spring crops had been sown—oats, peas, barley, and vetches

—and she looked forward to a splendid harvest that summer. On Shrove Tuesday, she told herself that no news was good news. And when the last day of February arrived and still no word came, she had almost talked herself into believing the synod had thrown Suger's claim off the agenda.

During the afternoon recreation hour, Heloise took Aristotle to the laundry house and dunked her in a trough of soapy water, the dog squirming miserably and staring at her with accusing eyes. The laundress was watching, arms folded in amused disapproval.

She said, "It's not spring, you know. She'll catch cold."

"No she won't," Heloise said. "Hand me that towel." She set Aristotle on the ground, watched her shake water in all directions, and began to rub her down vigorously with the towel. Outside in the yard, she could hear someone shouting. How many times had she told the children not to yell? A thousand, at least. A girl ran in, breathless.

"Lady Prioress," she said, bobbing, "you're wanted."

"Shhh. Who wants me?"

"Lady Abbess. Right away."

Heloise swaddled Aristotle thickly in the towel and gave her to the laundress. In the doorway of the abbess's apartment stood Sarazanne, her bovine face mottled red from weeping. She was waving a sheaf of crumpled parchment on which the bishop's seal had been broken. "Lady Abbess has gone to bed," she whispered. "You're to call a chapter meeting."

"Very well," Heloise said, taking the letter from her. Without further comment to Sarazanne, she went into the abbess's garden, sat down on a bench, and carefully read the letter once and then a second time. Disbelief welled up in her and, on its heels, helpless rage. Helpless because, for all Suger's lies, there remained a kernel of truth in his allegations. It was true that Argenteuil had had its share of, as Suger put it, "irregularities," but then, so had every other religious house, Saint-Denis not excepted. Indeed, some counted Saint-Denis among the worst.

An hour later, in the chapter house massed with bewildered nuns, Heloise read the bishop's fiat that the convent of Sainte-Marie of Argenteuil no longer existed. At her elbow, Lady Alais sat in the abbatial chair, her back very straight, her face congealed into an expressionless mask. The women ranged on the stone benches around the sides of the room stared at Heloise blankly. "Therefore," read Heloise, "it is decreed that the convent should revert to the royal abbey of Saint-Denis and that the nuns should be replaced by monks." She added, "We are given thirty days to vacate the premises."

"That's a barrel of muleshit," burst out Sister Blanche indignantly. "What ancient charter is the abbot talking about?"

"Evidently he has produced one," Heloise replied. "A copy has been sent to Rome."

Outraged, the nuns began to shout angrily among themselves, and even the dogs started to howl, until the racket in the chapter house rose to an earsplitting level. Heloise shouted over them, to restore order, "Sisters, sisters, I haven't finished . . ."

"Where did he find this obscure charter?" Sister Angelica asked. "Just tell us that."

"That information is not revealed," Heloise answered, her voice scratchy. "At Saint-Denis, I would imagine."

At the far end of the room, somebody screeched, "He wants our land and peasants!"

"It won't work!" another voice yelled. "There will be a papal inquiry, and Suger will be flung into the Tiber." The room exploded with nervous laughter.

"Think of public opinion," Sister Blanche said. Her blue eyes glinted with hope. "The people of France will never stand for it. This was an honorable retreat for women when the Capetians were still swineherds."

Sister Esclarmonde stood up, her massive shoulders as bulky as a man's. "We're going to appeal the decision, aren't we?"

"By all means," Heloise grunted. Her head was throbbing. Lady Alais had not moved. She wished that the abbess would say something, or at least give an indication that she was still breathing. Heloise let the women hop around and yell for another ten minutes, and then she waved them back to their places. "Make no mistake—we'll appeal. But it may not do any good."

"What do you mean—not do any good?" demanded Sister Esclarmonde. "What kind of negative talk is that?"

"There's another document here," Heloise said wearily. She paused to scratch her nose. The fragrance of laundry soap still clung to her fingers. The nuns were going back to the benches. She unfolded the letter that had accompanied the bishop's decree. "Now, listen to this and listen carefully."

The women stared at her.

"This is a charter drawn up by Matthew of Albano, the papal legate to the synod council." She began to read: "Recently in the presence of the illustrious lord and sovereign Louis of France, together with our brother bishops Reginald, archbishop of Rheims, Stephen, bishop of Paris, Geoffrey, bishop of Chartres, Gozelin, bishop of Soissons—"

"Get to the point!" somebody cried from the corner.

"—and others in great number, we were discussing the question of monastic reform. Suddenly, from the back of the hall, there was an outcry against the scandal and infamy prevailing at a nunnery called Argenteuil—" Looking up, she struggled to keep her voice steady; the chapter house was silent, and she noticed that the nuns were not looking at each other. "—at a nunnery called Argenteuil, where a small number of nuns were bringing disgrace upon their order and had long since polluted the entire neighborhood with their lewd and shameful conduct." She stopped.

Nobody spoke for a minute, and then Sister Judith roared, "Well, well! Our polluted neighborhood, is it? Our beloved brethren at Saint-Denis keep their whores in the dorter. God's death, there are more brats in this neighborhood fathered by monks than by lay folk."

Astrane spoke for the first time. "Sister, you are thinking of Saint-Denis under Abbot Adam. You know that Abbot Suger has reformed the abbey."

"Really?" Judith snapped. "I hadn't noticed." Her chest was heaving.

Astrane shrugged. "The abbot cannot abide immorality. There's nothing wrong in that."

"Which side are you on?" Judith glared. A chorus of ayes rang out.

"My sisters," Heloise broke in. Folding the papers, she glanced at Lady Alais, who was clutching her rosary. She said to her, "My lady abbess, would you like to speak?"

The abbess did not move or answer. Then, as if in a trance, she slid to the edge of her chair and stood unsteadily, fastening cold fingers on Heloise's arm. Every pair of eyes in the chapter house strained toward her. In a monotone so flat that most of her words were lost, she began to mumble. ". . . willful slander." She pressed her lips together and gazed down at her abbatial ring.

There was an embarrassed silence. Sister Angelica called out softly, "My lady abbess, what is to become of us?" Lady Alais did not reply.

After a moment, Heloise pried her fingers loose and toppled her back into the chair. Turning to the nuns, she said, "The bishop informs us that we are to be placed in convents of good repute, lest any of us go astray and perish through misconduct."

"Very funny," hooted Judith. "The flock has been scattered, and he worries about us going astray." A rumble of laughter floated through the chapter house.

Heloise reached for the letter. "Or he presents another alternative. Any nun who wishes may be released from her vows at this time." A gasp went up and, from the corner of her eye, Heloise saw Ceci's mouth drop open. "Of course, that must be your personal decision. I suggest that we adjourn now. In the days ahead, each of us should pray for individual guidance." Nobody moved.

Angelica's high voice sliced into the silence. "What about the appeal?"

"It will be made. But to be safe"—she sighed aloud—"it might be wise to apply now to the approved convents on the bishop's list. Then if the synod decision is overturned, we can always—"

"I'm going to wait and see," broke in Sister Blanche.

"So am I," squeaked one of the new novices.

Astrane said, "I wouldn't." Her eyes were perfectly calm—indeed, her face wore a look of satisfaction that was completely at odds with every face in the room.

"Why not?" said Blanche, frowning.

"I just wouldn't. Pope Honorius is certain to affirm the decision."

"What do you know about it?" asked the novice who wanted to wait.

Astrane smiled. "Nothing."

Giving the sign for dismissal, Heloise crossed the room to Ceci and swooped Aristotle from her lap. "Come on. It's over."

Ceci slumped her chin against her chest. "I can't believe it."

Heloise could not believe it either, although she had seen it coming for years. "Well, they say that seeing is believing." She lowered her voice. "Anyway, now I have my spy."

"Heloise, who?" She raised her head.

"Can't you guess?"

Ceci blinked. "Old Pisspot, isn't it?"

"Aye. I'm dead certain." She glanced back at Lady Alais, who was still sitting in her chair, her eyes filmy. At her elbow, Sarazanne stood stiffly on one leg and chewed her nails. Heloise and Ceci went into the cloister, where the sisters were beginning to assemble in small groups. The women made no effort to control their voices as they ordinarily would have, and the close vibrated with tears and curses. Heloise felt too weary to call for order. She staggered to a deserted spot under the eaves.

Ceci, rubbing her nose, followed. She said bitterly, "Astrane has sold her soul to Suger."

"Astrane has no soul."

"Neither does Suger . . . I wonder what he promised her. An abbacy, I wager."

Heloise shook her head. "She's too young."

Ceci asked, "What are you going to do now?"

"Do? About what?"

"We are released from our vows. You can go back to the world."

"I made my vows to Abelard, not to God. Abelard has not released me." Ceci was staring at her. "But Ceci, listen—there's no reason why you can't return to the world."

Ceci laughed sharply. She thrust her hands into her sleeves. "Where would I go?"

"Home. Angers."

"Heloise, I'm twenty-seven. They won't want me." She looked away, frowning. "Besides, I don't even remember what they looked like."

"Don't be so hasty. The chance won't come again. Think about it."

"There's nothing to think about."

They went in to eat.

From that day until Easter, the nuns at Argenteuil struggled to restore order to lives that had once seemed the most ordered, most secure, of all women. The children had been sent home. All semblance of discipline vanished, even the celebration of the divine offices being made late and once omitted entirely. The rule of silence that they had observed during meals gave way to half whispers and then to outright chatter. All of them, Heloise included, were waiting for the appeal to reach King Louis, but as the days passed without word, they gradually lost confidence. A few nuns, always in pairs, took bowls from the kitchen and walked out the front gate; they said that they were going to Rocamadour or Compostela. Some did not mention their destinations. To Heloise's surprise, Sister Judith, who had been a nun for thirty-five years, requested release from her vows so that she could live with her niece. And there were other women, young and aging, who renounced their calling, if it could be called that.

"Sister Astrane," Heloise said carefully, without looking at her, "the bishops wants a record of where each of us plans to go. You have not yet notified me of your plans."

"I'm going to Sainte-Catherine's."

Heloise frowned. "Where is that? I've not heard of such a convent."

"A new daughter house of Mount Sainte-Agnes. Near Senlis."

"Gramercy." She wrote Astrane's name on her list and, after it, Sainte-Catherine's of Senlis. She felt Astrane's eyes on her.

A moment later, Astrane was saying, "I'm to be prioress." Her voice was velvety with triumph.

"I see. Sister, I have work to do now. You have my permission to go."

The thirty-day grace period passed. Heloise sent a lay brother to the bishop to ask why Louis the Fat had taken no action on their appeal. The brother came back full of gossip. The king had left Paris for Rheims, where he intended to crown Prince Philip. In spite of her annoyance, Heloise was interested. That was unusual, crowning a thirteen-year-old prince as king while his father still lived. Louis the Fat was taking no chances with the succession. People said that Philip was arrogant, badly behaved, and disobedient, an all-round bad potato, and that the king could do nothing with him. Heloise hoped the king remained in good health for a while. She sent the lay brother to Rheims.

Uneasiness pervaded the cloister. The feeling of impending calamity grew stronger, and even those nuns, like Sister Blanche, who had hesitated, were applying to other convents. Lady Alais announced that she would enter Notre Dame-des-Bois and that Sarazanne would accompany her. She could not take the parrot; the abbess of Notre Dame forbade animals, and Lady Alais sold the bird to a merchant who stopped the night.

As for Heloise's own future, it remained a blank. Following her advice to the nuns, she requested admission to Notre Dame-des-Bois and several other houses, both for herself and for Ceci. Nothing happened. Either she received no reply, or she got letters politely refusing. Always there was some excuse—no room, or her application was being carefully reviewed and so forth. Heloise marveled at the power of Abbot Suger.

Ceci gave a lopsided grin. "Sweet, nobody wants us," she told Heloise. "Isn't that a coincidence."

"The abbot has done a thorough job," admitted Heloise. "But he doesn't control every nunnery in Christendom. Stop worrying."

"There's nothing to do but worry." Ceci laughed.

"Tomorrow I'm going to write to the abbess at Fontevrault. It's a fairly new community. Surely they'll be wanting people." She should have written earlier. At Fontevrault there were a convent and monastery together, but both were ruled by a woman, a unique arrangement.

Fontevrault had been founded by Robert d'Arbrissel, a Breton reformer who believed that women were more competent administrators than men. Heloise liked the sound of the place.

The next day, the lay brother returned from Rheims. Illiterate, he had not read the documents in his pouch, but he had been told of their contents and he arrived weeping. Heloise learned that Louis had endorsed the synod decision on the day of Prince Philip's coronation. Argenteuil was to be evacuated immediately.

Quickly the nuns began to leave, even though the final decision rested with Pope Honorius and he had not yet passed on the appeal. Nobody believed that he would save them. The wardrober opened her storeroom and distributed to each woman the personal belongings she had brought when she entered the convent. There were gowns, moth-eaten and mildewed, long out of style; faded ribbons and bracelets green with tarnish, dusty packets of letters, rag dolls, even a lute. Everyone got something painful. All that day the nuns wept. In the evening, when they were exhausted from grief, Heloise told the cellaress to make a fire outside the postern gate so that the nuns should be enabled to burn what they did not wish to keep.

In the schoolroom, she went through her bundle, those things that Abelard had brought on the day she had taken her vows. At the time, she had not opened it, merely handed the parcel to the wardrober. On top were Abelard's letters, tied with ribbon. She would never part with them, or with the Limoges box containing her wedding ring and the amethyst he had given her soon after they became lovers. The rest of the things she took out to the bonfire.

Heloise stayed at the convent for several weeks, saying that she must leave her records and accounts in good condition. It was an excuse. She thought, I once dreaded coming here and now I dread leaving. Each day some of the nuns departed, in small bands as well as large, and each day the courtyard shuddered with the sounds of weeping. After a while, Heloise learned to numb herself. By the middle of May there remained only the cellaress and three of her assistants. Sister Angelica, who had cared for the grounds and buildings for nearly twenty-five years, thought it her duty to personally hand over the convent to the abbot of Saint-Denis, or his representative. But now that Argenteuil officially belonged to the abbey, nobody seemed in a great hurry to claim it.

Four days before Pentecost, Heloise told Sister Angelica that she and Ceci would be leaving the following morning, after prime. She wanted no formal farewell, if Sister Angelica did not mind. The cellaress, her eyes pitted with rings of exhaustion, nodded; they kissed. Later that day, Heloise placed a bunch of rosemary on Sister Madelaine's grave, and afterwards she went to the schoolroom for the last time. Opening the cupboard, she took out a map she had been saving and slid it, folded, into her girdle.

The next day, Heloise and Ceci walked quickly through the cloister, Aristotle prancing at their heels. Already the place felt abandoned—no dogs barking or parrot screeching. Only birds sang. Along the south walk, weeds were choking out the mint; a brown apple core lay near the little statue of the Virgin. At the gate to the courtyard, Heloise kicked at the grille, not wanting to look back. Ceci stopped and turned.

"Look," she said, "the abbess's lemon tree. She forgot it."

"Oh, I don't think so. Probably she left it on purpose. You can't enter a convent with a tree." Suddenly she had in her mind a picture of Lady Alais approaching the gate of Notre Dame-des-Bois, trundling the lemon tree in a barrow, a parrot on her shoulder. She roared a wild peal of laughter.

Ceci jumped. "Sweet Mother of God, what's that all about!"

"Nothing," she answered, wiping her eyes. "Nothing. Let's go." She wondered who would water the lemon tree. It needed water at least three times a week. Sister Angelica for a while, and then of course the monks. The thought of men inside the gate made her feel funny. "Let's go," she repeated.

The sun had not been up long, so the air still felt cool and fresh. Crossing to the convent gate, they swung it open and then pulled it shut behind them. The empty road stretched out on either side.

"Which do you want to carry first?" Heloise said to Ceci. "The bundle or Aristotle?"

"The bundle."

Heloise hauled Aristotle to her hip. They started down the road toward Paris.

It took them five days to reach the Ile. Heloise made that about one mile a day and she had to smile over it. But there was no reason to hurry, no place they had to be, nothing they had to do. It felt good. Heloise's face turned golden tan below her wimple, and Ceci's nose began to peel. They walked slowly, talking to other travelers, enjoying the sights. The weather was fine and warm, and at night they slept comfortably in the fragrant fields with the stars for a coverlet. Seven times each day they stopped, wherever they happened to be, to say the divine offices. They might be nuns without a home but they were still nuns.

On the road, people were friendly and generous; the begging bowls that Heloise and Ceci thrust forward were always filled with food or coins, and it was a hardhearted person who could pass Aristotle without tossing her a bit of dried beef or a morsel of bread. On the Roman road they felt safe and exhilarated, as if it were a fair day.

Paris had grown. Fine houses were going up on the Right Bank, and the Templars were putting up a palace for themselves. Across the Grand Pont, on the island, many houses had been torn down and rebuilt; in the open shops along the Rue de la Draperie, merchants stood behind counters swaddled in brilliantly dyed linen and silk. Everything seemed to be colored rose. Heloise had forgotten that the light in Paris is pinkish.

The bakery where she had first seen Abelard still stood on the corner of the Rue de la Pomme, but the baker was different. Wondering, Heloise decided that the old one had probably died. It seemed unreasonable that everything should not be exactly as she had left it, ten years earlier. She and Ceci stood on the corner with their bowls. They had to watch Aristotle—she was not used to crowds and traffic, and once a horseman narrowly missed trampling her. After that, Heloise or Ceci held the dog.

They counted their coppers and bought cheese and ham pasties from a vendor. That was a foolish waste of money, because they were not good pasties, not like the ones Heloise remembered. Still, they ate slowly, making the pies last, and drifted east in the direction of the Rue des Chantres.

Somebody was living in Fulbert's house. She could see wet linen hanging near the stables. Ceci set Aristotle down, and they went cautiously up to the door. Heloise knocked. A sour-faced young man in clerical robes opened.

"What do you want?" he said.

"Who lives here?" Heloise asked.

"This house belongs to the Church."

"Yes. But who lodges here?"

Impatient, he answered curtly, "The Grand Penitentiary," and closed the door.

They backed off, still staring at the house. It looked as if it had shrunk. Ceci said, "What's a Grand Penitentiary?"

"I'm not sure. He's employed by the bishop. Or the Holy See."

"To do what?"

Heloise motioned her around the side of the house. "A sort of inquisitor." She peered over the gate, trying to see into the garden. The only things visible were the privy and part of the pear tree.

"Heloise. Really? You mean he questions heretics?"

"Ummm. Among others. Cases involving conscience." A suitable tenant for such a house, she thought, and turned away. They went down to watch the boats in the Port Saint-Landry.

18 ❧

THERE WAS A NICE feeling in Paris that lifted her—for a while. She knew it would not last. Sooner or later, she would glide up headlong against loneliness, the only thing about the Ile that she could rely upon.

Heloise and Ceci were too giddy to worry about much of anything. They slept along the river, under the willows, where the salt breeze overpowered the stench of dung and rotting garbage that hung over the Ile's streets. Day after day, that summer, they begged for alms. Most days they got enough to keep their stomachs reasonably full, with a little left over for Aristotle. When they were given little, or nothing, there were always the abbeys on the Left Bank: Saint-Victor, Saint-Germain-des-Prés, even Sainte-Geneviève, which was a bit of a walk. In the courtyards, they would line up with the other beggars and wait for distribution of leftover bread. Sometimes pea soup, but never with meat. By August, they were on friendly terms with the abbeys' porters and knew which days they could count on hot food.

On Assumption, they began following the Orleans road south, in the direction of Melun. Two years earlier, or perhaps more, Jourdain's father had died, and he had gone home to claim his fief. Heloise warned Ceci that Jourdain knew nothing of their coming, and most likely would not be living at Sancy. No doubt he had returned to Champagne and left the demesne to his stewards. In the end, after many days of debate, they decided to visit him, as they would be passing that way.

Without crossing the drawbridge, they shouted to the knight on the wall, "God greet you, is your master within?"

To their amazement, he immediately called back, "Aye, holy ladies. And awaiting you since St. John's Day."

They slept in beds again. Laughing, Heloise complained to Jourdain that the feather mattress made her back ache, so accustomed had she grown to months of resting on the hard earth. The beamed roof of the hall made her feel closed in, and she would catch herself looking up, expecting sky and clouds. Although Jourdain stayed with them much of the time, this was his busiest season. The villeins were bringing in the harvest, and after Michaelmas wheat and rye were sowed, plowing and harrowing began on the fallow fields, and hedges opened to the harvested fields so that cattle could graze on the stubble. Since it was also the end of the castle's fiscal year, the hall teemed with vassals come to settle their accounts.

Despite the remote location of Sancy, Jourdain seemed to know all the happenings of the world, and he spent the evenings chattering about the affairs of Church and courts. It was not all gossip. Heloise learned that Suger's expulsion of the nuns at Argenteuil was generally accepted, because people believed the sordid tales of their behavior. Jourdain told her that the Church was growing more corrupt each year, that while Notre Dame had banished her uncle, his name remained on its roll of canons.

"Why, in God's name?" sputtered Ceci. "He's a convicted criminal."

Jourdain shook his head. "Nothing was ever proved against him. So he suffers no dishonor. Only the loss of his canonry income."

"Which he didn't need anyway," Heloise broke in. "God, there's no justice in this world."

Jourdain shrugged. "They say he is senile now. I don't know. All I know is that he's rich."

Heloise said suddenly, "Is Agnes alive?"

"I suppose," he answered. "I've heard nothing to the contrary."

At compline, the two women went to the chapel for the office. When they returned to the hall, Ceci went up to bed and Heloise settled quietly on a stool before the hearth. The hall smelled of spices and sizzling fat. Beside her, Jourdain was throwing a ball of twine for Aristotle, tossing it into the air and trying to catch it before she did. Heloise laughed. The next time Aristotle, tongue hanging down, darted past her feet, she reached over to catch her. She tucked the dog firmly in her lap. "My treasure"—she smiled—"you're an elderly dame now. Those games are for pups." Jourdain was watching her. "Do you know something, my friend?" she said. "In my mind, I always date my entry into religion from the time I got Aristotle. Not from . . ."

Wordlessly, he nodded. He brought her a cup of wine, poured half into the flames, and filled up the space with water. His own he sipped whole, sitting on a chest. "We are approaching middle age, you know." Jourdain grinned.

"Aye. I don't mind." She watched his face with its slightly receding hairline, the beard glinting reddish in the firelight. Softly she said, "It must be lonely for you here. Sancy needs a mistress and you need someone. Why don't you marry, friend?"

"It's crossed my mind." He smiled. "There's a maiden the other side of the forest. I'm waiting for her to grow up."

"How old is this maiden?"

He pulled at his lip sheepishly. "Four."

"Jourdain."

"Well, I'm in no hurry, and neither is she."

Aristotle flipped her body into a ball, resting her chin on her paws. Heloise picked bits of rushes from her fur. "This child. Is she intelligent?"

"Very. Lively and smart."

Heloise glanced at him. "Pretty?"

He hesitated a moment, said, "Not unattractive," and they both burst out laughing. She remembered. That was what he had told Abelard, before they had met and Abelard had asked for a description. Not unattractive, Jourdain had said.

She said to him, "I could have killed you on the spot. Jesu, how vain I was."

"No, lady, you were right to be angry. It was not courteous of me." He fell silent. After a moment, he broke out bitterly, "Would to God I had told him you were ugly. Then none of this would have happened."

"No," Heloise said calmly. "Destiny can't be brushed aside that easily. What happened had to happen."

He took a long drink from his cup. "All of it?" he asked her, looking into the cup.

"No," she said slowly. "Not all. I serve God but I accuse him, as ever. Senseless cruelty, that's all it was."

"When are you going to stop fighting with Our Lord?"

"Never."

Jourdain stood and waved to someone at the side of the hall. His squire, André, came up with a fresh jug of wine. Easily, Jourdain moved around the hearth, refilling their cups. Heloise stared into the fire.

"In any case," she said finally, "my lord must be happy now."

"Well." Jourdain shrugged slightly. "He is an abbot, that's true."

"The equal of Suger and Bernard of Clairvaux and—"

"Aye." He paused. "Equal in theory but not in fact."

She jerked up her head, suspicious. "What do you mean?"

"I can't say. I've heard . . . things."

"Eh?" She sat upright, her heart banging.

"Ah, Heloise. You know that Saint-Gildas sits on some rock on the wild edge of the Atlantic. Miles from anywhere. What kind of life could that be for a man like Abelard?" He spat into the fire. "And there's been gossip about those monks for years. The Bretons can be bastards."

Frowning, Heloise lifted Aristotle to the floor. She stood and went to Jourdain. "What have you heard?"

"That they are unruly. But, mark me, all Bretons are unruly. It's likely just gossip." His face was guarded.

She said firmly, "Abelard can handle them. He's a Breton himself."

"Not very much. Le Pallet lies in Brittany, but it's more Poitevin than Breton. Besides, I doubt if Abelard even understands their dialect."

Her shoulders had tensed into two hard balls. Painfully, she arched her back, willing them to relax. "What are you trying to tell me?" she asked stiffly.

"Tell you? Nothing."

André brought up a dish of gingered pears. She scooped a handful and placed one on the tip of her tongue, sucking out the sweet flavor. "These are good."

"Suger did him no favor by sending him to Brittany."

"So? Why did he do it?"

"To get rid of him."

"But why? He's the most brilliant man alive today. I would say that even if he weren't my lord."

"This is the twelfth century. Holy Church doesn't want thinkers."

She said slowly to Jourdain, "Fair friend, I would not tell this to anyone but you."

He watched steadily, waiting.

"Abelard has always been a—" She hesitated.

"Troublemaker."

Half offended, she smiled. "I was going to say rebel. It stands to reason that a rebel, any rebel, would have many enemies."

Jourdain said, "He doesn't recognize his most dangerous enemy."

She raised her brows uncertainly. "Who's that?"

"Peter Abelard."

They were silent for a moment. Heloise could see they were getting nowhere. "Jourdain," she said, "what you say may be true. But God grant that it is not."

* * *

The following noon, at dinner, she said to Jourdain, "Have you a spare varlet and horse you could lend me?"

"Certainly." He smiled quizzically at her. "Where do you want to go?"

"To Uncle."

"God forbid!" he cried. "What do you want to do that for?"

As she herself did not really understand, she merely shrugged. "You think I shouldn't?"

"I didn't say that," he answered, composed again. "It just seemed curious to me."

"Mayhap that is my reason. Curiosity."

He did not question her further, and at midafternoon he escorted her to Fulbert's manor house, some thirty minutes' ride from Sancy. Under the autumn sun, the meadows were all gold and brown and the hills were drowned in a veil of apricot light. In the distance, Heloise could see the ramparts of a castle, sharp-edged against the sky. It was, Jourdain noted casually, Saint-Gervais. She looked again, then turned her eyes away.

Fulbert lived in a country house set on a wooded knoll. There was a shallow dry moat with dirt heaped on the far edge and a palisade that completely enclosed the house and its outbuildings. The gatehouse was empty, but the bridge had been left down and they crossed into the yard. Jourdain said, "I'll wait here."

Her mouth suddenly dry, Heloise went to the door and knocked. In a window to her left were hanging gourds full of aromatic spices. She braced her shoulders, expecting Agnes to open the door, but it was only a kitchen maid of ten or eleven. Without questioning her, the maid led her through a vestibule and into the *salle,* whose ceiling beams were carved with blue- and gold-painted fleur-de-lis. It was unusual to find such elegance in a country dwelling. Fulbert's ill-gotten gains, Heloise thought sourly.

At the sound of feet, she wheeled to face Agnes standing in the doorway. For a moment, the woman goggled dumbly at Heloise, as though she had seen a mirage, and then her gaze turned cold. She started to say, "What do you—" then stopped herself and bowed. "Lady," she murmured.

"Agnes." She glanced around at the furnishings, noting the carved chests, the scribe's writing chair, and the expensive chandelier hanging by an iron chain. She went on, "I wish to see my lord uncle."

"He's asleep. He can receive no visitors."

"All the same, I wish to see him."

Agnes did not move. After a moment, she said, reluctant, "As you please." In single file, they went down a darkened hall, out a back door, past a manger and pigsty. In an enclosed garden at the rear of the stockade, Fulbert reclined in an easy chair, a cup of brandy within reach. Heloise started. Tied to the foot of his chair was a monkey placidly licking its private parts. Agnes nodded dryly and hobbled back to the house.

Heloise waited, staring first at the monkey and then at her uncle. His hair, once silvery blond, had bleached out to a metallic white, and the hands that lay clasped peacefully over his abdomen were as yellow and wrinkled as the flesh on his cheeks. He did not look wicked, only old. And, as Jourdain had said, probably he was witless.

At last, Fulbert's eyes flickered. In the warm yellow light, he squinted at Heloise, glanced down at the monkey, and lifted his face to Heloise again. "Ah, fair niece." He smiled. "God's greeting to you. It's been many a year since I've seen your face."

"God be with you, Uncle."

He continued to smile at her. "God knows you don't resemble your fair mother at all. Hersinde was the baby of the family. When she was born, she had cheeks like unopened rosebuds." Heloise nodded. "She always reminded me of an angel. Too delicate to be real."

She nodded again. "Yes. My lady mother was a beauty." His pleasantness amazed her, as she had been expecting something far different.

Yawning, Fulbert said, "I'm well pleased to see you, niece. But I don't understand why you've left your convent. Have you run away?"

"Run away? No, I haven't run away. Argenteuil has been closed."

There was a long silence. Heloise was waiting for him to ask why Argenteuil had been closed, but he did not. Finally, Fulbert said, "I advise you to find another house, niece. The handmaids of Christ must not go into the world. It's not proper."

"Yes, my lord. I intend to enter another, you may be sure."

The monkey clawed at Fulbert's leg; hitching himself forward, he untied it and the animal hopped into his lap. "Hie, little monkeykin, have you had your nap?" He pummeled the monkey's chin. "Cunning, isn't he?"

"Yes." Then, with effort: "Are you in good health, my lord?"

"Good health, good health," he whinnied. "Of course I'm in good health. And would be in better health if Agnes fed me properly."

"You look well fed."

"Bah! She skimps on the honey in my sweet cakes. Says it's for my own good. Am I a babe? Don't I know what's good for me? I've money enough for all the bees and honey I wish." He waved at the trestle. "Give me my brandy."

He swallowed and wiped his mouth. "Ah. Yes, fair niece, I'm pleased to see you. Of course."

He maundered on for an hour or more, talking about his various properties, the current market value of his relics, his rent receipts, his will, the bowel habits of his monkey. There was no place for Heloise to sit. She rocked on one leg, then the other, nodding and murmuring responses from time to time and biting her lip. Agnes came and stood anxiously at the entrance to the garden, hands folded over her waist. Neither Heloise nor Fulbert glanced at her. He held the empty cup on one knee, the monkey on the other. Is it possible that he has forgotten? Heloise thought, full of horror. After robbing her of the things dearest to her, after destroying Abelard's career and reputation, was he not eaten alive by guilt and remorse? At last she made a farewell, screaming inside with awful laughter because she grasped that he lived untroubled, the suffering he had caused utterly forgotten. She left him to his monkey and his brandy.

Relieved, Agnes hurried her toward the house. She did not speak, and finally Heloise asked, politely, "Your daughter. God grant that she is well."

"She's dead," Agnes growled. "In childbed."

"Oh, Agnes," Heloise burst out softly, "I'm so sorry." She paused, searching for a word of consolation. "I—I have a child too."

Agnes pretended not to hear.

All along, Heloise had known their destination, but had not been able to name it, even to herself. "We are going to Brittany."

Ceci looked straight ahead. "He's an abbot now. He won't want his wife around."

Heloise said harshly, "You forget. I have a son in Brittany."

They stayed at Sancy, snowed in, until the New Year. Two days after Epiphany, the temperature rose to a springlike mildness, the snow unexpectedly thawed into a great dirty pond in the ward, and the roads became passable, if far from ideal. For their journey, Jourdain gave them a strong brown gelding and a wallet stuffed with money. He had not been pleased about their going, which he said was not a good idea in the first place, and if Heloise really meant to make the journey, she should wait until spring. But on the morning of their departure, he bade them farewell with tears and prayers, and at the last moment sent with them for protection a fourteen-year-old serf, John by name.

Among the trees, the air was smoky with snow; it lay so thick on the earth that it was hard to go forward in normal strides. Already the snow was starting to drift, confusing the trails and game tracks and transforming the forest into an immense white maze with neither beginning nor end. The two women were plodding now, lost, and they kept scanning the trees before and behind them, hoping to see a wisp of smoke from a chimney. On the rimed branches above their heads, hungry crows bleated and flapped. Under her mantle, Heloise hugged Aristotle to her side, leaving a tiny opening so that she would not smother.

Ahead, Ceci called over her shoulder, "Heloise, please. Let's stop for a while."

"No. Keep going." If they stopped walking, they would surely die. Earlier in the day, several times she had heard wolves howling in the distance; unlike the crows, they would not wait until their meal stopped breathing. She tried to walk faster.

Two weeks had passed since they left Jourdain, but once the blizzard had begun, it seemed an eternity. Under her breath, Heloise cursed the lad John. A sullen boy, who only spoke when asked a direct question, he had proved useless as an escort and, in fact, had slowed them down considerably, because the presence of a third person meant one of them always had to walk. And now the vile son of a sow had flown with the gelding and Heloise's wallet. When they had awoken that morning and crawled from the cave where they had huddled to sleep, it was snowing. There was not so much as a track to indicate in which direction the accursed boy had gone. Devil take him; she hoped the wolf pack got to him first. Keep walking, she told herself, walk or you will not live for long.

It was cold in the forest, and the wet snow numbed her feet through the soles of her boots. Wind whipped through the branches, and she heard Aristotle, a warm spot under her breast, begin to whimper. She unwrapped her cloak, kicked at the snow until she'd made a level patch, and set the dog on the ground. Bewildered, she stood dead still; Heloise, knee joints cracking, stooped and patted her soothingly.

"Hurry up, sweet. Do something." After a minute, she picked her up and thrust her quickly under the cloak.

The only things the serf had not taken were Aristotle, and Abelard's letters and the two rings, which had been sewn into Heloise's habit. But the map that she had been using to chart their way was in the saddlebag. Now she foraged her memory, trying to recall the look of the parchment sheet. They had been aiming for Blanchart, which could not have been more than three or four miles. But in which direction? By this time, she could not guess whether they were walking west, or deeper into the wilderness.

Single file, they went on all the rest of the afternoon, and when twilight came they perched in a tree, half dozing on a thick branch, their minds stupefied with exhaustion. All night long the dog whined with hunger, and the cold made sleep impossible. At some time during the night, the snow stopped.

Once, the next day, they heard oliphants blowing and the baying of hounds. But the hunters must have been far away; although Heloise and Ceci shouted until their throats were raw, the only sounds cutting the air were the echoes of their own voices. By midafternoon, they were walking aimlessly, slowly, to conserve their strength. Their toes and fingers screamed with pain of the cold. Under the broken branches all was quiet. Only crows beat the icy air, and under Heloise's cloak Aristotle keened through her nose, whether from cold or hunger she did not know. They ate snow and prayed.

To the south they saw a thicket of low hills and began stumbling toward them, hoping to find caves. They could not spend another night in the open. The sun had almost fallen when they crawled into a ledge beneath some tightly wedged rocks. There was no room to stretch out, but at least the ground was dry. Too exhausted for sleep, they huddled in each other's arms with Aristotle locked between their bodies. The sky darkened to jet and the stars came out, hard and white.

Ceci said, "Near Pamplona, we stayed at an inn once. It was really charming. There was a dear little garden and it smelled so—I don't know what kind of flowers, but it was like breathing perfume. You know."

"Did you dance there? I mean, at the inn."

"In a tavern nearby, at a wedding. It wasn't bad. But not as nice as the inn."

Heloise sighed. "Raimon. Was he—kind to you?"

That required thought. "I suppose," Ceci said at last. "He bought me lovely things. I had a yellow gown with a little blue overdress and a blue veil and—shoes, I had green silk shoes."

"Holy Mary, what a combination!"

"It was pretty, really it was. And I danced with castanets."

Heloise nodded and turned her head. "The prettiest gown I ever had was one that Abelard bought me. It was purple—no, more of a lavender, I guess. There was gold lace around the sleeves and I had a gold girdle."

"I love lavender."

"It was beautiful, the most beautiful gown in the world."

Aristotle, fussing, poked her head out for a moment and then slumped her chin against Ceci's knee. Ceci said softly, "We're going to die here." Heloise hunched her shoulders, not daring to answer.

In a thicket to their right something thrashed and then subsided. "I once had a hair crimper," Heloise said with forced cheerfulness. "Can you imagine that?"

"No."

"Well, I did. I made myself ringlets all down my back. Uncle was furious."

"He was a canon. They don't like women to look pretty."

"Abelard was a canon. He liked my curls." Ceci sighed against her ear. Heloise waited a moment and said, "Ceci, your Raimon. Was he—"

"Yes?"

"—lovely in bed?"

Ceci looked at her.

"I mean, did you like lying with him?"

Ceci shrugged. "It was all right. Why? Did you like lying with Abelard?"

In the darkness, Heloise smiled. "It was the greatest of all pleasures. The greatest."

They slept uneasily in each other's arms. The night trembled with sounds. Before dawn Heloise woke, her body paralyzed from the cold and from crouching in one position. Reluctant to wake Ceci, she disentangled herself and sat up. Suddenly a sense of something missing stabbed her, and she fumbled around heavily, groping for Aristotle. The dog was not there. "Aristotle!" she screamed. Ceci lurched upright.

As soon as the sky had lightened, they began to scour the crags and crevices, shouting, trying to distinguish tracks in the whiteness that might belong to a small dog. It did not take long. Some fifty yards from their shelter, in a glade fringed by black brambles, the snow was stained pink with gobbets of blood and bits of fur. The snow had been trampled down in a circle and whipped into a bed of brown and red slush.

Nothing remained except a few spotted bones. Gagging, Heloise closed her eyes and backed away. Ceci grabbed her arms. Dizzy with horror, they swayed over the rocks, and when they came in sight of their ledge Heloise could walk no further. She threw herself full-length in the snow, tears running into her mouth, cursing God for taking away her little lamb, her darling, her precious.

In the late afternoon, they crossed a frozen marsh and came out of the forest near a village belonging to the lord of Caudry. The villagers were poor shepherds, suspicious of travelers. They told of bad harvests the previous autumn. The children's faces were pale, their stomachs bloated with hunger. The headman had enormous hands and massive limbs and a face as black as charcoal, no water but rain having ever touched his face. If not for the pleadings of his wife, he would have chased them back into the forest. Heloise found the people repulsive, though the filthy thatched hut where they spent the night seemed a palace. The chief's wife offered them a pottage of leaves and roots, sour wine, and garlic. They took a few spoonfuls of the pottage, chewing slowly so that their empty stomachs would not throw back the food. The garlic Ceci put in her girdle. For sleeping, they were gestured to a corner far away from the peat fire. Ceci fell asleep the minute her head touched the ground, but Heloise, thinking of Aristotle, wept silently into Ceci's shoulder.

Early the next day, impatient to be rid of them, the headman set them on the road to Beaugency, which he said was a half day's journey on foot. It was not. They arrived in the town after dark and then had trouble finding a place where they could shelter for the night. Beaugency was full of horses, noisy people, and torches. After their nights in the forest, the flames made their eyes water. Light from the houses spilled into the snowy lanes, and the smoke of cooking fires smelled of roast meat. Stomachs cramped, they took a position outside a tavern and began to call, "Bread. For the love of Christ, a little bread," but nobody stopped.

It was late; soon the narrow streets emptied. From inside the tavern came drunken shouts and the clattering of ale cups. After a while, Heloise and Ceci went around to the side door and knocked. A woman opened and looked at them, closed the door, and opened it again a minute later. She held out a platter heaped with gravy-stained crusts and the carcass of a roast fowl. Heloise saw at once that flesh still remained on the underside of the bird and the wings had not been touched at all. Blessing the woman, she snatched the carcass and handed it to Ceci. The soggy bread she stuffed under her mantle. They trotted back to the street, eating as they went.

The winter was hard that year; there was rain blended with snow and chill winds, and the cold seeped into their very bones, felt all the more intensely because they got little to eat. When they came to a town, they quickly learned to find the church and sit with the other beggars. *Noble lord, good lady, a copper, a crust of bread, for the love of Christ.* Even so, it was not easy, because more than once they received a copper only to have it nipped from their fingers by fellow beggars. Hunger, they discovered, did not breed generosity, even for God's holy women.

The mornings were foggy, the roads deserted, and sometimes they walked for half a day without meeting another traveler. They stayed on the highroad along the bank of the Loire, not daring to turn off and attempt a shortcut lest they lose their way again. From time to time, they heard troops of armed men, soldiers in the service of some local lord, perhaps only a band of roving thieves, they did not know. Then they would plunge into the nearest thicket, crouching low to the ground for fear their black habits against the snow would give them away. Heloise lost count of the days; she knew it must be late in the month of February, but she could not have said how late. "Comrade," she said to Ceci, "spring is coming. When it's spring, life will be easy. You'll see."

Each day Ceci walked more slowly. The soles of her boots had worn thin, and she stuffed them with rags torn from the hem of her undertunic and, once, with one of Abelard's love letters. Still, her toes and heels erupted in sores, which soon began to swell with pus. It was bad luck. Limping, she hung on Heloise's arm. When they were covering less than a half mile a day, Heloise insisted they turn off the highroad and push toward a castle on the crest of a hill. Even though the guard in the gatehouse refused to lower the drawbridge—his master feared the plague—he did drop a basket of onions and rotting meat and direct them to Our Lady of Hope, a small convent down the valley.

They stayed at Our Lady three weeks while Ceci's feet healed. It was a poor house with only sixteen nuns; the prioress, Sister Maheut, herself cared for Ceci. Shaking her head, she chastised them. "You should have stopped when you saw the sores. Look how they are festered."

Ceci, who could barely endure to rest her feet against the floor, slumped back on the pallet bed. Now that it was unnecessary to move, there was nothing to prevent her sinking into sleep, and she did not wake the rest of that day and all that night. Heloise got up in the morning and went to say prime in the chapel. After the sisters broke fast, the prioress took Heloise into the chamber they used as a chapter house. She was a lean woman with a harried manner and penetrating blue eyes. The sisters at Our Lady seemed in awe of her. Leaning against the door, she said tightly, "Why do you wander the roads? Where do you come from?"

"France. Sainte-Marie of Argenteuil."

"And your abbess permits you to rove?"

"No, my lady. Our house was closed."

Sister Maheut was silent for a few moments. At last she said, "You may join us if you wish, but I can't take you without dowers. There are too many mouths to feed already, and we are poor. Surely you can see that for yourself."

"Yes, lady. I can understand."

"Have you any money?" Sister Maheut sounded embarrassed. "Anything at all you could give us?"

Heloise thought of the two rings in the bodice of her habit. "No," she murmured, "only the clothing on our backs."

Shaking her head, the prioress only sighed.

They kept going west. The ground began to thaw and ooze with mud. All about them the woods quivered with the chirping of birds, and the sap began to rise in the trees. As if drunk, they sucked eagerly at each ripening dawn, testing it for mildness. Happiness was warmth, Heloise thought; she never wanted to be cold again. With the approach of mild weather, the whole aspect of the road changed. Knights galloped smoothly by on their fine steeds, merchant caravans made deep ruts with their carts, pilgrims began to emerge from their huts and castles. The rich had mules and horses, the humble folk walked, and now and then a penitent with bare feet could be seen. Singing and laughing, people moved slowly and talked about the wonders they would find at Compostela or Notre Dame-du-Puy. In holiday moods, they smiled and opened their provision sacks to give a little to those who had less. Sometimes Heloise and Ceci had a loaf of bread or salted herring, and once a monk gave them a whole goat's-milk cheese.

Outside Tours, they fell in with a band of Normans, countryfolk bound for Brittany, and by Holy Week they were approaching Nantes.

Somewhere to the south, less than fifteen miles, Heloise judged, her son was running in the meadows. She wondered if he knew how to ride yet; surely he must have learned long ago and become a fine horseman by now. She could imagine the black outline of the pine grove above Le Pallet, remember its inner ward raucous with children's laughter. So many children at Le Pallet. Children and dogs. Not a day passed that she did not think of her little Aristotle; she had been the only living thing that had truly belonged to her, truly loved her. *O God! Kill my memory. Make me forget the sweetness of that tiny body.*

At Nantes, they parted company with the Normans and took the road north to Vannes. About sixty miles to Saint-Gildas, an alewife in the town assured them. Stay on the highroad, keep walking, they could not miss it. *O my Lord, you who send me only ill fortune, I do not judge your ways or presume to understand. But, Father, give Abelard back to me and I swear that I will obey you for the rest of my days. Thy will be done.* She knew better than to haggle with God, but she tried just the same.

The village of Saint-Gildas-de-Rhuys squatted on the Roman road running between Vannes and Port-Navallo. It was pretty, Heloise thought. There was a winding street that abruptly gave way to a square where fig trees had been planted. On the far side of the square stood a rather imposing church, surprisingly grand for such a small community. Beyond the church, silhouetted against the western sky, she could see the walls of the abbey, which had been built on a granite cliff jutting out into the ocean.

In the church porch, Heloise and Ceci sat down in the sunshine and watched some boys playing ball. After the quiet Seine and Loire, the furious hissing and thudding of the waves against the cliff sounded frightening, harsh. Heloise marveled that water could make so much noise, but none of the villagers seemed to notice. Approaching the village, they had caught quick glimpses of the sea, a dazzling blue shadowed by amethyst streaks, and it had looked beautiful but far from tranquil.

Ceci said, "This is nice. I'd like to stay here. We could get one of those little cottages we passed."

Heloise smothered a sigh. Abelard might object to their living so near the abbey.

"Should we eat first?" Ceci asked. "Or have a look at the sea?"

"I'm not hungry," Heloise said with a shake of her head. "Ceci, you wait here. I'll go up alone."

"No. I'm going with you. So let's not argue about it."

"He may not recognize me. It's been ten years."

"More likely you won't recognize him." She pulled a loaf of stale bread from her sleeve and broke off a chunk.

"What do you mean? I—"

"He's old now. What is he? Forty-five?"

"Fifty-one."

"Fifty-one! God's mouth, that's ancient."

They staggered up the rutted track that led to Saint-Gildas, the wind tearing at their wimples. A jowly-faced monk appeared in the doorway of the porter's lodge; he held a baby in his arms. Over his shoulder, they could see a woman spinning.

Heloise, disconcerted, remained silent a minute, and then she said, "Greetings, Brother. Is Abbot Peter within?"

"Not here," he barked.

Alarmed now, she tried to find out when the abbot was due to return. But to each of her questions the monk only shrugged. Finally, he took the child into the lodge and kicked the door shut. Heloise and Ceci started back toward the village. That Abelard should be abbot of such a place seemed incredible.

19 ❧

THE VILLAGERS KNEW all about Abbot Peter, and of course they never missed an opportunity to gossip about his monks, whom they regarded, simultaneously, with amusement and revulsion. Once Heloise and Ceci had settled down to wait, they heard everything. More than once, they were told how Abelard, newly appointed to his abbacy, had ridden into the village and left his horse and baggage at the tavern. Changing into a shabby cloak, he had climbed on foot to the abbey, where he had been given an offhand welcome and told to bed down among the beggars in the yard. The next day, returning in full regalia, he had been greeted ceremoniously and ushered into the chapter house, where the community had assembled. The first words he spoke to his new monks were a furious reprimand, a trick for which they had never forgiven him.

"Those swine," croaked a goodwife to Heloise. "They'd spit on Christ if they had met him ragged and barefoot." The woman insisted that she knew of what she spoke, because her aunt had five children by the cellarer.

Almost the whole of May passed, and still there was no sign of Abelard. The porter, Brother Alain, whom they visited daily, said nobody knew where the abbot was. On the second day of Whitsuntide, Heloise and Ceci went to the beach to fish. Returning to the village in late morning, they crossed the marketplace and heard people talking excitedly. Heloise edged into the crowd, trying to hear. Abelard was back; he had galloped through the village not an hour earlier. Trembling, she ran back to Ceci.

"He's here. They say he rode up the hill just after terce."

Ceci smiled. "I'll pray for you, sweeting." She took the cods.

Not caring if anyone saw, Heloise hitched up her skirt and careered up the hill to the abbey. Coming toward her were three monks, their faces locked with anger. She veered around them and loped to the gatehouse, breathing hard. The porter was not on duty, just a lay brother who said the abbot was in a temper and only a very foolish person would approach him now. Heloise pushed the brother toward the yard. "Find the porter," she said sternly. "Tell him I must see him at once." The lay brother went into the courtyard without answering. Heloise paced steadily in the road, her stomach churning. Twenty minutes later, the lay brother came sauntering back.

"He's eating now," he told her.

"Who's eating? Brother Alain? Abbot Peter?" She stuffed her hands into her sleeves to keep from shaking the man.

"Why, Brother Alain. Sit down. You're making me nervous."

Heloise sat near the wall. Brother Alain came, motioned, and led her into the yard. Her mouth was dry. She wanted to ask the porter if he had told Abelard her name, but the man looked surly. Monks were crowded around a door, screeching at the top of their voices. When they spotted her, they began to snicker. Brother Alain pushed them aside and gestured inside. "What do I do now?" she asked.

"In there," he muttered. "Wait."

The reception hall looked as if it had not been cleaned in a long time. The floor rushes smelled of rot and urine. She looked at a door at the far end of the hall, wondering if she should knock. She went over, bent her ear to the frame, but heard no sound; then she gave a soft thump. Nothing happened. She pounded.

"What is it?" somebody growled. She did not recognize the voice. Chest hammering, she pushed the door and went in.

Across the room, he was sitting behind a trestle strewn with papers and ledgers, writing, but he did not look up. When she cleared her throat, he finally lifted his eyes and stared at her.

Uncertainly he said, "Heloise?" Then: "Heloise?"

"It is I, my lord," she said, smiling softly. "It's Heloise."

"Lady." He looked puzzled. "I never thought to see you again in this life."

She wanted to reach for his hand, press her face against his chest, but she could not move. Outside, the monks' voices were raised in angry debate, and above that roared the thudding of the waves against the cliff.

"How came you here, lady?" Abelard was saying. "Forgive me, I—" He was hopping in circles about the chamber, finding a chair for her, bringing a cup of wine. She wished that he would touch her, just once. "Are you hungry?" he asked. "I can fetch you—"

"No, thank you. I need nothing."

"We must find a place for you to lodge," Abelard said.

"I have one," she told him hurriedly. "Ceci and I—we have been here a month."

Amazed, he stared at her. "A month! But—"

"No one could tell us where you were. So we waited."

"Please, tell me what you're doing in Brittany. Are you on pilgrimage?" He walked back to the table and sat down.

It was then that she noticed the chair, the same old armchair that he'd had at Fulbert's and later in his room on the Left Bank. The sight of it made a lump rise up into her throat. She said to him, "I came to see you. We came on foot."

"You walked!" He burst into delighted laughter. "Sweet heart, you walked. Wonderful. God, what a marvelous woman you are!" The grin stayed on his face, lighting up the blue eyes and curving the mouth with warm good humor. "God knows where you get your strength. There's nothing helpless about you, is there?"

She shifted uneasily on her chair, overjoyed to hear him praising her. "Oh, it was no large thing. People—" He was sitting back, smiling that old irresistible smile, and he continued to rave about her talent, strength, and good sense. It was not true, but she could not bring herself to tell him that. She leaned back and listened, soaking up his words like a drought-stricken field.

"Lady, my sweet sister in Christ." He spread his hands, palms up. "You do me honor, as always. You are—there is no woman like you in all of Christendom. Ah, Heloise, with all my burdens here. If you only knew. How often I've thanked Our Lord that you can manage for yourself."

Heloise said nothing.

"But of course you were never one of those helpless females. I insult you by even suggesting that you might have been a burden." He smiled comfortably. "My strong, capable Heloise. If the devil himself came to your door, you would find a way to deal with him."

Heloise smiled, not trusting herself to reply.

"When Suger reclaimed Argenteuil—but, lady, you have not told me which house you've joined."

"None," she said. At the shocked look on his face, she hurried on. "I applied to several but they refused me."

"Impossible!" he cried. "The most learned woman in France, in all of—"

"Mayhap it was Ceci they didn't want. I don't know. And then Suger —he dislikes me."

He frowned again, but did not comment on Suger. "We must remedy this." He gestured smoothly toward the ceiling. "You must have another prioress-ship. Or an abbacy. But we can talk about that later. Where did Lady Alais go?"

"Notre Dame-des-Bois." Heloise looked away, afraid that he would see the tears begin to well up at the corners of her eyes.

"And the rest of them?"

"Various houses," she answered. "And some asked release from their vows."

He flared, "What a waste," and got up and began pacing the floor. "What a hateful loss when holy women defile themselves with carnal pleasures." Heloise blinked, amazed. "How unseemly for holy hands to perform the degrading services that women are compelled to provide."

Heloise nodded several times, because she could think of nothing to say. She folded her hands in her lap to stop their trembling. Desperate to change the subject, she broke in, "Abelard, my"—she stopped herself from saying "my beloved"—"my lord, how fare you at Saint-Gildas? I've so longed for news of you." Immediately, she regretted her choice of words, for fear he might interpret them as a rebuke, but he did not appear to notice.

"Well." He gazed up at the ceiling. "Saint-Gildas. That would fill a book. A large book. Never, God knows, would I have agreed to take this house had I not been determined to outdistance my numerous persecutors. Who have an endless supply of persistence, I might add."

She could not bear to have him start on Soissons, so she said quickly, "I've heard that the monks here have a reputation for unruliness."

He sighed. "I've tried to reform them, but it's useless. I work, but I achieve nothing." He repeated bitterly, "Nothing. Brother Jacques still couples with his niece."

"They are your own countrymen," she said.

"Exactly. And who knows better than I what stinking sons of bitches the Bretons are." He paused. "It was for these swine that I abandoned the Paraclete and my students."

"Oh, Abelard." She wanted to weep for his loneliness and despair. He read her and grinned.

"So," he said lightly. "Here I am and here I will remain. God has put me here. Beside the harsh, roaring waves." He said it in Latin—*horrisoni undas oceani*.

Heloise nodded. The roar of wind and water. There was no escape from them.

Abelard murmured, "I never liked the sound of the sea. Now I've grown to loathe it."

"The headaches," she said. "Do you still get them?"

"Yes, yes." He sounded impatient.

The bell for nones began to toll. He glanced at her, turned away, and took a step toward the door. "Lady, I must leave you. Can you come back later?"

Heloise thought of staying until the office was over. But Ceci would be waiting, eager to hear what Abelard had said. He had said nothing—and everything. "Tomorrow," she said. "I'll return tomorrow."

"We must talk further."

"Yes." He was opening the door. "Abelard!"

He swiveled his head.

"I'm sorry," she said. "I mean, about this place."

He smiled at her. "Don't be. Truly the Lord is watching over both of us."

Then he was gone. She waited a few minutes, studying the cupboards lined with books, the familiar armchair, the worn inkhorn on his trestle. When she went into the yard, the bells stopped. Some of the monks were strolling slowly toward the church, but many ignored the summons. Three men knelt in the dirt, dicing; near the guesthouse a monk whom she recognized as the sacristan mounted a mare and headed in the direction of the gate. A falcon fluttered on his wrist. As she passed through the gate, the porter's child lisped, "Fare you well, pretty lady." The tears sliding around in her nose, Heloise went down the hill to find Ceci.

"I did not say I wanted to break my vows."

Abelard said, "That's the implication behind your words. What do you mean, then?"

Heloise kept her voice neutral. "I said that *if* I were to leave the order, our son would have a mother. It's one solution to all of our problems, that's all I said." She turned her head toward the wall, wishing that she were outside in the sunlight.

Abelard, silent, stretched back in his chair and pulled thoughtfully on his lip. At last he said, not looking directly at her, "Lady, I admire your efficiency. No doubt you can solve most any problem that needs solving." She opened her mouth to interrupt, but he turned her off with a glance. "But I fail to see that any problem exists. You have dedicated yourself to Christ."

"And our son?"

"Is accustomed to Denise. He's content at Le Pallet."

Heloise made herself ask the question that had burned in her gut for years. "And he thinks of Denise as his mother?"

"Well, yes. She is the only mother he's ever known."

Abelard could not know how his words cut her, true though they might be. "I wrote him many letters. But never did I get one reply."

He frowned. "Denise never mentioned any letters."

"Dozens. Why didn't Denise write me? Surely she did not imagine I'd forgotten my babe."

"Well," he grunted. "Well, I don't know. Mayhap she had her reasons. The lad is happy there with his cousins, and—mayhap she didn't want to upset him."

She shouted, "How could knowing his mother loved him upset him?" The wind had died down; the room was eerily quiet.

"Heloise, please—"

"Am I some slut who drops her babe in the field and leaves him there?"

"Stop." He clapped his hands over his ears. "You're distorting everything."

She got up and went to the window. Turning her back on him, she clutched the sill to steady herself.

"Lady, let's not quarrel. I know you love the boy, but there is no cause for worry. I swear it. He's a fine, happy lad. Just like the others at Le Pallet."

She did not want him to be just like the others. "Tell me, have you seen him?"

"Last year. Or the previous one. I don't remember. Lady, stop fretting. He's a fine lad."

"Yes, you said that. What does he look like?"

Behind her, Abelard's chair skidded on the tiles. "Why, like you. Tall, blond, handsome—" He sounded as if she should know all that.

He was standing behind her, quite close, but she did not turn to face him. "Lady," he said quietly, "put your mind at rest." She nodded, suddenly aware of the closeness of his body. Her chest began to pound.

She did not speak, nor did he. He slid nearer, so near that when she twitched her shoulder blade, it brushed lightly against his chest. An inch from her ear, through her veil, she could feel his breath. She closed her eyes, waiting for him to touch her, but he did not, and she sensed that his fists were clenched at his sides.

They stood, rigid, listening to each other's breathing, and still neither of them moved. At last, Heloise let the muscles in her back and hips slip, so that the whole back of her body eased against him. Instead of stepping away, he pressed himself against her. Through the rough cloth of his robe, she could feel his belly, ribs, thighs. Slowly she felt something move and stiffen against her buttocks. Inhaling a gasp, she let her mind race forward to clutch at hope. Her groin began to tingle. She wanted him inside her, and if he could not be, there were other ways to give and receive pleasure. Surely he remembered. Had they not once tried everything? She bit her tongue to keep from moaning aloud.

And then abruptly it was over. She heard him groan and he jerked back so suddenly that she almost lost her balance. Gracelessly she wheeled around. He was leaning against the back of his chair, his mouth working silently.

"Abelard—"

"Hush." She hugged her arms around her waist and stared at him. Stiffly, he said, "I beg your forgiveness, Lady."

"Please, no—"

"Lust. That has been the root of my misfortunes. Lust and pride." His voice swam with self-loathing. "The merciful Lord takes thought for the salvation of my soul, but I persist in my sins." He softened. "Go. Please go."

Numb, Heloise began to glide toward the door. Reaching blindly for the latch, she lifted it and stepped into the reception hall and out into the yard. Some monks were saddling their horses. She went toward them and then stopped, darting a fast look over her shoulder. Abelard was standing in the doorway, watching. She walked quickly toward the gate.

They left Saint-Gildas that afternoon. Ceci asked no questions, and for that Heloise felt grateful. They started back along the road to Nantes, leaving the sea at their backs.

After a week, Heloise was able to think of Abelard with a kind of detachment. Naturally, she had not expected to find him unchanged after a decade, that was too implausible an idea even to contemplate. Yet, at their first meeting, he had not seemed terribly different, and she had been able to jolly herself into believing him the man she had loved. She amended that thought—still loved, and would go on loving to the grave.

What she had not expected, what shook her at the core, was to find that he had been truly converted to God in a way that she had not dreamed possible. The things he said to her that morning, before she brought up the subject of Astrolabe, were what the most zealous of abbots or bishops might say. Rather, those extremely holy abbots, like Bernard, who despised the things of this world. Abelard the sensualist had vanished; Abelard the property of God stood in his place. And viewing it that way, she could not fault him. By anyone's standards, even her own if she thought calmly about it, it had been wrong of him to stand behind her as he had, making her want him. Although God and all the saints knew that she had needed no encouragement. But really he should not have done that.

South of Nantes, on the road to Poitou, they were picked up by a farmer hauling home a cart of provisions. Heloise remembered him because he had come to visit William occasionally, but he obviously did not connect the pregnant girl of years ago with the black-robed nun. She and Ceci sat on top of the cart, lazily watching the fields roll by. Throughout the morning, the sun beat steadily on their heads. The farmer grumbled about his vines and the avarice of a certain priest in Nantes and other matters of interest to him. The sky was full of lacy clouds.

A half mile from Le Pallet, he turned off, and they walked the rest of the way. The drawbridge was down, the gatehouse deserted. Heloise and Ceci went into the ward, where a dozen or more children were playing tourney with stick swords. Swiftly, Heloise scanned their heads for blond hair, but none of the boys was especially fair. One of the older girls ran up, breathless. She looked at them as though they had landed from the moon. The rest of the children had dropped their swords and stood gaping.

"Child," Heloise called, "we wish to see your lady mother. Is she about?"

"Agathe!" one of the boys shrieked. "Ask her what she wants."

The girl ignored him. "Holy sister, I think she's in the hall. Shall I fetch her?"

Heloise smiled. "Your name is Agathe?" The girl was thirteen or fourteen and her breasts were hard little apples under her bliaut. Heloise thought, This one was a babe when I last saw her.

"Agathe! Ask her—"

"Oh, shut up," Agathe threw over her shoulder. "Lady, I am Agathe. Do you want me to find Mama?"

Heloise resisted the urge to stroke the girl's head. "No. Go back to your game." She motioned Ceci up the wooden steps to the keep. This was going to be difficult. She must remember to keep a good control over herself.

The hall smelled of incense and fresh rushes. Somebody had picked sunflowers and scattered them over the trestles. Denise walked in, carrying a pile of bed sheets. When Ceci cleared her throat, Denise stopped and swung around.

"Greetings, lady," Heloise said.

Denise blinked at them, puzzled. "Good sisters—"

Heloise broke in. "Don't you know me, Denise? It's Heloise. This is my friend, Sister Cecilia."

The sheets tumbled to the floor, but Denise made no attempt to catch them. Her face was lined around the mouth and eyes, and patches of sweat stained her gown beneath the arms. "Heloise," she echoed in a dazed voice.

Ceci started to say something, but Heloise put a hand on her arm. She said to Denise, "Are you in good health, lady?"

Denise nodded blankly. She was watching Heloise and Ceci, her eyes darting between their faces. Finally she said, "I didn't know that you'd left your convent."

"The house closed," Ceci said quickly.

"We have not yet entered a new one," Heloise added.

"You are just passing through Brittany?" Denise asked thinly.

Heloise shook her head. "I've come to see Astrolabe."

"Astrolabe?" Her voice was stupid.

"My son. Astrolabe. What do you call him?"

Denise said slowly, "Peter—is what we call him."

Heloise looked carefully at the woman's face. She's afraid, she thought, frightened I will take him away or something. But why? She has a dozen others. "Is Peter well?"

"Yes."

"Good."

"What do you want with him? You won't make him feel bad?"

"I love my son," Heloise said. "You must know that from my letters."

At the mention of the letters, Denise flushed and stared down at the mounds of bed linen heaped around her feet. "Go away," she mumbled. "Go now before he sees you. I don't see why you've come back." She added in a small voice, "Have you no shame?"

Heloise swayed against Ceci. She struggled to keep her voice even. "Shame? Lady, I can't feel shame in loving my babe. Come now, send in my son."

"I've warned you. Remember that."

"Send him to me."

Denise scooped up the sheets and went out. Ceci glared at Heloise. "What's wrong with her? She's certainly disagreeable."

Sighing, Heloise walked over to a trestle and sank on a bench. Through the open shutters she could hear the children screaming in the ward. The minutes dragged. Ceci, at the window, called to her, "I see someone coming." Trembling, Heloise got to her feet.

The boy coming slowly across the hall was not one of the children she had seen below. He was tall for his age and gave the impression of being frail, even dreamy, although she could see that he was muscular and healthy and his arms, hanging loosely from the short-sleeved tunic, were covered with dirt and mosquito bites. Going up to Ceci, he smiled easily and said, "Sister, my lady mother said you wished to see me."

Ceci pointed to Heloise. He trotted over and bowed.

"Peter." Heloise made herself say the name. "Did Lady Denise tell you who I am?" It was a rhetorical question, but she did not know how else to begin.

"No," he answered.

Oh, Denise, she thought, how unkind you are. Licking her lips, she said gently to him, "Peter, Lady Denise is not your real mother. You know that, don't you?"

"Oh yes. But she is my mother." The boy's voice was confused.

She was going about this all wrong—she should have told him at once. She heard Ceci, at the window, cough sharply. Astrolabe was shuffling his feet and scratching his bites. She saw at once that he could not keep still a minute. She smiled at him. "Lad, I am Heloise. Your lady mother."

He opened his eyes wide. Obviously he was reluctant to accept that piece of information, but he did not want to be rude. "If you say so," he said at last. "But the Lady Denise is my mama."

The expression on his face was so full of pain and bewilderment that Heloise forgot her reserve. She went to him, took him by the hand, and sat him down on a bench. He did not resist, but next to her he began fidgeting. A lock of hair fell over his eyes. "Tell me, Peter. Don't you remember the letters I wrote you? About the convent and my little dog Aristotle? About the river with all the pretty boats?"

Puzzled, he tossed his head. "No."

"Fair son, mayhap you've forgotten. You were smaller then."

"No. I had no letter." He looked up at her impatiently.

Heloise knew there was no point in insisting. It was as she had always suspected. Denise had destroyed the letters. The boy was ill at ease anyway; he did not understand that the letters were meant to convey her love and longing for him. She wanted to fling her arms about those skinny shoulders, shout that she loved him. "Do you like books?" she asked cheerfully. "Tell me what you read."

The question seemed to surprise him. "Why, the *Disticha Catonis* and the *Eclogue* of Theodulus . . ."

Heloise nodded encouragingly. These were the standard beginner's readers. "And?"

"And my Latin grammar."

"Donatus. What else? Plato, Aristotle, St. Augustine?"

"No. I mean, I can't remember. Mayhap."

Questioning him further, she learned that a priest from the village came once a week to instruct the children at the castle. Astrolabe did not feel deprived in regard to his education, indeed he seemed to think that he showed more progress in his studies than his cousins, who were prone to tease him about it.

"At your age," Heloise told him, "you should be more advanced in your education. Your lord father is the most brilliant scholar in—well, in all of Europe."

"I know," he mumbled, a little sullenly. "He's a great abbot."

"And a very learned man. As you must be, too, when you grow up and become a man."

He stared at her, his eyes flashing. "I'm going to be a knight and ride in tourneys."

The racket in the ward had stopped. The children must have gone away somewhere. From the passageway leading to the kitchen, Heloise could hear the clanging of pots. She glanced at Ceci, who raised her eyebrows. She said to Astrolabe, "Your lord father and I love you very much, my sweet. Even though God has willed that we should be parted from you."

The boy did not answer.

She leaned toward him, carefully stroking the hair back from his eyes. To her astonishment, he flinched. "Sweet, what's the matter?" Suddenly Astrolabe burst into sobs. "What is it?" cried Heloise. "Are you ill? Holy Mother, Ceci, what ails him?" Ceci started toward them, then stopped. The boy continued to sniffle loudly.

"You're going to take me away!" he blubbered. "I won't go, I won't!"

To soothe him, Heloise stroked his hair. "There, there, I wouldn't take you away. We can be friends. There's nothing to cry about."

"You'll bewitch me and steal me—my mama said so."

Forgetting to guard her tongue, Heloise cried, "And who has a better right to you? You're my son. I would be the happiest woman in the world if I could be with you."

"You're a whore!"

"Son—"

"You're impure and wicked. I don't want you to be my mother!"

Heloise wrenched back. Astrolabe hopped to his feet and raced from the hall as if pursued by demons. For a long time, Heloise did not move. Finally Ceci said, gently, "Heloise, I think it's time to go." And when Heloise did not answer, Ceci said again, "Friend, let's go. There is nothing more you can do here."

Heloise rose quietly and clung to Ceci's hand.

For three days, they had been walking along the riverbank, looking in vain for a boatman who would take them across without wanting payment. Now it did not matter. Sweat bathed Heloise's body and her cheeks were an ashy green. She stumbled along until the middle of the day, when she crawled into a ditch and closed her eyes. When she woke, the sun was coasting down the sky and the afternoon shadows had lengthened. Ceci was sitting cross-legged by the side of the road. Heloise got up and they went on.

The fields were golden bronze with ripe corn. They crossed a little hill and descended into a valley where black and white goats were cropping on the slopes. Farther down the road, alongside a clump of yew trees, they saw tendrils of smoke. Relieved, Ceci warned, "We're stopping there. I don't care."

"I'm not sick."

Ceci snorted. "Don't be stupid. You're sick."

The cottage was a one-story building of wood, wattles, and thatch, all of dirty brown. Inside the fence sprawled an enormous dung heap, on which hens and pigs roamed nonchalantly. When Ceci shouted, a woman in homespun blouse and loose trousers hurried out. Heloise did not pay attention to their conversation. She leaned against the gate, watching. The yard seemed to be filled with long, lean cats, none of whom appeared friendly. The peasant woman was staring at the ground while Ceci talked, and finally wagged her head. Ceci came back and led Heloise into the hut. It was a single large room, the walls and ceiling timbers blackened by soot. There was no hearth, only a flat stone in the center of the room and a smoke hole in the roof. Several half-naked children playing on the floor goggled at the nuns and fell quiet.

The woman, whom Ceci called Marie, showed Heloise to a straw pallet and covered her with a blanket. The silence of the children changed to giggles and whispers as they began to play again. Ceci, crouching, put one hand on Heloise's forehead. With the edge of her sleeve, she blotted the perspiration from her face. She looked scared.

"Don't look at me like that," Heloise said abruptly. "I'm not going to die."

"I didn't—"

"Oh yes you did. God won't let me die. He's not through torturing me."

"Don't talk like that. It's bad luck."

Heloise closed her eyes. "He has emptied a full quiver into me. If he had a single arrow left, he could find no place in me to take another wound. And still he won't end my suffering."

After a while, Marie brought a crock of water, a ladle, and a rag. She set them on the ground near Heloise's pallet, and Ceci gave her small sips of water. "Shhh, shhh. God is with you, sweeting."

She opened her eyes and whispered bitterly. "God is *not* with me."

Ceci began to argue with her. "Mayhap that is because you refuse him."

"That isn't true. It is he who has refused himself to me." She slammed her lids shut again. Later, across the room, a man's voice rose in waves and receded. She thought, I have done nothing for the love of God, why should he reward me? Is it my fault that I love Abelard above him, did I volunteer for this madness? She could feel flies crawling on her face, hear the nervous swoosh of Ceci's hand as she shooed them off. Without opening her eyes, she plucked at Ceci's sleeve. "Comrade, why are you so worried?"

"I'm not worried."

"God has taken everything from me. I long for death."

"You'll get better. I'm going to take care of you."

Heloise drifted away, not listening. During the night, her bowels plunged to water and by morning the hut reeked of foul odors. Once she strained to open her eyes and saw Ceci crying. Quickly her lids fell together and she did not make the effort again.

Time passed. A week and then another week, perhaps more. She did not attend to the rising and sinking of the sun. Finally, one afternoon, she woke and swiveled her eyes around the room. It was empty, save for Ceci stirring a kettle at the fire. She called out weakly. Ceci ran to her and knelt. "Ceci, I'm still here."

"Oh, you're still here," Ceci said in a light voice. That night, Heloise slept deeply, without the fever dreams. Her eyes were sunk in great brown holes in her face, but she could not see that.

Ceci had washed her habit and veil and hung them on a hook near the pallets. Although Heloise could not get up yet, she sat propped against the wall and watched the family eating and talking. The man, Simon, said little to her beyond inquiring about her health, but one evening she called him to her. She asked him, "How much do you plow in a day?"

He shrugged. "An acre, sometimes more."

"Do you have a helper?"

"My oldest boy. He drives the oxen."

"And besides the plowing. There's more to do, isn't there?"

He could not understand the reason for her curiosity, but he smiled, wanting to humor a sick nun. "To be sure, a good deal more. I have to fill the oxen's cribs with hay and give them water and carry the dung— you know."

Heloise sighed, sympathetic. "It's hard work."

"Oh yes, it's hard work. Because I'm not a free man."

While she was listening to Simon, she thought of the whey and eggs that Ceci had been feeding her. The family was poor; she was taking food from their mouths, and she squirmed with guilt. Later that evening, she mentioned this to Ceci, who looked away uneasily.

"Heloise," she finally quavered, "I did something you won't like."

Heloise stared at her.

"I gave Simon your ring to sell."

"Which one?"

"The amethyst." Then: "Please don't be angry. I had no choice."

She slumped against the wall. "Well, it doesn't matter. I hope Simon got a good price." Ceci did not answer. A moment later something odd occurred to Heloise. She asked, "Did you give Simon all the money?"

"Only a little."

"But Ceci—"

In a rush, Ceci's words rolled out. "Heloise, I hired a man from the village to ride to Saint-Gildas."

"Ceci!"

"Shhh. I thought God was going to take you. I thought Abelard would want to come."

Heloise hugged her arms against her breasts. "But he didn't," she whispered. "See, he didn't come. Oh, Ceci, I could have told you that."

She was lying in the yard, under a yew tree, when he rode up to the gate with a young man in a clerk's gown. The two of them looked ridiculously out of place in front of Simon's hut. Throwing his reins to the clerk, Abelard dismounted and walked slowly toward her.

Without speaking, he dropped to the ground beside her and took her hand. A few yards away, in the doorway of the cottage, Ceci stood watching them. At last, Abelard began to ask her questions in a low voice—about her illness and how she felt and so forth. His manner was stiffly courteous.

Heloise broke in. "My lord, I didn't ask for you. It was Ceci who—"

"She did the right thing."

"No, it wasn't necessary. And she sold the amethyst."

He frowned. "What amethyst?"

"My ring. You gave it to me." Jesu, had he forgotten!

"Oh." He nodded slightly. "Oh, yes. That first summer."

There was a long, uncomfortable pause. Ceci went to the road and began talking to Abelard's clerk. Leaning back in the grass, Heloise closed her eyes. Abelard said, "You're not mended yet."

"I'm being well cared for. You needn't have troubled to come."

He looked away, gazing at the corncribs at the back of the yard.

Twisting back toward her, he said, "I want to give you something."

She made an impatient gesture, then let her hands fall slack. "There is nothing you can give me." She thought, I've never wanted anything from you except yourself, and that has been denied me.

He was stammering. "Lady—lady, must you make this difficult for me? You were dearest to me when we lived in the world, and now you are dearest to me in Christ. Our roads have separated, it's true, but we are still bonded together in the eyes of the Lord." He was breathing quickly, pleading almost. "I possess nothing, how could I as Christ's servant?"

Heloise swallowed. "Please. Don't."

"Lady, I own one thing. The Paraclete. It's still mine. Let it be my gift to you."

Dazed, she said the first thing that came into her head. "But what would I do with it?"

He stared at her. "Do with it? Why, build a convent dedicated to the service of Our Almighty Father."

"A convent," she repeated.

"I wish that I could offer you more, but it's all I have."

She looked up into his face, into the blue eyes trembling with tenderness or some emotion close to it, and she slowly nodded. So quietly that he did not hear, she said, "God's will be done."

20 ❧

Two DAYS BEFORE the New Year, their party reached the village of Quincey, which lay only a mile south of the Paraclete. In their baggage train were sumpters laden with kettles, pallets, blankets, candles, as well as sundry items they would need to live.

The great open fields of Champagne were broken by flat-topped blue hills and, now and then, strands of evergreens rising starkly against the chalky soil. The land appeared bleached to Heloise, bleached and silent. It was not an ominous silence, though. It felt reverent, almost dreamlike. Her feeling of unreality vanished once they rode among the clustered houses of Quincey. Lord Milo's bailiff, a barrel-chested man named Arnoul, came out to greet them, his manner displaying the utmost deference and even obsequiousness. The villagers stared with either dull curiosity or outright hostility. Immediately, Heloise sensed that the reappearance of Abelard did not please them, and it made her uneasy. Shivering inside her cloak, she watched their faces as they stood in their doorways, reluctant to leave their warm hearths and bowls of wine, even for the visit of an abbot.

Abelard took no notice of the silent, unsmiling faces. Smiling brilliantly, he waved Heloise, Ceci, and the clerk, Berengar, into Arnoul's house, where they sat down to bean soup and red wine.

Arnoul said, "My lord abbot, will you be staying at the Paraclete?"

Abelard did not answer directly. He began quoting the Book of Psalms about refuges in the wilderness, and then he quoted St. Jerome at some length. At last, he turned to Arnoul. "What did you say?"

"Your Holiness, you won't like what you find there."

"Eh?"

"There were brigands up there. Last year, I think it was. They used it to store their loot."

Unconcerned, Abelard grunted, "Well, now they must find another place."

In the midafternoon, they rode north along the river. Abelard rolled from side to side in his saddle, calling out in excitement.

"Wait until spring!" he yelled. "The waters are magnificently green. Cool, pure, the greenest river in the world. And do you know why that is?"

"No." Heloise smiled.

"Because of the reeds swaying in its depths. And reflections from the trees. Homer himself could not do justice to its beauty."

Behind his back, Ceci sniffed and flashed him a glance of disgust.

They dismounted by a knoll. Abelard strode across the field toward the river, and the rest of them followed slowly. Close to the water's edge stood a chapel made of limestone and wood; farther back from the embankment, a hundred yards or so, were two graceless rectangular structures, which looked like empty boxes.

Ceci said to no one in particular, "Is this all?"

"What do you mean?" Abelard asked, raising his eyebrows.

"There's nothing here."

Ignoring her, he said to Heloise, "I wish you could have seen them. Students, thousands of them. They gathered here from castles and mansions. Instead of delicate food, they ate wild herbs and made beds of straw and used banks of turf for their trestles." He sighed happily.

Ceci said, "That's all very nice. But if we are to live here, we can't eat off banks of turf."

Abelard answered sharply, "Sister Cecilia, our Lord Jesus reminded us to think of the birds—'for they sow not, neither do they reap nor store up food, yet their heavenly Father feedeth them.'"

Ceci said, "Well, didn't someone say that Our Lord helpeth him who helpeth himself?" Abelard turned away sharply and went into the chapel. Staring at his back, Ceci whispered to Heloise, "Men. They have no sense when it comes to practical things."

"He remembers it as it once was. Probably it was lovely then."

Ceci looked around skeptically. "I don't see how thousands of people could have lived here. Where? Tell me that." She clamped her lips together.

"They made huts from reeds."

"Where? I don't see anything."

Heloise was beginning to feel annoyed. "Ceci, that was six years ago. They've all blown away."

Berengar came up beside them. He was a bearded man of thirty or thereabouts, unfailingly courteous, with the gallant manners of the Poitevin nobility and the soft, drawling accents of the *langue d'oc.* "Ladies," he said, "if you would feel more comfortable, I can take you back to Quincey for the night."

Heloise shook her head.

He said helpfully, "There's another village about a mile to the north. Saint-Aubin. Mayhap you'd like to go there."

"We'll stay," Heloise said firmly. "Thank you."

Well, she thought, it does not look awfully promising at the moment. But from Abelard's descriptions, she could imagine it as it had been and as it would be again someday. With all those gnarled trees, the land seemed wild and desolate, despite the proximity of the villages. Its loneliness didn't bother her; rather, it gave her the same feeling as her rock at Argenteuil. There she had felt a serenity, a soul-soothing calmness, and she sensed it now too. Something could be done here.

She wheeled and walked toward Ceci, who was tugging at some object half buried in the ground.

Ceci whistled to Abelard's clerk. "Hie, Sir Berengar. Look here. What's this?"

He trotted over obediently and began kicking at the ground with the toe of his boot. After a moment, he bent down and lifted up a rusty iron kettle. He was about to toss it away when Heloise called out, "Save that! We may need it."

After compline that evening, they huddled around the fire that Berengar had made in the west building. Ceci dozed on a pile of hemp sacks, left by the bandits, probably, and Heloise, silent, was busy thinking.

"My lord abbot," she said at last, "these buildings need to be cleaned thoroughly and repaired. Could we get some villeins to help us?"

"Of course you can get villeins." He leaned over and poked at the fire until sparks flared up. "And men from Quincey and Saint-Aubin as well." He dropped the stick abruptly. "My lady Heloise, do you like this place? Tell me the truth."

"Aye, I do. But it needs work."

He nodded and shut his eyes. Heloise wondered if his head ached. There had been times, on the road from Brittany, when she had noticed his eyes glazed over, and then he would hold his neck stiff, as if only the greatest concentration would keep his head from bouncing off his shoulders. He did not look well to her. On his hands were patches of dry and itchy-looking skin; sometimes his face would flush bright red and he would sweat profusely. She pretended not to see. Under the circumstances, she had no choice. These past months, his manner had been formal, perfectly correct. It was as though Abelard and Heloise had died. When he spoke to her now—always in the presence of others, for he took care not to be alone with her—it was the abbot of Saint-Gildas talking to Sister Heloise, future abbess of the Paraclete.

She turned to watch his face. Worry lines grooved his brow. He had started talking to Berengar about the Church meeting that would take place at Etampes on January 20. It was to be an important occasion, because Pope Innocent would be consecrating the high altar at the abbey of Morigny, and other prominent men, such as Abbot Bernard of Clairvaux and Abbot Suger, would be there as well. Heloise knew that Abelard planned to ask the pope for assistance with his monks at Saint-Gildas.

She went back to figuring in her head, only half listening to the men. The room was full of the odors of dust and mold, and there were rat droppings in the corners. This will be my home, she thought, this land belongs to me. The thought made her feel good. A moment later, she realized that she had no idea exactly what belonged to her. Obviously, this property on which the chapel stood, but where did the Paraclete's boundaries begin and end? The field was not large, hardly big enough to make vegetable gardens. The next time Abelard and Berengar fell silent, Heloise said, "My lord abbot, God's pardon for the interruption. But can you tell me how much land belongs to us?"

Abelard stretched his legs. He looked surprised. "Well—enough, I suppose."

"How much exactly is enough?"

"This field." He motioned Berengar to bring him a leather bag. "And some other property in the neighborhood. I don't remember precisely."

Heloise fidgeted while he fumbled in the bag and finally drew out a paper, which he handed to her. "My lord Milo," he told her, "has been extremely generous. As you can see . . ."

While he was talking, she read the charter: "It is evident that Divine providence counsels the rich. . . . Wherefore I, Milo, by the grace of God lord of Nogent . . . wishing to make provision for my salvation, have found it right to dispose for the good of my soul of some of the temporal possessions which have been bestowed upon me . . ."

The charter went on to define the bequest: three cultivated fields, the villeins attached to the land, the use of the forest of Saint-Aubin in perpetuity, all the marshy ground adjacent to the Arduzon. Next were listed by name those whose souls were to be prayed for, mainly Milo and his kin.

Wearily, Heloise slid the charter into her girdle. Probably Abelard was right. It was enough, for now at least.

Nevertheless, she was soon to revise that hasty judgment. It was true that they owned three plots for cultivation, but under the three-field system, one of them must lie fallow that year. A second should have been plowed in October and sown with wheat, rye, or barley. But when Heloise went out to talk with the villeins, she found that nothing had been done. How could they have known that Master Peter would return? This all meant that she must wait until March to plow and that there would be no grain until after Lammas. Each day the stores they had brought from Sens were being used up, and while they all ate sparingly, she knew they would never last. She would have to buy grain in Quincey or Saint-Aubin, but with what? Abelard could give them a little money, but he would be returning to Saint-Gildas eventually. Surely they would go hungry before Lent was over.

It was ironic. Never, and certainly never since she had taken vows, had she spent so much time thinking about the material things of this world. Now these things that she needed—wheelbarrows, a proper well, plow, fishing forks—these worldly goods obsessed her so that even during prayers she could barely keep her mind on the words. There were so many things that she needed—and a few that she merely wanted. She struggled to remember that there was a distinction.

"Bees," she said to Ceci. "Wouldn't it be wonderful to have bees?" She craved a bit of honey.

"Aye. And a cow and some hens. Maybe we could get a dog, Heloise."

"No," she answered sharply. "No dog." Deep inside, memory knotted her stomach.

She sent Berengar and Ceci to the woods to gather sticks and fallen timber, and she began to mend the rotten beams under the chapel roof. Abelard helped to the best of his ability, but Heloise had to conclude finally that he had no gift for physical labor, especially not for carpentry. More often than not, he ended by smashing a finger under the hammer, and she dared not allow him to approach the saw.

Abelard and Berengar left for Etampes. That same day, Heloise rode the mare to Quincey. As she passed down the main street, she looked around more carefully than on the day of their arrival. Judging from the yellow clay houses, the villagers seemed to be a mixture of poor villeins and comfortable freeholders. Certainly, Arnoul's stone house was nice enough, and most of the wooden houses had chimneys. Now, for the first time, she noticed that Quincey had a small parish church, as well as a saddler, blacksmith, and carpenter. She made a mental note to find out which, if any, of the craftsmen would be willing to ply their trade on behalf of the Paraclete.

A crowd stood talking around the well. When they saw her, they stopped, and one of the women stepped forward, smiling shyly.

"Good day to you, Sister," she said. "I'm Melisende. My husband is Payen the saddler." The woman was young, pretty, and seemingly friendly.

Heloise smiled down at her, relieved to find a welcoming face. "God's greetings to you, madame." She reined in the mare and dismounted.

Melisende came closer. She said in a low voice, "Sister, how are you faring up there? Do you have firewood and food?"

"Oh, yes. Anyway, for the moment." She shrugged. "Later I don't know about."

"I wasn't prying, Sister—"

Behind Melisende, Heloise could see the town people staring, their eyes suspicious. She stared back, unblinking, wanting to smile but afraid.

"They say that Master Peter left today," Melisende said. "Will he be returning?"

"Certainly," Heloise said. "He's gone to Etampes." She added, "To see the pope."

Melisende lowered her eyes. Nodding stiffly, she murmured, "If there is anything I can do, Sister," and backed away toward the villagers. Heloise led the mare to Arnoul's house and tied her to the gate. She reminded herself that begging was nothing new to her, and, besides, in asking help for the Paraclete she was not begging for herself but for God. Still, she felt uncomfortable. She went to Arnoul's door and knocked. Arnoul opened. "Sister," he said nervously, "Sister, I thought you had gone." It was obvious that he had not expected her visit.

"Not at all. Abbot Peter and his friend have left for a time. But Sister Cecilia and I will remain." She decided to make clear to Arnoul that they were not transients. She said firmly, "The Paraclete belongs to us now. We intend to build a convent. We shall be your neighbors, Arnoul."

Arnoul signaled to his wife to bring wine, but Heloise shook her head. She could not remember what St. Benedict had said about the propriety of drinking wine in the house of a peasant. Probably nothing, but she was sure he would not approve. For that matter, St. Benedict's Rule did not seem to apply very well to a convent that had two members, three ruined buildings, and no resources. She shook her head again, and Arnoul's wife took the cups back to the hearth. He said, "We shall be honored to have a house of holy women for neighbors." Despite his words, he did not look pleased.

Heloise decided to come straight to the point. "Arnoul, you know that we have only two small dwellings and the chapel and those are in bad condition. Sister Cecilia and myself—we are doing our best, but we're not masons or carpenters." Perhaps intuitively she left Abelard out of it. "We have fields to plow soon, and we must borrow oxen and a plow." She went on rapidly without giving Arnoul a chance to respond, spilling out her plans to build a good well, a wall, a water mill over the Arduzon. He kept nodding, but when she asked for men to help repair the buildings, her most immediate need, he began to shuffle his feet. He did not know if anyone was available at the moment.

"Why not?" she asked politely.

"Friday is the feast day of Ste. Veronica."

"What about Monday, then?"

"The feast of St. Macarius." He shrugged helplessly.

She had never heard of either of those saints and told him so.

"Humble saints, my lady. Peasant saints. Many here observe their feast days."

Heloise turned away, tired. "I understand." She began moving quietly toward the door.

Arnoul came after her. "My lady, wait. You mistake me. If it's acceptable to you, we'll come next week. On Tuesday."

She remained with him for an hour discussing which tools she owned and which the men of Quincey must bring with them. Afterward, she left the horse tied to Arnoul's fence, burrowed her neck in her cloak, and walked up the street toward the church.

The place was empty and cold, and a single candle guttered on the altar. She said the office quickly, mechanically, and got up to leave. At the portal, as she was pushing the door, somebody pulled from the outside, and she sailed into the porch, struggling to land on her feet. A black-robed arm reached out to steady her. Looking up, she saw a priest chuckling. He was middle-aged, probably past middle age because his head was as bald as a walnut, but he had twinkling blue eyes and the grin of a youth.

"My, my!" He laughed. "I've never seen a nun fly. Sister, are you one of the Blessed Virgin's angels?"

Heloise straightened her wimple. "Sorry, Father. Only a clumsy mortal."

"Well," he said, "you look like an angel to me. Would you be one of the sisters from the Paraclete?" He did not wait for an answer. "Of course you are. You have your work cut out for you, don't you?"

Heloise could feel her shoulders relax. He was the first one in Quincey who seemed genuinely eager to meet her—and sympathetic. The priest took an onion from his girdle, broke it clumsily in half, and handed the larger segment to Heloise. They stood in the porch eating. His name was Father Gondry and he knew Abelard. He also knew that she was Abelard's wife, and when she expressed surprise that he should be aware of this, he only said that the world was small and the reputation of the learned Lady Heloise great.

"Father Gondry," she said suddenly, "tell me something, please. The people here don't like us. Why?"

He squinted at her. "That's not it exactly. They have nothing against you."

"Be honest. There's something amiss."

He chewed off another piece of onion and turned his head, jaws working. "The Paraclete is yours now. It belongs to women, not to Abbot Peter. Once the people realize that, they will love you, I'm sure." He looked at Heloise. "It's the abbot they're suspicious of. Not you."

She rocked back in bewilderment. "In God's name, how could Abelard have offended them?"

"Sister, it was not his fault, not really. All those students—why, you should have seen the place. Lord Jesu and all his angels, what a mess—"

"But Abelard said it was heavenly."

His blue eyes blinked. "Mayhap it was—for them. Not for us. There were, er, disturbances."

"What do you mean?" she asked.

Father Gondry blushed furiously. "Drinking. Incidents of various sorts. It wasn't safe for our maidens to go abroad without escorts. You know. It could have happened if there had been a dozen hot-blooded young men. There were thousands, for the love of heaven. Who bothered to count?" He offered her another onion. "Here, eat."

"No, thank you."

"Sister, I doubt if anyone could have controlled them. Best put it from your mind."

"Yes," Heloise said, and sighed.

Milo of Nogent sat on a great carved chair, which perched on a platform before the hearth. Heloise, on a stool, felt as though she were sitting in a hole; she had to crane her neck to see his face. "I don't think he should have left you without protection," he said. "There have been evil men in those parts."

"We've seen no one." She added calmly, "And if the bandits should return, what have we to fear? We own nothing they'd want to steal."

"You have a horse."

Heloise thought of Jourdain's serf; she wondered what he had done with the stolen mount. Sold it probably. Hurrying to change the subject, she said, "My lord, speaking of animals. We have plowing to do and no oxen or plow."

Milo smiled away her words. "See Arnoul. All that can be easily arranged." He signaled a page to bring wine. Heloise swept her gaze around the hall, trying to remember what Father Gondry had told her about Milo. A friend of Count Thibaut's, a man of shrewdness and craft, a womanizer, a rich nobleman who had forgotten God a thousand times and now wished to make reparation for his sins. Heloise thought him not unkind, but he was certainly representative of his class. She shifted uneasily on the stool. "My lord," she said loudly, trying to get his attention again. "My lord, if you please." Milo leaned back in his chair. "Here is what I have. Three arable fields, each averaging thirty acres. Five villeins who each have a cottage and five acres. That leaves me sixty-five acres. Each villein is bound to plow four acres for the Paraclete and work three days a week on our land."

Milo cut in. "Who's going to plow the rest?"

"I am. I mean, Sister Cecilia and myself."

The lord of Nogent raised his eyebrows sharply.

Determined to head off his objections, she said hastily, "St. Benedict ruled that holy men and women should occupy themselves with manual labor at certain times."

"St. Benedict. Surely he didn't suggest that nuns go into the fields with oxen. Such work was not meant to be done by women." He shook his head.

Heloise thought of the villeins' wives, who plowed, sowed, and threshed. "Thank you for your concern, my lord," she said. "It is true that the Rule of St. Benedict was written for men, but I believe that women must try to obey it." She paused for breath. "Your original bequest does not make clear our water rights."

"What do you mean?"

"Have we the right to fish in the Arduzon?"

"Certainly." His eyes kept studying her, as if he were trying to locate Abelard's mistress and wife under the baggy black habit. "Of course. Fish all you like."

"How far along the banks in either direction?"

"How far do you want?"

She had planned her answer days ago. "From Quincey to Saint-Aubin. And if it please your lordship, we humbly request exclusive rights."

He ended by giving her what she wanted, also the promise of seed grain, hens, and some razor-backed hogs. He told her to make a vegetable garden in the marshy land south of the chapel, which she had already thought of, and to plant vines, which she had not.

"My lord, begging your pardon—don't you think it would be a good idea for your clerk to take note of these gifts?"

"Don't you trust me?"

"I trust you. But it's always prudent to have business matters put down in writing. For your own protection, my lord." It was for her protection and he knew it.

Milo grinned at her, amused. "*La très sage Héloïse* is wise in more ways than one. You have a good head for business, lady abbess."

She smiled, trying to accept the compliment graciously.

They had snow twice in February, but it thawed quickly. Heloise's original assessment of the Paraclete as an isolated haven was proving to be inaccurate. Quite the opposite. The road between Saint-Aubin and Quincey was frequently traveled. There were merchants taking their wares to Troyes or Provins, and people from Traînel, Lisines, and Nogent-sur-Seine on the move through the Champagne countryside. Almost daily, people passed their encampment, for it could hardly be called a cloister at that point, and some of them came especially to see Heloise and Ceci. The saddler's wife brought seeds for the vegetable garden—beets, watercress, lettuce, leeks, and mustard—and she also was generous with advice. Their apple and plum trees must be pruned if they were to get good fruit in the summer, and Melisende showed them how to snip off shoots with a sharp knife. The bailiff of Saint-Aubin,

Galon, came with his wife, Adelaide; also a knight named Ralph Jaillac and his wife, Elizabeth; even Abbot Norpal of Vauluisant, who arrived on a mule and sniffed disdainfully when he realized that the Paraclete had only two residents. He found fault with everything.

"Recruit," he snapped at Heloise, "recruit or perish."

She tried to keep her temper. "Yes, we need novices," she said smoothly, "but no one has come forward yet."

"Come forward? You must go after them. And take only those with rich dowers."

Heloise shrugged her shoulders. No doubt it was sage advice. No doubt Abbot Norpal meant well, but she didn't care for his manner. He acted as though she were a fool who could not manage her own affairs. Besides, she had not asked for his opinion. She had her own ideas about the kind of women she wished to admit, and foremost among her requirements was that they be intelligent. Or, she told herself, at least not stupid. When he rode off, Ceci made a withering face behind his back. She said, "Oh my, recruit or perish. Pompous old ass. God's balls!"

Heloise laughed. "Sister Cecilia, is that any way to talk? You should be ashamed."

Abelard arrived the next morning from the Morigny meeting. He and Berengar stalked around the place exclaiming and vowing that Heloise had accomplished miracles. In her opinion, she had done practically nothing. Arnoul and the men of Quincey had helped repair the roofs and beams, and on one of the buildings they had added a room with a chimney, which Heloise was using as a kitchen. The well was still being worked on.

When Abelard had finished tramping up and down the riverbank, he came over to the marshy spot where Heloise was turning over the earth for her vegetable garden. "What are you going to plant here?" he asked.

"Lettuce, herbs, you know. I've already put in cabbage and onions."

"Any mint?"

"I might." Abelard had a great fondness for mint. She remembered that he liked to crush it into his wine. She sliced the spade into the mud and pushed with her foot.

"Here. Give that to me." Heloise stepped back, handing him the spade. "Why didn't you wait and have this plowed? Your hands will be ruined."

Heloise quickly hid her hands in her sleeves—they were already as calloused as any peasant woman's. "My lord, what news from Morigny? What did the pope say?"

"Lady." He straightened his back. "Innocent is a lion of a man, a prince and a fighter."

That meant something to Heloise. She had been worried about Innocent, because for many months the Church had been rent by schism and the Chair of Peter claimed by two popes. Innocent's rival was a former Cluniac monk who called himself Anacletus II. Heloise had suspected that Innocent would be seeking support from the important abbots of France, but whether he would grant favors in return was another matter. She said to Abelard, "What is he going to do?"

"Send a papal legate to Saint-Gildas. My old friend, Geoffrey of Chartres. No doubt the worst offenders will be excommunicated and expelled and the rest severely warned." Abelard leaned on the spade, smiling exuberantly.

Heloise nodded. If the legate planned to visit Saint-Gildas soon, it meant that Abelard would not remain with her long. She smiled back at him, trying not to think of it. "God be praised," she said. "Now everything will be fine."

He began digging again. "I spoke to Innocent about you. He's going to extend you papal recognition as the new owner of the Paraclete."

"That's splendid." She smiled. "My lord, I do thank you from the depths of my heart."

In the kitchen, she built a fire and looked fretfully at the basket of eels on the floor. Ceci had trapped them early this morning, before Abelard and Berengar had come, and clearly there were not enough to feed four. The two of them had been living on onions, garlic, acorns, and coarse barley bread—and the gifts of visitors. When they had time, they fished, but this was not always possible. She slapped the eels into a pan. Into a deep kettle she threw beans, onions, and water, and hooked it over the fire, hoping that by evening it would turn into soup. Oh, she thought, what I wouldn't give for a garlic sausage. Even a small one.

When she finally set the food on the trestle, it seemed more inadequate than she had expected. The eels must have shrunk during cooking. Nobody mentioned the spareness of the meal. Berengar, courteous as always, complimented her on her skill with the eels. He said, "Sister Cecilia tells me that you do not lack for visitors."

Abelard looked at him sharply. "What does that mean?"

Before Berengar could reply, Heloise said hastily, "People have been very kind. They wish to know us—and offer assistance."

For reasons which she could not explain, Abelard sounded cross. "Have men come here?" he demanded roughly.

"Certainly, my lord. Arnoul and some of the villeins from Quincey and—"

"Others?" Abelard ripped off a chunk of bread and lifted it to his lips.

"And others."

He was staring at her as if she had done something wrong. "Lady abbess," he murmured at last, "the more rarely you allow yourself to be seen, the more highly valued will be your appearances in public and your spiritual guidance."

Heloise's eyes widened. "But, my lord—"

"You must devote yourself to prayer and meditation."

She forced her voice patient. "Begging your pardon, lord abbot. How do you propose I do these things when there is no wall, no gate? There's no way to keep people out."

Suddenly he sighed, and the bad temper was gone. "Aye. I know. It's hard." He curled his fingers through the hair at the side of his neck. "Now, what was I thinking of? Of course, you must have a wall. I understand that."

Heloise looked at him across the trestle. Her chest burned with pity, and she longed to draw him into her arms and caress that dark head. It was curious; when she was separated from him, she squirmed with hot images of herself lying naked in his arms, their legs entwined. In his presence, however, those torturous pictures subsided and she felt calm, unaroused. She gazed beyond Abelard at Ceci, who was glowering at the wall. She was not eating anything; she would be starved by nones.

"Lady," Abelard said, "I nearly forgot. I have letters for you."

"Really?" She smiled. "Who would write to me?"

He called, "Berengar, get the abbess's mail."

There were two letters: on one she recognized the handwriting as Jourdain's and slipped it into her girdle to read later. The other she opened with some curiosity and immediately glanced at the bottom of the sheet to note the signature. "Astrane!" she exclaimed. "My lord, this is from a nun who was at Argenteuil. Ceci, it's from Astrane."

"Oh," Ceci said with a scowl. "That's nice."

Abelard said, politely, "What does she write?"

Heloise read silently. Everyone watched her. Finally she lifted her head with a dismayed expression. "She's at Sainte-Catherine's of Senlis. She has heard about our new convent." She shook her head in disbelief. "She and several others in the house wish to— She says here that she wishes to join us." She laid the letter flat on the trestle.

Ceci sat bolt upright and jabbed her elbows down hard against the board. "She said that! I don't believe it. What gall, what—"

Abelard's voice rose above hers. "That is good news indeed, lady. The Paraclete needs women. Write at once and extend an invitation."

At his elbow, Ceci was mumbling under her breath. Abelard swung toward her. "What did you say, Sister?"

"Pisspot. Limp-legged, nasty-minded pisspot."

"Stop that," Abelard warned. "Sister Cecilia, you may be excused from this table."

Ceci got up and ran outside. Heloise read the letter a second time, to see if there was something she had missed. There wasn't—Astrane was asking for an invitation.

In the evening, after the rushlight had been blown out, Heloise stirred restlessly on her pallet. She clamped her eyelids but they would not remain shut. Beside her, Ceci rolled over. "Heloise," she whispered, "what are you thinking about?"

"Astrane."

"You won't have her." It was a definite statement.

Heloise let a moment slip by in the darkness. Then she said quietly, "Yes. Yes, I believe I will have her."

"Heloise!" Ceci sat up.

"Didn't Lord Jesus tell us if someone slaps us on one cheek, turn the other too? And to treat others as we want them to treat us? How can I refuse her!"

"Holy Cross, she betrayed all of us."

"We must love our enemies." Heloise pulled the blanket around her neck. "We get no credit in heaven by merely loving those who love us."

Ceci kept silent. She flopped down on her back, and Heloise could feel her staring in the blackness. Finally Ceci said, resigned, "Mayhap she has changed."

Heloise laughed. "I wouldn't count on it."

After a while, Ceci said sleepily, "Hard to believe we shall have a cloister here someday."

"I know."

"Shall we get a lemon tree? In remembrance of Lady Alais?"

"I think that would be nice."

Ceci was asleep. As every night, Heloise began her prayers. *Our Father, who desirest that we all be saved, grant that we acquire thy love even as have the angels who do thy pleasure on high. Protect thy ser-*

vant Abelard. O Lord, watch over him from thy holy place. I beseech thee—to protect him in all adversity— In sudden despair, she broke off and buried her face in her hands. Why was it so difficult for her to pray? Why couldn't she love God as she loved Abelard, why was it so hard for her to serve God? Why? In fairness to herself, she sometimes felt that she did serve him. But certainly got no satisfaction from it. It seemed to her that all she ever did was remonstrate with him, as if she were some female reincarnation of Job. *Lord, I believe, even though I have suffered much at thy hands. Help thou mine unbelief and rebellion, my pride and lack of contrition.* She prayed, knowing that God laughed. He knew that she was neither resigned nor submissive.

21 ❧

THE SUN FELT WARM at midday now. The winter rains had stopped and the ground was beginning to dry up. Arnoul sent word that he was bringing a team of oxen and a plow to the north field.

After saying prime, Heloise and Ceci took the mare out through the fields. The strips belonging to the Paraclete were not adjacent. In addition to this one, there were two more to the east, each intermingled with strips held by Milo and the villagers so that it was difficult for Heloise to get straight where her land ended and theirs began.

It was still chilly, because the sun had just risen. They skirted the oak woods and came out into an open space where Arnoul was talking to the villeins who held their land from the Paraclete. Heloise swiveled her neck and gave Ceci a puckish grin.

"Keep your eyes open today, sweet," she said. "Because on Thursday they'll be working their own strips and the plow will be all ours."

"God's toes, when I took vows, nobody said anything about plowing." Pressing her mouth against Heloise's shoulder, Ceci began to laugh. "Look there. Those oxen look mean."

"Shhh. Act like a nun." Heloise jumped the mare over a balk of turf that divided the Paraclete's field from the adjoining one and jogged up to Arnoul. The hooded men inched back, trying not to stare. Several small boys kicked at the dirt. Heloise greeted them with a smile.

"Lady abbess," Arnoul stammered, "it was not necessary for you to come."

She slid gracefully from the mare and helped Ceci down. "Certainly it's necessary," she said quietly. "How else will we learn?" Ceci took the horse to a tree and roped it. "Besides, we've brought your dinners."

"As you wish, lady," Arnoul answered. He looked angry.

Ceci pointed to a wooden grid that lay flat on the ground. "What's that?"

"A harrow," Arnoul said.

"A harrow," Ceci repeated uncertainly, as if it were some exotic machine never before seen in Champagne. The children giggled and nudged each other.

Tugging at Ceci's sleeve, Heloise led her to a balk, where they sat down to watch. The oxen were yoked up. One of the villeins grabbed the plow handles and began guiding it over the ground. He started just to one side of the center of the strip, plowed the entire length, then turned at the end and plowed back along the other side. After a while, Heloise grew almost mesmerized by the repetition of the motions: the coulter cutting the earth, the share breaking it, then the wooden board turning it over. "Arnoul," she called, "has this field been manured recently?"

"No, my lady. By my records, four years ago."

Under her breath she clucked fretfully. The yields would be poor, unless God decided to be merciful and made a miracle.

Two men operated the plow, one of them grasping the handles while his partner walked alongside the oxen with a goad and shouted commands. Both of them swore a lot. After them trailed the men who broke up the larger clods with plow bats.

Above, the sun was climbing the sky. Heloise felt the warmth on her forehead and hands. Three men moved into the row scattering seed broadcast—peas and beans in the furrow, corn and barley on the ridges. Shrieking and squealing, the children ran up and down the field slinging stones at the crows. Arnoul was signaling to a villein, who immediately guided his horse and harrow over the furrows just sown. Ceci jabbed Heloise with her elbow. "Look how many men it takes to do this. There are only two of us."

Heloise smiled at her. "We'll manage."

"How?"

While watching the villeins, Heloise had been thinking about it. "I'll guide the plow. You drive the oxen."

"What about the seeding?"

"We can do half the strip, then come back and start seeding and harrowing."

"Sure. And in the meantime the crows will have a belly full."

"We'll get Berengar and Abelard to shoo the birds."

Ceci laughed.

"I'm serious."

"Berengar might do it. Abelard never. You're talking about an abbot."

Heloise shrugged. "We'll see." It would do no harm to ask.

Toward midmorning, they could hear the church bell tolling dimly from Saint-Aubin. While the men unyoked the oxen and fed them hay, Heloise and Ceci brought out the food. On those days that the villeins plowed for their lord, it was obligatory to provide them dinner. Wet—with ale. Or dry—without. Heloise had not tasted ale since Christmas, nor had she cash to buy it from the Quincey alewife. Her villeins would not be happy with their dry dinner, she knew. When they came up to get their fish, bread, and cheese, she made a little speech explaining the missing ale and asking for their indulgence. They said it didn't matter.

Heloise offered a brief prayer, and then everybody sat on the turf banks and ate. Arnoul, chewing noisily, said to her, "Lady, there was no need to apologize. These men don't expect ale." He talked about them as if they could not hear.

Heloise smiled. "It does no harm to express one's feelings. I'm truly sorry I had no ale for them." She took a crust of bread and smeared cheese on it.

Arnoul went to his horse and came back with a skin of wine. He offered it to Heloise. She shook her head. A few yards away, she could hear the villeins bickering roughly and cursing. The boys were happily stoning each other. Arnoul shouted at them, and they threw down their slingshots and sat on the ground.

Heloise said to Arnoul, "After dinner I would like to take the plow." He nodded, as she had already informed him that she and Ceci would finish the plowing. "Just once or twice down the field. To get the experience of it." He nodded again and fell silent.

After perhaps five minutes, he said, "Abbot Peter. He'll stay for a while?"

"A short while. He must return to Brittany."

"Does he know that you intend to plow yourself?"

She paused to glance at his face. His eyes were bright with disapproval. "I don't know if he knows or not. It is not important."

The bailiff wiped his forehead on his sleeve. "He should hire villeins to work your land. Two women can't do it alone. You need help."

Heloise stood up. "The abbot no longer owns the Paraclete. It is Sister Cecilia and myself who would be hiring, and we have no money. You know that."

Arnoul ground his heel into the dirt. "The abbot could find the money. He could preach."

Her back straight as a board, Heloise looked down at him. "With God's assistance, I shall plow. I'm not made of rock crystal."

Arnoul stood and shouted for the men. They yoked the oxen to the plow. Heloise grasped the handles; Ceci picked up the long switch from a ditch. The villeins stood against the turf balks, watching them. Cautiously, they moved off down the field. The ground was slightly uneven, the plow much heavier than Heloise had imagined. By the middle of the furrow, her arms were beginning to ache. She concentrated on keeping the plow steady. As they neared the end of the row, she heard Ceci shout, "How the hell do I turn these beasts around?"

"With the goad!" she yelled. "Prod them!" Ceci began to scream at the oxen. A villein came running down the field and swooped the switch from her hands. Roughly he beat the team until they had turned and were maneuvered into position. Heloise dropped the handles for a moment and wiped her hands on her skirt. She waited, inhaling the good smell of freshly turned earth. Once again her hands clamped the plow, and they started moving. When they reached Arnoul and the villeins, she noticed that the men were grinning. They let out a long cheer. Heloise dropped the handles and grinned back, her face dripping sweat. Arnoul barked, "Jacques, get going. Take the plow." He scowled at the men. "Move. This isn't a feast day."

In position again, the oxen began lumbering down the strip. Ceci, panting, untied the mare. The women went home.

Later, after vespers had been said, Heloise went down to the river to find Abelard. Beneath the trees it was dank and the deepening twilight brought an aroma of rotted reeds. Abelard was sitting against the base of a birch, a book on his knees.

"Lady." He looked up at her, his eyes sleepy.

"Abbot Peter," she said in a light tone. "If I remember correctly, you once told me that as a boy you were an expert with the slingshot."

He smiled jauntily. "Champion of Le Pallet. A regular David against any Goliath."

"Good." She smiled back. "The Lord has need of you."

All through the spring and early summer, while the earth covered itself with juicy grass and the cabbages rounded into pale-green ovals, Heloise and Ceci rose long before prime to begin their work. Abelard had been back in Brittany for some time, and even though Heloise prayed for a letter, none came. She told herself the pope's legate must have visited by now—the monks of Saint-Gildas surely had put their feet on a more righteous path. By midsummer, the days were long and they were in the fields from dawn to dusk working alongside the villagers. Heloise felt violently happy. People made whistle pipes from reeds and played tunes on them. Out in the hay meadow, moon daisies were in bloom and dragonflies skimmed overhead. The grass there was high enough for the children to hide in. Everyone said the harvest would be plentiful.

Months had passed since Heloise had written to Astrane, telling her that she was welcome at the Paraclete but spelling out clearly the primitive conditions she would find. Ceci, who had read the letter, said Heloise had painted such a dreadful picture that Astrane would be sure to give up the idea; she was glad of this. In time, both Heloise and Ceci forgot about Astrane. There was too much to do.

The Paraclete had acquired a sheep. One. It was an old, smelly creature, not at all lovable, and whenever Ceci looked at it, she began jesting about roast mutton. In July, on sheep-washing day, they drove the animal downriver to Quincey, where the villagers had built a big pen next to the water. It hardly seemed worth the trouble to have their one sheep washed and sheared, but Heloise felt they might as well. From early morning they could hear the Quincey sheep baaing a mile away, so much racket did they make.

Heloise and Ceci stood a little way off, watching. The sheep driven into the pen were all piled up against one another. Prodded with long sticks, they were pushed screaming into the water. Melisende came up and leaned against the pen, but conversation was difficult unless you shouted at the top of your voice. Yet somehow they talked, about the only things that mattered to any of them: the haying, when the corn would be ready for reaping, most often of the weather. It had been good so far, and if it held, if no rain spoiled it, they would give thanks to God.

At noon, Melisende's eldest son, a chubby lad of ten, ran up and said that three nuns had been seen in the village. Melisende said, "You must be mistaken."

"I saw them, Mama. They're all in black."

"Pilgrims," Melisende remarked absently.

After a moment, Ceci jabbed her elbow into Heloise's side. "Do you think—"

Heloise hurried toward the road, Ceci lurching along at her heels. There was no sign of any nuns. She walked slowly toward the village, shading her eyes. At the fork in the road, under an oak, sat Astrane and two other women. When they caught sight of her, they got to their feet and came forward hesitantly. Astrane called, "Sister Heloise. I mean, lady abbess—" Her face seemed saggy, apprehensive.

Heloise looked back. Ceci had stopped some fifty feet to her rear. She was not coming. Heloise turned, went up to Astrane, and kissed her on both cheeks. She stepped back and smiled at her, then at the two women behind her. "Welcome, ladies."

Her eyes glued to Heloise's face, Astrane said quickly, "We lost our way . . . somebody gave us incorrect directions . . . where's the convent, all I've seen are corn fields . . . I just can't—"

Heloise laughed. "Whoa, Sister, catch your breath. The Paraclete is up the road about a mile." She pointed north.

Ceci was stamping toward them, her face fixed in an expression that was half smile, half grimace. Heloise hoped that she wasn't going to be unpleasant to Astrane. Suddenly Ceci shouted at Astrane. "Well, Sister, we meet again on God's green earth. The Lord's will be done, I suppose."

Astrane looked away quickly, her eyes narrowed to slits. "God's will be done," she murmured, and introduced her companions, who stood smiling politely. Heloise glanced at the one called Gertrude. She was tall and her hazel eyes spouted curiosity. Whenever she spoke or looked at someone, she wrinkled her nose. The other nun, Marguerite, did not appear pleased to be there. Her eyes were bloodshot, and she kept swiping at them, and at her nose, with a wadded handkerchief. She told Heloise that grass made her sneeze.

They walked back to the pen to collect the sheep. Children and sheep and dogs clogged the dusty road. Ceci said to Astrane, "Forgive my curiosity, Sister. But how came you to leave a place where you were prioress? Surely that was not a wise move."

There was a long pause. Gertrude and Marguerite pretended that they had not heard. Astrane, shoulders sagging, was looking at the sheep. "I was not prioress," she said finally. "Abbot Suger promised me the position, but it did not come about." Her face was hard.

"So," said Ceci quietly. "You didn't get your thirty pieces of silver after all."

"Sister Cecilia!" Heloise said sharply. Sweet Jesus, Ceci could be cruel.

Astrane nodded, looking Ceci directly in the face. "No," she said, "I did not get my thirty pieces of silver." She laughed harshly.

Marguerite began to sneeze. They started up the road to the Paraclete, everyone talking at once, Ceci prodding the sheep with a stick. Heloise thought that Astrane's limp had improved slightly; or perhaps she had merely devised a way of holding herself that made the disability less noticeable. When they came in sight of the Paraclete, Heloise said loudly, "There it is."

Nobody spoke. Then Marguerite said, "Where?"

"Oh," Ceci said, laughing, "you have to look carefully, but it's there."

The three newcomers, including Astrane, who had been forewarned, looked about with undisguised confusion and dismay. Heloise smiled. "Sisters, we have very little. As you can see."

"Lady," Gertrude gasped, "anyone can walk right in here."

"And anyone does," Ceci called out cheerfully.

"We are going to build a wall," said Heloise. "In fact, now that you're here, we shall have one by the end of the summer." That was far too optimistic a prediction, but Heloise made it just the same.

Suspicious, Astrane asked, "Who's going to build this wall?"

"Ah, we are," Ceci answered.

"But I've never built a wall."

Ceci laughed. "Live and learn, Sister." She chased the sheep to its pen while Heloise led the women to the sleeping chamber. It was clear that they were exhausted. They fell on the pallets and slept until vespers.

On Tuesday of the week following, after sneezing and wheezing steadily, Marguerite told Heloise that she wanted to return to Senlis. It was the proper decision, Heloise thought, and she packed off the sniffling nun with a merchant caravan traveling north. She had neither the time nor the facilities for nursing the sickly, and she had counted it one of God's blessings that she and Ceci had kept in good health. All that week, and for several weeks after it, they were busy with the harvest. With hand sickles and flails, they reaped, stacked the sheaves, and threshed. Sacks were carried home on wagons and stored in every available foot of space, including the chapel. Gertrude and Ceci went to work on the fruit trees, which hung low with plums, apples, and pears, and they all picked blackberries, sloes, and nuts, knocking the acorns from the oak trees with sticks. For the first time in many months, they left the trestle with their stomachs full.

When the sacks of grain had been taken to the Saint-Aubin mill to be ground into flour, Heloise went to see Lord Milo's master mason for advice on building a wall. She had started the foundation before harvest, and thanks to the gift of a knight from Ferreux, stone had been floated downriver from a quarry north of Saint-Aubin and stacked behind the chapel. It was enough for barely one side of an enclosure, but it would be a start. The mason came to the Paraclete to show them how to mix the sand, lime, and water, how to lay the stones on top of each other and trowel mortar between the layers. He left them a level and plumb line so they could make certain the stones were laid perfectly horizontal.

Father Gondry came to bless the first stone and stayed to help with the lifting. He knew even less about wall building than Heloise. By noon, only five stones had been set in place.

Gertrude was proving to be the fastest learner of them all. She suggested to Heloise that they might cut the expense by mixing mortar with pebbles—if they filled in the spaces that way, the large stones would go farther. When Heloise told her to try and see what happened, she fell to work with such zeal that she demurred about stopping for food. Father Gondry went back to the village and returned an hour later with a crew of children. Mainly they ran around slopping mortar in their hair and getting in the nuns' way. Finally, Heloise sent them to the fields with sacks and instructed them to gather pebbles.

Astrane poured water into the bowl of mortar. "This stuff is getting hard," she said to Ceci. "You're working too slowly. Look. You're not putting enough on that stone."

Ceci slapped at the mortar with her trowel, ignoring Astrane's pointed finger. "Don't tell me what to do."

"Somebody has to." Squinting critically, she came up with the bowl and heaved a blob of mortar onto Ceci's layer. "That stone won't hold."

Ceci's teeth began to rattle. She stared down at her work, her mouth grim. Heloise called to them, "Please, sisters. There's no time to quarrel."

Ceci's temper was up. "Of course I'm stupid compared to the brilliant Sister Astrane. I'll bet Sainte-Catherine's was ecstatic to see you go."

"Go to the devil," Astrane growled.

"I would, if I weren't sure of meeting you there."

Gertrude had dropped her trowel and was chewing her thumbnail in distress. Everybody had stopped working. Heloise took a deep breath. "My sisters, this is awful."

Astrane grunted. "Lady, I meant no harm. I have a bad habit of finding fault."

Ceci looked away, pretending that she was not grinning.

Heloise said, "Tomorrow morning we'll have a chapter meeting. For the specific purpose of complaining." The women stared at her, surprised. "Then we shall make a list of all the duties here and divide them among us."

"Can I be the portress?" Gertrude asked eagerly.

Heloise threw back her head and laughed. She went over to Gertrude and stroked her cheek. "Sister, when we have a portal, you can be the portress." They picked up their trowels and went back to spreading mortar.

Without warning, Abelard came back after All Saints' bringing news that Prince Philip was dead. While riding along the Grève in Paris, the lad had been thrown and killed when a black pig darted from a dung heap, and now his younger brother, Louis, had been anointed in Rheims Cathedral. Abelard had attended the ceremony.

His return took Heloise by surprise, although it was what she had been longing for. He slouched at the trestle drinking watered wine and shamelessly allowing the nuns to wait on him.

Heloise could see that he was making an effort to be charming. He was feeling low, that much was clear to her, but he made jests and even succeeded in thawing Ceci. Heloise leaned near the entrance to the kitchen, studying him. In the light of the yellow candles, he looked fantastically handsome. Like the Abelard of their Paris days, but it was an illusion cast by the flames. Outside, in the light of day, his cheeks sagged, and his skin was blotchy and irritated.

Heloise thought of asking why he had come back, but she decided to leave the subject alone. Whatever his reason, he had wanted to come; perhaps he had even wanted to see her. Finally, she edged forward and said to him, "How goes life at Saint-Gildas?" He had not mentioned the legate's visit or the monks' reactions.

He shrugged, impassive. "We do not transform swine into saints overnight."

"Did your sons promise to reform?"

He drained his wine and set the cup on the trestle. "No." He split his lips in a grim smile.

"None of them?" Surely he was exaggerating.

"I told you. They're crafty bastards." His tone was deliberately light.

And final. He turned toward Gertrude again and began talking about Pope Innocent, who still did not feel safe returning to Rome.

Rebuffed, Heloise scooped up a platter and hurried into the kitchen.

Abelard had not been at the Paraclete a week when the uproar began. Father Gondry was the first to mention it to Heloise, but he made light of the gossip, saying that Abelard's return was none of people's business, and they had nothing better to do than meddle and criticize. Heloise sighed impatiently. What her neighbors said didn't worry her overmuch, and anyway she had more important matters to think about. Their pigs had been slaughtered—she was busy finding tubs to pickle the great pieces of pork and hanging sides of bacon near the fire to smoke. It was a job she did not relish, for handling the bloody meat made her want to gag.

On St. Martin's Day, Abelard rode up to Nogent-sur-Seine, to pay his respects to Lord Milo. Before noon it began to rain. He was away all day, and when he returned, his cloak soaked, he picked at his dinner and said barely a dozen words to the nuns. After the meal, Heloise waited until the others had left before she approached. She gave him some wine mixed with herbs. He drank without speaking. Hesitating, Heloise said, "Is there anything you would like to tell me?"

He looked up, wary. "Tell you? What would I have to tell you?"

"My lord. Something is wrong. I can see that."

He laughed, choking.

"Did something happen at Nogent?" She meant to discover the reason for his unaccountable bad temper.

Silence. Then: "People in these parts have a poor opinion of me." When she began to protest, he flicked his hands impatiently and would not allow her to continue. "When I left here in the spring, they said I had abandoned you, that I could have helped you and didn't. Now they're saying—" He broke off, leaning his head between his hands.

Heloise wondered who "they" were. "My lord abbot, I don't know what you're talking about. After God, you are the founder of this place. Surely you won't allow idle chatter to upset you this way."

He jerked back his head. "Idle chatter? Not at all. Malicious insinuations. Monstrous accusations."

Heloise, shaken, sat down across from him. She said quietly, "Tell me."

Abelard would not meet her eyes. "That I am still a slave to the pleasures of carnal desire—"

"My lord—"

"That I can't bear to be parted from the woman I once loved."

Heloise turned her head away, blinded with hurt. *Once loved.*

"For the love of Christ, I'm a eunuch! In my present condition, how can there be any suspicion of wrongdoing?" His voice snarled with pain.

Involuntarily, she stretched her hand to him, then laid it down awkwardly on the trestle between them. His eyes met hers briefly before jerking away. At last, Heloise said simply, "We need you here." There was no reply, and when she looked up, she saw that his eyes were closed, his body rigid. "Stay here. We need you."

He went on as if he had not heard. "What does it take to please them? I'm not a man anymore. I'm a thing. An it." He laughed hollowly, but the laugh made the skin on Heloise's neck crawl.

She waited for him to continue, but he did not. After a while, she slipped into the kitchen, sagged against the wall, and wept into her sleeve. The room stank of half-smoked flesh and dried herbs. She stared at the wall, thinking of Abelard in the next chamber. There were so many things she wanted to tell him: that she had been thinking of draining the marsh, that she was going to see the pope, that she loved him yet. She wished that he wanted to listen. It struck her that he was not really uninterested, only self-absorbed. She wiped her face and went in to him.

He was standing by the open shutters, looking out at the rain, which had settled into a steady drizzle.

"My lord, there is something I must speak about."

He glanced over his shoulder before turning to her. Her fingers picked nervously at her wimple. "My lord, I understand that the pope is at Auxerre."

"That's correct."

"Auxerre is but a short journey from here. I was thinking of—well, I had planned to—visit him."

Abelard's voice flared sharply. "By God, why! There's no reason to do that."

"I want to get a charter confirming my ownership of the Paraclete."

"Yes, yes. All that will be taken care of. Bishop Hatto promised me—"

"The bishop is a busy man," she said calmly. "We've been here ten months and still no charter."

"It is not proper for you to leave here." His face was turning red. "You must attend to your flock."

Heloise was surprised to find him so vehement. His own flock sat unattended, sometimes for months at a stretch. "I understand your concern, but my flock can do without me for a week. It's more important that I obtain recognition before the pope leaves France."

"Send someone else."

Heloise shook her head.

"I will go for you."

"No." She could feel her stomach knotting, waiting for him to forbid her, and then she knew that she would back down. "I wish to go myself."

Abelard lifted his shoulders wearily. He stared at her for a moment before murmuring stiffly, "Very well. Then go if you must. You give the orders here now."

Before she could answer, he had plunged into the rain.

At the end of the week, she set out for Auxerre, and she took with her as escort Arnoul's second-eldest son. Abelard accompanied them as far as Sens. The town was crowded, and she was in a hurry to find the road leading south to Auxerre. Aside from that, she sensed that Abelard felt uneasy with her, that he was anxious to make his farewell and return to Saint-Gildas. Before she cried, she wanted to be away from him.

The day was foggy, with a damp wind that ripped at her wimple. She left Abelard near the Troyes Gate. Tipping back in his saddle, he smiled pleasantly and gazed somewhere directly behind her left ear.

Heloise said, "My lord, you won't forget to send me the psalter and the abacus."

"Of course not. I'll send them the day I get to Saint-Gildas."

"Shall I give the pope your best wishes?" She was stalling now, dreading the moment when she must turn from him. Of all the things that she needed in this world, she needed him near her. But God had willed otherwise.

"Certainly," he said. "Please do that." He nodded vaguely.

Heloise's mare stamped impatiently. The bells in the cathedral began to pound. "Farewell," she said to Abelard, miserable. "Till we meet again, my lord."

"Till we meet again."

She spurred the mare, following Arnoul's boy down the path that led back to the highroad.

*   *   *

Pope Innocent, the second of that name, smiled and fingered his jeweled miter. A beefy, stoop-shouldered man with a hawk nose, he more resembled a smith than a pontiff. For a long while, he listened while Heloise talked about the Paraclete, and he continued to smile. "And when do you find time to read? Tell me that, child."

Heloise wanted to laugh at the word "child"—she was over thirty. It reminded her of Lady Alais. Arranging her face into a pious expression, she said, "At night, Your Holiness." That was only partly true. Most nights she was asleep before her head hit the pallet, but when she did read it was late in the day.

"The venerable Peter of Cluny has told me about you. He likened you to Penthesilea—"

"Your Grace," Heloise said, "I'm no Amazon. Only a frail woman in need of assistance."

Innocent shook his head. "I don't say that to flatter you. But it's clear to me that God must have set you apart when you were in your mother's womb." He scratched his nose vigorously. "Through the grace of the Almighty, you turned your zeal for learning in a far better direction."

"Yes, Your Holiness."

"Fortunately, you abandoned logic for the Gospel, Plato for Christ."

"Yes, Your Holiness."

Innocent beamed. "You bring supreme glory to the Creator, child."

Heloise stared at the floor, trying not to wince. After Innocent had assured her of a jeweled crown from the King of Heaven, he shouted for the clerk and began to dictate the bull.

". . . confirm to her and her sisters, as well as those who shall come after them, the perpetual possession of the Oratory of the Holy Trinity . . ."

Heloise listened, remembering Abbot Suger and his forged charter. His lies had forced her and Ceci into the road—and killed Aristotle. This time, perhaps, she would be safe.

". . . confirm the gifts which have been received and those they may receive through the concessions of pontiffs, the munificence of kings and princes, and the liberality of the faithful . . ."

The scratching of the clerk's quill grated softly in the small chamber.

"Given on this twenty-eighth day of November in the year of Our Lord eleven hundred and thirty-one."

Afterward, the pope offered to take the Paraclete under the personal protection of the Apostolic See, for which privilege Heloise would have to remit a sum of money annually to the Lateran Palace. Small as the amount was, it seemed enormous, and she wondered how she would be able to pay. However, she mumbled her thanks as she kissed Innocent's ring. She recognized a good bargain when she heard one.

22 ❧

HELOISE WOKE SHIVERING. Her chamber was icy, and the raw air clawed at her body through the blankets. Without opening her eyes, she knew that someone had come into the room. Abruptly, she sat up, squinting in the dark.

"Lady Heloise." Gertrude was whispering hoarsely.

A moment longer Heloise clung to sleep, and then she dragged her mind alert. "What hour is it?"

"An hour until lauds—lady, there's a knight at the gate." Gertrude's shoes rasped softly against the stone floor as she came toward Heloise's bed. "God's pardon for disturbing you, but I don't know what to do with him."

"Did you tell him we have no guesthouse?"

"Yes, lady, but—"

Now she could see Gertrude's face, a white blob in the shadows. She rubbed her eyes to scratch the sleep from them. "Surely he understands that we can't admit him to the cloister." She could not turn him away, either—it must be close to zero outside.

"Lady, listen, it's you he wants to see. He says it's of the most extreme importance. Otherwise I wouldn't have waked you."

Behind her head, the shutters rattled, and in the distance she could hear horses nickering. "Very well, I'm coming." Quickly she threw back the covers and fumbled for her shoes. "This man. Did he mention the nature of his business?"

"Take your cloak. It's very cold."

"Did he—"

"No, lady. Only that he's in the service of a Lord Jourdain of Sancy. Does that mean anything to you?"

Heloise stiffened. "Yes," she said, "that means something." Fear struck her in the chest. It had been more than a year since she had last seen Abelard, or had heard from him. There had been only a baffling silence. God forbid that Jourdain's messenger should be bringing news of Abelard. *Don't let him be dead, please don't let him be dead.* She followed Gertrude through the nuns' sleeping chamber and out into the half-built cloister.

Shafts of moonlight dusted bluish shadows against the snow. In the darkness, Heloise covered her mouth with her hand and sucked in her own moist breath. She puffed along behind Gertrude, her toes numbing before they had reached the gatehouse.

It was bitter inside Gertrude's lodge. A cresset flamed weakly on the wall. The knight, clutching his cloak around his ears, stared curiously at Heloise. When she held out her hand, he hobbled toward her on frozen feet and dropped to his knees. "Lady Heloise, excuse me for this discourtesy."

He was a young man with a short blond beard and watery eyes. As he pressed his lips to her hand, she realized that he threatened to collapse from exposure and exhaustion. "What is your name, son?"

"Garin, my lady. I serve Lord Jourdain, who is castellan of—"

Impatiently, she gestured him to his feet. "Yes, yes, I know all that. You have some message for me?"

Garin stood up. "My lady," he said, uncertainly, "I'm bound for the court at Troyes. My mission is to deliver this, er, letter—I mean document—to, er, Count Thibaut." He swallowed several times. "I can't tarry because I've been delayed, you see. The snow—" He began describing the drifts around Sens when Heloise gently broke in.

"I don't understand. What does all this have to do with me?"

"Oh, yes. Well, it has something." Scratching his chin, he glanced at Gertrude and then back at Heloise. "Lady, I'd better start again. I'm getting confused."

"I'm sorry. Go on." She waited.

"My lord Jourdain had given me this packet for Count Thibaut. I'm to show it to Lady Heloise. She may read it, but I am not to leave it with her. It's for the count. You see?"

Heloise nodded, smiling slightly. "I see." Garin did not move. "Well then, suppose you give it to me."

Garin crossed to a saddlebag that had been dumped by the door. A moment later, he handed Heloise a package wrapped in skin and bound with a string. "This is a treatise of some sort?"

"No, my lady. A letter."

"Really?" She tugged off the skin and saw that the bundle contained perhaps a hundred sheets of parchment. "A long letter. And when am I to read this?" She smiled at him.

"Why, now," Garin said. He yawned into his beard.

She smiled at Gertrude. "In the middle of the night?" In her opinion, the lad was a little simpleminded. She glanced at the first page; the handwriting was neat but unfamiliar. There was no inscription, but at the top left corner she noticed a few small words in Jourdain's hand. *Abelard's letter of consolation to his friend.* Heloise's throat dried up. She gasped, "This is a letter of Abelard's?"

Garin nodded.

"But it's not his handwriting."

"A copy, my lady."

She sent Gertrude to the kitchen to get food and drink for Garin. There was little in their stores, barely enough for one meal a day if they ate sparingly, but she trusted Gertrude to find some morsel. Garin dropped on a stool. Shaking with excitement, Heloise glanced at the opening lines of the letter.

"There are times when example is better than precept for stirring or soothing human passions; and so I propose to follow up the words of consolation I gave you in person with the history of my own misfortunes, hoping thereby to give you comfort in absence." Heloise frowned, wondering to whom Abelard had written these words. "In comparison with my trials you will see that your own are nothing . . ."

When she looked up, Garin's chin was slumping on his chest. "Sir Garin, I'll go now and read this. Sister Gertrude is getting food. You can sleep here—" As she turned toward the door, he called after her.

"I forgot something," he said. "Lord Jourdain said to be sure and tell you—he does not send the letter to hurt you. You may not like what you read, but he thought you would like to see it." He added solemnly, "My lord got furious over it."

"Good night, Sir Garin," she said, and went out with Abelard's letter pressed to her chest.

In her room, she lit a rushlight and began to read:

"I was born on the borders of Brittany, in a town called Le Pallet . . ."

The first twenty or so pages seemed to be purely autobiographical, describing Abelard's early years as a student, his disputes with various students and teachers, and then going on to recount his arrival in Paris and his rise to success as a master at the cathedral school. Something about the tone of the narrative jarred Heloise slightly—it was boastful, even bombastic in places. He constantly disparaged his teachers and colleagues, as if he felt determined to prove himself superior. Heloise thought, There is no need to do that; what need has he to exaggerate his achievements? When the lauds bell sounded, she reluctantly blew out the light and went out into the dark cold, to the chapel. The office dragged, as if time had slowed to a crawl. The chattering of Astrane's teeth echoed against the stone walls. Heloise's mouth opened and closed automatically; she did not bother to concentrate on the psalms. At the end of the service, she got up quickly and hurried back to her room.

Eagerly, she found her place on the page. More about Abelard's success. There was a rambling paragraph on pride, which disturbed her a little. Flipping the page, she was startled to see her name jump up. "There was in Paris at the time a young girl named Heloise, the niece of Fulbert, and so much loved by him that he had done everything in his power to advance her education in letters." Heloise blinked uneasily. "In looks she did not rank lowest, while in the extent of her learning she stood supreme. A gift for letters is so rare in women that it added greatly to her charm and won her renown throughout the realm. I decided that she was the one to bring to my bed, confident that I should have an easy success . . ." Involuntarily she gave an indignant gasp, reaching out one hand to steady herself against the writing table. Cold air from the cracks in the shutters whistled about her ankles. Angry, she pushed the page closer to the rushlight so that she did not miss anything, and, shoulders hunched forward, she kept reading.

When Heloise turned over the final page, it was still dark outside. She pushed the manuscript aside, blew out the light, and violently slammed her face against the oak slab. Tears crept down the sides of her nose, onto the table. Whole sentences came back to her, cutting, brutal words that denied their past together, rejected her as if she had been less than nothing to him. It was all there: the intimate details of their lovemaking, her pregnancy and the birth of Astrolabe, and then the marriage, castration, and taking of monastic vows. And so forth up to the present time. He had omitted nothing and he had omitted everything. His distortions and omissions burned at her memory. It didn't happen that way, she thought, you loved me once.

I am thirty-two. For half my life, my soul has loved you. And now you say that it was only an itch in the groin . . .

She concentrated on muffling the sound of her sobs. She was abbess of a convent and her daughters slept in the next chamber. She could not shriek and pound her fists against the wall like a seventeen-year-old girl. Clear your head, she commanded under her breath, think rationally. It was possible that Abelard's mind had been affected by his dangers at Saint-Gildas. He intimated as much himself, because the last ten pages of the letter centered on the attempts of his monks to kill him. They had put poison in the chalice during mass; they had held a dagger to his throat, forcing him to flee to Nantes. God knew, he might be dead at this moment. She sat up, dizzy with fear.

"A fugitive and a wanderer," he had called himself. "I carry everywhere the curse of Cain, forever tormented by quarrels and forebodings without and within."

He suffered. In comparison, her own pain was nothing.

Soon it would be prime; sniffling, she collected the sheets into an orderly pile and wrapped them up again. Darkness blanketed the cloister. When she came into the gatehouse, Garin was drinking soup. She said, "Sir Garin, perchance do you know the contents of this?" She laid the package next to his bowl.

He mumbled, "Aye."

Heloise's face reddened.

"Many have read it," he said, not meeting her eyes. "Lord Jourdain's clerk made this copy. There are more in circulation."

"How many?"

Garin shrugged. "Impossible to say. My lord got his copy from the Count of Dreux."

"But"—her voice cracked—"this is a letter to a friend. What kind of friend would circulate a private letter?"

Garin drained his bowl and set it down. He wiped his beard on his sleeve. "My lord believes that it wasn't written to anyone in particular. He believes—" He began picking his teeth with a nail.

"Yes?"

"—he believes that it was only a—a—"

"Rhetorical device?"

"That's it." Garin got up and took the manuscript to his saddlebag. Heloise followed him.

"I don't understand," she cried softly. "Why would Abbot Peter do such a thing?"

Garin shrugged again. "Mayhap to make known his plight at Saint-Gildas. He seems to be in danger. Lady, can you spare some hay for my mount?"

"Are you saying that Jourdain thinks this letter will release Abelard from Saint-Gildas?"

"Mayhap. Who knows?" He was not paying attention. Heloise sent Gertrude for hay; by the time dawn had broken, she had given him instructions for reaching Troyes and he was gone.

After prime, she went to the chapter house, where she had set up a makeshift office in the corner. The Paraclete had grown; now they had seven novices, a wall and cloister, and a refectory, dormitory, and chapter house. The new buildings were still in various stages of construction, but as long as they had roofs and four walls, they were used. What the Paraclete did not have was food; the harvest had been meager the previous summer. Bishop Manasses had promised her a portion of the tithes from the diocese of Meaux, but she doubted if it would amount to much. When half the district was going hungry, people had nothing to give the Church, not even for the salvation of their souls. Heloise opened her account ledger. She sat at the table, adding and re-adding and subtracting, until midmorning, when the novice Alys brought in a peasant with his daughter, a girl of about twelve. Both the man and his child were emaciated, the skin stretched tightly over white faces. The man began pleading with Heloise to enroll his daughter as a novice. He was not the first such father to appear that winter, nor would he be the last. In the end, Heloise sent him away, saying that the Paraclete had no food. His child would be no better off than at home. As they went out, Heloise watched the girl's eyes flash brilliant with relief.

At noon, they sat down to their daily meal: acorn soup, one small piece of barley bread, water. It was gone quickly. Afterward, Heloise's stomach was still rumbling. She wondered if she should make another trip to Nogent; Lord Milo had purchased grain from Flanders, and perhaps he would make her another loan. She decided against it, since she was already deeply in debt to him.

A weak sun came out for an hour, melting the snow along the north walk to a gray slush. The nuns worked in the refectory, as they had for weeks now, and cemented tiles on the floor. She wanted to tell someone about Abelard's letter, share it with another person as a kind of poultice for her wounds, but there was no one. She glanced over at Ceci, on her knees near the kitchen door. Not Ceci—she would call Heloise a fool. She bit her lip and listlessly laid down another tile.

Ceci looked up. "Heloise," she called, "remember the white bread we used to eat in Paris? Remember Agnes's lamb with garlic sauce?"

Heloise laughed grimly. "Cheese pasties. That's what I remember."

All of them daydreamed constantly about food. She slid a tile into place and pressed her weight down hard against it. Frantically, she struggled to keep from crying again. It would be impossible for her to go on each day without responding in some way to Abelard's letter. She could write to Jourdain, but probably he knew nothing. If he had had information, surely he would have entrusted it to Garin.

During vespers that evening, she made up her mind to write to Abelard, even though he did not want to hear from her, and afterward she closed the door to her chamber and took out parchment and ink. Once the blank sheet was before her, her mind froze. Presently she made an effort to begin, to put down something.

"Not long ago, my beloved, by chance someone brought me the letter you sent to a friend to comfort him. When I saw the superscription, I knew at once it was yours and I began to read eagerly because the writer is so dear to my heart. But nearly every line was filled, I remember, with gall and wormwood . . ."

At first she tried to conform to the formalities of good letter writing; she worried about her style and tried to keep her tone neutral. But in a little while, she forgot to be careful. Her words were emotional, she knew, and she also knew he would not like that. She pleaded with him for a letter, as she had done when she first went to Argenteuil, and she stressed his obligations to the Paraclete. Since his life was in jeopardy at Saint-Gildas, why did he not return to her and cultivate his own vineyard? And she said other things, too, things that had rankled with her for years.

"Tell me one thing, if you can. Why, after our entry into religion (which was your decision alone), have you so neglected and forgotten me that I have neither a word of encouragement from you when you are here nor the consolation of a letter in your absence?" Nor had he sent her the psalter and abacus he had promised when they had parted at Sens. But she did not mention those items.

"Tell me, I say, if you can. No, I will tell you what I believe and what indeed the world suspects. It was the flame of lust, not love, that bound you to me. Therefore, when you could no longer have what you desired, all your show of tenderness vanished too." Had it been show, could anyone, even Abelard, have acted that role so perfectly? She considered whiting out the phrase but decided to let it stand.

"This, my beloved, is not merely my opinion—it is everyone's. Would to God it were my belief alone and I could find someone to defend you, for that would comfort me a little. I only wish that I could find some explanation to excuse you and conceal the way you hold me cheap."

Write me, she thought, restore yourself to me somehow, so that I may find the strength to stay here and serve God. I have no love for this life. If you do not acknowledge my labors here, who will? I can expect no reward from God, for certainly I have done nothing yet for love of him. I would follow you to the flames of hell but I can no longer continue without your help.

Dear God, that was all wrong. She sounded weak and cranky.

"When in the past you sought me out for sinful pleasures, your letters came to me thick and fast, and your many songs put the name of Heloise on everyone's lips. Every street and house echoed with my name. Is it not far better now to summon me to God than it was then to satisfy our lust? I beg you, think what you owe me. Hear my plea, and I will finish this long letter with a brief ending. Farewell, my only love."

She read it over several times. There were many things she had neglected to mention. The wall was almost completed and he would not recognize the place; the harvest had been a disaster; she did not know how they would manage until summer. Had he seen Astrolabe? Abruptly she sealed the letter. Why bother? He would not answer; he never had.

The letter remained on Heloise's table for a week, until Father Gondry took it, and others, to Nogent, where he gave it to a courier heading west. Deliberately, she put Abelard into a corner of her mind. There was plowing to be done and seed to be sown. Lent began with a flurry of spring showers. When Heloise caught a glimpse of her reflection in a water bucket, she saw a pinched face and sunken eyes. She turned away quickly, knowing that she had become ugly.

Summer came early on a wave of blazing air. By the end of May, the nuns were baking in their habits, and Heloise gave them permission to go without stockings. In the warm evenings, at sunset, they went down to the river to bathe in their undertunics, giggling softly and floating among the reeds.

Every day now, people came to the gate, either pilgrims or travelers bound for the Troyes fair. The famine forgotten, their wallets and saddlebags were swollen with things to eat. In the Paraclete garden grew lettuce and cress, and the nuns picked tender little strawberries in the oak woods. Viscountess Margaret of Marolles sent her beekeeper with a round hive made of twigs, which they set in a corner of the cloister. In

July, they removed most of the combs and gorged themselves with sticky fingers. Heloise thought the gift of the hive a good omen.

All of the nuns spent the long mornings in the fields, weeding. Heloise came back at noon and worked at her table, but more often she took her ledgers to the gatehouse so that she could attend the visitors in Gertrude's absence. One afternoon in July, a messenger of Lord Milo's galloped up with a basket of cheeses. The convent entrance was intensely silent, lazy in the soft heat of midafternoon. Only the grasshoppers shrilled in the high grass by the roadside. After she had taken the cheeses to the storeroom, she hurried back with a bowl of cool water. As the man was leaving, he belatedly pulled a brown parcel from his saddlebag, apologizing for his forgetfulness.

Heloise took the package into the lodge to unwrap. It was a psalter bound in fine leather and gold traceries, but not until she had opened it did she discover Abelard's letter. When she had read it, she went to the chapel to pray, stunned. Then she returned to the gatehouse and read the letter a second time.

"To Heloise, his dearly beloved sister in Christ, Abelard her brother in Christ." She was surprised that he had placed her name before his; it was contrary to all custom of letter writing. Here was the letter for which she had yearned these fifteen years, but it gave her neither joy nor peace. She had wanted reassurance. It was not there. Only talk of death. If he had choice in the matter, he said, he would come back to the Paraclete. But if this was not possible during his life, then let it be so after his death. He instructed her to find his body, buried or unburied, and bring it to the convent. He asked for the nuns' prayers, enclosing a special supplication for his welfare. There was more, but her mind could not let go the part about dying.

A man and his elderly father came to the gate with begging bowls. In the shade near the gate, Heloise washed their feet and sent them away with cheese and onions. When the nuns and novices returned from the fields, she read them the portion of the letter that pertained to Abelard's difficulties. Gertrude began to cry and the novices imitated her. Ceci and Astrane, dry-eyed, murmured their sympathies.

Ceci said, "I'm sorry for him. I mean that, Heloise."

Heloise stared at the ground, choked with misery. They went to the chapel for vespers.

She lay sleepless that night, thrashing from side to side on the damp sheet. She knew that she should be praying, but she had nothing more to ask of God. He did not bother to listen to her anyway. At last, she fell on her knees by the bed and pleaded for strength to live through that night and the following day. That was all, just another twenty-four hours and then she would worry later about the days to come. Bitterness gagged her when she thought of Abelard's words. He denied that he had neglected her. The fact that he had never written or comforted her should not be attributed to indifference; rather, he had the greatest confidence in her strength and wisdom. That was what he said. He seemed surprised that she felt in need of help, emotional or spiritual.

She sobbed against the mattress. At dawn, she got up, her body screaming with exhaustion, and dragged to the kitchen to light a cooking fire. During the morning office, she kept thinking of the house in the Rue des Chantres. Summer mornings when she curled in Abelard's bed, gazing at the soft sleeping face and listening with half an ear to Agnes rattling her pots in the kitchen. The world was full of happiness then, and it slept next to her.

All morning long, she weeded and thought of bodies, his and hers. His whole, hers smooth and young. The wind blew loose dirt into her eyes and made them water. The crows snapped their wings above the treetops.

They went back and pressed clabber into cheese. The whey they saved for the youngest novice's supper. The new cheese was covered with marsh reeds and then wrapped tightly in leaves. At midafternoon, two monks on mules came to the gate; Gertrude raced into the cloister crying that one of them was Abbot Bernard of Clairvaux. Dismayed, Heloise straightened her wimple and sent the novices to put on stockings. She walked heavily to the gate, wondering what brought the renowned abbot to the Paraclete unannounced.

He stood beside his mule, beaming broadly as she approached. "Ah, Lady Abbess, there you are." His auburn beard was plastered to his chin, and his general appearance was that of an amiable ambulating skeleton. Heloise stared. "A fine place you have here."

She went up to him and knelt in the dust. "Your grace. Welcome to the Paraclete. You do us honor." His white robe was filthy and reeked of urine and God knew what else. She tried not to breathe deeply. She got up and asked Ceci to bring bread and ale.

"Milk," Bernard broke in. "If you please. My stomach won't tolerate much else." He was looking past her into the cloister, obviously pleased by what he saw.

"My sympathies," Heloise murmured.

Bernard smiled at her for a moment. His eyes were a clear, brilliant blue. "Not at all. Prayer and fasting raise the soul to God."

Bernard, son of the lord of Fontaine-les-Dijons, was the most beloved, most admired abbot in Europe, and already people were calling him a saint. In 1115, he had taken thirteen Cistercian monks and settled in a desolate valley not many miles from the Paraclete and, living on boiled beech leaves and sleeping on the ground, they had built the abbey of Clairvaux. Emphasizing poverty and manual labor, he had created an order which had spread to all parts of western Christendom and which now included more than fifty monasteries. He toured the Paraclete with its bare buildings and haggard, black-swathed women and, not surprisingly, pronounced the place perfect.

Like a sleepwalker, Heloise led the abbot through the grounds, keeping a little way from him because his breath smelled sour. The nuns were euphoric. The way Gertrude and Ceci fluttered around him, anybody would have thought Bernard an angel of the Lord instead of a mere man.

Heloise remembered hearing that Bernard loathed women. Once, his sister, richly dressed, had arrived at the gate of Clairvaux, and he had sent her away, calling her a whore. But at the Paraclete there was no evidence of any antipathy toward females. The women fussed over him, and Bernard laughed and told funny stories and spoke a great deal about love. Heloise forced a smile. Her stomach hurt.

At supper, along the trestle in the refectory, Bernard asked each of them their names, where they had been born, and so forth. At his elbow, Heloise struggled for control. Suddenly she was afraid of fainting. Bernard smiled at her and said something, but she did not hear the words. She had only to get through the meal, then she would retire to her chamber and it would be over. She thought, I can't go to pieces at table. I am Heloise, abbess of the Paraclete, I can't let go. An abbess, an abbess. What would happen if I fell apart in front of Bernard, but that thought only made the panic worse. She turned her face toward the abbot, a foot away. His mouth was moist, smiling. He said, "Now you, my lady. You, I know, have spent your life in study. The pope has spoken of you often."

She said nothing.

A novice brought up a bowl of onions, but Bernard waved her away. "Onions give me gas." He said to Heloise, "It's an excellent idea for holy women to study. As long as the knowledge is not acquired for its own sake."

"Alas," she replied, "we have few books here. It's a handicap in instructing our novices."

Bernard raised his eyebrows. "Books? You will find more in this wilderness"—he waved his arm in a wide circle—"than in all your books. No, the trees and stones will teach them more than any master."

"But don't you believe that reading helps a person to develop his powers of reason?"

"Faith is not dependent on reason," he said, very reproachful.

Giddy, she shook her head. "I suppose not, but reason sometimes illuminates faith, don't you think?"

"No!" thundered Bernard, snatching a crust of bread and stuffing it into one cheek. "Faith transcends reason and don't let anybody tell you differently."

"Of course," said Heloise, keeping her face straight. She said over her shoulder, "Alys, bring more clabbered milk."

Bernard was scratching at his hair shirt. "Lady, my health is delicate. I feel like a plucked bird." She was about to ask him about his ailments, since he clearly enjoyed speaking of them, when he jerked his head at her and said, "Your convent was founded by Peter Abelard, wasn't it?"

"Yes, my lord."

"And he provides you and your sisters with spiritual guidance."

Floundering, Heloise finally answered, "No, my lord. He is busy in Brittany." As she spooned clabber into his bowl, she could feel his eyes on her face. She wondered if he had read a copy of Abelard's letter.

"Tell me. You haven't let your mind be affected by schoolman's logic, have you? No, of course you haven't—you don't impress me as that type at all."

"What type?" Heloise coughed, suspicious.

"I'm thinking of those masters who bedazzle their students with their personal grasp of the sublime and sacred." He broke off a crust and dipped it into the milk. "You know. Sophists, bandying about the mysteries of God on the Petit Pont." His voice was thick with contempt.

"My lord abbot," she said firmly, "I never studied with a master on the Petit Pont. Shall we walk in the cloister? I would like you to see our new herb garden."

The abbot of Clairvaux rose and followed her meekly.

A storm blew up deep in the night, bumping thunder and lightning against the cloister. Twenty minutes later it was over. The eaves sloshed water steadily, the sound reminding Heloise of Bernard, who never stopped talking. Despite his extreme conservatism, she rather liked him. It was hard not to.

Her stomach ached. A stream of nausea rolled up into her throat. She went to the privy, vomited, and crept back to her chamber, where she sat down in the dark. After a while, she lit a tallow candle and picked up her pen. "To him who is her only beloved after Christ."

She laid aside the quill. What frightened her was this terrible feeling of helplessness. Hundreds of miles away, Abelard would be murdered and someone would bring her his body, gutted, embalmed, wrapped in leather to keep the corpse from stinking on the journey from Brittany. If he died, she would collapse. She wrote: "A heart overwhelmed with anxiety knows no calm. A mind beset with anxiety cannot devote itself sincerely to God." God. She had not once thought of God since yesterday, when the letter had come. Not even during prayer.

"What have I to hope for if you are gone? What purpose to prolong this charade"—she marked out "charade" and substituted "pilgrimage" —"in which I have no support but you?" She said to herself, But I have no support from him, save the knowledge that he is alive.

Sticky with sweat, she leaned back in her chair, away from the circle of candlelight, and tasted herself with revulsion. Scared and sick, helpless. Appalled at her helplessness. Where was the efficient Lady Heloise who fed her starving nuns, dickered with barons and popes for favors, gave pious advice to half the neighborhood? In the shadows, she clung to the table and laughed at herself, knowing that there was no Abbess Heloise. Hypocrite, she screamed inside, poseur. She wrote: "Men call me chaste; they do not know the hypocrite I am. I can win praise in the eyes of men but deserve none before God, who searches our hearts and loins and sees in our darkness.

"For a long time, my pretense deceived you, as it did many, so that you mistook hypocrisy for piety . . .

"Do not feel so sure of me . . ." She pushed strands of damp hair behind her ears.

"Do not suppose me healthy . . .

"Do not believe I want for nothing and delay helping me in my hour of need. Do not think me strong, lest I fall before you can sustain me . . .

"Stop praising me, I beg you!" His praise was the most dangerous of all because she hungered for it.

He had said that she was strong, independent, but he knew nothing of her. She cast about herself, hunting down in memory the girl she had once been, so long ago in the Ile-de-France. That person had gloried in her love for a man, in the sweet touch of his body, and although time should have killed that girl, it had not. Into her head came an image of herself and Abelard, flesh intertwined, in the room high above the Seine, and with the picture came words and she wrote: "The lovers' pleasures that we shared have been too sweet—they can never displease me, and can scarcely be banished from my thoughts. Wherever I turn they are always there before my eyes, bringing with them awaked longings and fantasies that will not even let me sleep. Even during mass, my thoughts are on wantonness instead of prayers. Everything we did—everything—and also the times and places are engraved on my heart, along with your image, so that I live through it again with you. Even in sleep I know no respite. Sometimes my thoughts are betrayed in a movement of my body . . ."

Shaken, she got up and threw herself on the bed. She shut her eyes and rolled over onto her stomach, riding the prickly tension that throbbed through her thighs and swept up along her breasts. Later, spent, she slept.

In the morning, Bernard offered to preach a sermon before leaving, and the women filed into the chapel, excited over this great honor. He chose as his theme the mortification of the flesh, clearly one of his favorite subjects. The only things they should worry about, he told them, were loving God and punishing their bodies. Heloise, kneeling to one side, observed his scabby bare feet, his skeleton chest, and then she concentrated on his voice. Not for nothing was he called Doctor Mellifluous—the Honey-Sweet Doctor. Like Abelard, he had a gift for speaking, and she could understand his enormous popularity. The man was lovable, if you did not think about what he said.

Behind her, she could hear someone crying, probably Gertrude, who took sermons quite seriously.

At the altar, Bernard was saying, "Listen, handmaids of Christ. Look at those bodies which you clothe with such diligent care, nourish as if they were royal offspring." He wiped his forehead on his sleeve. "Are they not a mass of putrefaction? Are they not worms, dust, and ashes?"

Under her breath, Heloise grunted. She thought, He hopes to merit heaven by making earth a hell. Everything he said revolted her.

"Don't think about what your body is now," Bernard cried. "Sisters, you had liefer consider what it will be in the future. Pus, slime, decay."

He tucked his fingers together happily. "The filth of obscene corruption."

At the back of the chapel, one of the novices began to sob.

"Tears!" exclaimed Bernard, smiling. "Tears which are from God assure the remission of our sins. Tears are spiritual delights, above even honey and the honeycomb, and sweeter than all nectar."

Bernard went on for a while longer, but Heloise did not listen. She squirmed back on her heels, waiting for him to finish so they could say the Lord's Prayer and go out to the fields. There was work to be done today.

Bernard knelt. The nuns began to pray, "Our Father which art in heaven . . ."

Heloise wondered what the storm had done to the corn. It should be ready to pick soon.

". . . Give us this day our supersubstantial bread, and forgive us our . . ."

She must give Bernard some food for the journey. It would not be courteous to send him away empty-handed. Perhaps some cherries or plums. No, he would not eat them.

". . . deliver us from evil. Amen."

She opened her eyes to find Abbot Bernard leaning over her, furious. "Lady," he hissed, "what kind of prayer is that!"

"My lord," she cried, scrambling to her feet.

"I can't believe that I heard it. What happened to daily bread? Answer me that, madame!" The veins in his neck were stretched taut. "What is this supersubstantial? Don't you know how to recite the Lord's Prayer?" He tugged at her sleeve with a bony hand.

Startled, Heloise freed her sleeve. "We follow the old *vulgata* version of St. Matthew," she replied carefully.

"And who told you to do that?"

"It may not be common usage, but I don't see anything wrong in it. It's a literal translation of *epioúsios*."

"Don't argue with me. This is your innovation?" He was shouting at her now. "You presume to change the wording of Our Lord's prayer?"

She was at the point of shouting back. "I—we use those words because the founder of our convent suggested it." Furious, she turned and walked out into the cloister, Bernard grunting at her back.

By the time they reached the north walk, he had cooled off. "About this supersubstantial bread—I've never heard of anything so silly."

Heloise shrugged, anxious to get rid of the man. "It's an ancient practice, I believe."

"Ancient or not, it sounds stupid. You tell Abbot Peter I said so."

"I'll do that." No use saying anything more to Bernard.

Suddenly he shrugged and smiled, angelically. "Ah, well. What else can you expect from a man who spends his time arguing with boys and consorting with women?"

Heloise felt her face grow hot. Amazed, she watched him trot to his mule and pat its nose.

"Are you certain?" Heloise asked, and gave the woman a penetrating look. "Are you quite certain that you want to make this decision?" She leaned forward, riveting her eyes on Hermeline's elegant forehead as if to peer into her mind.

Hermeline sat very straight on the stool. "I've given it thought, if that's what you mean."

"You're young and very pretty. And you've been wed." She folded her hands in her lap. Some of the best nuns were widows, but only those who had lived out the span of wife and mother and wished to withdraw from a life they had sucked the juice out of. Heloise had reservations about accepting a childless widow who was a mere twenty years old. She said, "How did your husband die?"

"Killed in a tourney at Rouen."

"Did you love him?"

Hermeline met her eyes. "More than my life."

Heloise nodded. "But surely you want children. There will be another man—"

"No." The word thudded against the stone wall behind Heloise's head like a boulder toppling onto an iron plate. There was a fierceness in her tone that made Heloise go weak-kneed.

She said carefully to Hermeline, "Do you have a sincere desire to serve God? Or do you merely hope these walls will dull your memory?"

The young woman's gilt hair was drawn back tightly under her wimple, and when she moved her head the room smelled of rose water. She whispered, "No walls could dim those memories." She paused. "I will tell you this, lady abbess. I will serve God with the same devotion that I served my lord. More I cannot promise."

Nodding again, Heloise stood up. "Go home, lady Hermeline. On the first day of May, if you still feel inclined, you may return and I will accept you as a novice."

With a sweep of yellow silk, the woman fell to her knees, kissed Heloise's hand, and went out. Heloise stood quietly for a moment. This one knew her own mind, which was more than she could say for most of the applicants she interviewed. Astrane said it was a wonder they took any new members at all, so mercilessly did Heloise grill them about their motivations. Even so, the convent of Paraclete now comprised some twenty women, and they continued to come in a steady stream.

She went to the window. In the cloister, Ceci was talking to Astrane, grinning sarcastically, waving her hands in Astrane's face. Maybe they were arguing again. Or perhaps not; they had, over the years, come to terms with each other. When Astrane turned away with a shrug, Ceci stood a moment before walking slowly toward the river. Heloise followed. When Ceci saw her, she called, "There you are! And what did that fine lady have to say?"

"She wants to join us."

Ceci began to smile. "She's a very rich widow, if I recall correctly."

"Yes, she is."

"She owns the vineyards at Crèvecoeur—"

"And woods and meadows at Lisines and property in Provins and much more. She would bring a considerable dowry to the Paraclete."

"Havo!" Ceci let out a long, admiring whistle. "God's nose, sweeting, you didn't let her get away, did you?"

Heloise walked past her and sat on a tree stump near the water's edge. Suddenly dizzy, she bent over and plunged her head between her knees. Her shoulders began to twitch silently.

Slowly Ceci came to her. "Heloise. Heloise, what's wrong?" She reached out and grazed her palm against Heloise's head.

"Nothing," she mumbled.

"You've been ill these past months. Don't deny it."

Before Christmas, when she had received Abelard's brutal reply to the letter she had written in the summer, she had been violently sick at her stomach for two days. The vomiting had passed, but she still suffered from periodic attacks of faintness.

"Sweeting, tell me."

"No. You won't understand."

Stiffly, Ceci jerked away her hand. She did not speak. After a few minutes, Heloise reached into her girdle, reluctantly drew out the letter, and handed it to Ceci. Slowly she pulled herself up and walked to the water, her shoes slipping in the mud. She had never shown Abelard's letters to another soul, as if doing so would have been a kind of betrayal. But it did not matter now. She strode back and forth, gulping cold air.

Behind her, she heard Ceci saying, "This is the writing of an old man."

Heloise spun around. "It's from Abelard."

"That's what I mean." Ceci was sitting against a tree, reading slowly. She did not look up. From time to time, she muttered under her breath. Once she remarked, gravely, "He would have you without memory."

"How can I stop remembering!" Heloise cried. "Just because he doesn't remember—"

"Ah," said Ceci, "you're wrong there. I think he does remember. But it pains him. Stop pacing up and down. It makes me nervous."

Heloise settled herself on the stump. Ceci growled, "Idiot."

"Who? Him or me?"

"Him." She grimaced. "But you, too." A moment later, she yelped, "Mother of God! Can you believe this? He says that you were born to be the instrument of his salvation. Wait—let me read that again. I can't believe he wrote that."

Heloise murmured, "He wrote it. Ceci, mayhap it's true. We don't know God's will sometimes."

"That's right. But neither does he. You would think he held daily conversations with God."

"Ceci, please—"

"Shhh. I'm nearly finished." She read silently, and when she had completed the last page, she folded the letter and balanced it on her knee. She sat chewing her lip a while before saying softly, "Heloise, remember Sister Madelaine? She always used to say that it does no good to beat a dead mule."

Her eyes brimming with anger, Heloise yanked her head away. She should have known better than to confide in Ceci, with her old hatred of Abelard and her rough expressions.

"But I would say this mule is still breathing."

Startled, she said, "What do you mean?"

"He still loves you. Doesn't he say somewhere"—she tapped the letter thoughtfully with her forefinger—"doesn't he say he loves you beyond counting?"

"He said loved. Past tense."

"Oh, well." She shrugged. "He talks about being parted in this world and united in the next."

The bell for sext rang. Ceci stood and walked alongside Heloise. She handed back the letter, and they hurried toward the chapel. Finally Ceci sighed. "Sweeting, don't grieve."

The novices were lining up outside the chapel door, waiting for her. Heloise forced a smile and moved toward them.

That afternoon, she worked at her writing table. A pile of letters waited to be answered. Walter of Courcemain wished to give the Paraclete eight quarts of rye annually. Thierry Goherel donated the quitrent from one of his meadows, amounting to twelve deniers annually. Bishop Hatto of Troyes asked if she could use beeswax candles for Candlemas. And so on. One by one, she wrote replies steadily and set them to one side.

There was another letter, too, one she had saved for last. Her cousin Louis of Saint-Gervais wrote that Canon Fulbert was dead at Christmas; in his last testament he had specified that his books, amounting to a sizable library, should go to his beloved niece, Heloise.

Something sharp turned inside her. With tired eyes, she reread Louis's announcement, bloodless and brief. With Fulbert's passing, something had ended. She could not define it and did not try. The sun creeping through the open shutters was warm; she yawned. She thought of the dead, of Sister Madelaine and then of her mother and Fulbert, and of Astrolabe, who was as good as dead to her. Perhaps wisdom only meant the ability to recognize endings, to accept them and go on somehow.

Heloise reached for the ledger that she used as a necrology. She dipped the quill into the inkhorn. "December 26. Death of Fulbert, uncle of Abbess Heloise." With finality, she closed the book.

23 ❦

In the spring, after Lent was over, she replied to Abelard's letter.

"Since I would not want to give you reason for finding me disobedient in anything, I will set a bridle upon my lips. Thus in writing at least I may moderate what is difficult, or rather impossible, to suppress in speech. For nothing is less under our control than the heart . . ." God help me, my golden falcon, I love you.

"I will therefore stop my hand from writing words which I cannot restrain my tongue from speaking. Would that my heart would be as ready to obey as my writer's hand!"

That reassurance made plain to him, she continued to write until her wrist sagged. Once, when someone rapped at her door, she pretended not to hear. When at last she had finished, a stack of forty sheets lay in a heap on her table, each of them impersonal, businesslike. She told him that she was experiencing problems in administering a community of women under rules that had been originally devised for men, which was true. Scarcely a month went by without the appearance of applicants eager for novicehood, and many Heloise had to turn away; she had no place to put them in the overcrowded dormitory. The buildings that had seemed so spacious a year earlier, the gifts that had appeared to offer a solution to their financial troubles, suddenly shrank, and Heloise again faced the prospect of borrowing money. With the community strained to a breaking point, she realized for the first time that the Paraclete would survive, not only for her lifetime but perhaps for generations to come. While she had definite ideas of her own about what kind of religious house she wished to create, still she was open to suggestions, and therefore she asked Abelard to compose a new Rule, one that would apply to females.

To her surprise, he responded enthusiastically, and that summer and fall she received, in installments, a treatise on convent administration. His concern and care overwhelmed her, for there was no small detail that he overlooked, even down to what sort of undertunics the women should wear. Abelard also wrote for them sermons and over a hundred hymns, magnificent, sensitive works that might have been composed by some holy troubadour. If something between them had ended with the exchange of their intimate letters, a new beginning had been made. Of that Heloise had no doubt. It almost seemed as if the writing of Abelard's troubled letter to "a friend," and his letters to her, had acted as a catharsis in a way that she could never have imagined. His letters to her now were full of good humor, affection, news of their son, even light gossip.

"He jests," she said to Ceci one day in amazement. "What do you think of that?"

"I think"—Ceci grinned—"that there's life in the old mule yet. Although God knows he doesn't deserve a second chance after the hell he put you through."

Heloise retorted, "God doesn't know any such thing." She leaned forward and thumped Ceci on the shoulder. "God in his mercy sees into his heart and knows him for what he is."

"Good," said Ceci dryly. "I'm glad to hear it."

There was, of course, a reason for Abelard's buoyancy. Perhaps because of Heloise's urgings, he had requested permission of Pope Innocent to relinquish his abbacy at Saint-Gildas and return to teaching. By the following summer, in the robe of a monk, he was back on the hill of Sainte-Geneviève in Paris. Jourdain wrote to Heloise, saying that people told him it was as if Master Peter had never left the city, so enormous was his popularity. While Jourdain had not actually gone up to the Ile to see for himself, he had his sources; Abelard, he said, was teaching and writing and drawing to himself, as before, thousands of awestruck young men. One of these youngsters was Astrolabe.

Now sixteen, Heloise's son was personable, earnest, and intelligent. Or so Abelard wrote to her. Denise having died the previous Michaelmas, he felt it was time for the boy to leave Le Pallet and begin his serious education; he had brought Astrolabe to live with him on the Left Bank. What Abelard failed to mention was whether their son ever spoke of his mother, and this Heloise feared to ask.

In early July, after sheepshearing, she made Astrane prioress of the Paraclete, or rather she made it official. At the same time, Ceci was designated cellaress, Gertrude portress, the elegant Sister Hermeline sacristan, and so forth. The next morning, Heloise handed Astrane the ring of keys that always jingled at her girdle and, with Sir Arpin of

Méry-sur-Seine and a band of knights for escort, she struck west for Paris.

Despite Abelard's insistence, in his new Rule, that the abbess remain cloistered, Heloise had not paid strict attention to his wishes; the previous winter she had gone to Troyes and, for that matter, she had made several short trips throughout Champagne. Secretly, she adored to travel, although she was not as bad in this respect as Lady Alais had been, and she took care never to venture out of the Paraclete unless there was a good reason for doing so.

For months—in fact, ever since Abelard had returned to the Ile—she had shamelessly sought an excuse to visit Paris. Now she had one. At the prompting of the bishop of Troyes, King Louis had been moved to grant an important tax privilege to the Paraclete—perpetual exemption from the payment of duty on anything they might buy throughout the kingdom of France. This was, to put it at its mildest, a considerable coup for Heloise, and she notified the Royal Curia that she would come personally to accept the king's charter.

The air on the Mount Sainte-Geneviève smelled like clover and fruit. The abbey's special guesthouse, reserved for important church visitors, stood in a grove of plum trees, and when Heloise woke the morning after her arrival, her nose filled with the sweetish smell of ripening fruit. After breakfast, she walked down the hill, to Abelard's lodgings on the Rue de Garlande. Descending the slope, she stopped to look across the river at the Ile. From where she stood, the island appeared serene, the masses of hurrying legs, the murky streets strangely mute. There was only a tangle of willows along the riverbank and turrets pointing at the sky.

She headed for Abelard's door. A servant opened and gestured her into the solar. The room was plainly furnished, spotlessly clean, the residence of a monk. She stood by the window, tucking her hands into her sleeves. Behind her back, a door opened cautiously and someone said, low, "God's greeting, lady mother." She wrenched around.

"Father will be back shortly." Astrolabe scratched his ear, blushing. "I'm to entertain you."

Heloise smiled, tremulous. "Don't you want to?"

"Aye, I didn't mean—" He stood on one leg, fidgeting.

She went to him, brushed the hair from his eyes, and kissed him lightly on the forehead. Under her touch, she could feel his body locked tight with tension. She said lightly, "My dearest love, you're a *very* handsome young man." He didn't answer. "I'm glad to see you, son."

He nodded, looking uneasily toward the door. She studied the dark-blond hair that curled around his collar. He was very tall, but thin, vulnerable-looking. She thought, He does not have his father's aggressive temperament. She could feel tears stinging her eyelids. "Son," she said swiftly, "are you well, how do you like Paris? Oh, it is so wonderful to see you, this is the most wonderful day of my life, you don't know." She broke off, conscious that she was babbling like an idiot.

Astrolabe glanced at his mother's face. "Lady," he said gravely, "would you like some ale? I could get you something to drink."

She dabbed at her eyes. "Please don't go to any trouble—"

"It's no trouble."

When the servant had brought bowls of ale, they sat on stools by the window and drank and talked. Or, rather, Heloise talked. The boy, uncomfortable, answered her politely in as few words as possible. He kept darting his eyes into the road, obviously anxious for Abelard to return.

"I think," she said to him at last, "that you are greatly ill at ease with me. Mayhap I should leave and come back later when your father is here."

He shook his head roughly. "Oh no, madame. I mean, lady mother. Don't mind me." He added, sighing, "That's just my manner. I'm sorry."

Heloise almost reached out her hand to touch him. "Don't be sorry. I could never be displeased with you. I—you're a little frightened of me, aren't you?"

"No."

"But that's natural. You don't know me."

"No. But my father often speaks of you."

Surprised, Heloise said, "He does?"

"Often."

Heloise edged the stool closer. "What does he say?" She grinned conspiratorially.

Smiling for the first time, Astrolabe said, "That you are the most admirable woman he has ever known, and a fighter, and nobody but you could wage war with the Lord for fifteen years." He gave her a covert glance of amusement.

Heloise threw back her head and laughed. "He said that?" She set her bowl on the windowsill. "Well, I don't fight as much now as I once did."

There was a pause. "Lady," Astrolabe said, "what is it like in Champagne?"

"Lovely, perfectly . . . lovely."

"Is the Paraclete a small abbey? Do you still go out to the fields and plow? Is the river really emerald?" Coltish, he bounced to his feet and began hopping about the room.

"Whoa!" she laughed. "Would you like to visit me? You can see everything for yourself."

"When?"

"At the end of the summer. After Lammas, possibly."

"My father won't permit it."

"Of course he will. I'll speak to him. By then you'll be ready for a holiday from study, won't you?"

He smiled shyly. "Lady, when you were a student, did you have difficulty with logic?"

"Sometimes." She remembered her first lessons with Abelard, those boring treatises of Boethius. "I should be happy to help you with your lessons, if you like."

He stopped pacing and faced her uncertainly. "Would you?"

"Certainly." He ran into the bedroom. Heloise got up and followed. The inner chamber was large, with two narrow beds and a table piled with papers and books. Next to the table sat Abelard's old armchair, the carvings worn and chipped. She closed her eyes, struggling for control. Turning, she went back to the solar and sat down. A moment later, Astrolabe came in carrying a stack of books and a wax tablet; he dumped the armload at her feet. "You're reading all of these? God help you, child."

Astrolabe laughed. She reached down for the top book. He said, "That's my father's. For his theology class."

"Didn't he promise the pope not to teach theology?"

The boy shrugged. "I know nothing about it. Only that this work is too advanced for me. Father said so."

She glanced at the title. *Sic et non.* Yes and no. Pro and con. She looked up. "If it's too difficult, drop it. Work on something at your level."

He faltered. "But it's your book."

Startled, she said, "What do you mean?"

He sat down across from her, shrugging a little. "Why, my father said that you gave him the idea, that you had done much of the research as a girl. Don't you remember?"

"Sic et non," Heloise exclaimed. "Dear God, it can't—" Quickly she leafed to the first page and scanned the prologue. This work, Abelard wrote, was the attempt of an inquiring mind to arrive at a positive truth by means of logic. She flipped to the first hypothesis: *That faith should be founded on human reason—and the reverse.* She thought, laughing to herself, Abbot Bernard would love this. After the proposition came a list of quotations, some pro, some con. Many of the contradictions Heloise vaguely recognized as the results of her searching through the Bible and the Holy Fathers, but there were others that Abelard himself had added, and he had gone on to analyze the differences among them.

At her knee, Astrolabe said, "Do you like it?"

"I like it."

"It's very critical. I've heard people say so."

"It's honest," she murmured. Silently she read, "The first key to wisdom is assiduous and frequent questioning. It is through doubting that we begin to seek, and through seeking that we eventually perceive the truth." She said aloud, "Your father is not afraid to explore the unknown."

There were 158 hypotheses in *Sic et non.* She was relieved to see that Abelard drew no conclusions; instead, he presented the contradictions as a subject for investigation. He had taken Heloise's seeds, those scraps and scrawlings that she had mislaid in her travels between Paris and Argenteuil, and he had given her, fifteen years later, a full-grown oak. Wanting to cry again, she sucked in her breath and said, "Sweet heart, why don't we start with mathematics?"

An hour later, when Abelard came in, they were sitting with their heads bent over the tablet.

Heloise rested her head against the trellis in Abelard's garden, lazily watching the moon touch bright patches on the hedges. The night was pleasantly warm, and a tentative breeze ruffled the July leaves. She watched Abelard, half sprawled in the shadows, then gazed down at Astrolabe curled into a sleeping bundle at her feet. All day she had been studying the boy. He was odd, alternately diffident and hungry for affection, still babyish in his longing for attention. She had wanted him to be a copy of Abelard. He was not. There was no reason, of course, why he should be, and she reminded herself of that.

"Lady," Abelard said softly.

"I thought you were asleep."

"No." He paused a moment. "Lady, everything has come out all right. Surely you must see that now."

Heloise tried to peer into his face, but it was no use. There was only his voice coming at her in the darkness. "Mmmm. But it has not been what I would have planned."

He said, "Your plans did not take into account God's schemes for us."

How many tears had she shed? Now she would weep no more. Still, this evening, she felt empty and stupidly happy. "God's will be done," she said lightly, because that was what Abelard wanted to hear.

The breeze shifted, a lute song died away, then abruptly wound closer. She turned slightly, straining to catch the tune. It came to her now, familiar as the skin on her face, a sound of warmth, love, the crystal music of remembered happiness.

Abelard was humming softly, "Ah, would to God that night must never end."

"Nor that my lover far from me should wend."

"Nor watchman day nor dawning ever send. Ah God, ah God, the dawn!" Impulsively he reached for her hand. "It comes so soon."

Louis the Fat lay sick in the royal bedchamber at the Cité Palace, struck down some weeks earlier by a sudden flux of the bowels. His advisers were eager to remove him to his hunting lodge at Béthizy, where he could escape the fetid odors of the city. But moving the king was a major engineering problem; his extreme corpulence prevented him from sitting or getting to his feet without help. He could no longer mount a horse. A litter stood in readiness for the departure, because the king's condition had improved greatly, but still Suger delayed. A few more days, he said, and he ordered his master and beloved old friend carried to a couch in the great hall and propped against pillows.

Heloise rode in through the iron gate, Astrolabe at her side. But when she had dismounted and was about to ascend the broad stone stairs leading to the hall, the boy suddenly took fright and insisted that he would remain with the horses. She left him behind finally and went in alone. The dark hall buzzed ceaselessly with knights and courtiers, everyone's mouth going. Heloise, wondering how a sick man could mend amidst this commotion, stepped inside and announced herself to a chamberlain. Gesturing her to follow, he began pushing through the crowds. When they reached the dais at the front of the hall, the chamberlain halted abruptly. A knot of barons surrounded the king, and at the foot of the divan crouched a blond boy, his eyes sad and lost. When he noticed Heloise, he flashed a delicate smile, as if to say, *This is all too noisy for me.* He was about Astrolabe's age, a year younger, she thought. She smiled at him and inclined her head slightly. The gentle boy did not look like a king.

All at once, someone's voice rose sharply, the barons and the prince quickly dispersed, and there remained only one person at the king's side, the short, stolid Abbot Suger. In a loud voice, the chamberlain bellowed Heloise's name. She gulped a large breath and started toward the dais.

Just behind Louis's head, Suger was staring at her. He gazed from Heloise to the king, and back to Heloise once more.

Heloise knelt briefly. "Sire—"

"Lady Heloise," Louis said formally, "venerable abbess of the Paraclete. Lady, your immense renown echoes through our kingdom."

Blushing, Heloise got to her feet and looked at him. Never before had she seen such a fat human being. Vast mounds of flesh rippled in waves over the couch, so that it was impossible to imagine a frame of bone underneath. He bore no resemblance to the plump, robust man she had met so many years ago in the palace garden. Suger handed him a goblet; Louis drank, his hand twitching with palsy. He beamed at Heloise. "I've been wanting to meet you."

"Sire, you would not remember, but we have met once."

"Really?"

"Years ago. In your garden. I twisted my ankle, and you got a horse to take me home."

"Really?" he repeated. "I don't remember."

"Oh, of course you would not. I was a young girl then."

Louis smiled, his bleary eyes bubbling among the folds of flesh. He waved a page to bring a stool. "Please. Come up here and sit."

Heloise went up two steps and sat down. A foul smell suddenly lashed at her nostrils and she tried not to sniff. Near the king's couch she noticed a chamber pot and quickly darted her eyes away.

The king handed his goblet to Suger. He said to Heloise, "The Paraclete. This place was wilderness when you arrived."

"True. It was not inhabited."

"Rumor says that you yourself plowed the fields and constructed shelters. Is that true?"

"Aye." She grinned at him. "I have become a passable plowwoman."

Louis nodded. "Like our sainted Abbot Bernard. He built Clairvaux in the same way. Lady, tell me this. Does your vineyard prosper?"

Heloise looked over to Abbot Suger, who was appraising her with expressionless eyes. It was impossible to know if he remembered her from Argenteuil, but surely he must. She turned back to Louis. "We prosper, Sire, because of the love and goodwill of our neighbors. If it were my choice, the Paraclete would remain a small house. But we are flooded with applicants, and it seems that the Lord sends more women all the time. We are forced to expand, and yet we have not the means to do so."

Louis nodded again.

"Our requirements grow faster than I can meet them."

Suger bent close to Louis's ear, whispering. The king said to Heloise, "Lady, I have promised to help you—"

Suger broke in. "We mentioned duty exemption on all goods bought in the kingdom. I believe that was the gist of the grant." He spoke in a clipped voice, without looking at Heloise.

"That would be a tremendous help," Heloise said fervently. "Equally helpful would be exemption on any goods we might wish to sell." She stared at the floor, swallowing at her boldness.

Louis glanced at Suger and said, "Of course. They must have exemption on both buying and selling. I'd forgotten that. What do you think?"

Suger sniffed. "That sounds reasonable," he said haltingly. Shifting his weight, he gestured to a cluster of clerks standing against the wall. One of them ran up with a table, another with parchment and ink. Louis began to dictate. When the royal charter had been prepared, a clerk carried it to the couch for the king's signature. The great seal of France was brought, the scarlet wax melted on a small brazier, and the document completed. The king smiled. "And your lord, my dear abbess. Is he in good health?"

Surprised, Heloise managed to answer coolly, "Splendid health, Sire."

"He teaches again in the Ile. We are delighted to have him back."

"Yes, Sire." A chamberlain appeared at her elbow. Heloise rose and bowed and thanked the king. Behind his head, she saw Suger watching her with tight lips. The chamberlain beat a path for them through the courtiers. At the main door, he said politely, "Lady, may I fetch your horse?"

"Thank you, no." She went out into the brilliant sunlight and looked for Astrolabe.

For another week, she stayed on in Paris, although her business had been completed. She was waiting for the arrival of Abelard's nieces,

Agathe and Agnes, from Le Pallet. The two sisters wished to become novices at the Paraclete, a decision that caused Heloise some concern. "Are you positive they want to?" she asked Abelard. "This may be a childish whim. Have you spoken to them?"

"Agathe is determined to take vows. And Agnes goes wherever her sister does. They're inseparable." Abelard moved around the lecture platform collecting books and notes. "But you should speak to them just the same. Better to make sure of their minds. They're young."

Youngsters. She watched as two young men bounded into the hall, grabbed tablets they had left on the floor, and raced out again, yelling in a peculiar accent. "Those boys," she said to Abelard, "where are they from?"

"England."

"Oh. No wonder they speak so strangely."

Merry, he laughed over his shoulder. "That's Norman French, for your information, plus a smattering of Saxon. A linguist like you should be interested—you might ask them to give you lessons."

She smiled. "Mayhap I will. What are their names?"

"Tom Becket. And John of Salisbury. Good lads."

They went outside. It was a mild, amber morning. From the road came a rising chant of rumbustious voices yelling for Master Peter. Enveloping him, the boys began firing a torrent of questions. Heloise stopped at the corner and waited.

She thought, Tomorrow, or the day after that, I shall go back to the Paraclete and I'll be alone again. Once I would have dreaded the parting, but now it does not seem so terrible.

Abelard sent the boys away, and Heloise followed him down the hill. Before they reached his door, it opened and Astrolabe waved at them furiously. "Mama, hurry up! I'm starving."

24 🌿

HELOISE STOOD AT THE rectory window behind the church in Quincey and watched the sun trying to stab feeble rays against the dun-colored sky. In the road, villagers had begun to gather with the tapers they would carry later in the procession. Down near the marketplace, an entourage of richly dressed horsemen wheeled their mounts in capering circles. Wearily, she turned back to the room where Ceci and Astrane were anointing the body. The twisting fragrance of balsam stung her lids. She thought, Blessed man with your onions and angels. No doubt you must be with those celestial ladies now.

She had ridden to Quincey in the middle of the night, in time to see Father Gondry receive extreme unction. At the last, he had asked to be laid on the ground, on a haircloth sprinkled with ashes, and he had departed smiling. ("Sweet lady, pray for me when you kneel in your chapel—the Lord smiles upon you in your humility and kindness.")

From the day she arrived, even during those times of agony when Abelard had turned from her and when she had longed for death, he had been her rock. His voice counseled reason, assured her that she would survive. And so she had, somehow.

"This is nearly finished," Astrane said. She wiped ointment from her hands and arms.

Heloise smiled at her. "Sister. You are weary." Astrane's eyes were puffy and red. They had all wept, earlier. But now they concentrated on the work to be done. In the corner, on a narrow bed, stretched the linen shroud. Carefully, she lifted it and carried it to the table. Ceci and Astrane rolled the priest to the edge; Heloise spread the shroud flat.

"All right," she said. The body was positioned in the center of the cloth and then, methodically, they began to enfold it like a parcel that must be protected from the rain. Outside, the crowd had grown; sounds of wailing broke jarringly into the room. Heloise's mind drifted. Her thoughts ran back to one day last summer, when he had come to see her. No, it was not last summer, but the one before that. That very hot summer when Louis the Fat had died and Prince Louis had gone to Aquitaine to wed the magnificent Duchess Eleanor. That had been a worrisome time, because the sun blazed every day and the fields lay cracked and dry. They had prayed for rain, which came finally. Not in time, though. On one of those miserable days, Father Gondry had come to her office, his round face puckish as a squirrel's, and told her that he had made his will. To the Paraclete he was giving his property at Traînel, a large manor house with fields and vineyards. It was, he suggested hesitantly, an ideal place for a convent. She might consider opening up a daughter house, but, of course, she could dispose of the property as she liked. He would not presume to tell her what to do.

Someone rattled at the door. Heloise could hear Ceci whispering with Payen the saddler, and then she came back with a sheet of deerskin. Once more they lifted the corpse and wrapped it up. With needles and lengths of leather string, they started to lace the ends together.

The wind smacked against the shutters. Heloise stabbed the needle into the soft skin, pulled it out, stabbed again. From the corner of her eye, she watched Ceci's cheek bent over the table; suddenly she saw that Ceci was no longer young. Thirty-seven, she must be. Or at least thirty-six. They did not keep track of natal days. Ceci had always seemed a babe, a little black-eyed maiden who jogged at her heels. Yet, under the wimple, Ceci's black curls were silvered with gray; her full, pert face must have thinned long ago, but she, Heloise, had not noticed. She was thankful they were not permitted mirrors—the shiny steel would have reflected a face she could not acknowledge as her own. Last year, she had lost two teeth, rotted slowly during years of poor diet and empty stomachs, slipped out of her mouth as easily as an icicle dissolves in a spring shower. She had been surprised.

"Payen is bringing the coffin," Ceci said hoarsely.

They sewed silently until the strings had been snipped and tied. Needles put away, Heloise looked around the dingy room one last time. Bed, chest, a bowl of onions gilded by the candlelight. There was nothing to put in order.

"The new priest," Astrane murmured. "He's young."

"It won't be the same," Ceci said.

"No." They filed to the door and went out. The rest of the women from the Paraclete stood in the road, waiting. Some carried crosses and censers; Gertrude held the sacred books. At a nod from Heloise, Payen and Arnoul went into the house and emerged moments later, the coffin hoisted on their shoulders. They laid the box across two wooden poles that served as a bier. Chanting, the new priest walked to the coffin with measured steps, draped it with a black pall, fell back. Arnoul and the saddler lifted the poles. The keening cortege shuffled into the church, leaving a trail of muddy footprints inside the chancel gates.

Father Aimé started the dirge. He had a good, bold voice. Dry-eyed, Heloise stared at the draped box. Father Gondry had not lived his span. Last night, someone had told her that he was only forty-three. He had appeared old. Yet Abelard, who was much older, seemed ageless to her.

The priest was sprinkling holy water on the coffin, bobbing his head as he went. Ahead, in the front row, Heloise caught a glimpse of Lord Milo and two of his sons. Father Aimé chanted the antiphons of forgiveness and deliverance from judgment. The cortege began to reform. "Move aside there," someone hissed. "Let the Lady Abbess through." Heloise walked to the head of the line. Astrane handed her a wooden cross, which she braced against her chest. She moved off, followed by the bumping coffin, the file of nuns, the villagers in their black tunics. The light was failing rapidly—if they did not hurry, it would be dark before the grave was completed.

At the entrance to the burial ground, Heloise halted and waited for the cortege to catch up. Candles bobbed rosy in the dusk. She started to move again, swerving toward the shadowy back wall, where a shallow trench had been dug in the shape of a cross. After making the sign of the cross, Father Aimé threw handfuls of holy water, and the grave-diggers bent over their shovels. Sister Hermeline's voice, calm and crystal in the winter twilight, started the psalms.

After a while, the mounds of moist earth were heaped high; the coffin disappeared. Silence. People coughed. The final collect for forgiveness. Hastily, the shovelers began cramming the earth back into the hole. In the matted leaves near her feet, Heloise saw a mouse slither desperately for shelter in a thorn hedge.

The priest turned and went past her; people began to stumble into a queue of sorts, and children whined softly for their suppers. Very slowly, Heloise inched against the wall where it was darkest. The November blackness fell silently on the tombstones, save for the funeral torch that smoked at the head of the grave. For the hundredth time that day, she thought of Abelard and of their son, who was now grown—tall, well formed, sweet tempered but for his occasional moods of silent apathy. If she could only hold the two of them forever. These last years had been good to her; hurriedly she corrected herself—*God* had been good to her. And to Abelard. Without bowing her head, she prayed: *Almighty Father, do not still that golden voice too soon—I'm afraid to live in this world without him.* A mouse—the same mouse?—brushed the hem of her habit. Darting her eyes among the shadows, she hunted for the tiny creature, but all she glimpsed was her own insecurities, old companions that would follow her to the end of the road.

The snow had stopped. The sounds of romping children echoed across powdered roofs. Heloise sat in the bishop's court at Troyes, waiting for her case to be called. Across the chamber, Abbot Norpal ate apples and crooked his arm around his monks. They talked loudly without much interest in their surroundings. Now and then, the abbot would glare in Heloise's direction. Shortly after sext, one of his monks came to her.

"The abbot wants to give you a chance to drop your complaint," he announced.

"The abbot has delayed this case for two years," she said quickly. "He wastes my time and the court's time. I want the matter settled." If she dropped the case, she would have to pay a fine.

"And who told you to sue the abbot?" the monk demanded angrily. "It's you who have wasted our time." He strode back to the abbot of Vauluisant.

She ate bread and cheese from her bag, and then the bishop's steward called her to his table. After the oath-taking, he asked her to state her plea. She explained that the oak wood lying south of the Bagnaux road had been given to the Paraclete by Sir Ralph Jaillac in the year of Our Lord 1136. The following year, she discovered that the abbey of Vauluisant was cutting firewood and feeding its pigs on her land. When she brought this fact to the abbot's attention, he had informed her that the wood had been the abbey's property since the time of Sir Ralph's grandfather. She spoke slowly, very careful to follow the traditional wording for her charges. Finally, she handed Bishop Hatto a charter confirming her right to the wood, and swept back to the bench.

The steward called Abbot Norpal, who could produce no charter of ownership but claimed that everyone knew the wood belonged to Vauluisant. Drawling, he reminded the court that Bishop Hatto himself, while visiting the abbey in 1132, had hunted fox in that very same wood. And so on. The abbot, smiling, drowned the courtroom with wind. Bishop Hatto nodded from time to time.

Heloise leaned back, impatient. She wanted to get home.

362

* * *

Halfway up the empty river road, she reined the mare to a walk. Through a rolling veil of snowflakes, she could see the chimneys of the Paraclete smoking gently. The land and sky were white, shredded, comforting. Every time she rode back from Quincey or Saint-Aubin, she felt compelled to have a long look. There was a new gate, and within the snowbound walls, kitchens, infirmary, library, and a guesthouse with a special wing she had added for Abelard. New buildings had gone up swiftly, old ones had been expanded and renovated, including Abelard's original chapel, which was now a sizable church. The Paraclete was larger than Argenteuil, it suddenly occurred to her. She nudged the mare forward.

"They've cut pine branches to decorate the church," Gertrude told her. "And Cook says she is making beef and raisin pies."

"I thought it was anise cakes," Heloise said. Christmas pilgrims were singing around a bonfire, filling the yard with a rousing carole. "Where's Master Peter?"

"Writing."

"How can he work on a lovely day like this?"

Gertrude wrinkled her nose into a smile. "He asked for you a while ago."

"And my son?"

"I've not seen him today," Gertrude answered.

Heloise made her way slowly to the east wing of the guesthouse, past women eager for her blessing and men who dropped on their knees in the trampled slush to kiss her ring, all the formalities that accompanied the position of abbess. There were children, too, and they chattered like blackbirds and squeezed around Heloise with running noses and snow-dusted bonnets. The air smelled of fish soup bubbling in marjoram and dill, and that bland wetness that comes with a fresh snowfall. Under Heloise's boots the snow squeaked. Her feet were dry, but her cloak had become crusted with snow. Outside the door, she flung it off and shook the snow from it. She knocked and went in.

At the writing table, Abelard sat very still, a quill in his right fist. It was a peaceful room, the walls whitewashed, the floor tiled in blue; blasts of warm air fluttered up from the brazier. When he saw her, he tossed the quill aside and said happily, "Who won?"

Heloise made an impatient gesture with her hand, as if the matter were trivial. "We did. I suppose."

He raised his eyebrows. "Don't you know?"

Throwing her cloak over a chest, she brought a stool to the table and sat down. "We get to keep the wood."

"Wonderful."

"But Abbot Norpal gets the acorns. Which means we can't feed our pigs there."

"Huh. Clever decision, I would say. I'll wager Norpal was burning."

Heloise smiled and shrugged her shoulders. "I expect he knows that he got more than he deserves."

Abelard laughed at her. "Lady, he should have known better than to tangle with you."

She bristled. "What's that supposed to mean?"

He twisted his body toward her, still smiling. "Tell me, how many lawsuits do you have pending?"

"Why, three—against the monks of Saint-Jacques, the monks of Saint—"

"There—see what I mean?"

"My lord," she cried, indignant, "those monks are trying to take advantage of us. Because we're women, they think we won't defend our rights."

"Lady, lady," he broke in. "I'm not criticizing you. Fight on. I think the Lord fights on your side."

She smiled uncertainly. "Do you think so?"

"No doubt." He turned his eyes back to the parchment on which he had been writing. And then, unexpectedly: "I only pray that the Almighty will aid me against my enemies."

She stared at him, startled. "Enemies? You have no enemies—"

He smiled easily, as if it was of no importance. "'Enemies' is the wrong word. Let us say, instead, critics. Your friend Abbot Bernard has been to visit me twice this year."

That surprised Heloise. Generally, Bernard did not travel about making social calls. "What did he want?" she asked. "Was he friendly?"

"Oh, very. But it seems that somebody has been reading my books and taking exception to some of my statements."

"I don't know what there is to find fault with."

"Brother William is outraged—he says I treat Holy Writ as if it were dialectics. He claims I invent a new novelty each year."

It seemed to her that Abelard, while smiling, was telling her something dangerous. "Who is this William?" she asked.

He shrugged. "Used to be abbot of Saint-Thierry, but he decided an abbacy was too grand for him. My dear old friend is now an ordinary monk. Cistercian."

"You know him?"

"Once that rascal loved me. Now he calls me a public evil. In any case, he sent Bernard a letter of protest that listed thirteen offensive statements in my *Introduction to Theology*." He got up, stretched, and slouched to the window. Heloise turned her eyes to follow him. He laughed. "Brother William plans to search *Sic et non* for mischief—when time permits."

"Bernard." Heloise took a deep breath. "What did he want of you?"

"To get me to correct my errors." He opened the shutter a crack and reached for a handful of snow. Before he could draw it in, the flakes had melted in his hand.

"You're not going to, are you?" Heloise asked very quietly.

"Certainly not." Abelard snorted, wiping his hand on his gown. "Certainly not. It would mean the end of me as a teacher and writer." He came back to the table and sat down, smiling slightly. "Bernard kept saying, 'Faith does not discuss—faith believes.' Any departure from that stance is rank heresy to him. The thought of my standing before a class of beardless young men and asking them to question Christian doctrines is enough to try the patience of a saint. His words."

She answered wryly, "He's aiming for sainthood."

"Do you think he'll get there?"

"No." She hugged her fingers to her sleeves, suddenly chilly. "Abelard, all knowledge is good. Even the knowledge of evil. Because a good person can't guard against evil until he knows what it is."

"Precisely. It's not wrong to know anything. The evil is in doing wrong. Besides, all knowledge comes from God and therefore must be good. That fire needs charcoal."

She nodded, getting to her feet. "I'll send somebody to fix it. My lord, did Bernard go away satisfied?"

Flippant, he answered, "Well, he went away. Tell me what there is for dinner around here."

"Fish soup. But if you want meat, I think Cook could find some ham for you—"

"I'll have both. And apples and cheese. And clabbered milk, if you have it."

She went for her cloak, slinging it over her arm. "Aren't you worried about getting fat?" she teased, moving toward the door.

"It's this country air. I—" Abruptly, his voice cracked; Heloise wheeled around in astonishment. His head sagged over the table, his shoulders crumpled beneath the black robe.

"Abelard!"

He seemed to be paying no attention. His face was hidden and she could hear him mumbling under his breath. "Dizzy—go fetch Astrolabe—"

Loath to leave, she ran to him and turned his face toward her. The eyes were shut fast. Under her fingers, his jaw was limp. Panicky, she raced into the yard, yelling for Gertrude as loudly as she dared. Across the way, Astrolabe was hurling snowballs with one of the children. Waving wildly, she called him to her. Behind him hurried Sister Gertrude. Heloise shouted to her, "Master Peter has fainted! Run to the infirmary." She caught a glimpse of Astrolabe's face, suddenly white and scared, but pulled him toward Abelard's chamber without speaking.

"Mama, wait—"

"Hurry up." Dashing ahead of him, she snatched up a fistful of snow, packed it hard between her palms, and ran inside. Hands dripping, she smacked the snow on Abelard's neck and face.

"Mama, wait—" Astrolabe grabbed his father by the shoulders, levered him off the chair, and stretched him full length on the floor. "He'll be all right. It only lasts a few minutes."

She bent down to him, catching him by the wrist. "This has happened before?" she demanded. "For God's sake, why didn't you tell me?"

"He didn't want to worry you."

"Oh, well, he didn't want to worry me. But look at what's happened now. He's ill. We must do something." She sank on her knees next to Abelard.

"He made me promise."

"Never mind your promises." Sister Claude came in with a goblet of herbed wine; she crossed the room without speaking, raised Abelard's head, and forced a little of the wine between his lips. Heloise hissed at her son, "He's ill. Why didn't he tell me?"

Abelard stirred. He opened his eyes briefly, then closed them.

Head bent next to Heloise's ear, Astrolabe whispered, "Please, Mama. It's not serious. The spells only last a few minutes, and then he's all right again. Sometimes he forgets. Listen to me. Go outside now so he won't know you saw this. Please, Mama, I'll call you when he's himself."

Sister Claude said, "I'll be here, lady. I think he's coming out of it now. These faints don't last long."

Heloise grunted. Reluctantly she got to her feet. Abelard's face shone waxy, but she could see that he was breathing normally. She backed toward the door and eased out. Two priests from Baudement were crossing the yard; they pointed at her and waved. She smiled and bowed. Her breath was coming fast. Astrolabe said it was not serious, but he was wrong. Fainting fits in a man of sixty were always serious. Crouched in the doorway, she nervously licked her lips and tasted snowflakes.

At last, the latch clicked behind her back and she spun around to see Astrolabe beckoning. She stepped into the room. Behind the table, Abelard was sitting in the chair again, talking to Sister Claude. His fingers were curled around the goblet. When he saw Heloise, he called, "Lady, what can I have to eat?" and threw her a quick smile.

"Fish soup, my lord. Ham."

"Do you think I could have a bowl of apples and a little Brie?"

"My lord, I told you—" She looked from him to Astrolabe's expressionless face.

"If it isn't too much trouble, I might take some clabbered milk."

"Yes, my lord." She turned away, shaken.

Astrolabe said, "I don't believe the faints have anything to do with Bernard. He had them before all this fuss started."

Heloise had led the boy to a quiet place next to the water mill, impatient for explanations. "Son," she said, "you say 'all this' as if it were not yet ended. I want to know—"

"Abbot Bernard has visited Father."

"Yes, yes, I know all that. But your father refused to change his books. What more can Bernard do?"

Astrolabe, leaning against the stone wall of the mill, had his back to Heloise. Hesitantly, he said, "Oh, he has written a treatise refuting Father's views. Very nasty, too. You know, sarcastic."

The wind lifted a cloud of cobwebby snow. The waterwheel creaked softly, subsided, creaked again. Heloise, staring at his back, tried to think. It was not wise to make an enemy of Bernard, of all churchmen, and Abelard should have known better. But when had Abelard been cautious? "How sarcastic?" she demanded. "Do you mean hostile?"

"Amusing," he said. "He calls Father a dragon who has been lurking in his den and now comes into the open." He picked at an icicle with his fingernails. "He said Father was setting degrees and grades to the Trinity and was trying to compute eternity. It's all silly. Everybody in Paris is laughing."

Heloise smiled to herself—Bernard was high-strung, extreme. As usual, he had managed to overstate his case. On the other hand, he was not a fool, nor would he allow himself to be made one.

Grinning, Astrolabe turned to her. "It's a good fight. Father wrote a point-by-point rebuttal of Bernard's charges, and somebody made a lot of copies and took them around to all the taverns." He flung back his head, tossing the long hair out of his eyes. "He called Bernard a devil disguised as an angel—now, isn't that funny?"

Heloise, frowning, did not answer.

"Oh, Mama, you worry too much. The pope and the whole Roman Curia are on Father's side. He told me as much." Then: "I think Father is enjoying all this."

"Hunh," Heloise grunted and snapped her mouth closed.

They went back to Paris after Epiphany. Before their departure, Heloise gave a string of instructions to Astrolabe—he was to stick close to his father, try to get him to see a physician, of whom there were several in the Ile. Most important, he was to write her if there was news of any kind. The boy promised, although it was clear that he felt disloyal to his father.

A letter arrived from Jourdain telling her that he planned to visit the court at Troyes in the spring. It had been a bad winter at Sancy; a pox had broken out and half his villeins were sick with it, also Jourdain's wife and youngest son, but they had recovered nicely. If all went well, he was determined to travel to Champagne and naturally he would come to see her. Idly, Heloise wondered what Jourdain might look like now. There had been many letters over the years, and she knew that he had not changed in any discernible way. Still, she persisted in thinking of him as a youth, which he was no longer.

On Candlemas, she made a trip to Traînel, a half day's journey, to inspect the legacy left by Father Gondry. She had meant to wait until Lent, but an unexpected climb in temperature had melted the snow, and she wanted to take advantage of the clear roads before they had another weather change. With her she took Ceci, and they went to see Lord Anselm, who ruled in that part of the country west of the Arduzon. As she told Anselm, she could sell the property or she could use it. The more she thought about it, the clearer it became to her that here was a solution to one of her problems. The Paraclete, despite its expansion program, was undeniably overcrowded. Nearly a hundred women, and still the novices came. If she could siphon off a dozen or two and put them someplace else, living would be much easier.

The limestone manor house on the edge of town was quite spacious. Attached were vineyards and a few acres, not enough to produce much in the way of crops but certainly adequate for vegetable gardens. She strolled around the house, thumping walls and talking to herself. The place gave her a nice feeling. There was no chapel, but that could always be added.

"It's cozy," Ceci said, lagging at her heels. "No privy, though."

"We'll make one."

"It needs a lot of fixing up."

"I can see that," Heloise murmured. "But when it's done, I think we'll have something lovely." She rammed open a shutter and looked out over the brown fields. "Ceci?"

"What?"

"I think," she said deliberately, "that we should name this convent after Ste. Madelaine." And in honor of Sister Madelaine, she thought. "How does this sound? Sainte-Madelaine of Traînel."

When she turned, Ceci was grinning. "The old witch will be very pleased, wherever she is."

Unbidden, the prioress's face leaped before her eyes, the schoolroom at Argenteuil, and the flat rock above the Seine which she had used as a refuge from Madelaine's sharp tongue. How she had longed to get away from the woman, from the high walls of the convent. The stern schoolmistress and the dreamy, unhappy girl. What had she dreamed about then? Love, pretty gowns—the things all little girls want. Madelaine had wanted her to take vows, become an abbess, because she could imagine no other life for a clever woman. She had understood nothing of Heloise. Ceci was clearing her throat. Heloise closed the shutters before the tears started to form in her eyes.

Songbirds returned to the willows along the Arduzon and the Easter pilgrims to the highroads; the plowing and sowing and harrowing were finished, the vines tended. The Paraclete's tenants brought their sheep tithes. On the other side of Ferreux, a serf killed his master and burned the manor house—it was a bad business. Just before noon on Good Friday, Jourdain came to the gate with a large party of horsemen, among them Count Thibaut and Countess Mathilde. There was a frantic rushing about while Gertrude tried to decide where to put such distinguished guests. In the end, Abelard's wing was made ready for the noble couple and the rest of them tucked into odd corners of the guesthouse.

During Easter weekend, between the many special services, Heloise made time to speak privately with the Count of Champagne, and by the time his party left on Tuesday morning, he had promised to donate a barrel of wheat annually, together with the produce of the fishing grounds near his mills at Pont-sur-Seine.

"He adores you," said Jourdain, who had remained behind. After three days of walking all over the convent grounds that were open to guests, he had told Heloise that she had created a miracle. He was still shaking his head, his plain, amiable face vaguely astonished.

Heloise searched his face, still looking for the awkward boy. "I told you," she said. "People have been incredibly generous to us. God be thanked."

"Because you are a model abbess and this is a model convent."

"Oh, certainly," she said lightly, turning away from him. "People see only the façade."

Jourdain fingered his beard. "You still," he said softly, "think of yourself as a failure." He had grown stout, and his hair had thinned on the crown.

She smiled, her mouth tight. "I built this house for Abelard. Nothing was done for God."

"No, I think you're wrong." She wheeled to face him. "God works through people. Mayhap by serving your lord, you are serving your Lord."

Heloise shrugged. "Intention is all that counts." She merited no applause from heaven. The sun was going down. She led him into Abelard's apartment, lit the candles, and ordered wine and wafers. Jourdain sat drinking white wine from the Paraclete's own vintage.

He gazed about the room. "Master Peter must find this to his taste. Peaceful." Abruptly, he went on. "You've heard about the joust, of course."

Heloise tried to smile. "Joust? Is that what it's become?"

"It's no longer a private quarrel. Bernard has been writing letters to various cardinals and bishops."

There was a long pause. Heloise said finally, with an effort, "Denouncing Abelard for heresy."

"He's gotten no support."

"It makes me nervous."

Jourdain smiled at her, his forehead pitted with tiny wrinkles. "I think Master Peter will fix the abbot of Clairvaux once and for all at Sens. Bernard will retire to his cell and never come out again."

Heloise frowned and sat up straight. "In heaven's name, I don't know what you're talking about."

"Sens," he answered impatiently. "The octave of Whitsun. There's to be a big display of relics, and even the young king is coming. I thought you—"

She had received the circular invitation weeks ago. Archbishop Henry Sanglier had summoned abbots and abbesses and rural priests from every corner of the archdiocese. It was to be a great assembly—churchmen of every rank, as well as nobles and commoners.

"Are you going?" Jourdain asked.

She nodded.

"Then you will see Master Peter there. He's challenged Bernard to a debate."

Heloise stared. "That's very interesting. But whatever for? Bernard isn't a debater."

"He's going to outline his views and defy Bernard to refute them. Inspired plan, isn't it?"

"Do you mean to tell me," she said sharply, "that the archbishop agreed?" Outside in the yard, she could hear someone shouting; she hoped that Gertrude would quiet him.

Jourdain, yawning, drained his goblet. "Why should he refuse?"

"Jourdain," Heloise murmured, moving her stool closer. "You've known me since I was a girl—you know that I worry about everything. But isn't this something to worry seriously about? Isn't this very foolish of Abelard?"

"I don't think so. Because this way he can show everybody how pure his teachings are. It's the only way now that he can expose Bernard's attempts to discredit him."

"I don't know." In a debate, Bernard would be demolished. She could not imagine the frail little abbot defeated. "Bernard has accepted?"

"I told you. It's going to be the theological joust of the century."

"Has Bernard grown stupid, do you think? Do you think he realizes what he is doing?" Her voice climbed to a high-pitched laugh of jubilance. "Abelard will win, won't he?"

Jourdain grinned. "He can't lose."

25 ❧

THE ROADS LEADING TO Sens on that first day of June swarmed with travelers on horseback and foot, and Heloise and Jourdain were among them. Student and priest, king and commoner, all jounced along to witness the display of relics, to have a look at the rising cathedral with its novel arches, and if possible to hear Abbot Bernard argue the Trinity with Master Peter Abelard. Because the town had no place to lodge this invasion, people camped outside the sand-colored walls, among the fields and vegetable gardens and the wild hyacinths.

When Heloise and Jourdain rode up to the Troyes Gate, the mob was so great that they had to wait in line to enter. They inched over the drawbridge into the noisy commercial quarter with its three- and four-story houses and shops shouldering into the streets, their corbeled upper stories looming precariously overhead. Shopfronts were painted blue or garish red, many faced with tile, and a clutter of merchandise spilled from the stalls into the street—boots, cloth of gossamer and wool, savory spices, rosaries.

The foot traffic separated Heloise's mare from Jourdain, and she had to rein in sharply to keep from riding down the honking geese that nipped around her mount's hoofs. Twisting in her saddle, she called back, "Jourdain! Rue du Temple, in case I lose you. Third house." He nodded.

At the Knights Templars' house, she stopped and waited for Jourdain. A goodwife, white wimple bobbing, smiled at her and boldly asked for a blessing. Jourdain came. "This is incredible!" he cried. His voice was thick with glee. "Every monk in France must be here."

Heloise tipped back in her saddle and laughed. Carefully, they picked their way down the Rue du Temple to the house of a widow who had donated a water clock to the Paraclete and counted it a great honor to lodge its abbess in her home.

The Montauban family was lined up in the vestibule, the children washed and combed like little archangels. Each of them scrambled forward, knelt down, and brushed a kiss on Heloise's ring. "Lady abbess," murmured Mme. Montauban, "are you alone? Where is your maid?"

"I have no maid," Heloise said, smiling. "We are all equal at the Paraclete."

"Lady, this is a great honor for our house—" Chattering nervously, she escorted Heloise to a second-floor chamber, where Heloise washed her face and shook the dust from her habit. She immediately went out again. On foot, she walked quickly to the cathedral to say vespers. As she returned to the house, a red sun flamed and slipped behind the roofs.

A servingwoman told her that a young man had come, and she had sent him up to the abbess's chamber. Heloise swung up the stairs, breathless with excitement. The door slammed open. "Mama!" Astrolabe pulled her to his chest in a hug that cracked her elbows. "Mama!" he shouted, "did you ever see anything like this, did you?" and danced back.

She caught him by the arm, planting a kiss on his cheek. "No"—she laughed—"I never have. Sweet heart, you need a haircut. Where are you lodging?"

He ran his fingers loosely through the glossy strands. "The archbishop's guesthouse. Mama, Queen Eleanor is here. I saw her this morning. She has golden hair and the whitest skin."

Heloise paid no attention. Astrolabe, face flushed, tunic askew, was prowling about the room like a caged lion. "Your father, is he well?"

"Quite well." He threw her a surprised look, as if that were an irrelevant question. His eyes were dark and shining. "He's in splendid spirits."

"Son, he has no idea I'm here, has he? You didn't tell him?"

"You asked me not to. I can't see why—"

Heloise smoothed his hair, loving the touch of him. His skin smelled like musk. "He doesn't like me to leave the Paraclete."

"Well, you do."

She looked away, smiling a little. "I know. But we're not going to tell him."

"Everyone is here! Father's students followed us all the way from the Ile. Gilbert and Berengar and Arnold of Brescia—"

Heloise started. Arnold was a well-known agitator, banished from Italy by the pope for his political activities and charged with heresy. She had not known him to be one of Abelard's students. She said, "That's wonderful."

"They've all gathered at the Tournelles Inn. You should see them. Mama, come with me, you can meet them." He jabbed at her shoulder.

She stretched out her arms and hugged him, saying, "Son, I'm too old to frequent taverns."

"Oh, lady, you're not old. Please."

She backed away and went to light a candle. Dappled light gashed the room with shadows. "Don't be silly," she said gently. "My sweet boy, I'm an abbess."

He turned to her, face sheepish. A moment later, he was hitching up his girdle with a delighted smile. "Nobody will sleep tonight. We're going to stay up and talk."

Heloise could see that he was impatient to get back to the noisy taverns and the cheering young men who would be thronging around Abelard. Kissing him, she sent him off into the darkness.

Later, she stretched on the bed, watching the moonlight quiver in milky pools on the tile floor. She slept and dreamed of Fulbert's turret above the Seine.

At daybreak, the great bells of the cathedral began to bellow.

Heloise and Jourdain hurried toward the main thoroughfare, doubled back over the Grand Rue, and threaded their way through a warren of muddy little lanes. "Jourdain," Heloise said, "Astrolabe came to see me last night. He said that Arnold of Brescia was with Abelard. Isn't he a heretic?"

Jourdain looked at her with no particular interest and shrugged. "That's what they say. I think he's merely a hothead. Talks a lot."

"But isn't that bad for Abelard?" she demanded.

"Lady, there are hundreds of his students here. And former students. Some radical, some as orthodox as you please."

They turned a corner and came out alongside the apse of the cathedral, into an area that looked like a work yard. There were sheds sheltering forges and a carpenter's shack next to a large pit where saws and long pieces of timber had been stacked. Some ten years earlier, Henry Sanglier had decided to rebuild the church, and he had hired the eminent master builder William to draft a ground plan. At Sens, as at Saint-Denis, a daring new style of engineering was being used, and people raved about the wonders of ribbed vaults and flying buttresses. Jourdain said, staring in awe at the scaffolding soaring into the hot sky, "This is going to take fifty years to finish."

"More like a hundred," Heloise answered. "It's lovely, isn't it?"

The yard, frosted with stonecutters' dust, stood empty today. They skirted the sawing pit and started around the side of the cathedral, only to run up against a solid wall of backs. Although the service had already begun, the bronze doors were jammed and people stood in the aisles at the rear of the nave. When Heloise presented her billet of admission to a Knight Templar, he advised her of the futility of trying to reach her place. People were climbing on tombs and hanging from the marble pillars, and when the knights herded them down, they crept back an instant later. At last, Heloise and Jourdain were crushed against a statue of the Virgin, and there they stayed, squeezed tight. They could hear, but seeing was more difficult. After the service came the presentation of relics; the golden reliquaries encrusted with rubies and diamonds were brought forth with their treasures—the Crown of Thorns, fragments of the True Cross, a drop of blood belonging to St. Clement, one of Judas's thirty pieces of silver. Or so Heloise heard, for she could see nothing but a blur of incense and tapers and billowing gonfalons.

When knights tried to clear the aisles, the mob heaved back. There was silence. Slowly down the nave moved King Louis carrying a gold cross. He walked sturdily, the boy that Heloise had last seen huddled at his father's feet in the Cité Palace, and his eyes were downcast in an attitude of humility. On tiptoe, Heloise caught only a glimpse before he moved on, followed by a queue of bishops and monks. There were not only the prelates of the diocese—Elias of Orleans, Hatto of Troyes, Manasses of Meaux—but many others whom she did not recognize. Jourdain whispered into her ear as they went by: the archbishop of Rheims; Abelard's old friend, Geoffrey of Chartres; and on and on they came. A thousand necks stretched to goggle at the jeweled miters, the vestments gleaming with gold.

The procession wound down the center aisle, turned, and headed back along the north aisle toward the choir. The aisles filled again as the crowd surged forward. The chanting of the choristers trumpeted along the stone walls. The air inside the cathedral reeked of sweat and incense. As the morning wore on, sweat gushed on Heloise's face, and she felt on the verge of suffocating.

When Jourdain grabbed her arm tightly and began dragging her through the bodies, she followed blindly. Outside milled hundreds of people, but here at least there was air. They stood together on the porch, next to pilgrims speaking German, and gasped at the breeze. "Let's wait a bit," Jourdain said, panting. "It will be over soon and the court will be coming out. You don't want to miss that, do you?"

Heloise did not care, but she nodded. All during the procession, she had been thinking of Abelard, hoping it was less crowded where he sat. She turned to Jourdain, and said, "I don't mind." Ceci would ask her if she had seen the young queen and demand to know every detail. Eleanor, duchess of Aquitaine, had been queen of France three years and she was still less than eighteen. Incessantly, people gossiped about her, even the nuns of the Paraclete. This granddaughter of William the Troubadour was supposed to be spectacularly beautiful—and spoiled. From Aquitaine she had brought troubadours to the Cité Palace, an incident which caused the pious Queen Adelaide to move out, and people also said that Eleanor did not get along well with the king either.

The crowds wedged into the bronze doors parted, and Heloise could see the royal bodyguard shoving through roughly. Trumpets brayed and people began to shout, "Vivat Regina!" Behind Heloise, somebody said, "Three years and no babe. She must be barren." Another voice, full of mockery, answered, "It's the king—he's too holy to fuck." Heloise choked back a smile.

Clouds of silk—red, rose, yellow, and orange—drifted through the summer afternoon like blossoms of dust raised by stallions' hoofs. Behind them sailed a radiant girl loaded down with bracelets and winking ear pendants. Heloise drew in her breath sharply. The queen's gown was made of magnificent lavender tissue, and over her blond hair, fastened to her brow by a circlet of wrought gold, flowed the sheerest of wimples. She had draped it around her neck and shoulders, and one corner cascaded over her left arm. When the crowd cheered, she scanned their gaping faces and smiled beautifully.

Jourdain nudged Heloise. "She's got rouge on. Nobody has cheeks that pink."

"Rouge?" she said dully. "I wouldn't know about that, friend." Staring at the long train on the queen's gown, she felt drab and ugly. "Let's go." She turned and stumbled down the worn stone steps to the street.

"If you wish to understand the Word, you must love!" For more than an hour Bernard had been talking about love, and now even some of the most mesmerized of his admirers were beginning to shuffle their feet restlessly. "A cold heart cannot understand words of fire—"

Heloise, bored, crossed her arms over her chest. Bernard performed all the difficult religious duties—he fasted, he suffered—but he could not endure the easy ones. He did not love. She let her attention drift to the abbot of Clairvaux's face. He seemed on the verge of collapse, but when had he not looked frail? A plucked bird, he had called himself at the Paraclete; he looked in worse condition now, if that were possible. She stretched her neck and shoulders, sweeping her gaze around the jousting ground, over the swaying heads and faces. Suddenly, Bernard's words jolted her back to the wooden platform above her head. "This man," he was saying, "our theologian, says nothing about love or mystery, although he speaks a great deal." Around Heloise people began to buzz Abelard's name. Furious at herself for wandering, she began to push her way closer to the platform. She could see Bernard lashing out wildly with both arms.

"—his arrogant manner. Of all the expressions in heaven and earth, there is only one that Master Abelard appears not to know." He paused and looked around. "The expression—I KNOW NOT!"

Heloise blinked hotly. A ray of reddish sunlight struck Bernard's hair, throwing a rosy nimbus about his face and his white robe. From where she stood, he looked like some cadaverous emperor delivering judgment, his fiery head seeming to touch the clouds.

"Master Abelard is a monk without a monastery! A prelate without an office! He adheres to no law, has no rule to restrain him!" Whistles from the crowd corkscrewed through the fading light. "This man sweats hard to prove that Plato was a Christian. But he only ends up proving that he, Abelard, is no better than a pagan himself!"

Shocked that he would dare stoop to this low, spiteful attack on Abelard, Heloise rattled her rosary in helpless frustration. Imbecile! He knew nothing of Abelard's philosophy. Bernard was hammering out venom: "He's a Herod in the trappings of a John the Baptist!" He hopped to the edge of the platform. "He was condemned at Soissons, but his new errors are even worse than his old!" Under her breath, Heloise screamed, "Liar!"

"Master Peter and Arnold of Brescia—that pest that the pope threw out of Italy—these two heretics are actively in league against God and his Christ. This evil must be stamped out!" Bernard rocked convulsively from side to side.

Eyes burning hard, Heloise stood there for a moment, and then she turned and plunged through the onlookers. She would listen to no more. Over to her left, a woman called out, "Devil, Abelard is a devil!"

Heloise thrust her hands out, fumbling for open space. Two men passed a wineskin over her shoulder. Behind them, Bernard thundered, "This man is a teacher. His pupils idolize him and, mark me, he influences their minds and hearts. His books are spreading beyond the seas and the Alps, flitting from province to province, from kingdom to kingdom." He was gasping hoarsely. "THIS MAN'S VOICE MUST BE STILLED!"

At the edge of the field, under the shady green oaks, the air rushed spongy and cool. A sickle moon pierced the sky. Bernard was asking the crowd to pray for the unbeliever, Master Abelard, his words floating down over the field as careless as snowflakes. Heloise gathered up her skirts and ran.

It was just after matins when she lay back on her bed, yet sleep would not come. Her mind revolved like a rusty wheel on all that Abbot Bernard had said at the tourney field. Abelard no Christian . . . voice stopped . . . pest. The savagery behind his words still echoed in her ears. She stirred restlessly, picturing Bernard as a fanged hound on the trail of a bleeding lamb. Except that Abelard was no lamb, nor was he wounded. Tomorrow he would devour Bernard. That was the only thought that comforted her.

Heloise closed her eyes, but a moment later, it seemed, the serving-woman rapped on her door, saying that her son waited below. She shrugged on her habit and hurried down. The fire had gone out in the solar; only a single rushlight burned with a slim blue flame. Astrolabe, his face grimed with dust and sweat, stood very still in the center of the room. "Mama," he breathed quickly, "something bad has happened."

She groped for the doorway. "He's fallen sick."

Astrolabe shook his head. "He's well. It's Bernard, that bastard, son of a dog—" His eyes were murderous.

Heloise, confused, stared at him.

"—he's condemned Father. He's got all the bishops to condemn him!"

"No!" She flared in irritation. "How could that be? This is not a trial. God's love, it's only a debate."

"It's what I said. Tonight, Bernard invited all the bishops and abbots to a private meeting. It was a supper at the canons' chapter house." His voice rose, excited. "When they finished dining, Bernard sent for Father's books."

"Go on."

"I hate him!" Astrolabe cried wildly. "He started to read certain passages. Out of context. Somehow he persuaded them that Father must be condemned. And nobody—not one—uttered a word of dissent."

"How do you know this?" Heloise asked quietly.

"Geoffrey of Chartres was there. He came to Father's room afterward and told us."

Heloise took a step toward him, keeping her eyes on his face. "So then Bishop Geoffrey must also have told you that it was all a farce. A man cannot be sentenced without a trial." Her head began to pound. She heard the servant tramping about in the pantry.

Astrolabe wiped his face on the shoulder of his tunic. "Wait. Geoffrey said that everyone was drunk. The wineskins kept going around the trestles, and the men were laughing and making jokes. They called Father names."

"Bernard was drinking?" Heloise said, startled. "I can't imagine—"

"He got them drunk!" Astrolabe shouted. "By the end of the meal, most of them were half asleep and the rest were wagging their heads. When Bernard asked for condemnation, people started mumbling, *'Namus.'* "

She broke into harsh laughter. *"Namus?* We swim?"

"Mama, they meant to say 'We condemn.' *Damnamus.*" He turned his face into the shadows, breathing hard.

Heloise cleared her throat and said, "What did Bishop Geoffrey have to say about that?"

"I don't know—nothing. He only said that Father should expect to be called to public account tomorrow, that he must either defend his views or repudiate them."

"Ah. Then the assembly is no longer a forum but a court of law."

"Geoffrey was very angry. He said that Father should refuse to appear. Go back to Paris."

"Flee?" She frowned. "He wouldn't—"

"No, he'll stay." He sank on a stool and hunched forward, his head cradled in his hands.

Heloise came to him and wrapped her arms around his shoulders. "The servant is still awake. Can I order some wine?"

"Please." He stared at the floor. "Mama, why do people hate Father?"

Heloise was silent. After a moment, she said softly, "Did you notice the ribbed vaults in the cathedral? It's an entirely new principle of building. They appear to soar into the air and stand alone without any support."

He lifted his head and nodded wearily.

"Well," she said, "those vaults are like Abelard's thoughts."

He began to cry in tiny hiccuping whimpers. Heloise kissed his hair and went to find wine.

She woke at dawn. Through the cracks of the shutters, the sun was probing spears of brilliant yellow. It would be warm again today.

She slipped out of the covers and dressed quickly. Around her, the rest of the household still slept. She went downstairs to the pantry, took a loaf of yesterday's bread, and tucked it into her sleeve. Latching the main door quietly behind her, she set out for the cathedral.

Already there were several dozen gowned students sprawled in the nave, having slept there all night in order to get a place. Heloise briskly marched up the aisle to a small section near the front that had been set aside for nuns. Scrambling under the rope barrier, she settled on the floor and bowed her head to say the morning office. Afterward, she brought out the bread and forced herself to chew.

By terce, the cathedral was thronged. It was just like the previous day, except that this morning's crowd was noisy and unruly. They had not come to a religious service, but to witness a tournament and defend their champion. The more blood the better, Heloise thought bitterly. The mob grew restless, stamped its feet, and spat impatient whistles. Around Heloise, the women swaddled in black whispered discreetly, while the abbess of Notre Dame-aux-Nonnains complained about the heat and the town's poor accommodations for visitors. Heloise craned her neck. The nave was packed to its last cranny.

Presently, the choir began to fill up. On one side were seated the bishops and abbots, gorgeously robed. In their midst, she caught sight of Bishop Geoffrey, who was the papal legate. Next to the bishop, stiff as a carved capital, sat Abbot Bernard in his white Cistercian wool, his hands folded in his lap. His eyes were closed, as if to shut out the vulgar assortment of humanity. On the opposite side of the choir had gathered the lay dignitaries—King Louis and Queen Eleanor with their courtiers, Count Thibaut of Champagne, the crabbed old Count of Nevers. There were many others whom she did not recognize. Everyone was sumptuous in his spring finery. A little lower down, near the choir steps, was a section crammed solid with black-robed monks. Heloise leaned around the head of the nun in front of her, trying to pick out Abelard. The crowd banged feet against the stone floor.

Abbot Bernard stood and walked briskly to the center of the choir.

Silence dropped. Heloise waited to hear how he would open the assembly. It was a few moments before she realized, to her intense astonishment, that he had no intention of opening it. Instead, he was beckoning to somebody at the side of the choir. A white-robed monk advanced, his arms laden with books, and he laid them on a table near Bernard.

The abbot ignored the books. He took a step forward and said, "At Master Abelard's request, the archbishop of Sens wrote to me and asked if we might meet, so that Master Abelard might defend his propositions which I have condemned. My initial reaction was to refuse." A murmur eddied through the nave. Bernard gave a fey smile. "For one thing, he has been a debater from the cradle, just as Goliath was a warrior. Compared to him, I'm merely a child."

Heloise grunted under her breath.

Bernard was going on. "For another, I felt it was unseemly that the cause of the faith should be defended by the feeble arguments of one man."

The abbess of Nonnains twisted to the nun at her side. "What did he say?" she shouted.

"That he didn't want to come," said the nun.

Heloise looked up sharply. "Shhh."

An angry voice growled, "Pox take you! Get on with the debate!"

Ignoring the catcalls, the abbot said loudly, "On several occasions, I've asked Master Abelard for a statement of his faith. He has been given the opportunity to deny that he writes heresy. Or to amend his works in a spirit of humility." Triumphant, he gazed about the choir. "He has refused!"

In the monks' section, men were muttering openly and darting comments over each other's heads. An angry claque began down in the nave, awkwardly bawling, "Master Peter, Master Peter . . ." Something sailed through the air, splattering against the choir steps, and the claque still yelled, "Master Peter . . ."

Face working intensely, Bernard lifted his arms. "It is not I who condemn his writings. He is condemned by his own words." From his sleeve he whipped a sheet of parchment and unfolded it. "Those who have ears to hear, let them hear." Without pausing for breath, he started to read: "Heresy Number One. Christ is not one of the three persons in the Trinity. Heresy Number Two. Free will is sufficient, without the help of grace"—suddenly Abelard sprang to his feet—"to ensure our ability to do good."

Heloise straightened and watched Abelard's face. Scarcely breathing, she waited for him to interrupt Bernard. But he stood motionless, rapt and shockingly white, his lips pressed together. The claque swung into clapping, and some of the monks in the choir picked it up. Reluctantly turning to face Abelard, the abbot shouted over the racket, "Master Peter, do you deny writing Heresy Number Two? Feel free to answer without fear and in whatever way you choose."

Instantly, the enormous cathedral was quiet. Her habit clammy with perspiration, Heloise strained to see. Abelard's face was glazed; he did not move or speak, and after a moment he looked down at his feet.

"Heresy Number Three," Bernard said, rattling the parchment sheet. "There is no sin without consent to sin." He darted a quick shake of the head to King Louis. "The man stubbornly refuses to speak. Heresy Number—"

Swaying like a man walking in his sleep, Abelard slowly began to move forward. Bernard broke off. Stepping into the aisle that divided the choir, Abelard stopped, turned his head toward the bishops, and then swiveled and slowly surveyed the young king. The voice that had enthralled two generations of scholars filled the choir and nave. "I refuse," he cried out, "to be judged like a guilty clerk. I appeal to Rome."

The choir enclosure broke into a hum of confusion, like a wind scattering sleet through the forest. Bernard shrugged. Wheeling, Abelard made a gesture toward his right and strode down the choir steps, down the aisle past Heloise, back through the nave to the west portal. After him ran Astrolabe and a half dozen others.

The cathedral broke into a roar. The dismayed prelates sat gaping at the astonished faces in the nave. Only Abbot Bernard appeared unperturbed.

With a flourish of disgust, the abbess of Nonnains turned to Heloise and demanded loudly, "Do you mean it's over? Where has Master Peter gone? What on earth—" Heloise paid no attention. She sat like a ghost, shivering and invisible, and rocked forward until the half-eaten bread crumbled in her sleeve. She felt sick to her stomach. All around her, people were muttering and yelling; they had come to be entertained, but the main attraction had suddenly bolted the arena. Rising slowly on trembly legs, she pushed her way to a side entrance and staggered into the hot sunshine. A monk rushed up to her. "Sister," he asked, "do you know why Master Abelard left? Is it true, did he walk out?"

"Aye, Brother. I—I don't know the reason." He was not well, no matter what Astrolabe said. So far as she could judge, he had teetered on the edge of fainting.

"Thank you," said the monk, and turned away.

In the afternoon, she had Mme. Montauban send a servant to find Astrolabe. An hour passed. The man returned, saying that neither the lad nor his father was at the archbishop's guesthouse. Their belongings were gone. Jourdain came, sad and exhausted, and murmured soothing words. She nodded politely, not answering. In the solar, she sat by the window, twisting her girdle into knots and peering into the road for a sight of the boy.

"Don't torture yourself," Jourdain said. "Master Peter said he was going to Rome, and he's probably on the road by now. You should leave too."

Heloise shook her head stubbornly. It could not end this way.

Jourdain said, pleadingly, "Do as I tell you—I'll take you home. The assembly is over."

In the street, a black dog was foraging for scraps. Heloise curled her fingers until the knuckles whitened. "The assembly is over," she repeated dully. "Did they judge him a heretic?"

Jourdain burst into an ugly laugh. "In secret session, may God forgive them. They have sent their decision to Rome. Heloise, friend. It's time for us to be off."

"Please," she said. "I beg you. Go and try to find out what happened to him. If he has truly left Sens, then I'm willing to depart."

Sighing deeply, Jourdain agreed and went out.

She sat at the window a while longer, too tired to climb the stairs to her chamber. The youngest Montauban child prattled hesitantly in the doorway. "Lady," she quavered, "are you going home? Why, lady?"

Heloise smiled vaguely at her. "It's time, that's why." She turned back to the street. Farther down, she heard the frantic pounding of hoofs on the cobbles. When the horseman came into her line of vision, she gasped to see that he was Astrolabe. Before she could get up, the door banged open and the clatter of feet rang in the vestibule. She ran, seizing him by both shoulders. "Where is he?" she cried.

"Gone. Set out for Rome an hour ago." The child flattened herself against the wall, frightened to see the wild-looking youth. "I tried to make him wait—"

They stared at each other. Heloise said swiftly, "What ailed him? Why didn't he speak out against Bernard?"

"He told me that at that very moment his memory completely deserted him. He couldn't remember what Bernard had said, or what he was doing there in the choir."

"Dear God." Heloise clung to his arm. "You should not have left him. He's in no condition to travel anywhere."

"Mama, he insisted." Astrolabe fumbled in his girdle. "He wrote this letter for you. He thinks you're at the Paraclete and he wanted you to get this tonight. Before you had news of—today."

Swallowing, she took the letter, unsealed it, and began to read where she stood.

"Heloise my sister, once so dear to me in the world, now even dearer to me in Christ, logic has earned for me the hatred of the world. The perverse, for whom wisdom is nothing short of perdition, say that I am a master of logic, but I cannot understand St. Paul. They acknowledge the brilliance of my intellect but question the purity of my faith as a Christian.

"I do not want to be a philosopher if it means rejecting Paul. I do not wish to be an Aristotle if it cuts me off from Christ, for it is in his name, and none other under heaven, that I must find my salvation. I adore Christ who sits on the right hand of the Father.

"And so to remove all anxiety, all doubt and uncertainty, from your heart, I want to reassure you that I have established my conscience on the rock on which Christ built his Church. I will give you, in brief, my testimony:

"I believe in the Father, the Son, and the Holy Spirit, God who is one in nature, the true God who comprises the Trinity of person. I believe the Son to be equal to the Father."

She glanced up. "When did he write this?" she asked Astrolabe.

"Last evening."

"You're sure."

"Positive," he said.

"I further believe that the Son of God became the Son of Man and having completed his mission, even unto death itself, he rose again and ascended to heaven whence he shall judge the quick and the dead. Finally I believe that all sins are remitted in baptism and that those who have erred may be reformed by penance. As for the resurrection of the body, what need have I to speak of it? I could not call myself a Christian if I did not believe that I would one day live again. This then is the faith by which I live and from which my hope finds strength. Thus safely anchored, I do not fear the barking of Scylla; I laugh at the whirlpool of Charybdis; I care nothing for the siren's deadly songs. Let the storm rage, I am not shaken. Though the winds blow, I am not moved. For the rock of my foundation stands firm."

Slowly she lifted her eyes to the boy. "This is the confession of faith that Bernard wanted." He could have saved himself with this statement, but he had not. Instead, he had given it to her.

Abruptly, she thrust the letter into her sleeve. "How far south has he got, do you think?"

"Not far. Mama, you—"

"Saddle my mare."

They careered south along the river road that led to Auxerre, saying nothing. Heloise kept her eyes straight ahead and watched the dust rise like brown moths in the dying light. Mounted monks came into view, loitering toward their monasteries and grumbling loudly about the abortive affair at Sens. Heloise and Astrolabe kicked up their horses, passed, and churned on, dodging a party of pilgrims on foot.

Twice they stopped at inns to make certain that Abelard had not turned off for the night. Heloise thought about the road to Rome, how it wound treacherously through the Alpine passes. It was a hard journey, even for those in the best of health. Her fists tightened on the reins. He would not reach Rome, that she knew as surely as if God himself had told her. She ached with loving him, the man with the silvery voice and the pain in his eyes, but she would not add to his humiliation by pressing him to return to the safety of the Paraclete. Let him climb the long road home, let God watch over him.

An arm's length away, Astrolabe called out, "Mama, darkness is coming. Mayhap we should stop."

She looked away from him, into the woods that snapped with twigs and the whirring notes of birds. "No," she said in a tight little voice. She must see him once more; she needed a picture of him to keep in her mind during the endless years ahead.

At the hour of dusk, finally, they came upon Abelard in a clearing beside the road. Beneath an ancient oak, he was sitting on the trampled grass chewing bread, and he did not look up until they had reined in. Then he rose and walked toward them slowly, as if it hurt to move. The skin across the bridge of his nose, along the sides of his cheeks, and down over the neck was fiery red, scratched raw in spots.

Heloise dismounted and swayed toward him. He dipped his head, smiling, as if meeting her on the highroad were an ordinary occurrence. "Is it you, lady?" he asked softly.

"Aye." Behind her back, Astrolabe cleared his throat. "You will want company. It would be best if the boy goes with you."

"And it will be a good thing for him to see Rome." He spoke without glancing at Astrolabe.

"Have you money?"

"Some. Enough." He shrugged. "I shall travel from monastery to monastery. We won't go hungry, God willing."

She felt her tongue dry in her mouth. "At the passes. You must hire a guide to take you through."

"That's right," he said absently. "Lady, you look weary."

"I'm all right."

Abruptly, he rasped, "I'm finished."

She looked up, startled.

"Let others carry on the fight for truth. My young men—let them look to other teachers." He spoke very quickly and looked beyond her shoulder at Astrolabe while he talked.

She shook her head, hunting for an argument, but in the end she said nothing.

"You need not grieve. Nothing can be changed now."

"How do you know?" she said. "Mayhap it will come out differently."

"Once I wrote verse. I sang songs. When I was done with poetry, I put aside my lute."

Under the great tree, they stood quietly for a few minutes. Each looked at the other without speaking. Dark blue was staining the evening sky, pricking it with pinpoints of white. The wind was still.

"Lady?"

"Yes, my love."

"If I've caused you pain in this life, forgive me."

She did not trust herself to speak. At last, he reached for her and she tangled her fingers in his. He put his cheek against the coarse black wimple.

"Ladylove," he breathed.

26 ❧

IT WAS MICHAELMAS AGAIN, and the sacks of grain had been counted and duly recorded in Heloise's ledgers, the tithes collected, and the villeins blessed and twice blessed. With the coming of autumn, she turned her efforts to the renovated house at Traînel and prepared to install her women. Each day the packing progressed a little; barrels and boxes were deftly filled, wagons loaded with beds and trestles and chests. Keys swinging from her girdle, she moved briskly through the whitewashed rooms and arcaded walks of the Paraclete, and her eyes, deliberately smiling, cloaked all evidence of her thoughts. Three months had passed since Abelard had been condemned at Sens, less than two months since Pope Innocent had issued his edict: guilty as charged . . . heretic . . . sentenced to perpetual silence. Abelard's books had been burned ceremoniously in St. Peter's. Now it was over, Heloise had thought. Now, silenced, he would never write again. Jourdain had said that Abelard undid himself, that a man of different temperament, less contentious, more humble, would not have attracted so many enemies. Well, possibly Jourdain was right, but she did not believe it. Since Sens, the anger had rushed out of her, and all she felt now was a vast sadness that it should end this way.

The Saturday after the fall quarter day, the nuns going to Traînel assembled in the yard, twenty of them, and Sister Gertrude, whom the chapter had elected abbess. With them came Astrane, Ceci, Hermeline, and those of the senior nuns who wished to attend the installation ceremony. In anticipation of the trip, the women chattered and giggled, behavior not ordinarily encouraged at the Paraclete. Heloise pretended not to see. Some of them had not passed through the gate into the outside world for years; let them have this one day. Horses were brought up, wagons for those who did not ride. After some early-morning fog, the sun broke out.

The caravan straggled north along the river road to Saint-Aubin, where they would make a crossing. The woods were thick with colors of apricot and russet; the air smelled of fungus and burning leaves. Ceci trotted her horse close to Heloise. "You're sure the archbishop is coming in person," she said. "He's not sending an assistant."

Heloise nodded. The archbishop of Sens had requested the honor of presiding over the opening of Traînel. Not Henry Sanglier, who had died suddenly, but his successor, Hugo. Heloise had been surprised that Hugo was bothering to come all that way. She lifted her head into the air and dragged deeply, thinking of the pine-strewn plains of Burgundy, thinking of Abelard and the abbey of Cluny, of its abbot, whose name was Peter also. Peter the Venerable people had begun calling him, although he was only six or seven years older than Heloise. One day in July, Abelard had ridden up to the gate of Cluny. He was still there, and now he would never leave. A temporary resting place for a wanderer, he had written to her shortly after his arrival, but it had become more than that. She did not know what Abbot Peter had said to Abelard, what tact and patient persuasion he had used, but it was clear to her that he had immediately recognized one thing: Abelard had reached the farthermost limits of his endurance. Within weeks, he had persuaded Abelard to join their congregation, and he had assured Pope Innocent that heresy was abhorrent to Abelard. Most astonishing to Heloise, Peter had reconciled Abelard with Bernard, but how he had managed that feat she could not imagine.

After Lammas Day, she had received a letter from Abbot Peter: "The pope has granted that Master Peter may spend the last days of his life, which are perhaps not many, in our abbey of Cluny. Nothing shall be permitted to disturb the sparrow from its place under the eaves, the dove from its nest."

His kind words brought comfort to her. This man, Jourdain's boyhood friend whom she had been hearing about for half a lifetime, would care for her lord. She wished that it could have been herself. But that was not God's will.

The wagons clattered down the main street of Saint-Aubin. The villagers trotted alongside them, calling out questions about their destination. It was an unusual sight, scores of nuns out in the world on a September morning. They skidded down a short hill and onto the rotting quay, where barges bobbed. The Saint-Aubin people stood on the bank, watching. Heloise gestured to the boatmen, and they pushed off. The river was narrow, a duller green here than at the Paraclete. The nuns leaned over the sides of the wagon like small children on a holiday and peered down at the slack water.

"Lady," Gertrude said tearfully to Heloise, "I shall never cross this river again."

"Don't be silly. You'll come back to the Paraclete once a year for instruction. I told you that."

Gertrude answered, "Traînel is such a long way from home."

Heloise smiled gently. "Sainte-Madelaine is your home now. And it's not so far. You'll see. We will be there before sext."

Home, she thought. The Paraclete was Abelard's home. Strange that God sent him to Cluny. She had faith in Abbot Peter—he was well known for his skill with medicine and herbs, and he had written that Abelard suffered from scabies and perhaps some other disease for which he knew no name. She trusted him, but she trusted herself more, and she had sent a lay brother to Cluny with ointments for Abelard's skin and baskets of fruit for the abbot. Over to her right, she saw the smoking chimneys of Traînel. They crossed the Orvin River, wound through the town, and drew up at the gate of Sainte-Madelaine. The nuns crawled out of the wagons and stood wobbly in the road, mouths sagging with excitement. Ceci had already dismounted, her horse wandering off with its reins trailing in the dust, and she threw open the gate. "Sisters," she yelled, "come on. Let's look around."

Heloise sent a nun after Ceci's horse. She followed the women into the vestibule and passed out a side entrance into the garden that would serve them as a cloister. On a bench, half hidden by a leafless apple tree, sat the archbishop with his face buried in a handkerchief. He sneezed explosively. When he saw Heloise, he rose and sneezed again. "My lord archbishop." She went to him.

"Lady Heloise." He sniffed. "What a glorious day." He flashed her a watery smile.

"My lord, you sound ill."

He waved away her concern. "It's nothing. A mere cold, a simple matter of some sneezes and a sore throat." Hugo was a small man, and his voluminous archiepiscopal robe made him appear even smaller. He went on at some length about his cold. He thought that he probably caught it at his coronation, but he was not sure. In any case, he was glad of an opportunity to get out of Sens, into the pure air of the countryside, which he expected to cure him by sundown. He sat on the bench again and gestured with his soaked handkerchief that she should join him. "Tell me now, what is the schedule?"

"Dinner first. Then later the installation ceremony. Lord Anselm should be arriving momentarily."

"Amen. And the abbess. What is her name?"

"Gertrude," she replied. "A capable woman."

"Well, then," said Hugo. He blew his nose. "There is nothing for me to do but wait for dinner." Abruptly, he added, "Did you bring wine?"

She suppressed a smile. "Aye. From our own vines. My women are unloading the stores now."

"That might help, some spiced wine. With cinnamon and nutmeg. Soothes the throat, you know." He extracted a clean handkerchief from his sleeve.

She got up and went into the house. In the kitchen, nuns had brought in wood and lit a fire, and her niece, Agathe, was laying trout in a long pan. Heloise said, "Sweet, get someone to unpack the wine and make up a spiced henap for the archbishop."

"He's a big drinker?" Agathe grinned.

"A cold." She looked at Agathe and memory caught at her heart. She was Denise's daughter, but still it was hard for Heloise to remember that. Denise had done her harm, and she had forgiven her. Not forgotten, though. Agathe had inherited nothing from her mother except her piety. "We must unpack the kitchen utensils first," she said. "Later this afternoon is time enough to start on the beds."

A group of nuns balancing part of a trestle on their shoulders inched past her in the direction of the refectory. Heloise swung around them and hurried back to the garden. Hugo was dabbing at his eyes. "Wine is coming, my lord. Now, what can I tell you about Sainte-Madelaine?"

He smiled. "There's no need to give me a report, if that's what you mean. Your order is well known. Anselm has been generous with you?"

"Very. He built a chapel and stables. And he will do more in future. He has sworn to be our protector."

Hugo muttered something. He shot a quick glance at her and said suddenly, "Speaking of protectors, what news of Master Abelard? I've heard that he joined Cluny. But mayhap that is rumor."

Heloise looked down at her lap. "You heard rightly. He is teaching there. Abbot Peter has made him master of the oblates' school." Astrane was coming into the garden with a goblet. "Here," Heloise called.

Hugo took the cup and drained half of it. "Strong," he said. "That's what I wanted." Astrane backed away, hands folded. She bowed and went into the house. "Abbot Peter is a good physician. Smart. Knows that minds should not stand idle. Abelard's health—is it better?"

"Worse."

"A pity. Terrible thing—what happened at Sens. Unfair. But Peter will look after him." Hugo finished off the cup and laid it on the bench between them. Agathe must have put the fish on the fire, because aromas were drifting into the garden.

"The abbot?" Heloise said, almost tentative. "He is a good man?"

"Largehearted," Hugo said. "Always smiling. Serene temperament, but he has plenty of spirit, if you know what I mean."

Heloise nodded. Astrolabe had written her that his father occupied himself with things of the mind—reading, prayer, and meditation. His habit had grown shabby, but he did not seem to notice. At Cluny all was peaceful, and his favorite spot there was a lime tree where he rested with his face turned toward the Paraclete. Hugo coughed and mumbled something. "Pardon, my lord."

"I said that Arnold of Brescia has been teaching Abelard's classes at Sainte-Geneviève."

Startled, she answered, "I didn't know that."

He fingered the goblet. "And having little success, I might add. His students have dwindled to a handful. Has your son returned to the Ile?"

"No. Not yet." There was a commotion in the house, and she heard the bark of a man's voice. Lord Anselm.

"He plans to continue his studies, doesn't he?"

"In the spring. For now he remains with his father."

"Wise," Hugo murmured. They sat in silence until Astrane came out to announce Anselm.

All afternoon, she smiled automatically, her mind elsewhere. Lord Anselm's wife was there and his three sons, boys of Astrolabe's age more or less. Anselm had brought the keys to the house. Nose dripping, Archbishop Hugo drew up a charter of foundation and charged Anselm, overlord of the region and benefactor of the Paraclete, to care for the daughters of Christ. He was to look after their needs, for the love of God and for the health of his soul. Heloise, standing a little apart, watched Gertrude accept the charter.

Hugo pressed the keys into Gertrude's hand. "Welcome," he said, smiling, "welcome to this place in which henceforth you will love and serve God."

Heloise shut her eyes. She wondered what Abelard was doing.

Abelard insisted that Astrolabe must return to Paris. He did not want to, but Peter the Venerable talked to him and explained things. On his way north, the young man turned east and headed for the Paraclete. Heloise felt uneasy when she saw his drooping face, although she assured him that he looked splendid. Later, she told Ceci that he looked as if he had not slept for weeks.

"He doesn't like being ordered around," Ceci said. "I don't see why he couldn't have stayed."

Privately, Heloise agreed, but she knew that Abelard must have a reason. In the morning, she brought Astrolabe bread and ale, and sat on the edge of his bed while he ate. She talked, but he sat stiff and silent, not meeting her eyes. At last, she said, "Son, I'm sorry to see you so troubled."

"I'm not troubled," he mumbled.

"Well, then. Whatever it is that's ailing you." He had a mulish temper, like his father. And his father's moods, too.

He blurted, "Father's leaving the abbey."

Her lips twitched imperceptibly. "He's leaving. Where is he going?"

"Saint-Marcel," Astrolabe said.

"And what sort of house is that?" she asked evenly.

"A small priory of Cluny's. Near Chalon-sur-Saône." He tipped the ale cup, drank, and wiped his mouth. "The climate is mild in that part of Burgundy."

She took the cup from him. "Saint-Marcel. What's wrong with it?"

"Nothing. I didn't say anything is wrong with it." He sank against the pillow and squeezed his eyes shut. His face showed nothing. He repeated, "It's a fine place."

Was it really? From his description, it sounded like a house for monks who were seriously ill. "I think," she said, choosing her words carefully, "that it sounds lovely. Your father will be well cared for there?"

"Oh, very."

"Then there is no problem."

"None," he said dully.

"Astrolabe—"

"Yes?" His eyes opened.

"Look, you have a life of your own to live. Things to do. You must return to your studies." She waited for a reply. Nothing. Standing, she said at last, "Don't you want to get dressed this morning?"

"If you want me to." When she reached out her hand to stroke his hair, he pushed her away. She saw his eyes filling. He said, "Leave me alone, stop looking at me—"

Heloise reared back and looked at the wall. When she glanced at him a moment later, he was digging his face into the pillow like a rabbit homing into its hole. She could think of no words to console him. Finally she murmured, "We are all in God's hands." The words came out stiff and flat—and meaningless. He did not answer, for which she couldn't blame him. She went out.

Three days later, he set out for Paris, still grieving over a loss that had not yet taken place. In that, he was her son.

Easter fell late that year. The guesthouse was unusually crowded with pilgrims, among them the Countess of Champagne. The purpose of her visit was to discuss with Heloise the founding of another daughter house —Baldwin of Closfontaine would donate the land and she, Mathilde, the funds for building. It was an interesting proposal; Heloise said she would think about it. As it turned out, most of the talk that Easter was about war, a subject that concerned all of them a great deal more than any new convent. Count Thibaut was feuding with King Louis, or perhaps it was the other way round, Heloise was not certain. It was over some family matter that sounded absurd to her. Countess Mathilde told her that Louis had threatened to invade Champagne. Heloise could not imagine the monkish Louis invading anything and said so.

"Those kind are the most vicious," Mathilde retorted. "The ones who look innocent."

Heloise raised her eyebrows. "But he seems so sweet," she insisted.

"He's a Capetian, isn't he? Which is why, dear lady, blood will flow."

The Monday after Easter, the countess went back to Troyes; the guesthouse emptied and the yard was strangely silent. The lull that comes after a big feast day. Heloise sat at her trestle, catching up on correspondence. She reread a letter from Astrolabe. Not really a letter, more of a memorandum. The boy could be maddeningly uncommunicative on occasion, and this was one of them. He had signed up with a master but neglected to mention names or course titles. Paris was extremely crowded and he had had trouble finding a room. Finally he had taken lodgings on the Rue de Petite-Orberie, which, he explained, was near Notre Dame. Sometimes he seemed to forget that she had once lived in the Ile, or perhaps he did so deliberately. Heloise remembered the street; it was not far from the Rue des Chantres. A picture of Fulbert's house blinked into her mind. Just as swiftly she pushed it out, got up, and went to the window.

In the cloister, the morning sun was washing the ferny new grass and the gravel paths bordered with fleur-de-lis and pansies. A group of schoolgirls huddled around the fountain, dipping their fingers into the water and spraying each other's bliauts. As Astrane came by, they stopped and sprawled gracelessly on the grass. When they noticed Heloise at the window, they laughed and waved.

She walked around to the door and went out. One of the children called, "Lady Heloise, come here! Marie, tell her."

Smiling, she came slowly down the path toward them, and turned to the youngest of the boarders, a girl of five with an aureole of frizzy blond hair. "Tell me what, sweeting?"

Marie said eagerly, "We're going to get a war." She said it as if she were talking about a sweetmeat.

"Do you know what a war is?" Heloise asked gravely.

Marie shrugged her scrawny shoulders. "When soldiers fight with swords," she piped proudly.

"Yes. And when many people who are not soldiers get killed and their houses and fields burned."

The child's mouth gaped into an O. "Dead, you mean? People get dead?" Heloise nodded. "Why does King Louis want us to get dead, why, lady?"

Heloise kicked a clump of loose dirt back into the flower bed. "King Louis doesn't want us dead. He's angry at the count."

"Why?" Marie insisted. "Tell me, I'll understand."

Heloise sat down on a bench and pulled the child into her lap. Marie twisted one arm around Heloise's neck. "Because," Heloise said, "the king's cousin put aside Count Thibaut's niece so that he could marry Queen Eleanor's sister. Now, does that make sense to you?" It certainly made no sense to her. Marie nodded vigorously. The portress was hurrying across the walk, signaling Heloise. When Marie saw her, she scrabbled off Heloise's lap.

"Sister Elizabeth, listen—do you know something?" The portress ignored her. "Sister, I have something—"

Elizabeth stopped a yard from Heloise. "Lady abbess, a visitor for you. A monk. Brother Thibaut."

Heloise looked up vaguely, still thinking about Queen Eleanor and her sister. "What does Brother Thibaut wish to see me about?" She stifled a little yawn.

"Wouldn't say. For your ears only, he told me." Elizabeth scowled. "Shall I send him away?"

"No, no. Don't do that. I'm coming."

Marie tugged at Elizabeth's skirt. "Sister—"

"Later, lovey," she said. "Later." She wheeled briskly and started toward the courtyard. Heloise strolled behind.

The yard was deserted. Brother Thibaut sat on a shady bench under the wall, his hands folded. When he saw her, he stood and bowed. Heloise came forward, smiling. "God's greeting. What can I do for you, Brother?"

"Lady." His voice was the texture of cobblestones. "I come from Saint-Marcel."

Heloise tensed. She raked his face with her eyes, asking the question without speaking.

He nodded.

"When?"

"Nearly a week ago." He watched her curiously. "The twenty-first day of April."

The twenty-first. Frantically she cast back in time, struggling to remember that day. It must have been the Wednesday after Palm Sunday. What had she been doing that day? She couldn't remember. Abelard had gone and she had not missed him; no dream, vision, or portent had warned her. She thought, I have been living without him for five days. She said to the monk, "What hour of the day did he die?"

"Around nones. Shortly after."

"In bed? Was his mind clear? Brother, don't hold back." Her voice rose quietly. "Tell me everything."

"He was sitting under a walnut tree. Reading, I think. He was always bent over his books. Never let a moment pass without praying or reading." He added, "Insofar as his health would permit."

Heloise nodded. She looked up at the gatehouse. A crow strutted along the edge of the roof. "Yes," she said.

Brother Thibaut said, "His sickness worsened during Lent. But he wouldn't keep to his bed. He said that he felt better when he sat outside. He had his chair—"

"He was awake until the end?"

"Until the last. He confessed his sins in so Christian a manner—such eagerness for his journey. Any of the brothers can bear witness to that." The monk scratched his chest through the coarse habit.

"He passed—quickly?"

"Quickly. Are you all right, lady?"

The pain ricocheted around inside her head. She stepped backward.

"I'm all right," she said calmly. "Brother, rest with us until the morrow. Sister Elizabeth will attend to you."

He bowed slightly. "If it please you, my lady."

She turned and reeled toward the cloister, passing Ceci without speaking. It was nearly time for dinner, and the children were leaving the fountain. She went quickly along the south walk to the chapel. The sanctuary was empty, only one candle shivering on the altar. Lacking the strength to kneel properly, she threw herself into a heap and her keys clanked against the stone. A dragonfly, trapped in the darkness, buzzed near her ear; she shook it off. After several minutes, she lifted her head and tried to crawl toward the altar. The flame swam. She lay down again, grinding her cheek against the cold stone. *Abelard is dead.* Her fingers were stuffed between her teeth, and she made herself bite down on them until the salty taste of blood filled her mouth. Pain threaded through her hand, the alive sensation of being hurt.

"Oh God, you know everything about me. You know that I am afraid. My dear beloved is gone. Don't make me stay here without him. I am old—release me."

Footsteps clumped on the stone behind her. "Dear friend," Ceci whispered. She came to Heloise and knelt, holding a goblet. "Drink." She twined Heloise's hands around the cup. The heavy sweet liquid burned her throat all the way down.

"Cry," Ceci crooned to her. "There's no one to hear."

Heloise rocked against Ceci's shoulder, trying to focus on the blurred outline of the candle's flame. She said at last, "I have no tears." Her voice faltered.

"Stay here. I'll have Astrane call a chapter meeting and make the announcement."

"No." Heloise pushed to her knees. She wiped her bleeding fingers on her skirt. "I'll do it myself." They went out into the sun-drenched cloister.

"He died a monk of Cluny," Brother Thibaut said. He shuffled his feet near the doorway of the abbess's parlor.

"I don't care about that."

"It's the privilege of our order to keep the body in our possession."

"Brother Abelard wished to be buried here," she almost shouted. "I have letters in his own hand to that effect. He specifically stated that wherever he might die, his body should be brought to us."

Brother Thibaut shook his head. "I wouldn't know about that, lady. All I can tell you is that he's already been buried. It's too late."

She snapped, belligerent, "You can unbury him."

"Lady!" The monk gave a small sputter of astonishment.

For the first time today she felt like screaming. She knew that it was unfair to vent her irritation on Brother Thibaut, who was, after all, only a messenger. "Tell me. Where is he buried?"

"In the chapel, of course, as befits a great philosopher. In a niche along the south wall." Brother Thibaut threw up both hands. "Lady, the site is very close to the hole in the floor."

"What hole?" She looked at him sharply.

"The hole that—the opening of the well where the heathen threw our martyred St. Marcel. It's a great honor to be buried near the hole." He rubbed his hands nervously and glanced into the yard, anxious to get away.

"I don't care," Heloise repeated. "You tell Abbot Peter—"

Thibaut broke in quickly. "The abbot is not at Cluny."

"Where is he?"

"Traveling. In Castile."

Heloise looked around the chamber. No use haranguing the poor monk. "All right," she said quietly, "all right. When is the abbot due to return?"

"Sometime after Lammas, I think. Mayhap Michaelmas."

"Very well. I'm sorry to have bothered you with all this." She turned away, mortally tired. She felt her shoulders burning with tension.

The monk took a step toward her, the corners of his mouth flattened down with sympathy. "In time you'll feel differently. Brother Abelard is very happy where he is. I swear to you, lady. Truly it's a nice tomb."

"Yes. Thank you."

Astrane said, "These arrived before sext. I forgot to give them to you." She dropped a sheaf of letters on Heloise's writing table.

Without looking at the seals, Heloise stacked the packets with other unread correspondence. "The pile mounts," she sighed. "Before sundown I will read them all if it kills me." She picked up a quill.

Astrane limped toward the door. "Oh. One more thing." Heloise lifted her head. "There's a monk in the yard. He wants you."

"Did Sister Elizabeth inquire of his business?" God forgive her for complaining, but with all these visitors she had little time for her duties.

Astrane grimaced. "I doubt it. She was annoyed with the fellow, I could tell that. He insisted on squeezing his wagon through the gate. Parked it in the middle of the yard. I think he's selling something."

"Since when do monks peddle merchandise?" Heloise sighed again. "Very well. Ask the good brother if he would mind waiting a few more minutes. I must finish these tithes—"

"He won't mind. He's a jolly fellow."

Heloise reached for the abacus, not listening. "Good," she murmured. "Show him to the guest parlor."

The harvest had been abundant that year. Good thing, she thought. If there is fighting before the spring, who knows if we will be able to get our seed in. She had heard that King Louis had no intention of calling up his vassals for forty days' winter service; he was planning to hire mercenaries. Which meant that Champagne would be plundered. She flexed her fingers and totted up the column of figures. Perhaps it would be wise to have the gate strengthened with iron bars. *Routiers* had been known to sack convents. She wanted to take no chances.

She rose, washed her hands, and walked to the courtyard. The day was half gone and she had accomplished little. She felt slightly annoyed with herself. A huge wagon was standing in the middle of the yard. Objects with odd shapes had been stacked under the canvas, so that the entire thing resembled a misshapen pyramid. Nearby, four black-robed monks were sitting on their heels chewing dried meat; their habits were gray with dust. She stopped to look, then stamped around the wagon and went toward the guesthouse. She thought, Those shutters need painting. A bearded monk was sitting on the steps, reading. As she approached, he lifted his head and flashed her a wide grin.

Her steps faltered. It was something about the man, his smile, the expression of complete kindness around his mouth. She had never met him, she was certain of that, but still—she squinted, searching his face.

"My very well beloved Lady Heloise." He got to his feet eagerly and started toward her, the book tumbling to the cobbles.

Intuition sent her plummeting to her knees. "Your Reverence," she cried. "I had no idea—"

"Of course not. Forgive, my lady." His eyes shone. "I should have sent word ahead."

Heloise's poise scattered. "I'm amazed," she stuttered. "I can't tell you—" She felt like a fool.

Peter of Cluny smiled. He caught her by the wrist and lifted her up. Heloise thought, Other than his smile, he looks like an ordinary man. There is nothing exceptional about him but the grin, which is joyous.

Now she burst into delighted laughter. "Your Grace, permit me to welcome you to the Paraclete."

He broke in, sawing the air expansively, staring around the yard. "You don't know how much this means to me." His eyes fixed on her face. "Lady, may I be frank with you?"

She nodded happily.

"Dear lady, I love you." He uttered those odd, inappropriate words simply, and when she gaped at him, he laughed. "Oh, it's not today that I have begun to love you—this is an old malady. I was not even a young man yet, hardly more than a boy, when I first heard about you."

"From Jourdain."

"No." Peter shook his head. "No, I knew about you before Jourdain met you. Don't ask me where. There was talk of this girl who devoted herself to the pursuit of knowledge, and nothing could distract her. Not even the frivolities that young girls usually indulge in. You surpassed all women—and nearly all men."

She shot him an anguished glance. "You overpraise me. Please."

"My very dear sister in Our Lord," he said. "I don't say it to flatter you." He stooped to pick up his book, which lay open on the cobbles. Straightening, he said quietly, "It's my humble way of encouraging you."

Heloise squinted at him. "To do what, Your Reverence?"

"Safeguard this place, finish what you've begun. You must go on firing the hearts of your women—and other women too. Does that sound reasonable?"

"Aye, but you're speaking of something that's not easy for me. Firing people's hearts."

He grinned. "Don't think about it. You burn and illumine naturally. Don't think about it."

"Easier to say than do." Abruptly, she clenched his arms. "I miss him so terribly!"

"Ah well, but that is always the temptation. To dwell in the past. Your life is far from over."

Staring down, she kicked her toe against the cobbles. "No. It is over."

His voice boomed out forcefully. "Dear lady, would you deny reality?"

She looked up, surprised.

"Your Abelard is dead. That is one reality." He shook the dust from the hem of his habit. "You have your own life to live—that is an even greater reality and that's what you must cling to. Everything else is unimportant now. What do you think?"

She smiled crookedly. After a long pause, she said, "I suppose—you're right."

Across the yard, Sister Elizabeth was opening the gate. A party of merchants, trailed by several packhorses, rode in and reined their palfreys near the well. Heloise swept her gaze over the merchants, past Sister Elizabeth, and up to the covered wagon that Peter had brought. She froze. The abbot was saying, "This is a large convent. I don't know why I expected something much smaller."

Unable to speak, Heloise pointed dumbly to the wagon. She weaved toward it, her legs suddenly unsteady. Peter followed. She turned to look at him. "How did you—"

"The rules forbid," he said solemnly, "the removal of any monk who dies in our order. So there was only one way."

Her eyes widened.

Peter grinned the tiniest of grins. "I stole it. Naturally."

"Oh."

"I think God will understand." He called to the monks sitting alongside the wagon, asking them to cut the ropes.

Heloise swayed toward him. "Didn't your sons at Saint-Marcel object?"

Peter looked at the monks tugging at the ropes. "If they'd been given a chance, they would have." He turned back to Heloise. "I pretended to make a visitation to the priory. One night while they slept, I had the body disentombed, and we loaded it on the wagon and left. See?"

Incredulous, she said, "In the middle of the night?"

"I'm afraid so."

Languidly, the monks wound the ropes into coils. One of them reached for the canvas and pulled. The first thing Heloise saw, perched high atop the wagon, was Abelard's armchair. A monk scooped it from the cart and set it jauntily on the cobbles. The four of them returned to the wagon and began to haul up the coffin, wrapped in black linen. Easing it over the side, they grunted and levered the box to the ground. Heloise went to it; she stroked her fingertips across the cloth.

Peter came to stand beside her. "This man," he said, low, "belonged at your side. But Divine Providence gave us the honor of his presence for a while. He was a true philosopher of Christ, Master Peter was."

She swallowed hard. "Can they take him into our chapel?"

He went to the monks and said something. They hoisted the coffin on their shoulders and started toward the cloister gate. Heloise and Peter walked slowly behind, Peter swiveling his neck from side to side. "Wonderful. This is truly an astonishing place. Master Peter told me there was nothing here but a chapel when you arrived."

She did not answer. Eyes on the coffin, she felt a sob start somewhere deep in her chest and bubble up into her throat.

"Lady Heloise," Peter said softly, "your Abelard is not in that box."

"I—know."

"He's in a far country. Never doubt that he will be restored to you."

They turned down the west walk of the cloister. Two nuns leaned from a window, whispering behind their hands. The heads disappeared and the shutter slammed. Heloise said, "I never wanted to possess him, the way other women want their husbands. I only wanted him near me at times. Our Lord did not grant that desire."

Peter said calmly, "He is the other half of you. God is keeping him for you."

God was keeping Abelard for her. His words wrapped around her like the heady fragrance of good incense. She thought, My beloved is not dead, only waiting. Astrane darted around the corner and slid to a breathless halt at Heloise's elbow. Heloise smiled. "Sister, the abbot of Cluny has brought Master Peter home."

Astrane knelt for his blessing; the cloister began to fill with nuns. Straightening her spine, Heloise watched as the abbot strolled a circle around the cloister, smiling a greeting at even the smallest child. When he returned to her side, she said, "Your Reverence, this is a day of rejoicing for us. A visit from you—" She was going to make a speech, but he smoothly cut in.

"My spirit must have visited here before," he said lightly. "I feel at home. Even though this is a flying visit."

"You'll stay the night, won't you?"

"Of course. And say mass tomorrow, if it pleases you." He smiled. "You know, this is a dangerous country at the moment. With young Louis's cutthroats expected momentarily."

"Then you believe there will be war?"

He shrugged. "Pray God not. It looks bad, though."

Slowly, they made their way back to the cloister gate. "Elizabeth," Heloise called, and the portress came running. "Show His Reverence to the guesthouse." She turned to Peter. "What is your pleasure? Ale, a bath—"

"A nap, lady." His eyes twinkled wearily.

"Then I'll see you at supper. Sleep well." Turning away, she heard him call her name. When she swung around to look back, he was pulling from his girdle a packet tied with string.

He murmured, "These were in Master Peter's chest when he died. Perchance you want them."

"Thank you." She glanced down at the packet, startled to see her own nunnish handwriting. *Saint-Gildas-de-Rhuys.* Abelard had saved her letters.

Hurrying across the cloister, she pushed a door and followed the corridor into her room. She went straight to the corner and loosened a stone, and from the niche she drew out a small locked box. Hesitating, she held the box in one hand, the letters in the other. She should burn them; it was madness to keep those incriminating pages, so full of her despair and unspeakable longings.

After a moment, she turned and went to her table. The stool was gone, and in its place someone had left Abelard's chair. Smiling, she sank down very slowly on the seat and set the letters and the box on the table. Tomorrow was time enough; tomorrow she would destroy the letters, hers and perhaps Abelard's as well. She rested her cheek against the coolness of the chair's carvings. A dying sun sprayed rays of fire across the table.

May 16, 1163 🌿

IT WAS PAST COMPLINE NOW, and the nuns were coming back from chapel. The stars had gone behind some clouds, and there were shadows all across the sky; the infirmary room seemed to have grown brighter and smaller. Heloise writhed her head to the side and watched Father William as he opened a box and drew out a small black vial, which he set lovingly on the trestle. Sister Claude was perched on a stool next to the bed.

"Father's preparing the oil," the infirmarian said. "Are you comfortable, can I get you anything?"

"No." There was nothing for Claude to do now. Then: "Sister?"

"Yes, my lady."

"I'm so very—happy."

Claude stroked her hand. Eyes blurring, Heloise saw her gesture with her head to someone near the doorway. Moments later, there was the sound of oak smacking against oak, a single crash, then echoing silence, then another crash. The smacking noise receded as the sister with the death board shuffled slowly into the cloister to summon the nuns.

She thought, Twenty-one years since Abelard died. And still she woke each morning hungry for his face. Sister Claude got up and brought a standing candle and placed it behind Heloise's head. She looked at Claude and scratched her fingers at the coverlet. She breathed, "Bury me"—Sister Claude inclined her ear close to Heloise's lips—"with my lord." Claude, white-faced, nodded.

The nuns filed in so quietly that she was not aware of their entrance, only, later, of gold-flecked shapes massed above her head. Claude glided back, and the priest took her place; the prayers began. He tipped the vial, and she felt him trickle a drop of oil onto her eyelid. "Through this holy unction and his own most tender mercy, may the Lord pardon thee whatever offenses thou hast committed by sight." The hand moved away. She sensed it, rather than saw it. The priest's voice dived lower, surfaced again, but she did not listen.

Unbidden, fragments kept weaving their way into her mind. She had seen the world rush on: all the events, great and small, that the chroniclers set down; all the people, good and evil, who had made them happen. She had stayed behind her cloister walls, removed supposedly from worldly matters; but she had watched. The war in Champagne had not touched the Paraclete, but a thousand souls in Vitry-sur-Marne had been burned alive in their church when Louis's soldiers set it afire. She remembered that, and of course the crusade that had failed. So when poor Louis got back to France afterward, there were some who wanted him to abdicate. But, in the end, people forgot. In her mind, she saw Abbot Suger, who had ruled France for Louis, the little fat man who had hated her and who was dead now. And Queen Eleanor, who had got Louis to divorce her and only a few weeks later married Henry Plantagenet, a lad young enough to be her son. And the boy Tom Becket, who had risen to the archbishopric of Canterbury. The same boy who had been Abelard's student long ago. How many years had that been? She did not want to count. There were no great masters at Paris now. Oh, there were plenty of teachers, men who called themselves philosophers, but none with the wit and brilliance of her Abelard.

She had not returned to the Ile since his death. Nor had she heard the sound of a lute for twenty years. She knew why.

At the Paraclete, after the crusade, they had become prosperous, and the hard years when they had plowed and built walls faded to curious memories. Papal bulls from a half dozen popes, royal charters, six daughter houses founded in twenty years. Their property holdings extended from the Marne to the Yonne. She had done her duty.

"Whatever offenses thou hast committed by touch—" Father William was repeating the unction; the oil dribbled over her hands. It would soon be finished. Absolved, shriven, unblemished as the moment she had come into the world. Where had the years gone, those billion lungfuls of breath inhaled and exhaled, squandered without her noticing? She thought, We begin to die from the moment we are born. This is but the end that was promised at the start.

She remembered the day that Ceci left, a bright September afternoon with the leaves rioting to saffron and Ceci tramping off into the oak woods to walk, or perhaps run—Heloise never knew exactly what she did there. That was something Ceci had never learned—to stay meekly within the cloister. And she remembered Sister Elizabeth streaking across the cloister with her skirts swirled up about her knees, and she, Heloise, coming out to see the hunters whose arrow had glanced from an oak. They had carried Ceci home under a rag blanket, her bloody corpse pierced like a wild boar. How many Septembers ago had that been? Five, and she remembered ramming her head against the door of the gatehouse, howling, *Ceci, don't leave me, what will I do without you!* and being amazed that she had felt that, let alone uttered it.

Ceci killed in a freakish accident. Jourdain, who had ridden off to the crusade with King Louis, killed by a Saracen arrow in the cucumber gardens outside Damascus. Astrolabe, whose lungs had fatally hemorrhaged the year after he became a canon at Nantes. Peter the Venerable gone too. Names drifting down the stream of time, beloved souls that touched hers and floated on, leaving her behind.

All at once, she thought of the letters, her black secrets hidden behind the wall of her chamber. Why had she not burned them, as she intended to do all along? She had never read them again, never even taken the box from its niche. Well, she thought. Well, there was nothing she could do about it now. They shall stay there until they crumble to dust; and she smiled.

Sister Claude's lips were moving, but Heloise could not hear the words above the roaring of her own breath. A column of mist closed upon her, and she felt herself being pulled, floating through a dark corridor. Somewhere behind her, she knew that women were weeping softly, but she didn't want to look back.

From a long way off drifted the sound of bells moaning, or perhaps it was only the wind. She came out of the blackness into a meadow, violently green. She had never known color to be so vivid.

Across the field, there was a stone wall, absurdly low. Not much use for keeping anyone out, she thought. Someone was sitting on the wall, and when he saw her, he grinned and stretched wide his arms. She rushed forward.

Note 🌿

WHILE THIS IS A work of fiction, I have followed the outlines of Heloise and Abelard's lives and used nothing but historical facts, when those facts are known. At certain periods, their lives are extremely well documented by their own writings: Abelard's *Historia calamitatum* (Story of His Misfortunes) provides valuable details about his early life, his relationship with Heloise, and the castration.

In addition to Abelard's autobiography, I have used as my chief source the eight letters exchanged by Heloise and Abelard. Extracts from this correspondence are quoted verbatim in the text. Certain unlikely incidents in the novel, such as their lovemaking in the refectory of Sainte-Marie of Argenteuil, are described in the letters. Heloise's letters in particular are memorable for their frankness, and even today they retain the power to shock. It is difficult to reconcile the pious abbess with these erotic outpourings. But it is not Heloise, abbess of the Paraclete, who is speaking; it is Heloise the woman. Not for another eight centuries would a woman write so openly of sexual feeling.

The personal letters, along with Abelard's letters outlining a Rule for the nuns, were kept by Heloise at the Paraclete during her lifetime. Unfortunately, the circumstances in which they were first made public are not known. It has been suggested that sometime in the late thirteenth century, more than a hundred years after Heloise's death, they were brought to Paris and copied. At present, there are nine known manuscripts of the letters, but no trace of the originals.

Aside from the surviving writings of Heloise and Abelard, I have made liberal use of the letters exchanged between Heloise and Peter the Venerable; the letters of Bernard of Clairvaux; and various twelfth-century chronicles, charters, and documents. All of these I have combed for details and woven into the narrative. For example, it is a fact that Astrane was the first prioress of the Paraclete, that Peter the Venerable illegally removed Abelard's corpse, that Heloise brought a lawsuit against the abbot of Vauluisant over the disputed oak forest, and so forth.

In the few biographies of Heloise, she is presented as either a classic case of the helpless young woman, seduced and abandoned, or as a self-sacrificing cardboard saint. In this novel, I have tried to portray her as I believe she must have been: a highly intelligent woman who struggled with the demands imposed on her sex by twelfth-century society. In one sense, she was very much a woman of her own time, and certainly it is impossible to understand many of her actions without taking into account the twelfth-century mind. In other and perhaps more important ways, however, she was an alien in her own century, and in that sense she speaks directly to our own. In an era when learning was limited to a select few (and most of them men), Heloise shines forth as the most brilliant woman of medieval times. Her contemporaries, never quick to admire female intelligence, nevertheless praised her as surpassing in erudition all women and—the highest acclaim—nearly all men. But in the twelfth century, her gifts could only be counted as an embarrassing superfluity. There was nothing she could do with them, and it is interesting to speculate on the probable course of her life had she not met Peter Abelard. In all likelihood, her uncle, despite his encouragement of her studies, would have eventually married her to some wealthy baron.

The tragedy of Heloise and Abelard was well known during their lifetime. It is mentioned in the chronicles of William Godel of Limoges and the English courtier, Walter Map. In the thirteenth century's *Great Chronicle of Tours,* a fanciful entry about Heloise recounts: "It is said that when she was lying in her last illness she gave instructions that when she was dead she should be laid in the tomb of her husband. And when her dead body was carried to the open tomb, her husband, who had died long before her, raised his arms to receive her, and so clasped her closely in his embrace."

The romantic historian disregards the fact that Heloise was not placed in Abelard's tomb. In the necrology of the Paraclete, it is recorded that she was buried alongside Abelard in the crypt of the abbey church. For three hundred years they rested undisturbed. Then, in 1497, Abbess Catherine de Courcelles had the bodies exhumed and moved to either side of the altar in a new church, which had been built farther back from the river. Between that year and 1780, the remains were relocated several times within the church.

At the time of the French Revolution, the Paraclete was sold, the nuns dispersed, and its buildings, apart from the residence of the abbess, destroyed. A few days before the sale, several citizens of Nogent-sur-Seine took the bones of Heloise and Abelard to the church of Saint-Laurent in Nogent. In 1800, the artist Alexandre Lenoir requested permission of the state to bury them in Paris, at his Musée des Monuments Français. Lenoir acquired a sarcophagus from the monastery of Saint-Marcel, which he believed to be the one in which Abelard was first buried. Fifteen years later, the museum was closed and the bones moved to the cemetery of Mont Louis, now called Père-Lachaise. There they remain today.

Enclosing their sarcophagus is an elegant Gothic-style structure, its canopy adorned with gargoyles and spires. Around it has been added an iron fence to deter visitors from cutting their names in the stone. Through the railing, flowers are still sometimes left by Parisians, tourists, and lovers of all nationalities.